BETRAYED

Scott Ray

Copyright © 2023 **Stellar Literary Press & Media**

All rights reserved. No part of this publication may be reproduced, distributed, or transmitted in any form or by any means, including photocopying, recording, or other electronic or mechanical methods, without the prior written permission of the publisher, except in the case of brief quotations embodied in critical reviews and certain other noncommercial uses permitted by copyright law. For permission requests, write to the publisher, addressed "Attention: Book Rights and Permission," at the address below.

Published in the United States of America

ISBN 978-1-959173-40-3 (SC)

Stellar Literary Press & Media
222 West 6th Street
Suite 400, San Pedro, CA, 90731
www.stellarliterary.com

Order Information and Rights Permission:

Quantity sales. Special discounts might be available on quantity purchases by corporations, associations, and others. For details, contact the publisher at the address above.

For Book Rights Adaptation and other Rights Permission. Call us at toll-free 1-888-945-8513 or send us an email at admin@stellarliterary.com.

This is a work of fiction. Names, characters, places and incidences either are the product of the author's imagination or are used fictitiously, and any resemblance to actual persons, living or dead, events, or localities is entirely coincidental.

PART ONE

Chapter 1

AFGHANISTAN 1986.

It's the time of the year when the weather is transitioning form winter to spring in Afghanistan. The heavy rains have pretty much subsided, leaving behind wet, clinging mud everywhere. The warming sun is beginning to dry up the landscape, exposing the ruts in what passes for a road in this territory.

This kind of weather seems to bring out the fight spirit in the local male population, in fact it's called the Spring Offensive, and this year was no exception. The Afghanis were beginning to make positive strides in their fighting abilities. Their enemy from the USSR was growing weary of an opponent who never seemed to quit and was always ready to fight no matter how many fighters they lost. The tide of the war had been turning in the mujahideen's favor in the last nine-twelve months and finding recruits, especially among the young, was too easy. Hence, the numerous requests for weapons instruction.

The Americans and their allies wanted to maintain the momentum the mujahideen was developing. The supply of light arms, along with the Rocket Propelled Grenades (RPG) was serving to even the match on the battlefield. And with rumors the surface-to-air Stinger Missile would be debuting later this year, it was a fine time to further apply pressure to convince the USSR to pull out of Afghanistan.

The Americans, in particular, were really enjoying themselves. The US never forgot how the USSR involvement kept the Viet Nam conflict alive; blaming them for guiding the North Vietnamese leadership until the bitter end when American forces fled the country in disgrace. Now it was time to return the favor in spades.

****

CIA Paramilitary operator Dirk Winter has traversed this region of Afghanistan several times since his assignment to assist with training mujahideen fighters in their war against the Soviet Union. He has slowly learned the best routes around the area as he tries to minimize the bouncing ride he encounters. A particularly hard swerve to avoid a massive hole resulted in his Jeep behaving like a bucking bronco, threatening to loosen the fillings in his molars.

Today started like any other when a request to assist a small group of fighters under a want-to-be warlord sent him for a late afternoon meeting with the local mujahideen fighters to discuss tactical battlefield assessments in addition to training on the use of Rocket Propelled Grenade (RPG) launchers.

Winter was a specialist in small arms training and battlefield tactics who was embedded with a Special Forces unit. He had been working along the Pakistani/Afghan border for the last three months, slipping effortlessly back and forth between the two countries. The US trainers succeeded with small teams of fighters attacking the slow-moving Soviet armored vehicles. They showed them how to create diversions to draw the quarry in and then spring the trap, leaving behind smoking shells of twisted metal. After they completed their task, they would meld back into the countryside. When, or if, Soviet reinforcements showed up, there was no one to attack.

The trainers settled on four four-man teams as the ideal number for tactical purposes. Each armored-vehicle hunter-killer team Winter would assemble had four RPG shooters. Each man would be shown how to fire the shoulder-mounted weapon to overcome the guaranteed casualties they would suffer.

****

Winter arrived about ten minutes late for the meeting, parking his Jeep about one hundred fifty feet in front of a sand colored building that may have been a warehouse at one time. He meets his interpreter, Khan, who is already outside waiting for him. Khan was a wisp of a young man with wavy black hair, black eyes, and a face framed by glasses. He received his education in Egypt, fluent in both English and Arabic. "Everything good?" he asks.

"Not bad," comes the reply. "Only hit one major hole this trip", Winter says, "but it was big enough to cause my helmet to fly off my head, ricochet off this equipment bag and bounce onto the road. Had to stop and go back to retrieve it."

Kahn smiled and nodded, not sure if he understood the humor of everything Winter said. As they walk through the door the local commander, Mohammed, was impatiently pacing back and forth. The fifteen Afghani recruits he had with him were more than anxious to join the fight against the Soviets. They were as green as grass, too rabid and a bit trigger happy. Hence, keep them busy.

Through Khan's words Winter explained that although the road leading to the village had been cleared of Soviet soldiers and was considered safe, caution was always observed. Sporting a 'let's get going look', Mohammad said he understood.

Winter started his session by explaining the most effective tactical use of the RPG weapon was in areas where armored vehicles were confined to a single path (a mountain road, swamps, snow, urban areas) in and out of a location. The RPG teams would trap the convoys by destroying the first and last vehicles in line, preventing movement of the other vehicles. This tactic was especially effective in cities. Snipers could lure their pursuers into ever smaller, narrower streets until there was no room for the large vehicle to maneuverer, then the turkey shoot could commence.

Khan suddenly stopped speaking and had a quizzical look on his face. Winter was sure his companion had no idea what a turkey shoot was. After a brief pause Khan spewed out his explanation and everyone laughed; message and meaning received.

Mohammed found this information to be of prime importance as the goal of his full group, about one hundred fifty fighters, was to infiltrate a city about twenty five miles west of this village and drive out the Soviet invaders. Mohammed spread out maps over a make-shift table to detail their planned route to the city. Switching between Arabic and broken English, Mohammed pointed out potential problems; but his rapid, clipped, speech indicated an enthusiastic view of the plan. Khan's interpretation further highlighted the confidence Mohammed was expressing.

After about an hour of standing around, a burst of raucous noise brought Mohammed and Winter's attention back to the fighters. Although the heat was nowhere near as bad as it would be in a few weeks, when combined with boredom it served to make the environment intolerable. Winter divided the Afghanis into groups of four and began to demonstrate how to carry the weapon, to load it, aim and fire. Each fighter went through the paces until they felted comfortable handing the weapon.

Chapter 2

Beyond the far rise, over a hill about two miles from where Winter was conducting his training, another meeting was taking place. A group of scrubby looking men, a local militia mixed with some irregular fighters from other nearby areas, had gathered. Adrenaline was running rampant against the background of rumors telling of an impending battle and they all want in on the action. They were carrying automatic rifles and small rounded objects that resembled grenades. Dirty looking, grubby beards and wearing mismatched clothing, they certainly looked the part of a rag tag bunch of misfits.

They were milling around in the midday sun, impatiently wasting time, going a little crazy, a tinderbox looking for a fuse. Several of their scouts had gathered information of a meeting not too far from where they are standing around and they were, what, looking for a signal? The enemy had gathered, why are we not killing them?

Their brothers had identified them, a young group of rogue tribesmen, working with the Soviet Satan, to betray their true calling, the jihad. To betray their own kind. The Qur'an was very specific in their mind; all who do not answer the call to jihad are also the enemy and must perish as well. They were hungry to take action.

The grumbling among the men was becoming more passionate, the desert heat increasing their ardor to fight. Several men began to jostle against each other; this thing could quickly explode into violence. Finally, a man wearing cleric robes, followed by two thick bodied men, bodyguard types, strides through the chaos, and turns to address the group.

"Our scouts have confirmed the enemy has gathered about two kilometers from us and have begun engaging in their unholy work. The only way to stop their evil is to attack and destroy all of them. We must send an irrefutable message that all who oppose our jihad shall be expunged. Leave no survivors and take all of their weapons. Go with the blessings of Allah; knowing that you are doing his work. May he grant you victory." With the speech over several men start giving orders to the fighters.

Hearing the words from the cleric that they about to enter battle with Allah's favor, their blood thirst has been whipped into a fever. Some of the men were driven to such a frenzy that they began walking towards their destination. Others were in a little more control of their emotions, choosing to ride in their vehicle of choice; the dirty, banged-up Toyota Hilux, the Afghan version of the Toyota Tacoma compact pickup truck.

The compact pickup truck is the chariot of mid-east warfare. Their mobility and speed make them ideal for desert fighting. The four-wheel-drives can tackle almost any terrain. Since they are light trucks they don't weigh much, allowing them to cross weak bridges and fragile roads that would be impassable to armored vehicles that weigh multiple tons. The pickup's bed is the perfect size for ferrying fighters or smaller weapons such as machine guns or mortars. In fact, just before leaving, a mortar was loaded into one of the vehicles.

Amid chants and shouts the fighters took off at a spirited clip. A whole lot of fast-moving mean with some nasty firepower was headed Winter's way. His afternoon was about to be turned upside down.

About a kilometer out the procession is halted. The fighters clamor out of their vehicles and gather around their commander. Raising his hands to quiet the assemblage, he speaks. "They are to split up and flank east and west. When in position a signal would be given to begin firing. Aim for the infidel brothers first in your initial barrage. The firing, coming from multiple direction, would confuse the young fighters. The ensuing chaos should eventually cause them to panic; they may even end up shooting each other. Keep yourselves at a distance and hidden as much as possible."

Glancing at the sky he noticed the encroaching darkness. Once he has surveyed the battlefield he should be able to determine further tactics. If lucky they could complete their task before the lack of daylight will hamper their vision. If not, they would hopefully be successful enough to simply conduct a mop up battle at first light. Also, in a new day's light he would be better able to determine how and when to deploy the mortar. That would be especially valuable if there are any buildings to reduce to rubble, thus eliminating hiding spots.

"Remember my brothers, patience," as he signals them to move forward. "Do not make any unnecessary noise, we don't want to tip them off we are here. Victory is ours."

Chapter 3

Winter was just finishing his hands-on instruction, and the fighters were laughing and smiling, definitely impressed with the new weapon they had been using. Suddenly, at the last possible moment, something would go terribly wrong with his mission.

Pop! Pop! Pop! Thud! Thud! Thud! Winter quickly drops into a crouch, scanning the scene around him. He's thinking *are those morons playing with their weapons?* He opens his mouth but before he can utter a sound, he feels something hit his body, then grunts in response to a wet, burning sensation. Falling to the ground and screaming at Khan he says, "What the fuck, did those assholes just shoot me"?

He reaches up high on his right thigh and finds where the blood is oozing from his leg. The gun fire is increasing in intensity as he hears Mohammed screaming at his fighters. He grits his teeth and crawls under his Jeep trying to find a safe haven. He feels someone bumping his elbow; turning to see Mohammed also seeking cover.

Clearing his head a bit and catching his breath, Winters looks out and sees the young Afghanis firing their weapons indiscriminately as they scatter around the grounds, trying to find a place to hide as the bullets keep zinging at them. Mohammed's commands don't resonate with them. Turning back toward Winter, with a quizzical look on his face, Mohammed stammers out, "turkey shoot?"

"Something like that," Winter answered. It's just not that funny when your ass is the one being shot at.

A brief lull in the firing lends an opportunity for Winter to pull himself cautiously up the side of his Jeep, and he begins searching for something behind the driver's seat. The pain from his leg is burning into his brain like a mother-fucker. Bumping into something hard he wraps his hand around the object and lifts it up; a first aid kit. No sooner than he finishes that task, the firing starts again.

Ducking down for cover he opens the kit and begins flipping through the contents. Bandages, bandages, ahh, a syringe and a small bottle, morphine. He loads the needle and jams it into his leg, soon feeling relief from his pain. Winter tears at his pants, exposing the wound. The bleeding had stopped, and Winter found a small hole, a nick more than anything. The burning makes him believe the fragment must have creased a nerve. Muttering to himself, he secures a bandage over the wound and tapes it into place.

Winter turns around to scan the area, trying to assess the situation. The gun fire, while not as heavy as it was, is still coming at his position. Mohammed doesn't appear wounded. He's barking orders, still trying to direct his inexperienced fighters who are in a wild frenzy. Winter believes the firing is coming from a small rise he passed about two hundred fifty yards back up the road. It's not very high but it still provides an elevated advantage to whoever the hell is shooting at them. Winter counts four, five, six fighters on the ground, not moving. Dead, he figures. He sees three more hiding behind the makeshift table they turned upright for a shield. The others have scattered; maybe even fleeing the scene.

So, who the hell is shooting at them Winter wonders. If the Soviets have been cleared out.., Afghanis attacking each other? It's certainly not unheard of in this country. The tribal warfare here has raged on for decades, even centuries, Winter figures. They basically stopped fighting with each other long enough to unite to drive out foreign invaders, then it's back to business as usual. If one tribe thought another was gaining the upper hand, well...

Where the hell is Khan, I don't remember seeing him when I looked over the scene. Could he somehow be involved in this carnage? Nahhhh. Although new to Winter's unit, he had been thoroughly vetted, working as an interpreter for other units with no issues. Still…..*Enough with that shit thinking; it's getting dark and we need shelter before the shooters begin to move on them.*

Remembering the building he parked in front of was about one hundred fifty feet away, he grabs Mohammed's arm, signaling him to follow as he duck walks toward the building. The ground to the building was wide open with only the make-shift tables and a couple of oil barrels as barriers. If they stay low maybe they can reach the building and, do what exactly? His radio was with him when the shooting broke out and now, who knows where it is. Still, the building may give them a fighting chance; if their enemy wants them bad enough they will have to enter the building to kill everyone. If they aren't that important the building will at least provide shelter.

After what seemed like an eternity, with bullets whizzing around them, Winter and Mohammed, joined by three other fighters, reach the building. The door is cracked a bit and appears to be opening ever so slowly. Finally, the door opens quickly, and a hand reaches out to them. Kahn! Once everyone is inside the door is pushed closed and barricaded by some tables and a desk type object.

"Kahn," Winter says, "I wasn't sure what happened to you." Kahn, who had been speaking to Mohammed and the other Afghanis, turns to Winter.

"Shortly after the shooting started I was immediately knocked on my ass. When I realized I wasn't dead I made my way into this building. I tried to coax the others into the building with me, but they were scared and started running around, blindly firing their guns. Four of them were shot as they tried to hide behind the building. I dragged two of them into the back of the building, they died soon after I got them in. They had their weapons and some ammo belts on them. I removed them and put them in that pile behind you." Kahn reaches up and removes his helmet, tossing it to Winter. "Thanks for making me wear this."

Winter sees the hole at the top of the helmet; probably an inch lower and Kahn wouldn't have made it. "You're welcome." *Four Afghanis, me and Kahn.*

Looking over Kahn's pile he notes there are enough rifles for everyone and some ammo. If whoever is out there comes looking for us we will be able to rattle their chains a bit. We may even be able to take out a small force. "Did you find any food or water?", Winter asked.

"No nothing," came the reply.

Soon the building is engulfed in darkness; there hasn't been any shooting for quite a while now. "All we can do now is wait," Winter says to no-one in particular. Silence is the response. May as well try to get some sleep.

Chapter 4

Winter shifts and turns over, slowly waking up. After a few moments his head clears and his eyesight refocuses. He noticed a ray of sunshine beaming into the building, dawn's early light. He hears noise, voices, talking behind him. Suddenly he hears a single gunshot. He turned around to see Kahn and Mohammed in a rather animated exchange. After another minute or two they approach Winter, with Kahn doing the talking.

Kahn explained that two of the other fighters had slipped out during the night instead of taking guard duty. The third one was getting ready to leave when Mohammed shot at him. The fighter looked back at Mohammed, raised his weapon, then lowered it and kept on walking. Mohammed aimed again but Kahn prevented him from firing. Their argument resulted in Kahn convincing Mohammed not to kill the fleeing figure.

Winter was now questioning how long Mohammed would stick around and, for that matter, Khan. Kahn wasn't a trained fighter and Winter wasn't sure if he even knew how to fire a weapon. However, one thing he was sure of, Kahn wasn't a coward and would do his best in a battle. Still...

The three of them scattered throughout the building looking for places where they could fire at the encroaching enemy while at the same time providing some cover. Most areas where they would be able to see the front of the building and fire from are extremely vulnerable to return fire.Although no natural cover is available in the building they managed to move several sturdy metal objects to hide behind without blocking their line of sight onto the open ground in front of them.

Mohammed and Kahn take cover on the left side of the building while Winter is on the right. They each have an automatic rifle, and four ammo belt clips; not a lot to sustain a long firefight. Their best chance stems from the fact the enemy will need to engage across the open field and grounds leading to their building. If the goal is to take the building and kill or capture them, the enemy will suffer casualties. If the attacking force is large in number they will eventually succeed, Winter thinks. He still can't reason why this building or they, are so damn important.

As the gray of the early dawn gives way to brighter sunlight, Winter watches as fighters begin to move from the fading shadows toward the building. As he repositioned himself, the first volley of bullets begins striking their position. After three to four minutes of steady firing, things go quiet. Winter quickly checks his group; no one was hit. His best guess is the shots mostly struck the ground in front of the building as he heard nothing to make him believe the building had been hit. He's not sure why, doesn't really care, and begins their response by firing back across the terrain in the direction he thought he had seen movement earlier.

In an effort to conserve their ammunition they each fire off ten shots and then stopped. Looking over the terrain Winter tries to assess the effect of their efforts. He doesn't see anything to make him believe they inflicted any casualties. He also doesn't see any movement to indicate the enemy is advancing towards them. It seems they are content to keep them pinned down from a safe distance.

However, about five hundred feet beyond his Jeep, left in front of the building, he believes he sees a rather large, partially camouflaged object. A bright glint of sunshine makes him believe the object exists, however, the same reflection renders him unable to more clearly identify what he has spotted.

A loud, thunderous boom; a screaming, whistling sound, then the explosion at the end. Sounds like a mortar round was fired towards them. Winter looks out and sees his Jeep has been destroyed. Another thunderous boom and the explosion to his left; this round struck the building, leaving a monstrous hole right where Khan and Mohammed had been secluded; collapsing the building inward. Winter calls out, no reply. If either of them survived they are most likely buried beneath the rubble.

A lull in the gunfire allows Winter to look out and see two distinct groups with several figures in each, moving toward the building. It appears they are readying to storm his position; as to why, unless maybe it's an inter-Afghani squabble, he has no idea. Still no noise coming from the destroyed part of the building, so Winter is assuming its him against however many fighters are thrown at him.

The gunfire starts again, but Winter notices a difference in what he's hearing. This round of firing seems to be emanating from a further distance, behind the location of the first firings, and a bit west. Winter sees the fighters, two dozen or so, gathered together maybe one hundred twenty five yards from him. It seems like they are waiting for a signal before storming the building. Well, let'm come, Winter says to himself; I may not survive but I'll take a lot of them with me before I go down. He cocks his head and listens. Is that the distinctive whopping sound of a helicopter? Who the hell wants me that badly?

At the sound of the helicopter the fighters rise up and charge toward the building. Multiple burst of shots, coming from Winter's left, ring out and eight fighters are cut down. What the hell, Winter thinks, where did those shots come from, and who fired them. Winter's turn and he mows down three more himself. The figures temporary halt their charge to regroup.

Winter still hears the whopping of the helicopter in the distance background, behind the current position directly in front of him. There appears to be one hell of a battle going on over there; punctuated by a loud explosion. One thing for certain, the mortar fire has ceased. Whoever is in the chopper must be on his side. He quickly peers to the west and spies two figures in uniform. They must be soldiers and they are flanking the fighters. Whoever they are they are definitely on his side.

Round two and it appears more fighters have joined the fracas. This time about a dozen men charge his position. Winter cuts downs the front wave of three fighters and ducks for cover. The building is peppered with bullets. Another line of fire from his left, eliminates several more. A brief lull in the firing allows Winter to look over the terrain; it looks like six fighters will reach his position. Winter quickly drops back a few feet to regroup.

Suddenly a burst of automatic weapon fire from behind him takes out three Afghanis. What the hell! He quickly spins on his heels, seeing someone in a military uniform to his left and slightly behind. He looks back to the front; no one in sight, they must be hiding behind the rubble created from the mortar shell which struck earlier. Noticing movement in front of him and to his right, he crouches, sights and fires. Damn, his rifle has jammed!

Nothing and then, an explosion like a hand grenade has gone off. Automatic weapon fire is being exchanged outside the building, then silence. Three fighters are running towards him, this is going to be hand-to-hand combat. At least it's three -on-two.

A shot echoes out and one fighter is down. Winter spins to his feet and meets the second fighter with a karate kick; however, his buddy slides in and delivers a solid blow to the side of Winter's face. Winter rolls to his right, barely avoiding a kick to his head. As the second fighter lines him up again for another blow, a blur flies through the air; taking him out with a tackle. The first fighter, momentarily distracts, misses a punch and Winter grabs his arms and flips him over his head, watching him land with a thud. He turns in time to see the soldier drop his opponent with a spin kick to the face. He picks up the fighter he tossed and spins his head; a distinctive crack, and the fighter slumps.

Winter turns his attention back to the fighter who received the spin kick. He staggers back to his feet, swinging a knife. Before he can move, a shot rings out from his left and the fighter drops. Winter hollers out "I had it under control."

"I know," came the reply in a distinctly English accent, "but he wasn't going to surrender and this was faster." Before Winter can answer back, the soldier raises his hand; "sshhhh. Listen." Winter quickly closes his mouth and listens. Nothing; no weapons fire, explosions, or helicopter noise; just dead, eerie silence.

Chapter 5

Winter is startled by noise from his left, near where the front entrance to the building was before it was blown in; where Kahn and Mohammed were buried. Instinctively Winter raise his rifle as he whirls toward the noise. The soldier with him recognizes the uniform and says to Winter, "Hold it, he's with me."

"Thernopolis," comes the call from a voice with a bit thicker English accent. "Everything alright here? Did we get our man?"

"I didn't get around to introductions yet, had a little mop up work to finish first," answers Thernopolis, "But I sure as hell hope we saved the right Bloke, otherwise this firefight ain't over yet." Turning towards Winter, who has a quizzical look and his rifle at the ready, the soldier asks, "Are you Dirk Winter, United States CIA officer?"

"Who wants to know?", Winter asked, warily eyeing the soldier who helped out of his jam, not sure himself if the fight is truly over.

"Thernopolis." Comes the answer, "MI6." Pointing at the other soldier with them, "that's Williams, British Special Forces."

"What are you doing here?" Winter demands.

Williams, "We just happened to be headed to your forward command yesterday afternoon to meet with you when chatter came over the radio that the Afghanis had a Soviet commander pinned down in an abandoned building with a group of Afghani turn coats. The coordinates matched where you were supposed to be training Afghani fighters. We radioed ahead to your command to report what we had heard. They had also heard the conversation. They didn't have a rapid response team available for immediate action; hoping you would be able to hold out until morning. We hid our vehicle about a mile back and snuck in on your west side. Just as we advanced to about one hundred meters away from your position, all hell broke loose."

Thernopolis' turn, "We weren't sure, but it appeared some of your trainees may have fired at you and each other in yesterday's chaos."

Winter nodded, saying "That's what I thought, that some of them were involved with the ambush."

Thernopolis continued, "Anything's possible, that's why we didn't fire, we weren't really sure who was the enemy. The bulk of the fire seemed to originate from over the last roll of terrain before here, which was out of our range. We stayed out of sight and radioed our position and your location back to your base, then hunkered down for the night. Your guys came in with a chopper this morning after the Afghani attack started and took out their position. Once they took out the mortar unit we took out part of the first wave advancing towards you. We fought our way in to look for you and provide any further assistance you might need. Were you alone here?"

Winter: "No, I had an Afghani interpreter with me, along with several Afghani fighters and their leader. My interpreter and the leader stayed behind while the others fled during the night. They were holed up behind that pile of rubble to your left that used to be a wall. The second mortar round scored a direct hit on us and took it down."

Williams, "Sorry to hear that."

Winters asks Williams, "How did you end up with an MI-6 partner?"

Thernopolis, "I got that one. It's a new type of deployment we have. The big brass figured it was just as easy to place a few of us with regular combat units. We're here basically to observe combat positions and tactical decisions. Strictly hands off. However, if the situation requires defensive action, and in your case we are helping a friend and ally, we can deliver rapid response to neutralize the bad guys.

Winter, "What have you learned?"

Williams, "Officially we are here to help an ally. Look, everyone knows the U.S.'s main purpose is to return the bloody nose to the USSR that you got from them in Viet Nam. Can't say we blame you. And with the Afghanis you've got a tough group to deal with; they don't quit regardless of how tough the odds are. They fight amongst themselves, but they will unite to fight a common foreign intruder.

"We Brits have had a tussle or two with them during our past imperial rulings. We have learned that some of these guys are just plain nuts, and others, not so bad. And to think your country is arming these guys indiscriminately. Who knows who they'll shoot at next, maybe both of our countries."

Winter half heard Williams as his attention was focused on Thernopolis walking to the back of the building. There was something different about that guy, he just wasn't sure what. Maybe just an unusual walk. He whispers to Williams, "What's up with Thernopolis? There's something a bit different with him but I can't put my finger on it. You know, the funny walk; just different."

"That's because he's a she."

Confused, Winter replies, "Huh, Who's a she? What are you talking about?"

"Thernopolis, he's a she. I mean, she's a woman, Thernopolis." Changing the subject Williams asks, "What's with the liquid on your right leg?"

Winter reaches down and feels the wet spot on his leg. In the ensuing action it apparently started bleeding again, a slow trickle. "Nothing really, just cut myself shaving."

"Interesting response," Thernopolis pipes up, which elicits a grin from Winter. Noticing the grin and Williams' deadpan expression, she says, "Ahhh. You Yanks, not sure I understand your humor." She walks over to Winter, "I've had some medical training, let me take a look." Winter hesitates a bit, prompting Thernopolis to exclaim, "Don't worry, I won't bite. Maybe just a small nibble or two. Don't worry, you can keep your pants on if it makes you feel better."

Williams inquires, "Would you two like to be alone?" In unison they both reply, "Shut up!"

Thernopolis pulls the bandage aside and examines the wound. Nice and with a little seepage. Winter says, "If I'm lucky my first aid kit is somewhere near the shell of my Jeep."

Williams hustles outside and finds a square box fully intact near the back tire. He scoops it up and returns inside, handing the box to Thernopolis. Shaking his head he says, "The weird thing about the destruction of objects is what survives. Your Jeep is a total mess and the first aid kit is fine."

Thernopolis opens the kit, rummages a bit and finds fresh gauge. She opens the package, removes the old bandage from Winter's leg, and secures the new one in its place. "As good as new," she proclaims. "I would still have it checked out when we get you back to your base."

Winter examines her handiwork. "Thanks," he says. "I'll have it looked at."

Just as the Brits load Winter into their Jeep and prepare to depart, a helicopter takes one last flyby. An individual, peering over what looks like a long gun instead is aligning his sights for something else. Click. Click, click, click, click.

Chapter 6

Williams and Thernopolis drop Winter off at the location where the Americans have established a camp along the Pakistani border. After Winter's wound is checked out, nothing serious; it's cleaned, and a few stitches are used to close the small hole. Winter's boss, Ed Jeffers, appeared for a debrief on what happened as soon as the doctor finished his work. Winter goes through the events of the last 24 hours, hitting the high points on how his training session was interrupted when they were attacked by unknown forces.

"After holing up overnight in a building, all hell broke loose the next morning when a major onslaught was launched against my position. The majority of the Afghanis I was training were killed during the initial firefight while the survivors took off during the overnight. Their leader stayed behind and was lost during the battle, along with my interpreter.

"Just as things were getting dicey in the building, Thernopolis and Williams showed up to help me destroy the onslaught. Meanwhile, our rescue team had arrived and were mopping up the remainder of the fighters that didn't assault the building. Then my new British friends brought me here."

Jeffers just nods with no response; everything Winters has told him matches to the information from the yesterday's radio chatter and the report from the leader of the helicopter unit.

Sensing that Jeffers isn't going to say anything Winter asks, "So, Ed, any idea as to what may have happened?"

Jeffers, "Our best intel picked up chatter that you had been identified as a Russian arms dealer looking to make a deal with non-Afghani fighters. The local Mujahideen then rounded up fighters to attack you.

From your description some of the fighters you were working with melded back into the countryside. We'll let those assholes deal with each other.

"I have a new assignment for you. You are going to Cairo, Egypt, to conduct the same training you were doing here. We have made contact with an individual we believe to be an Egyptian spy who is training anti-Soviet fighters en route to Afghanistan. You will assist with the instruction on RPG launchers".

Winter's made a 'damned, not this type of assignment again' face. This work was getting old fast. He wanted action, just not as crazy as the ambush earlier today. Jeffers picked up his body language, adding, "Our MI-6 counterparts have picked up information on arms dealers trying to make connections with the Iranians to receive shipments of Chinese Silkworm anti-ship missiles. Our belief is the transaction, if concluded, will see the missiles end up on the Al-Faw peninsula where they will be used to harass shipping in the Strait of Hormuz. Who knows, the Iranians may even get lucky and actually hit a ship or two and sink it.

"Anyways, the data is considered raw, but promising. And it's possible you will get to take out a launch site if we find one. Questions?"

Winter shakes his head no although the thought of a positive response to the weapons smuggling gets his attention.

"Good, a vehicle is waiting for you out front to take you back over the Khyber Pass to Peshawar. From there you will catch a flight to Cairo. Move out, keep your eyes and ears open, and trust no one. Egypt is still a hell hole with a lot of weapons, making it tough to figure out who is a friend and who is your foe. The same person may be both depending on how the wind blows. And, good luck."

Winter walks out of the building, thinking overall this job sounds as bad as Afghanistan. Hmm. MI-6 again. Sounds like the cooperation of our allies' spy agencies is the real deal. At the thought of MI-6, he scans the area to see where his British compatriots are. Off to his right he sees Thernopolis loading gear into a camouflaged truck. Walking on over he calls out while waving, "Heading out?"

"Yep."

"Where to?"

"Cairo."

"So am I. Hey, wait, the boss said MI-6 was tracking arms dealers running in North Africa. Are you involved?"

"Yep, running the mission with your CIA. I understand you will be observing and learning when you're not providing weapons instruction. Always good to have another set of eyes on the street, so to speak."

She pauses a minute then says, "Since this truck is your mode of transportation, how about you finish loading this equipment while I try to find some grub?"

Thernopolis walks across the compound towards a greenish, tent-like structure. Winter watches her trek; one, to see where she's headed and two, now that he knows the story, he decides he likes the ever so slight sway in her hips as she strides purposefully over the ground. As she disappears through the door he turns his mind to complete the task at hand.

After a few minutes of hauling gear he realizes he's famished. He quickly finishes loading the truck and hustles over to see if Thernopolis was successful in finding food. Walking into the 'building' he notices a chow line has been setup. He steps up, grabs a beverage and some semi-warm sandwiches; then turns to look for Thernopolis, finding her at a corner table, where he joins her.

"Not exactly a five-star café but it will do," said Thernopolis. "The food is good enough to fill the hollow spot. All finished with the truck?"

Winter nods while chowing down. "All loaded up and ready to go," comes the reply. "Who's driving?"

"I was told there will be a driver ready to go in about half an hour, forty-five minutes."

They casually chat about nothing in particular to pass the wait for the driver. They each go grab seconds; who knows when they will eat again. While dining Thernoplois isn't wearing any head gear. Winter notices her jet black hair and beautiful green eyes. She smiles easily as she teases him about his "American" colloquialisms, which he spits out rapid fire. Just as Winter believes he has run out of things to say a soldier approaches and announces it's time to move out.

Chapter 7

Peshawar, Pakistan
Near the Sunehri Mosque

Down an alley, about a stone's throw from the Sunehri mosque, stands a nondescript sandstone structure, similar in appearance to many buildings throughout the city. On the second floor a group of Islamic fighters are holding a meeting. The men are dirty and grubby looking, caked in sweat like they have spent the entire day rolling or crawling through the desert sand. They are wearing drab olive green or brown, semi-military looking clothing; all are sporting the traditional beards. They are hot, thirsty, hungry, yet excited.

The assembled group is comprised of individuals representing many ethnic groups/tribes, mostly from Afghanistan and Pakistan, with a few stragglers from other mid-eastern countries. They are all either commanders, warlords, or close to their local warlords. They gather in Pakistan to plan strategy and then move to the battlefield.

Rumor has it that tonight is the promise of an appearance of a great leader of the resistance. While not a decorated fighter, cleric or military tactician, he will use his vast personal fortune to help fund the mujahideen by funneling arms, money and fighters from the Arab world into Afghanistan, earning respect and popularity among many Arabs.

The assorted groups have come to Afghanistan for one reason, jihad. They know the battlefield has been rapidly shifting in favor of the mujahideen and they are eager to fight. The infidels must be defeated and driven from the holy lands of the Muslim world forever.

The deal they have made with the Americans is one of necessity, not of mutual trust; after all these are Jews and Christians, sons of the long-ago Crusaders. There are to many obstacles to ever develop trust with any of them. Still, in this case a deal had to be made; the old adage the enemy of my enemy is my friend is once again in human history, adhered.

The Americans are still smarting from their disgrace in the Viet Nam War which was accomplished through heavy, some believe solely because of, the involvement of the USSR. The Afghani resistance knew the only way to counter the military prowess of the USSR was to turn to a military power of equal or greater prowess.

Taking advantage of the Americans eagerness to get involved, the conditions demanded by the leaders of the jihad was relatively simple. We will accept your weapons, training, tactical assistance and so forth. When the war is over you will leave your military equipment behind so we will be able to defend ourselves from any future attacks. In addition, you will leave our lands. The US quickly agreed to the terms, recognizing that from time to time they might have the opportunity to strike at their common foe.

Finally, the din in the room dissipated as men entered from the back of the room to control the meeting. Many of the new arrivals were dressed in clerical robes, some donning elaborate turbans. A tall, he towered over the others by a good head in height, distinguished man was accompanying the religious men. When quiet was establish one of the religious leaders, a fat, one-eyed man, stopped conferring with the tall man, and began to speak.

"Brothers, we have gathered to tell you the latest happenings of our great crusade." Gesturing towards the tall Arab he continued. "Our devout brother here are secured many more arms to aid us in our jihad." A buzz of excitement permeates through the gathered masses.

"So many men have been swept up in the fervor, their desire to join our great cause attracting so many fighters that we are having problems keeping proper track of the recruits. It will be your responsibility to keep them separated by ethnicity and tribal loyalties so they won't turn on each. Don't worry if you lose some men in battle; those men will live forever in glory in the presence of Allah. Plus, there are many others ready to replace them on the grounds of glory. Victory is ours; it just requires perseverance and faith. Remember, everything is possible through Allah.

"My second announcement is to inform you of a highly successful attack on a Russian encampment. Our fearless brothers swooped down on a Russian commander training a group of our fellow tribesmen, infidels, in the use of weapons against us. The glorious battle resulted in the death of all of our enemies. We captured many weapons to use in our future fights."

A loud din of enthusiasm is alive among the commandeers as they listen of the great victory.

The cleric wraps up his presentation, "Now, my brothers, use the news of this great success to go forth and meet the enemy. Destroy them in their nests, knowing that you have the blessings of Allah."

Never is the actual truth of the events ever mentioned; about how the only ones killed were their fellow mujahideen who wanted to be warriors. That all of the attackers were killed by the American forces, not Russians, who came to rescue their trainer embedded with the resistance. The truth; obscured by the other hallmarks of Third World warfare: bad intelligence, weak leadership, poor planning.

As the meeting broke up the speaker hurried over to confer with their honored brother. "Just a little bit coloring of the truth, wasn't it,?" he asks.

"Just a small bit," the cleric responds. "It's the excitement of success that keeps the faithful going. Besides, those who were killed were of a different tribe than the raiding party. They would probably end up killing each other at a future date. We just sped up the process."

A calloused son-of-bitch thinks the honored one. "As you say my brother, you know what's best for our jihad. Now, onto other business. I've just secured a vast cache of weaponry for our cause. Come help me devise a plan to send them into Egypt under disguise so they won't be intercepted." Smiling he continues, "You seem to me to be quite devious when it suits you purpose."

"Yes, yes," is the reply. "Let me reach out to some of the field commanders from Egypt who were in attendance tonight. They should be able to identify many supporters to aid us in our quest. I've heard some of the intelligence agencies haven't expressed worries over our ultimate intent in this war. They seem to wish that their weapons only reach 'approved' groups to help exact revenge of a prior grievance. And they accuse us of harboring grudges forever. I believe an expression goes, it's like the pot calling the kettle black. Indeed!"

"Hence the need for your wise guidance," says the tall one. As the rotund cleric leaves, he is left alone for a few minutes to ruminate. *Maybe I could grow to trust the bastard, especially if I can manipulate him to achieve my goals. I just need to be wary of his vast ability to manipulate others. We're like the cobra and the mongoose. What's his name again, Mullah something or other. It's not important now. We need to focus on moving the newly arriving weapons.*

Shortly the cleric reappears with several other men, intruding on his private thoughts. Gesturing at the men the cleric says, "These are the leaders from Egypt. They know all of the important and not so important players in their territory." Pointing towards a table he says, "Come, let us put our heads together and try to develop a successful plan. Our future success depends on bringing more weapons to the battlefields."

Yep, thinks the tall one, this partnership just may work out. Besides, if he betrays I will just kill him, holy man or not.

Chapter 8

US Embassy
Cairo, Egypt

At the American Embassy in Cairo two men are sitting at a large, weathered wooden table in the far corner of the room. Maps, photos, and satellite images are attached to the walls as well as scattered across their table. The younger looking of the two men, an American, speaks.

"So, lets discuss what this mission is about and the people involved."

The other man removes an ever present pipe from his mouth, and, speaking with a clear British accent replies, "This is a joint mission with your CIA and our MI-6 into the tracking of weapons shipments into and out of the Mid-East."

"I know that," interrupts the American, a little bit of arrogance in his tone. "Let's get to the crux of this great exchange of spy agencies."

Ignoring the tone, his colleague plunges on. "A lot of war materiel, including fighters, are flying all over the place, so to speak. Your country and my country currently are racing to keep up with all of this activity. Our biggest concern is that the deliveries are falling into the hands of "unapproved groups". By combining our somewhat limited sources we can increase our firepower and perhaps slow down the flow. If we are lucky we may even determine a point of origination."

Pondering the thought for a moment, and not really sure how to respond, the American adds, "Interesting idea. My guys and your guys banding together to chase the bad guys. It just might work."

The biggest thing bothering him is that the Brits seemed to have more input in running this operation than he does. Still, when briefed by his station chief he voiced only one objection; he didn't want to be window dressing. He wanted to be sure his ideas will be incorporated into the overall strategy. No problem the station chief assured him.

Time to test this Brit's honesty, he thought. "So, tell me about your man heading up your part of the operation? I would like to know a little bit about him."

The other man briefly pauses; he knows the American has seen the file on his point person, just like he has a file on his man and has read it. If he wants to test my integrity, so be it. But first, some fun. He takes a draw from his pipe and then blows out the smoke, a nutmeg aroma. "I don't have a point man in charge of this mission."

"What are you talking about?"

Trying to maintain his poker face and definitely winning this battle, the British accent responds, "I'm telling you I don't have a point man running this operation."

"Sure you do, his name is Thernopolis," the American fires back. *Oh shit, he says to himself, I just told him I pulled the file on his operative. Oh well, that what spies do, we spy, even on our friends.*

Knowing the sex of Thernopolis wasn't included in the file that was tapped, the Brit continued. "It's not a he, he's a she."

"What in the hell are you talking about?" The American's voice is starting to exhibit a little bit of frustration.

Setting his pipe down to prepare himself for a story, the Brit continues, "My MI-6 officer is Maya Thernopolis, a woman, and if I may say so myself, she's one of the best officers that we have in the entire service." A smile creases his face as he is clearly delighted in putting one over on his CIA counterpart. He continues with the basics.

"She comes from good stock. Her father is Greek, an engineer who works for British Petroleum (BP). The mother is a British citizen who works for the British Embassy; including working for us at MI-6. The father was transferred to BP headquarters in London during Maya's senior year in high school with the family joining him after her graduation. After she graduated from the University of London she applied to us and was accepted."

His chest puffed a bit, like speaking of his daughter, he continues. "She has distinguished herself from day one, quickly rising through the ranks. She an expert in hand-to-hand combat, as well with all types of small arms weapons, including qualifying for Marksman and Sniper designations. She's a cracker jack intelligence analyst, well versed in interpreting satellite photos and tying it to human intelligence. Also, she's more than capable of leading teams in acting on that information. The sky's the limit for her in our operation. Now, what about your guy, assuming he is, indeed, a he?"

Funny, funny. Boy, never did I think his officer was a woman. Very impressive resume.

"My guy is indeed a guy. Name is Dirk Winter. He's also a college graduate, a member of the school's Reserve Officers' Training Corps (ROTC). He joined the United States Army, ending up in the Army Special Forces, colloquially known as the Green Beret. He became an expert in unconventional warfare in addition to becoming a combat weapons instructor.

"He is qualified as an expert with explosives, he blows things up quite well. "In addition to the highest ranking with both rifles and pistols, he's proficient in the use of Rocket Propelled Grenade launchers and Bazookas and a qualified in instructor with both weapons.

"We recruited him for our paramilitary group, thus he's a Paramilitary Operations Officer. In my opinion, putting Thernopolis and Winter together should be a very unique pairing."

With the interlude of testing each other and swapping the bios of their leaders over, they return to pouring over the intelligence laid out before them. While the data is voluminous, something is missing; and it's the 'what' that's driving them up a wall.

Chapter 9

A jarring ride through the Khyber Pass nearly loosened their teeth and a few other things. Once at the airport in Peshawar they took a military flight to Cairo. The flight was smoother than the trek to Peshawar but still quite noisy; not allowing for any real sleep or conversation. Finally, twelve hours after they left Afghanistan they arrived in Cairo, deplaned and scrambled into an official car for the journey to the embassy.

The afternoon sun was quite warm coming through the car windows. Since there was no airconditioning, or simply not turned on or not working if it existed, the windows were opened as far as they could be lowered. The driver deftly negotiates the twists, turns and bumps along the route, finally pulling into the underground parking garage of the embassy and discharges his passengers.

A waiting security guard escorted them through the garage to a back elevator which they take to the third floor. The doors open into a waiting room outside a large conference center. The guard punched in a code, escorted them into the room and then left.

Two men are staring at satellite images that show a seaport and rail yard as they walk in. They keep on talking between themselves, asking and answering questions; totally ignoring Winter and Thernopolis.

A soft throat clearing by Thernopolis is quickly followed with a louder one from Winter; that seemed to break the men's concentration. "Come in and close the door," one of the men says as he gestures at the images; both still have their backs turned toward Winter and Thernopolis.

"I believe you may be right," comes the reply in a British accent. "And, if I'm correct," he continues, "the people who just entered our domain will hopefully provide the answers to our questions."

Turning to face them the taller man, lean, fit, red haired and freckled, extends his hand to Winter. "Rob Wilson, CIA Officer in charge of this mission. You must be my man, Winter?"

Shaking the extended hand, "That's right, Dirk Winter, paramilitary operations officer."

"And, you must be Maya Thernopolis," says the other man, "that makes you my mission operator. Charles Scott, lead MI6 Officer for this detail" as he reaches for Thernopolis's hand.

Scott, a slight bit of grey at the temples of his dark hair, looks trim with an aristocratic jaw line and sports a vice-like hand grip. He definitely the oldest of the two command officers, probably in his late forties.

"Sir," Thernopolis says, "As we walked in I believe you commented that the people who just entered the room will provide answers to our questions. We weren't provided with any information prior to leaving Afghanistan."

"Nor were you supposed to have any. Follow me over to the satellite images and I will explain myself." Crossing the room to the far wall, he continues his talk. "Egypt remains a hot bed for arms trafficking due to its unique location and its history of Islamic militarism. Arms flow into Egypt to militants and out to other fighters both east and west while some weapons are kept for internal operations.

"What we are focusing on is traffic traversing the coast and the associated ports along the Mediterranean Sea. A lot of the weapons are transported in small vessels, such as fishing trawlers. These boats are hard to detect and even more difficult to intercept. There are many official and unofficial "stops" along the way where weapons can be loaded or unloaded, and the boats hidden from prying eyes."

Pointing to the first image, Scott explains; "This is the Port of Alexandria. It about 180 kilometers, or 110 miles, in distance you Yanks understand, from here. It takes about three hours to travel between the two cities. We have intel from agents that we are trying to coordinate their locations via the satellite images and their intelligence reports.

"Mostly what we've received from the photos and human reports is raw data indicating potential shipments of arms, either going out or coming in, and to who and where, the weapons may be going. We also have similar satellite photos for several other ports including each port on the Mediterranean Sea.

"Your role, Thernopolis, will be to interpret the raw information. You will monitor the intel coming in, correlate the satellite images to written reports, identify potential targets and plan interdiction efforts. The goal is to take weapons out of the hands of the 'bad guys', either capturing or destroying shipments as needed. Thus, we believe you will be providing the answers at some point in the near future."

"And you will have two responsibilities", Wilson says to Winter, "First, provide weapons training to groups identified by CIA agents as friendlies before they reach the battlefield. While we believe the training you provide will be to "acceptable allies", one can never be 100% positive. Therefore, you will also be alert to any indications, hints, that the groups will be diverting weapons or themselves to unauthorized purposes.

"Second, any pertinent information gathered will be relayed to Thernopolis. If anything becomes actionable you will team with various assets on the ground to guide the surveillance and participate as needed."

Winter, "Meaning?"

"Meaning, use your judgment to act as necessary. If action is taken, you will assist and coordinate any efforts through Thernopolis and her team. All efforts will be taken so your cover won't be compromised. So, while you can lead a team to a certain location, we prefer you to lay back while others do the heavy lifting."

Winter frowns at that statement; but, before he answers, Wilson raises his hand, a signal to hold your tongue. "However, if it's necessary to blow your cover to conclude an operation, then by all means do so. In the event of blowing your cover, you will need to be pulled as a trainer and reassigned. Therefore, use great discretion before acting."

Scott adds, "Interpreters will be available to help you with the language barriers. All information obtained will be fed back to central intelligence here to develop any interdiction efforts. In addition, our agents will be providing oversight of the fighter groups.

"And, Winter, be careful. While our agents and assets will do their best to vet the people you will deal with, remember these assholes will shoot at each other over the slightest provocation. You can easily get caught in the crossfire."

"Don't I know it," Winter responded.

****

After Winter and Thernopolis depart to find quarters to get themselves situated, Wilson says, "So..tell me a little more about your officer."

"Sure. Thernopolis was the youngest woman to graduate from the service's revamped training program and also the youngest woman to achieve field operation officer status. She has participated in numerous missions on foreign territory, proving herself on many occasions. She achieved a reputation for bold leadership, decisive action and fearlessness. She very proud of her service; she has been called a natural operative and has devoted herself to it, heart and soul.

"She expanded her talents to include intelligence after a mission she led went sideways and she was captured. For a while we thought she had bought the farm, but she escaped, leading a special ops team that was looking for her back to where she had been tortured to help free her fellow captives. To say we believe she can walk on water would be a fair assessment."

"Very impressive," says Wilson, mulling over in his mind what to add about Winter. "I don't have the same to add about Winter. We recruited him from the Army to add to our Paramilitary Operations Group. We have the option to recruit from our military when we seek to add specialists to unique units. We liked his abilities in unconventional warfare, in addition to his skill as an explosives' expert and weapons' instructor.

"When we reached out to him he was ready, after three years of active duty with the Army, to try something different. He has led assaults on facilities to rescue hostages and to destroy positions deep behind enemy lines. To say anything about certain operations he's been involved with would be to reveal highly classified information. We consider him to be a cracker jack operative, one of our best."

Scott listened closely to what Wilson had to say. He found himself agreeing to Wilson's earlier assessment that teaming up Winter and Thernopolis should be a very unique pairing. He hopes they aren't too much alike.

Chapter 10

Their mission headquarters was located on the far end of Cairo; close enough to easily walk to, yet far enough away from the busy daily activity of the city proper. A compound that consisted of barracks, a mess hall and other buildings established a field operation presence.

The first three weeks in Egypt were relatively quiet for both Thernopolis and Winter. The human intel wasn't uncovering any activity beyond unconfirmed rumors of the movement of weapons to "undesirables", i.e., unapproved groups. The satellite images Thernopolis was working with also didn't provide anything promising. There was some suspicious movement of a group of small boats hugging the coastlines. The agents on the ground found nothing to support the opinion they were anything besides small fishing vessels. To be sure, a small group snuck onto one of the boats and found nothing but fishing nets and a rather modest haul of fish. Fortunately, the boat was unoccupied during the boarding; no skirmish, no harm, no foul.

Winter's time was also kind of low key. On day three he spent about three hours training a local group of police recruits in the use of small automatic pistols and assault rifles. The day wasn't much different than his last training adventure in Afghanistan; trigger happy, green recruits who really shouldn't be carrying weapons into battle. Oh well, you train whoever they send you with no questions. At least he didn't get shot at this time.

This exercise reminded Winter of last excursion into Afghanistan, which had him training fighters in the use of RPGs. Those fighters were also as green as the grass and didn't appear too skilled in the proper use of rifles in fighting let alone knowing how to use advanced weaponry like an RPG.

In fact, they didn't exhibit the discipline necessary to be an organized fighting force. If they were simply going into battle with whatever small arms they could muster the Soviets would soon turn the war back in their favor. Therefore, he understood the need for helping to get the new guys battle ready.

A major problem in Winter's estimation, was the number of Afghani recruits that were streaming into battlefield. They arrived armed with automatic rifles and other small arms. The question, which they had no answer for, where are the weapons coming from? If the weapons were being transported into Afghanistan, no chatter was picked up hinting they were passing through where he was camped out in Egypt. Then why was he here?

There were active skirmishes occurring throughout the middle east, including a long engagement between Iran and Iraq, yet the CIAs main event still seemed to be centered in Afghanistan. This was not a Muslim vs Muslim battle like the Iran and Iraq war. This fight was clearly about a foreign infidel, the Soviet Union, that needed to be destroyed. And the 'farm', as the CIA covert training facility, was referred to, wanted in on the action.

The lack of training work led to him accompany other intel guys on the local rounds, which even included him attending a militia recruiting effort. He stayed pretty much secluded in the back of the room in an attempt to learn some Arabic phrases. Such was the life of a weapons trainer when there was no one to train. Even the local CIA assets commented on how slow the action was.

While convinced this wasn't the best use of his skills, he decided this problem was meant for those above his pay grade to tangle with. He was a key operative from the farm and if they decided this was the best way to utilize him, so be it. He would continue to tag along with the other agents until something broke or not.

****

One advantage of the slow operational pace was that it provided Winter with an opportunity to become better acquainted with Thernopolis.

Thernopolis. To say she was unlike any other woman he had ever met was analogous to saying the desert heat was unlike any other heat he had suffered through. He had seen her fight like a warrior when saving his butt; laser focused and brutally efficient. He had also seen her soft side when consoling a small child's tears who had lost her mother in a local marketplace they were strolling through. She could pound down the beers with the best of them, and, when so moved, could swear like a trucker. The complete package of…just one of them. She fit in.

They were quite a contrast in physical appearance and personality. Thernopolis stands six-foot-tall, maybe even a smidge over, medium length shiny, black hair, flashing green eyes, olive skin and a very toned, muscular body. She easily caused one to evoke thoughts of the mythical Amazonian warrior. Thernopolis was always a little more serious, perhaps because she was a woman. She believed she was always in the spotlight and felt she had to constantly prove herself.

One illustration of the extra scrutiny Thernopolis faced resulted during the routine of physical training. Since this field assignment came with plenty of down time, it meant they had ample opportunity to maintain their combat skills, including shooting and physical training. Thernopolis excelled at everything and was probably the most skilled of the group. In the process she earned enormous respect for her abilities.

In fact, in one hand to hand combat session she easily turned a 200-pound instructor into a sniveling mess with blood pouring from his nose after he got a bit too handsy with her upper body and laughed; daring her to do something about. Wrong move on his part.

The incident with the combat instructor was witnessed by both Scott and Wilson. They looked at each other and without saying a word it was clear they were impressed with her skills and pissed at the instructor. After the session ended Wilson called her over and explained to her they had seen the entire incident. Waiting for a reprimand, perhaps even a harsher response, she was surprised when Wilson asked if she wished to press charges.

Needing a moment to process what he had said, she responded she was fine, and the incident was closed as far as she was concerned. Then she added, "If that jackass complains" … Scott cut her off, saying, "If that pussy does I will tell him he'll need to discuss it with you first." That remark elicited a chuckle from Thernopolis.

Winter, on the other hand, has sandy, brown hair, hazel eyes and a ruddy complexion, also about six-foot tall, maybe six-foot, one inch, and given that he was in the army special forces before joining the CIA, was in tremendous physical shape. He was serious on the job, a quick study with a near photographic memory. When off duty however, he was a natural jokester, his mission to keep everyone loose.

Eventually he was able to get Maya the Serious to loosen up away from the job. She even started to understand his 'Yank' humor, adopting the philosophy of smiling when unsure how to react. They soon laughed at each other's jokes and came up with a special facial expression that could instantly crack the other up.

The abundance of free time they spent together and the way they clicked as a team, led them to believe a bit of a personal relationship was developing. They enjoyed the time they spent together when out with the rest of the gang; and, also, on the rare occasions when they were alone together. Thernopolis also noticed that Winter was stealing lingering glances at her, checking her out physically. No problem as she was doing the same to him.

One early morning they happened to alone after a late dinner with their buddies. While not drunk, they both had a nice buzz going as they weaved toward Thernopolis's quarters. Just as she was about to open the door, she thought she saw someone in a crouched position go behind the building, as if casing her place.

Winter took the lead as they slowly crept around the surrounding shadows. After they completely searched the area as quietly as possible, finding no one or nothing, Winter quickly turned around to ask Thernopolis if she was convinced someone was back there. As he spun around he bumped into her; his mouth opened as he prepared to say something. Instead, since they were eye-to-eye Winter planted a quick kiss on her lips, then took a step back.

I'm still standing so it must be okay. Before he could put together another thought, Thernopolis reached out and pulled his face back to hers and gave him a real soul-searching kiss. Winter reached out and lightly traced his index finger along her jawline. Her skin was velvety soft as were her lips.

After a moment she breaks and smiles at him. That kiss was much more than he expected since he really wasn't sure what to expect, just hoping she wasn't going to bounce her hand off his face.

Without speaking they walk back around to the front of the building and he escorts her inside. In the dark they share one more kiss when Thernopolis says, "See you in the morning cowboy?"

"I think so; umm, sure, uhhh, yes," he stammers, as he leaves the building to walk back to his quarters; sporting a big shit-eating grin. It was difficult to tell who had enjoyed the activities more; probably a draw. And, definitely something they would like to explore further.

Thernopolis' smile was from ear to ear and glowing brighter than the overhead moon. She liked him; no question about it. And yet, was this the time, during a mission, to start thinking about personal things of such a..? What? As she got ready to hit the rack she reminisced. She had been through a relationship in the past that started with another operative…

It was during a raid where she met her first serious love interest, at least that's what she thought initially he was. She had been on the job about four years and had rarely set time aside for intimacy or love. She was very cognizant of her position within MI-6 as the first female recruited into the revamped service. Thus, she was very task oriented and wanted no outside distractions. Maya the Serious.

That all changed when Maya was assigned to a forward team during the Falkland Islands War. Their mission was to launch an attack deep in enemy territory on a heavily fortified Argentinian defensive position and destroy it. Maya, along with several other commandos hit the battery after suppressing fire was laid down. As she was clearing a bunker near the end of the battle a fellow commando blinded sided her with a tackle seconds before an Argentinian soldier fired. Landing on top of her as the burst flew over them, Maya was able to free her hand, pull her pistol and fire a kill shot into the enemy combatant.

Briefly starring into each other eyes, her comrade stood up and reached out his hand to help her to her feet. "Nice shot", he said.

"Nice tackle," she replied as she rubbed her right shoulder and searched for her helmet.

"Sorry about that, it was totally an instinctive move. Hope I didn't hurt you.

Putting her helmet on her head and still sitting on her butt, "Nothing to apologize for; I will be fine."

We haven't been properly introduced, Maya; I'm Brian Bailey," as he extends his hand a second time.

Shaking his hand, she replies, "You know my name?"

Flashing her a flirtatious smile he says, "Come on, you're the only female in the unit so everyone knows who you are. I really extended my hand to help you to her feet."

Returning the smile, she grabs his hand and stands up. *It's the first time a guy tackled me to get my attention. Of course, he did save my life.*

That unusual introduction lead to a friendship once they got back home. The first date was arranged after a session at the shooting range. They both had fun just hanging out and sight-seeing around London. They had similar interests beyond work requirements; although competitions at the firing range were fun, even if, or because, she won all of them. But regular interests, like food, movies and music also clicked. They laughingly discovered they both were into punk rock during their rebellious periods while in school.

Anyhow, the enjoyable first date was followed by a second and third date, then Maya went overseas on assignment for three weeks. Probably the end of everything, she thought, especially when she had trouble locating Brian when she returned. Still, she assumed a fellow operator would understand the requirements of the job and the long absences involved.

After being back three weeks and just as she was ready to write off the friendship, Brian walked into the restaurant where she was waiting to dine with some friends. Since her table was empty he sat down; explaining that he had been on an assignment that he had just completed. Since you were in the field I couldn't contact you.

"So, we're cool?" he asks.

"Everything is ok with me. Thanks for the explanation, I feel better."

Over the ensuing months, consisting of a little over a year, she and Brian hung out on a regular basis when they weren't off on assignments. This arrangement worked perfectly in Maya's opinion; both knew the hazards the other person faced on the job and they were able to adjust and adapt. And the time away from each other reduced any pressure to find things to talk about when they were together; their assignments provided plenty of action to rehash.

Perhaps the best thing about the relationship was that she could be herself; with no apologies. The strong, dominant woman she was didn't scare Brian. She felt very comfortable spending time with him. And yet…comfortable wasn't that real, toe tingling spark that made a person light-headed, breathless at the sight of the other person. The forever love; it never really developed. They both came to realize at about the same time that they were great friends, friends with benefits, but that was the limit of their relationship.

One evening they had a heart-to-heart about what the future would hold for them. They agreed neither wanted marriage at this point in their lives as their careers were still the driving force in their life. While they remained close for several more months, things slowly did begin to change. After about a year and half they drifted apart.

Soon she drifted off into slumber land.

****

Across the compound in his own rack Dirk was wondering too. He also didn't invest a lot of time looking for love; a hazard of the job. In the past, when he would leave for extended periods of time, and couldn't offer a real good explanation beyond it's the job; the women he dated just couldn't deal with it. Are his stories legit? If so, was he working a real dangerous job; and they wondered was it legal or illegal activity? Or, worse, he was just a two-timing lying S.O.B. playing with other women.

After a while it didn't matter. The women simply wanted no part of that lifestyle. They liked knowing where they stood in a relationship and didn't like to be left alone, sometimes with little warning. Some demanded him to choose between them or the job. Whatever the reason, attempts at romance had always failed.

But maybe with Maya it could be different. They each knew what the other's job required. They understood the risks and accepted them personally, so accepting them for another could be accommodated. They had much in common and enjoyed spending time together. And, who knows, maybe...*ZZZZ*.

Chapter 11

As much as Thernopolis and Winter were enjoying their time getting acquainted they knew sooner or later the mundane would need to end or the team would be deployed elsewhere, maybe even broken up. Finally, midway through the fifth week in Cairo another analyst noted an interesting deployment of several small boats making their way across the Mediterranean Sea.

Gathering photos over the last twenty-four hours, he watched as the ships, while staggered, appeared to be moving towards Port Said in a zig-zag pattern. They gave the appearance of a loosely formed group trying to purposely hide and confuse anyone who may be surveilling their journey.

He calls Thernopolis over and shows her the photos. He explains, "The photos appear to show a group of ships, staggered, that are moving in unison toward Port Said."

Shuffling the photos in time sequence order he points to several small images. "All of the boats, four at this time, are following this larger ship, here, in the lead. Each of the lead ship's maneuvers are followed on a time delayed basis by the others."

He points to the pictures that detail how the group, after approximately an hour's delay, perform the exact maneuvers to change position. "An interesting choreographic dance," he adds.

Thernopolis ponders while she studies the photos; absorbing his interpretation. After a few minutes she inquires, "And, what makes you think they aren't fishing trawlers,"

"I originally had the same thought. The number of boats is a tell-tale sign. Most trawling operations are one ship, on occasion there will be two.

Unless they were to split off at some point, I don't buy the trawling operation."

Thernopolis nods in agreement. "I understand your position, it's a reasonable assumption. Anything else?"

"Yes. This last photo, which provides a good close up of the lead vessel. Notice the open deck, which would allow cargo to be loaded onto the boat. Furthermore, where are the fishing nets? Or, for that matter, the winches needed to lower and raise the nets? I don't buy their ruse."

Nodding her head in agreement she says, "Good catch, I'm convinced. Write up a brief summary and I will forward it out to the field assets. That lead boat could be here in forty-eight to fifty-four hours based on its current speed. Thanks," a quick read of the name tag, "Myers. These photos seem to be about six hours apart, with new pictures due in about two hours. Let me know when the next ones arrive, and we'll track them for a while to confirm our suspicions."

"Yes ma'am. And thank you, too."

Thirty minutes later Thernopolis is with Scott in his office reviewing the photos and briefing him on the latest intel. A thoughtful draw on the pipe, a vanilla aroma today, then Scott buzzes Wilson on the intercom; "Can you come over; I have some interesting information to discuss with you."

"Be right there."

In short order Wilson appears, notices a vanilla aroma, and asks, "What's up, something good I hope?"

Scott sets his pipe down and shows Wilson the satellite photos, providing him with the theory Thernopolis and the analyst believes the photographic intel is showing.

Wilson closely examines the data, evaluating the analysis. Nodding, he says, "It does appear this group of boats is moving in a rather coordinated pattern. And, as you point out, the close ups of the boats show that, if they are indeed, 'fishing trawlers', they have been stripped of the normal trawling gear, making them appear ready to serve another purpose.

"The intel briefing with my officers this morning didn't disclose they are picking up any chatter about this potential movement. Silencio. Nothing on weapons movement across the land or sea and no chatter on unusual characters entering the territory."

Scott, "It is very interesting. So, if our assessment is correct, then somebody or somebodies, are playing this close to the vest. When is the next set of photos due?"

"In about an hour," Thernopolis replies.

"Very well. After you've had a chance to compare the ships position with the material you have here, we will meet again and formulate several courses of action."

"Winter and two other officers are continuing their training with a group of Egyptian soldiers today," Wilson says. "This group is regular army and has been thoroughly vetted. I personally know their commander. They could break away quickly if needed. Keep me posted."

****

Ninety minutes later Thernopolis is back in Scott's office where Wilson and Winter have joined the discussion. Thernopolis attached the latest photos to the wall and leads the group through her and Myers' analysis. Pointing to the photos she begins,

"There is no question, in my mind, that the lead boat is heading on a direct path to Port Said as documented by the last four photos," pointing at each photo as she talks. "They originally didn't appear to be on a fast track and may have been stopping from time to time to provide the illusion of drawing their non-existent nets through the water."

Tracing an outline on the last photo she continues, "But, our analysis of this last shot shows the boat in an unexpected location, according to our previous projections. We now believe this first boat has significantly ramped up its speed, perhaps discarding the illusion of fishing entirely. The lead boat could be arriving in port, based on new estimates, in roughly forty, maybe forty-six, hours."

Thernopolis walks to the far wall in the back of the room, "These photos over here, show the next two closest boats are still following a very similar pattern of movement. They have also increased the knots they are traveling at. Since they were lagging the first boat from when we first spotted them, the spacing between them doesn't appear to have changed much.

We now expect the second boat to arrive at the port approximately seven or so hours behind the first boat. The time lapse would allow an efficient loading operation to be completed with the first boat gone well before the second one arrived.

Furthermore, we have calculated approximately the same amount of lead time after the second boat leaves and when the third boat would dock.

"The last boat, just barely in this photo, seems to be thirteen hours behind the lead boat and perhaps has even completely stopped in the water. There could be several reasons for this behavior, including the fact that boat may not be needed if the other boats can handle all of the cargo they will be picking up.

"They could also simply be in a holding pattern cruising just off-shore. It's also possible they may be waiting to simply turn around and return to where they departed from.

"Another possibility is the last boat could be an armed boat and/or carrying soldiers. It will remain offshore in case a problem developed with the handling of the cargo. At that point they would provide support for the other boats.

"Once again, based on the pattern of concerted movement, we've concluded they are part of the same group and/or deployment and that they are not simple fishing trawlers. We believe they are coming to retrieve some type of cargo and transport it elsewhere."

The others in the room study the photos while listening intently to Thernopolis's presentation. They are paying particular attention to the analysis of the change in speed and the new projected time of arrival. The calculations seem to indicate a bit of urgency in the boats travel as they come closer to the port. The photos, ten in all, did tell a story that they interpreted pretty much the same as Thermopolis had. Someone is in the process of moving precious cargo.

Returning back to the front of the room, Thernopolis has displayed four sheets, each contained a question. The main questions to find an answer to are; Where is the cargo now located? Can we interdict while the goods are being taken to the port and stop the transfer? What will be the fall-out if we take forcible action, including the exchange of gunfire? Failing at preventing the cargo from reaching the port, can we do undertake any action at the docks to prevent the loading of the ships?

After each was satisfied they had sufficient time reviewing the intel, a brief discussion followed where everyone presented their opinions. While Winter thought the last boat could possibly be an outlier and not part of the group, he agreed, as did everyone else, that the boats appeared headed for the port to pick up cargo of some type. In his mind there are only two questions to answer, what will they be receiving and what is our course of action in response?

Following a brief pause, Wilson finally spoke up in favor of preventing the cargo from reaching the port. "Port Said is about one hundred miles north of us. There is one main road connecting the two destinations. We could establish roadblocks and monitor the traffic, stopping anything, vehicles, farmer's wagons, that looks problematic. Not sure what problematic would be, perhaps we could just randomly stop traffic or maybe stop all vehicles. Again, our assets in the field are not hearing any chatter or activity to lead them to believe a big smuggling operation is underway, so I'm not sure what we will accomplish."

Scott, who has been following everything holding his pipe but without smoking it, adds, "When we stop someone and find something of value, then what? How do we determine if the cargo is going from "friendlies to other friendlies? If a driver refuses to stop, will that action triggers us to take aggressive measures to interdict?

Thernopolis adds, "And, what if its drugs, fighters, refugees or a combination of all three, instead of weapons.? What is our response? Our purpose here is to monitor and if necessary, redirect or intercept weapons traffic."

Wilson, "Good questions, all of them. And while we believe we have a good handle on who is "trustworthy" and who isn't, I'll be the first to tell you we don't know everyone we encounter; not by a long shot. I guess we could ask those we stop to produce credentials and anyone without them will be taken off the road. Still… I just not sure. And what if they don't want to cooperate, do we force the issue and risk a firefight with potential friendlies?"

Winter, who has been pondering for several minutes, chimes in; "I not sure I like the idea of stopping traffic and examining their contents, because I'm not sure how successful we will be. If we wave someone off to check them out and they agree, so be it. But what if they don't agree? We can delay and hassle them a bit, perhaps changing their timetable. But when push comes to shove we have to let them proceed. Therefore, how practical is this action?"

To Thernopolis he asks, "If we let the vehicle continue through, would it be possible to track the vehicles that voluntarily turn away?"

Before she can answer Scott asks why.

"Sorry, Winter says, "I don't trust anyone; whether we think we know them or not. If this is a big operation, they could simply reload their cargo onto another vehicle and inform that new crew what we are doing."

Scott nods in agreement, acknowledging the opinion of someone on the ground, although he doesn't necessarily concur as most vehicular traffic is over the main road.

Answering Winter's question, Thernopolis doesn't believe it would be beneficial to attempt to recalibrate the satellites to track what could be numerous vehicles going in several different directions. She prefers they remain tracking the immediate waterway into and out of Port Said.

Winter, "Alright, let's try to rationalize this. The consensus of the three of you seems to be in agreement with trying to prevent some type of cargo, weapons are our best guess, from reaching the port by stopping traffic. As for myself, I don't think this will work too well. Why?

"Anyone we stop and can't convince them to turn around, even after a strong amount of harassing, we are simply going to let them continue their route rather than risk starting a firefight that could in the long run create more problems than it solves. Yes, the word will spread that if you strongly resist the roadblocks, you will get through. The only positive is if we do nothing more than disrupt a timeline, it may spook a ship's crew, and maybe convince them to leave without receiving anything. I'm not sure that result justifies the operation.

"Another big negative is the reaction to our roadblock. The story will also quickly spread that the foreign trainers have a hidden agenda to interfere in the locals' freedom of movement. Thus, we could open up ourselves to guerilla attacks, putting our mission in jeopardy, and perhaps, starting the firefight we want to avoid.

"Now, if we don't care about any repercussions, then bring in some of my colleagues from the special forces and stop everything from moving. If a driver refuses to voluntarily cooperate then we forcefully stop them. We may start an all-out war, but no weapons will move from here to the port."

"A bit extreme, don't you think, starting an all-out fight?" Scott asked while searching for tobacco to restoke his pipe.

"Precisely, which is why we need a less extreme plan then setting roadblocks." A pause then Winter continues. "What if we do nothing about any cargo movement unless it falls into our lap?" We could allow the boats to be loaded and leave Egypt, then track them to their next port."

Looking at Thernopolis he asks, "That would be possible, right?"

Thernopolis thinks for a moment then answers, "Yes, it would be possible to track the boats to their next destination. Then what, intercept at the next port?"

Winter; "If it weapons, which again is our primary purpose, then yes. However, if the weapons are transferred to trucks or other modes of transportation, the best action may be to continue tracking them to a final destination. That would provide time for us to develop several different plans of action to take. If we have a clearer idea of the final destination, I think we'll have a stronger case for whatever action we decide to take, including using lethal force for interception purposes.

"If the cargo is fighters, then perhaps we track their movements to a battlefield or set up an interception plan to keep them from joining a battle. Anything else, simply report it up the chain of command."

His pipe restarted and oozing smoke Scott simply says, "I like it. Although I would prefer immediate interception of any weapons, this alternative allows us to find, track and possibly destroy a major weapons' smuggling operation."

Thernopolis adds, "We can certainly have the satellites continue to monitor all sea traffic as they currently are. I also like maximizing our time to strike, hopefully a clean, decisive action."

"If everyone is in agreement," they all nod yes, "then it's a go," says Wilson. "I will have some roadblocks set up just because I can; besides, you never know what may shake out."

That statement causes Winter to turn away and to wince and roll his eyes in exasperation.

Wilson ignores Winter and adds, "Winter, I don't want you on the front lines but rather as a backup. Remember, if something goes sideways your cover is likely blown. Thernopolis, you can also accompany Winter as backup if time allows. Just remember, your primary role right now is the photo analysis."

As the meeting breaks up Thernopolis calls out to Winter, asking him to wait for her to walk back to her office. "Nice plan," she says, "Do you think it's the best option?"

"Actually, it was originally a 'fly by the seat of your pants' proposal. But the more it played out in my mind, the more I liked it. I think what Wilson wants is basically a waste of time, but he's command so we have to follow along."

As they enter her office he leans in closer and whispers, "Get together tonight?"

She gives him a mischievous smile, "You devil, you; what do you have in mind?"

"We'll just play it by ear, or maybe I'll nibble one of your ears."

She cocks her head to one side, nonchalantly flips her hair and beams back a wide smile. "I like that plan," she coos.

Chapter 12

Later in the day a series of blockades are established by Egyptian police along the highway from Cairo to Port Said. As Winter suspected nothing of value was found. Most of the vehicles were transporting farming equipment, farm animals, and the like. The police found no evidence of weapons, drugs, or people moving in the direction of Port Said. All drivers were cooperative, thus requiring no muscle from Winter or the other CIA/MI-6 people.

Eighteen hours later and the blockades were yielding the exact same results, nothing. Wilson has a quick meeting with Winter, telling him his prediction was correct; stopping traffic revealed nothing and was basically a waste of time. The locals were cooperative with no one trying to run the blockade or turning around to retrace their route. Confusion was the order of the day as drivers waited to have their vehicles searched. Since the police removed nothing, they just shrugged and continued their journey when told they could leave. If anything was moving from Cairo to Port Said, it wasn't being routed over the main through fare.

Later that morning Wilson contacted his operatives at Port Said to find out what was going on at the docks. This was the second time he had spoken with his chief officer. Wilson had a brief conversation with him shortly after the roadblocks had been set up to inform him of the interdiction effort down in Cairo. The intelligence put together by Wilson's people provided reason to believe there would be weapons movement to the port in about thirty hours, thus the reason for roadblocks being established. The chief officer, Dave Myers, reported they were hearing stories about some type of action happening in a day or so, but nothing rock solid at this point.

Eighteen hours can make quite a difference in tracking a fast moving operation, as Wilson learned from call number two. Myers reported the scuttlebutt on site is about a ship docking to pick up a major cache of cargo. While there is no clear evidence as to what the cargo is, the rumors are saying it is definitely weapons. Myers and his contacts have also noticed increased activity at one dock in particular with equipment being moved around the port in preparation for a loading or unloading event. Everything Myers has told Wilson dovetails with their analysis and assumptions. The scene at the docks will be hot soon.

Wilson informed Myers of the latest intelligence scenario that had been developed from the satellite photos. "If our analysis is correct, this is the boat the rumors are talking about. And, tomorrow appears to be only round one as we have identified definitively two boats headed in the same direction. Those two boats are staggered far enough part to allow for the preceding boat to be loaded or unloaded, and to then clear the dock. We also have a third boat waiting in the waters that we aren't sure what its purpose is; in fact, it's possible this boat may have stopped and may not advance to a dock. We just don't have a strong conclusion at this point in time.

"A major problem developed in our deterrent actions down here; we haven't been able to identify the vehicles that are transporting the material to the port. The traffic stops have been followed by the locals with no pushback; however, they have netted nothing but typical deliveries like farm equipment, food stuff, and so on. Therefore, we are unable to tell you if the quantity of weapons arriving port side will be large or small; what exactly is being shipped, who may be involved, or any proposed time of arrival. We turned up a complete goose egg.

"The latest projection had the ship coming into Said in approximately fifteen hours from now. You and your men have to get as close as possible to the dock tonight to watch the preparations for a ship scheduled to arrive early tomorrow morning. You'll focus of all your resources on that dock's happenings. In addition, you will monitor the warehouses for signs of the movement of men and equipment dockside.

"The reason I want your team there right after sunset tonight is to determine exactly what activities are occurring at the dock. You should be able to observe the scope of the operation, the amount of equipment in place to transfer the cargo, the number of dock workers involved and if there are any armed guards on site. These activities will give you an idea of how extensive the operation is. Armed guards will attest to the serious of a successful transfer and tell you how valuable the cargo is. Overlook nothing, if you can think of things once on site that we haven't discussed, by all means, check it out."

When Myers asked if they should attempt to intercede, Wilson was non-committal. "The decision to attempt to disrupt the cargo exchange will be entirely up to you. It will be your command decision based on your analysis of the prep work being performed at the docks, and the actual cargo movement; whether loading or unloading. In addition, the presence of armed guards will also be factored in. If you believe it's possible to make a move, then do so. If not, just watch from a safe vantage point and report what you see. Do not, repeat, do not, attempt a heroic, but suicidal mission, that accomplishes nothing more than a high casualty count."

****

Myers and his unit arrived shortly after dark. They were able to split up and conduct an unimpeded visible sweep of the area. At this particular moment the port area was sparsely populated, enabling them to move undetected; in several locations they were within twenty feet of the buildings. Interesting situation for a scene they expected to be highly active. The men had prepared for the possibility of armed patrols.

They observed that several large cranes and similar equipment had been moved into position near the dock to handle a loading or unloading operation. That indicated that something had either happened or would be happening. Although on two occasions they had to duck into the shadows to avoid people, the general quietness was very eerie, haunting even.

One thing of particular interest to Myers was the fact they encountered no trucks coming into the dock area, even prior to their arrival at the port.

If weapons or other cargo was arriving from Cairo then where the hell are the transport vehicles? Was Wilson's intel wrong?

Myers and another man came upon a warehouse that was one hundred-fifty, maybe two hundred feet from the dockside. Several lights in the building had been left on, an indication of prior activity and perhaps foretelling of future work. Extreme caution caused them to steer wide of that building. Satisfied with what they had seen they turned around to rendezvous with the rest of their team. As they rounded one building they dove back into the shadows as they nearly walked into a truck headed in their direction. After several minutes of non-movement to be sure the truck didn't stop, they skirted through the shadows until they found the rest of their team. The other men reported they encountered increased activity as they returned to their checkpoint. Time to stay in the shadows and watch the show unfold.

****

The next day the first boat arrived at Port Said. It arrived about forty-two hours after it was flagged by the satellites, pretty much in line with the revised timeline the analysts projected about twenty-four hours earlier. At approximately twelve o'clock a.m. local time the bay sprang to life. A work crew drove trucks to the ship where cranes began efficiently loading the cargo.

The CIA officer, Myers, along with six other CIA and MI-6 officers monitored the work from the shadows of several buildings at the far end of the port. They were close enough to observe but far enough away to be safely secreted. They confirmed what the intel photos revealed, this boat was definitely not a fishing trawler but a cargo ship. They watched as large containers were loaded onto the boat. Whatever the cargo was, and weapons was definitely the leading possibility, it was already in the warehouses prior to the alert issued in Cairo. That explains why they didn't observe any vehicles entering the docks on their rounds and why they found nothing of value from the Cairo roadblock. The intel operation, for which Myers will have to report on, was a bigger failure than they knew.

Their surveillance also noticed what they discerned to be a fair amount of heavily armed men on-site. They were definitely outmanned and outgunned; therefore, no one complained when Myers said the decision to interfere or not was his, and he ordered his men to stand down. There was no back-up readily available, meaning any attempt to intervene mostly likely would have created a large firefight that may have ended up as a disaster.

As suspected, this was serious business. Whoever was running this operation definitely wanted the loading of the vessel to occur under the cloak of darkness. And, they gave the impression they were willing to kill anyone who had thoughts of interfering.

Chapter 13

It's mid-morning when the boat is loaded and is readying to depart to its next destination. The cranes are returned to an equipment building. The armed men clamor into trucks and leave at the south end of the port about a mile from where the CIA/MI6 guys are secreted. After the dock is completely emptied out Myers calls back to headquarters to give a quick synopsis of what transpired. "What now?" he asks.

Wilson has placed the call on speaker phone so Winter, Scott and Thernopolis are listening. Thernopolis took that question. "The satellite intel still shows, as you and Wilson discussed yesterday, three more boats spaced on the sea that appeared to be headed towards Port Said. The second boat, based on our analysis, has slowed down but should come into port approximately ten to twelve hours from now. Our guess is that a similar cargo transfer will occur.

"At this time there doesn't appear to be anything more your team can accomplish at the port. We need you to disburse to a safe house about five miles out and south of where you are now. Are you familiar with its location?"

Myers; "Yes."

"Good. We need to regroup on our end, try to hash over what just happened and then develop a new plan of action. Once we are ready you will need to be able to regroup on our confirmation. Any questions?"

No response.

"Good, stay in touch."

Scott, "And guys, do not increase your firepower at this time. You are to operate in observation mode only. If you receive any pertinent information from your field people, catalogue it and report the data back to us."

"Roger that," comes the reply.

Scott sets his pipe down and says to Thernopolis, "You're on the clock. Get a satellite recalibrated and let's find out where that boat is headed. They appear to be carrying a large cargo for a ship its size which may slow their speed. And, since the transfer was designed to provide as much natural under the radar coverage as possible, my belief is the end designation is not to a nation we consider friendly."

"On it sir."

After she exits Scott addresses the other two; "Thoughts?"

"From the description of the care to hide the mission and the amount of firepower at the docks, the level of seriousness surprised me. If any hostilities had broken out our boys would have been picked apart," says Wilson.

"If the weapons passed through Cairo it occurred either before we had knowledge of the ships, via a different route, or worse yet, somehow we were duped and they drove them right under our noses and past our roadblocks as we watched them go by. I wonder if the police could have been in on the whole deal."

Loudly clapping his hands together, Wilson finishes by bellowing, "Damn, we had no idea anything like this was about to happen? Who in the hell fell asleep at the switch?"

"There are times when we don't know," replies Scott as he relights his pipe. "A lot of our intelligence is still hit and miss in this part of the world as we seek to increase our presence. This appears to be a very tight-lipped event with some very disciplined people involved. Hopefully we can track it, determine a final destination and have our people take action at the other end."

Taking a draw from the pipe he asks, "Winter, you're very quiet; what gives?"

"I still not too happy we lost everything at Port Said." A quizzical look from Wilson. "I know, I know, given the circumstances at the docks we made the right move, but hear me out. The fastest way to know where that boat is going is the information located at that dock's warehouse. Let me go up there with a couple more guys and with ten of us in total we will hit it after the next ship is loaded. We will catch them off guard and wipe the warehouse, seizing every document we find. A quick power sweep on the place hopefully results in no casualties. If time allows we can do a quick analysis on site; if not we'll bring back everything we grab."

Scott, "You're right, there probably are some documents at the warehouse office that will tell us the final destination of all of the ships, in addition to the type of cargo they are carrying." A brief pause, a puff on his pipe, a quick glance at the ceiling; mulling over Myers' report on the heavily armed guards they observed. "Ok, do it, but not until you report from on-site first; we aren't looking for a bloodbath."

Looking at Wilson he adds, "Can I assume you agree?"

"Absolutely, but let's do our best not to shoot our way in," nodding in the affirmative as he looks at Winter. "If we can take them by surprise and strike quickly it should work. Winter be ready to leave in thirty minutes. Remember, just yourself, there are already seven guys on site."

As Winter is leaving the room, Wilson says to Scott, "Let's meet with Thernopolis in an hour for the latest update. I'm not sure where my greatest area of concern lies, whether it's where the first ship is churning off to, or when we can expect the other three to arrive, whatever. It's just a big information black hole that I don't like. I hate being in the dark, especially when people's lives may hang in the balance."

****

"Come on in guys," Thernoplois says, waving Scott and Wilson in as they enter the conference room. "I chatted briefly with Winter before he left," she continues while arranging the latest photos. "We have set him up with another communication's link, so there are two hook ups at the docks once he arrives. He should meet up with the rest of our guys, in about forty-five minutes," as she checks her watch.

She walks to the conference table and lays out six new photos. "Hot off the wire."

The first snapshot details the first ship arriving in port and the next two highlights the loading operation at the docks. The detail has a reasonable closeup of the activities; they are using some good-sized cranes that were run by highly skilled operators.

Thernopolis, "While we can only guess at the amount of time involved to load that ship, it was a very efficient job. Also, note the present of heavily armed men at the docks, not just near the loading activity but also further back, as shown in photo number three. A tremendous amount of security for an innocuous event to say the least.

"The next two shots are of the trail boats. We still believe the second boat will arrive in about four hours. I was able to inform Winter that he should arrive roughly two to three hours ahead of the second boat. Since this will be a daylight event, they will try to blend in as workers at the dock. It should be easier for them to assess the situation and determine the best method for hitting the warehouse after the loading is over, the ship leaves and the dock empties.

"The last photo of the remaining boats shows the third boat still steaming towards the Port, perhaps seven or eight hours behind the second boat. An interesting aside, the fourth boat didn't make this picture. At this point we have no explanation why it's not visible; hopefully it will appear in a later satellite pass.

"The last photo shows the loaded first boat clearing the port, initially in a northernly direction. Comments?"

Before either of them can speak a clerk knocks, is waved into the room and announces a call for Scott from London. He excuses himself, leaves his pipe behind and goes into the front room to answer the phone.

With a grimace Wilson says, "Well, it seems to be the same old story we been living since we deployed here, hurry up and wait. The photos confirm what we suspected, but, I don't know," as he starts to ramble a bit. "I just think the paramilitary group could be better deployed where there's some action. There was a big operation at the port, and most of us are here where we couldn't accomplish a damn thing no matter how hard we tried, and…, I don't know…just frustrated. It seems like we missed a big opportunity, that's all. Sorry, no offense to you, Thernopolis, or the other intel analysts."

"None taken; the analysts only wished their work could have yielded better results. But I hear you. When you are used to action and you basically end up shining a seat with your ass…, well, I too am frustrated."

"Mark it down as the three of us here are frustrated plus the entire leadership in London," says Scott as he re-enters the conference room; apparently he had heard their complaints as he walked back in. "As the clerk said, that call was from London. Officially, they are very pleased we showed the sound judgment to stand down and strictly observe the port operation. We avoided a disaster by using common sense.

"Concerning the operation at the dock they were also totally in the dark as we were. No, repeat, no intelligence group, British, American, Israeli, and so on, had uncovered any prior chatter foretelling the massive cargo transfer that transpired earlier today in Port Said. The information they gleaned from their sources had zero knowledge on where the weapons came from, who controls them, who transported them to the port and what the final destination is. Command buys our theory that the ship is destined for a nation or nations unfriendly to us.

"I informed them of our new plan for a document sweep at the warehouse, seizing shipping manifests, bills of lading, journals and whatever else we find. After assuring command we have no intention of an offensive firefight at the port, that this is a stealth operation, they agreed with our decision. They are probably more embarrassed at the intelligence failure than we are. As such they are just as interested to the learn the final landing spot of at least that first boat. Any other information, as you Americans would so elegantly phrase it, would be icing on the cake.

"So, Mr. Wilson, as much as we all hate it, we will play defense for a while longer. Once again, any loading or unloading of a boat is not to be interrupted. That order was repeated to ensure I received the transmission clearly."

That remark caused Wilson to raise his eyebrows, furrowing his brow. Rather than taking the risk of making a dumb comment, Wilson respectfully decides to hold his tongue for now.

Scott, realizing he is without his pipe, continues talking while searching for it. "Now, Mr. Wilson, some good news for you. Unofficially, you are to tell Winter and the others in Port Said, if they can intercede and stop the transfer of cargo to the second boat, they are free to use their discretion and operate accordingly. Any success will be warmly welcomed and explained to the Egyptians authorities as intercepting weapons bound for Mubarak's enemies. Of course, if they create a total fucking mess, command will brand them as rogue assets. If they survive a mess and the Egyptian authorities want them, they can have them."

"Nothing new there," grumbles Wilson. "We are always being asked to put our asses on the firing line, unofficially of course, to do the dirty work. That's so the big brass can maintain 'plausible deniability' if we fuck up."

Somewhat ignoring Wilson comments as a 'steam-blowing' incident, Scott adds, "And cheer up Thernopolis; and get your ass up there to help out. There's a vehicle ready to go now. The rest of us can handle the satellite info. And, remember, we are sending you on site to be the adult in the room. So, think with your head up there, not your emotions. We want this but not at all costs. You will pay harshly for stupidity."

****

After Thernopolis leaves, Wilson asks what else was said. "Really not much else. They are disappointed and unsure where the intelligence fell short. Both the CIA and MI-6 believe they have solid assets and officers in the field. Hell, even Mossad had nothing to offer, either leading up to the operation or any knowledge of who's behind the action. A total fuck up like this, while not the only time it has happened, is still very a rare occurrence. They will be chasing their asses for a while trying to figure out who fucked up.

"In the meantime, us guys in the field are expected to soldier on. The future of this particular mission may well depend on what happens in Port Said."

Wilson nods in agreement, then adds, "Let's keep this between us. We don't need to pile on additional pressures up there, perhaps causing someone to make foolish decisions because they believe their ass rides on the outcome. After all, while we believe there will be a treasure trove of documents in the warehouse, if it turns out they find nothing, then they find nothing."

"Absolutely, this stays in this room; however, finding a major document or two would be nice."

Chapter 14

Thernopolis jumps into the waiting Jeep and heads for the highway at a rapid pace. She was more than ready to head for where the action will be happening, even if the plan was on the docile side. A person like herself can stand being cooped up for so long and she was definitely at the stir-crazy point. She made contact with Winter while en route to Port Said to find out where they were located. The squad has rendezvoused at a private residence serving as a CIA safe house a couple of miles away from the dock.

On arrival she had a brief chat with Winter to inform him of the latest information from London. Again, the main thrust is to watch, learn and employ a lightning fast strike to secure the warehouses after the boat is loaded and departed. Ideally, no gunfire will be needed. However, if they ran into a mess with heavily armed thugs like the ones guarding the earlier loading, they are to use their discretion to deal with the situation. Don't be stupid!

Thernopolis also details the latest from the intel photos. Checking her watch, she says, "The best estimate for the arrival of the second boat should be about an hour from now."

Winter, "Alright, we will stay here for three hours, then contact Scott for confirmation the boat is in place to be loaded, then proceed to the docks. There are two trucks here on site we can use. We will stop a thousand or so yards from the entry point and then cover the remaining distance on foot. We will spread out, try to stay covered by the buildings, and find observation points for viewing."

The group, with Thernopolis their new addition, now numbers nine. They are sufficient in number to set up a decent perimeter in a semi-circle spacing facing the water. The outer building and structures should provide them ample places to hide.

No one is packed heavy as the weapon of choice is the SIG Sauer P226, a semi-automatic pistol. If they are challenged the cover story is they are simply additional dockworkers looking for a job. The goal is to keep your weapon hidden. If they are lucky they will blend in and become part of the background.

****

The latest satellite photos back in Cairo were starting to tell a new story which was much different than the scenario that had been developed earlier. After thirty minutes of back and forth with the analysts currently interpreting the photos results, Wilson agreed with their conclusion. He placed an urge call to Scott; one ring, then another and a third; shit, he's not in. A few more rings then a clerk picks up; Mr. Scott is in the field; probably for an hour or more. Alright, Wilson says to himself; this is why I get paid the big bucks. He checks his watch; it's been about two hours since Thernopolis left; at worst the loading process should be underway. He can imagine the fuming going on at the staging area. As he reaches out for his phone to call Thernopolis, it rings.

"Is this Wilson?" A brief pause, then, "Hey, what's going on back there; we're getting a little stir crazy here. You can only check and recheck you plan so many times," says Winter.

"I literally was reaching for my phone when you called. We have checked and rechecked the photos showing the latest movements of the vessels. As a result, we have a major change of plans. The second boat has come into the port, but it is moving into the Suez Canal. At this time, we wouldn't even hazard a guess as to its ultimate destination.

"Boat number three has also changed course and appears to be steaming toward the port in Alexandria. We have alerted our people there and they will watch that boat. The fourth boat has apparently stopped in the water. The interesting thing is we have received clearer pictures of that boat and they show what may be several machine guns on board. This means this boat was acting as a "muscle" boat; bolstering weapons in case the other boats encountered problems. When the first boat loaded without incident they decided to maintain alert status at a safe distance."

Winter, "Don't tell me we've wasted a lot of time accomplishing nothing. I have a group up here ready to take some kind of action. And, another thing…"

Wilson is only half listening, a lot of cussing and swearing about an intelligence fuck up, coming in loud and clear from the other end. He's just listening, not answering; deciding it's best to let him vent and get the frustration out of his system. Also, while Winter is talking he's trying to formulate some type of action they can take. Finally, Winter pauses for a moment and he jumps back into the conversation. "Are you guys ready to move out"?

"Damn right we are."

"I've got an idea. We are 100% comfortable that the second boat is out of the picture and the third boat, even if it reversed course, wouldn't reach Port Said for at least three hours. We consider this action on their part to be highly unlikely."

"Go on," replies Winter.

"Take your guys and raid the warehouse as planned. As you so eloquently explained, our intelligence has absolutely no idea what's the purpose for this flotilla of boats. We don't know what cargo was picked up and where is it headed. As we have speculated, there may be a wealth of information on the dock. Go get it. Hopefully, there will be no resistance and you will be able to walk in and walk out with what we want. Plan your mission and let us know your thoughts before you hit the place; maybe we can receive a photo or two of the dock to assist you in the raid."

"Sounds good to me."

****

The trucks are loaded, and Winter takes his group to about a thousand yards from the dock. They park behind a restaurant type building and disembark from the trucks. "Remember," Winter reminds everyone, "if anyone is discovered and challenged, you are here to look for work loading or unloading the next boat due in. We will meet back here in twenty minutes." The group splits up, nonchalantly walking from behind their cover in staggered departures, making their way towards the dock. There are plenty of buildings and equipment to hide behind as they conduct surveillance of the area.

About fifteen minutes later everyone has returned back to where they parked the trucks with the same report; except for two men who are meandering round as pretend guards, the area is empty. The lack of activity clearly indicates no one is expecting a boat anytime soon.

Winter checked his watch, it been a little over an hour since he talked to Wilson. He grabbed the sat phone and placed a call.

Wilson reaches to answer the phone as Scott walks in. "What's up at the front?" he says.

"Listen in" comes the reply.

"Winter, we received a series of photos about five minutes ago. The position of the boats hasn't changed. We show no heavy human activity at the docks, maybe a couple of guards."

Winter, "Roger that. We conducted some surveillance and can confirm the two guards on site. We walked the around the premises some and didn't appear to attract any attention; we looked like dock workers. Beyond that everything is quiet."

Wilson, "Then everything is a go from our standpoint. I know you hate to hear this, but, use discretion. Easy in and easy out."

"We will tweak our plan a bit and execute the raid," answers Winter. "There are nine of us, we should be able to grab the two guards before entering the warehouse. There shouldn't be any problems."

Hanging up, Wilson says to Scott, "Maybe we can catch a big break on this and find something to fill the major gap in our intel."

Chapter 15

Seven Hours Later in Scott's Office

"The raid went down exactly as planned with no improvising needed," Winter said. "Thernopolis, Myers and I went in with two other guys, leaving the other four behind to provide premises surveillance. We advanced to the building through the shadows, grabbed the two guards and secured them behind the warehouse. We checked the surroundings to make sure our action didn't attract attention and then entered the warehouse through a side window. Once inside Myers picked the lock to the office door.

"As we went through the office we found a treasure trove of hard documents, floppy disks, photos and two computers. A document which appeared to be a shipping manifest was written in Arabic. Thernopolis and Armstrong provided the deciphering and determined the listed destination of the first boat as the Port of Alexandria. They noted a listing of both large and small weapons, including mortars and RPGs, as the cargo that was loaded. Depending on the final destination of that cache, that could be a bad sign for us, as a small army could be well armed with that load.

"The second boat is headed down the Suez Canal to the Red Sea, docking at Al Wajh, Saudi Arabia. The boat's cargo was to be unloaded and placed on several trucks to be taken to the King Faisal Air Base in Tabuk. Since Saudi Arabia is an ally, the ship's cargo, hopefully, will end up in good hands. The document detailed military weapons as being on board the ship; mostly missiles for the Saudi Royal Air Force, along with RPGs and howitzers.

"Boat three is mostly farming supplies such as grain, farming tools, etc. Boat four was indeed a bad ass boat as it contained several mounted machine guns and soldiers. Its sole purpose was simply to provide fire power in case of conflict. It was definitely a great call on our part to stand down and simply observe the transferring of the cargo. It seems even if the cargo transferred was harmless the intent was to ensure no interference at the dock.

"Thernopolis and the analysts here examined the computers, the photos and the floppy disks." To Thernopolis he says, "You're up."

"The floppy disks basically contained a lot of schematics and diagrams of the port area where the boat docked. They described the water depth, markers for guiding the boat into port, where the moorings were located, the equipment to be used for loading the boat, etc. The photos simply showed the identifying information on each boat so the workers could be sure they were working with the right boats. It also detailed that all four boats were Norwegian flagged ships with crews of various nationalities," explained Thernopolis.

Continuing she added; "In addition to dock information it told the first boat was indeed headed to the Port of Alexandria while the second boat was to travel down the Suez, docking in Tabuk, Saudi Arabia. The disks showed the types of munitions intended for the Royal Air Base. I use the word intended, because as we know, weapons have a habit of being "side-tracked" to other players. All of this information has been packaged up to be sent to London.

"And, just one more observation. We didn't find any information as to where the boats originated from, nor do we know where the weapons came from. Either the people at this end didn't know because it really was none of their business, or we were unable to decipher it from the documents we examined. There were several notations that were unknown to us. Those were marked and hopefully the crew in London can crack the writings."

"Nice job you two. I also called Myers to give our congratulations to the rest of your team members," said Wilson. "I informed them to remain alert for other similar activities at the port. If there's a next one, maybe we can be more proactive.

"Time for other news regarding new assignments. While the two of you were at the docks I received a call from Fort Bragg, North Carolina, headquarters for the U.S. Green Beret. They have received intelligence reports from the United States Central Command, (Cent Com) that has identified a major shipment of weapons and fighters moving from Libya into Egypt.

"Long story short, Winter's old unit is about to undertake a mission on the Egyptian-Libyan border to smash that smuggling operation. They knew we were operating an interdiction unit and wondered if we could supply some assistance. I volunteered both of you to assist."

Winter's eyebrows rise at the mention of his former comrades. He pauses before he answers, "Wow. Always glad to help out. What exactly will we be doing?"

"They specifically mentioned the need for a long-range sniper, which is Thernopolis's specialty," comes Wilson's response. "As for what you will do, the guys believed they could work you in once they had conducted an on-site evaluation. Just like the old days they said. In fact, you may be involved with surveillance exercise."

"Sounds like a plan," chimed Thernopolis. I haven't had live sniper action in several months."

Scott has been puffing on his pipe for several minutes, looking for an opportunity to weigh in. "Excellent," he adds. "I figured the two of you would be happy to get out into the field and experience some real action. Plus, you may be able to stop something this time as opposed to performing a document grab."

"What is the estimated time on site and where will we go after the task is over," asks Thernopolis.

Wilson jumps back into the conversation. "This action will go live in twenty-eight to thirty-four hours, so you will need to assimilate quickly once you arrive. The total time at the border shouldn't be more than three, maybe four days, tops. Once the assignment is over you will be returning here. Any other questions?"

Silence.

"Okay," says Wilson. "Go grab some gear and weapons; Thernopolis remember to take your favorite sniper rifle.

"Winter, the guys will have explosives for you when you arrive at the border; sounds like they know your habits well."

That remark elicits an ear-to-ear smile from Winter.

"There will be a helicopter ready in an hour; it's about a two-hour flight from here. Good luck!"

****

Once outside the weather slams them in the face. The early afternoon sun is very bright as it reflects intensely from every object in sight, making it difficult to see. The temperature is rising rapidly; yep, another scorching day in the desert.

Thernopolis and Winter, squinting in an effort to block the sun's rays, walk out together heading towards their quarters. Winters comments, "It's always good to see action, I've been far too inactive for my liking. Hopefully we can make up for what we missed at Port Said and actually remove some weapons from the field. This should be even better if there are fighters to be removed from action before they even reach a battlefield. Prevention, the best way to stop the bad guys."

"I'm with you on that one," she says. "Tracking the ships positions via the satellite photos was important but also kind of boring. I liked stretching my legs a bit like we did yesterday afternoon."

"Sniping, hey? Sounds like the work will be a lot more intense when we swing into action. Know anything about where we're heading?"

"Other than the fact it will be hotter than hell? Nothing, except we are going west," she replied.

They stop at Thernopolis's quarters. "Meet you at the heliport in thirty minutes."

"Sounds good to me," Winter replies as he strides across the compound towards his place.

****

Twenty minutes later Winter meets her at the heliport; she always seems to arrive first wherever they go. He noticed the long bag she carried in addition to her duffel.

Walking behind a building they arrive at the helicopter pad. The copter is somewhat smaller than a combat bird but since it not a combat operation it shouldn't be a problem. However, to show it belongs, it still sports the ugly brown desert sand camouflage; everything must blend into its background. The engine has been turned; the copter's long blades are gradually gaining speed at it prepares for takeoff.

Crouching down as they walk to the copter, the pilot is there to load their gear. After he stows her duffel bag he reaches for the long bag. Thernopolis hesitates and draws the bag away.

Puzzled by her action he asks, "Something special?"

"Sniper rifle," she replies. "I would prefer it near me."

"I understand, not a problem."

Winter hands him his bag which is stored.

"Where are your chutes?"

Winter, "I didn't know we needed them, no one informed us to bring them."

"That's alright, I have extra." the pilot says. "Jump or not, we have them handy, just in case. The worst you should run into would be the need to fast rope down. Don't worry, I have extra gloves as well.

"Musaid, huh. Not the greatest place to fly into. There are no normal landing spots out there. Also, there can be action close to the border, if you get my drift."

"I know," said Winter as he buckled himself in and checks on Thernopolis. She is tightly packed in, almost to the point of restricting blood circulation.

"The people we are meeting out there said you will be able to land in a nearby field with no difficulty. They assured me there has been no exchange of fire in several weeks."

"Always easy to say by the nonpilots. They seem to believe we can land these birds anywhere."

"Can't you?"

"I suppose," the pilot huffs. "Hang on," he says, as the chopper, with a rattle and a clatter begins lifting up into the bright, blue sunny sky.

After they are seated Thernopolis leans over, "Have you ever jumped from a helicopter before?"

"I have both jumped from a helicopter and fast roped down. You?"

"I jumped just once and that was from a military transport plane."

"And…"

"It went well. Bigger bird and all. This is my second copter ride. Just to let you know, I threw up the first time, so I'm not promising anything."

"Good to know."

The copter lurched a bit as the pilot maneuvered it. This action caused her to apply a white-knuckled death grip on Winter's right arm. She probably turned a bit white in the face as well. She wasn't sure but she thought she saw the pilot smile. Jackass!!

The flight ended without further incident; the landing was relatively smooth, and there was no weapons fire. Thernopolis kept everything down although she came close once. She also didn't release her grip on Winter's arm until they landed. *Maybe I'll just drive back, she thinks.*

The pilot unloaded the two bags he stowed and sets them on the ground. Thernopolis is clutching her sniper rifle as she steps off after Winter.

Rummaging around behind his seat, the pilot emerges with what looks like a five-gallon water container and three plastic cups. Filling them he hands one to each of his passengers. Taking a swig he says, "This container was frozen solid when we lifted off, now look at it. Still, not too bad."

They each nod while drinking, it was indeed refreshing and appreciated. Thank you, they manage to say.

"No problem," he said while pouring a refill. If there's nothing else I can do then I will return to Cairo."

"Thanks for the ride," says Winter.

With that, crouched over, they walk about one fifty yards or so from the chopper and watched as the bird flies away.

Chapter 16

Siwa Oasis, Egypt
Near the Libyan Border

"Here we are, somewhere in Egypt and it's hotter than hell," Winter groused. Putting on his sunglasses, he continues carping, "The damn sun is so bright these stinking shades have little effect. Maybe this wasn't such a great idea after all. What the hell was Wilson thinking, volunteering us to be sent to this hell hole."

"Now you complain. You didn't second guess him when you had the chance earlier."

"Yeah."

"Hey Dirk, over here."

Winter recognizes the voice and begins to look around. About one hundred seventy yards from where they landed he spots someone waving at them. He crouches down to avoid the dust and dirt kicked up as the chopper lifted off, then started walking toward the waving figure.

"Eddie Fallon, what the hell are you doing here? Were you the loser in a contest to see who would get stuck picking us up?"

"Yeah, I'm happy to see you too, dickhead. Eddie is a somewhat short, bull of a man with a powerful looking chest stretching his t-shirt and arms to match dangling by his sides. As Winter gets close Eddie reaches out and envelopes him in a big bear hug, lifting him from the ground in the process. He's laughing as he turns Dirk loose.

"Are you kidding me, when the guys heard you were coming back, even for a temporary job, there was a race to see who would get to come here to meet you."

By this time Thernopolis, who carried all of the gear, had caught up to them. Turning from Winter, Eddie has to look up as he comes face-to-face with Maya, who is a few inches taller than he is. He looks over her from head-to-toe, trying not to fall over his wide open mouth. After a brief period of silence Fallon says, "Nobody told me you were bringing the reigning Miss World along. So, who is this vision of loveliness?"

"This is Maya Thernopolis, MI-6. And let me tell you, she is a straight up badass; one of the best operatives I've ever had the pleasure of working with."

Eyebrows arched and a smirk on his face he responds, "Oh yeah, how good is she?"

"Eddie, I'd trust her with my life in any operation, and you know I don't usually make comments like that. As a matter of fact, we've been in combat together and she bailed my ass out of a tight spot in Afghanistan. She has earned my full respect."

"Afghanistan, what the hell were you doing over there? We not exchanging fire with the Russians, are we?"

"Kinda. Long story that maybe I'll tell you about someday. And, now that you mention it, she is great looking, although I've never noticed."

Thernopolis smiles, in fact blushes a bit. It's the first time either one of them has spoken of the other with those type of words to anyone. She liked it hearing them, especially the great looking compliment.

"Eddie, is it?"

He nods and extends his hand. "Hope I didn't offend you, that certainly wasn't my intent.

"No offense taken." Playing him a little bit Maya, grinning, continues; "In addition to being a kick-ass and gorgeous, I'm also the sniper you ordered," as they shake hands.

Eddie just nods. no longer surprised at anything. Staring at Winter, he said, "It's just...well, you know, a little heads up would have been nice."

"Nah," Dirk said. "I've had too much fun watching you fall all over yourself."

"Thanks a bunch pal. And to think, we used to be good friends…"

"Only a brother could do that to you," a grinning Dirk replies.

"How do you put up with his crap Maya?"

"You get used to him after a while. He evens begins to grow on you."

That remark elicits a chuckle from Eddie. "So, you do know him. I'm sorry for that."

With the introductions over they follow Eddie across the sand to a Jeep parked about a hundred feet away. "Jump in," he says, "we have an encampment about four miles west of here. Boy, are the guys going to be surprised when I bring you two back!"

Maya climbs into the back along with their gear while Dirk parks himself in the front. Over the din of the engine he asks, "So, where are we headed?"

"A little place called the Siwa Oasis, about ten miles from here."

"What do you know about it?"

"Well, we are still in Egypt, but just barely."

Maya is learning forward from the back seat trying to get an idea of what the guys are talking about. She thinks they are talking about we they are headed. Straining, she finally gives up as the clatter from the Jeep's engine and the noise of the wind whistling makes the effort futile.

"There's a lot of history in this land that stretches back thousands of years to ancient Egypt. I'm not familiar with a lot of the story, no reason to be actually. But I do know that the oasis lies eighteen meters below sea level, along the rim of the Great Sand Sea. Because of that natural formation the area has a vast agricultural presence with a lot of date trees in particular. The trees provide natural camouflage."

A hard bump nearly pitches an off-balanced Maya, who's still somewhat trying to listen in, from her perch in the back. Turning around quickly to look back to make sure he hasn't lost his passenger Eddie yelled out; "Sorry about that; you can't always see the dips in the road."

Dirk asks, "Anything else about Siwa?"

"There's a real old fortress in the middle of downtown, Shali, built in the early 1200's, that's kinda cool. That place dominants everything other building down there. There are some ruins along with a 17th-century mosque that is still standing. And the ruins of the Old Town are quite impressive. This landscape plays an important role in our mission.

"In the downtown area are a hotel or two, and some eating places. To enjoy the luxuries of home we have set up among the desert camps outside of town near the mountain of Jebel Dakhrour, about three miles east of town."

Approaching a dessert camp Eddie down shifts to slow the Jeep, finally coming to a complete stop next to a large tent-like structure. "Hey guys, we're back," he hollered out.

Two guys emerge from the tent just as the three climb out of the Jeep. Striding towards them, Robbie Smith, the taller of the two, yelled, "Holy shit, it is him." Grabbing Dirk's arm and slapping him on the back he says. "Man, it really is you. How long has it been, like forever?"

Grinning Dirk responds, "It almost seems like it has been that long." Looking him over as they shake hands over he adds, "Man you look great."

Feeling himself being spun around Dirk goes with it and almost crashed into Allen Jordan. Bear hugging him much like Eddie did, he says, "So, they haven't shot you ugly ass yet?"

Dirk laughs. "Nothing serious yet, although some have tried."

Allen is only half listening as he spies a shapely backside on someone bent over pulling stuff out of the back of the Jeep. Releasing Dirk he walks on over to introduce himself. *I'll eat my hat if that butt doesn't belong to a woman.*

Allen is two steps away from Maya as she turns from the Jeep. Allen immediately sees the long bag; must be carrying some type of rifle. "Maya," she says, noticing him staring at the bag. "Sniper rifle," she adds while extending her hand.

"Allen," as he grabs her hand. So, you're our sniper? Welcome aboard."

"Thanks."

Allen, also on the shorter size with the powerful arms and upper body, sees that Maya's skin is almost as dark as his. "You a sister?"

"Come again?" she says.

Perplexed Allen tries to explain. "A sister, you know, African-American. I'm from Maryland."

"Ok, gotcha. No, my father is Greek and my mother is British. Obviously, my father skin tone is dominate."

Seeing Robbie staring at Maya, Eddie gives him a poke in the ribs. "Where's Dave?" he asked.

"Out doing a little scouting, trying to get more information on this place," Allen replied.

Robbie looked at his watch. "Left about forty-five minutes ago. Said he was heading for the ruins to look them over. Should be back soon. Maya, is it?"

"Yep, I'm your shootist."

Perplexed, since he had no idea what a shootist is, Robbie just nodded his head. "Cool."

Eddie leads everyone into the tent.

"Eddie, is this the entire team now, the six of us?" Dirk asks.

"You betcha. You remember how we always flew; traveled fast, deadly and in small numbers."

"Right. Where exactly are we, besides in the Siwa Oasis, which you alluded to as barely being in Egypt."

Eddie walks over to a table, reaches under it and pulls a map from a weathered, brown satchel. Spreading it out on the table, he points. "We are so deep in Egypt that we are thirty miles from the Libyan border, here," as he taps on the map. "Technically we are in a military zone. Usually permission is required to officially enter here. However, one of the village elders contacted us through an intermediary to seek our help. So, we're cool in that regard."

"Some suspicious men have been floating in with the Bedouins who travel through here. They pretend to be traders, but people have spied them carrying large boxes into and out of various buildings around town. After a day or two they load the same crates onto trucks. They also have roamed among the ruined tombs and around several desert camps, and performed the same ritual of hiding crates.

"Cent Com has been watching their movements via satellites; they are convinced that weapons are being passed through here. Our task is to intercede and destroy as much of the operation as possible through whatever methods are required. They want to send the message that this route is permanently closed.

"Our only handicap is to perform our work outside of the town. Under no condition are we to engage in hostilities around the civilians. We need to be very surgical, precise and clean. I promised command no problems; hence the heavy scouting."

"What's the game plan?" Maya asked.

Eddie responded, "Based on our intel, both satellite and reports we've gathered from sources here, the men show in the middle of the night and hide their crates. They move among the ruined temples, graveyards, what have you. After a full slinking through the downtown area, scouting maybe, the following day or maybe two, they load up different trucks and then everyone leaves."

"You trust the people in town you're working with?" Dirk asked.

"Dave and I have been talking with the people since we both have a basic understanding and are conversant in several Arabic dialects," Robbie responds. "The reason I trust them is the anonymous source who contacted us identified these individuals who have the same concern for the general well-being of their fellow residents. They have assisted with our surveillance of the area both in and out of town."

As they continued to talk Dave popped in. Sporting dirty blonde hair, he's taller than the other guys, not as quite as wide as well; but still with the look of someone you wouldn't want to mess with.

"Just the man I've been waiting for," says Eddie. "First, introductions. Dave Robitelli, this is Dirk Winter, the man you replaced on our team." They exchange handshakes and a nice to meet you.

Turning to Maya Eddie added, "And, this young lady, is our sniper, Maya Thernopolis."

Handshakes again.

To Dirk Dave says, "I've heard a lot of about you."

Dirk replied, "All good I hope?"

"Not too bad, but there were somethings that I can't repeat in front of a lady." This line of conversation caused Dave to blush a bit.

"Ah, yes, perhaps it is best to skip over that," Dirk answered.

"Maya, you are the first female operative I have encountered. Welcome," Dave said.

"Thank you," she says. I hear that a lot. We Brits are more progressive in that area than you Yanks are."

Eddie interrupted; "If you ladies are done with your ass-kissing, let's get down to business. What did you learn on your scouting mission?"

"The latest scuttlebutt from our people is to expect a group tonight," Dave answers. "If the smugglers follow their recent pattern of movement they will secrete the weapons in the ruins outside of town and move them the following night. Our question is when do we hit them and where."

"Are all options available to us or are we operating under restrictions as to where we can execute our raid?" Maya asks.

Robbie, "As long as we avoid undue endangerment to the civilians, we're good to go. Since the smugglers work under the cloak of darkness where there are no lights, there shouldn't even be any tourists wandering around."

Dirk asked, "Do we have any idea how many men are usually involved in the operation?"

Eddie takes this question; "They arrive in plain farm trucks with two men per vehicle. They fit in as farmers that are delivering crates of dates, vegetables and other crops for sale at the various markets.

"The vehicles that are loaded later are usually small pickup trucks like the Toyota Tacoma. The number of men accompanying the pickups are also two per vehicle."

"Well," Maya offers, "if we hit them upfront, after they arrive at the ruins, there should be fewer total combatants. That will make the battlefield easier to control."

Allen, "Okay, what happens when their comrades arrive and finds no waiting smugglers? Will they go searching for them in town and, perhaps, create havoc and hurt innocents?"

"Good point," Dirk responds. "The best option may be to wipeout everyone involved; send the message this area is being watched and its best not to bother returning here again. Eddie, do we know anything about the smugglers?"

"Nothing about their identity. Since the weapons are traveling a long distance through Libya, starting at the port of Tobruk; it wouldn't be a big surprise if the Libyan army was involved at some point in the operation. Remember it wasn't that long ago that Gaddafi attacked Egypt in a short war. While Egypt kicked their asses, they may still relish screwing with the Egyptians whenever they can. Imagine the embarrassment if Cairo found out weapon shipments to their enemies were passing right under their noses."

"Would the involvement of Libyan solders make our job harder?" Maya asked.

"Not necessarily," Eddie responds. "The Libyan soldiers aren't the best fighters in the middle east. It's possible the smugglers could be tougher than they are, especially if they have been fighting in Afghanistan or other 'hotspots'. Therefore, we will be prepared to engage in a nasty firefight from a battle-tested foe. Of course, we'll prevail."

"Naturally," everyone shouts in unison.

"There's about two hours of light left before dusk starts to set in. Let's go into town, take a look around and then eat. There are a couple of decent places for food, so I've been told," Dave said.

"Dirk, you and Maya come with me and Dave and we'll do a quick look see around the area," Eddie said. "Robbie and Allen will stay behind in town since they snuck into this area about two weeks ago. They already have a pretty good knowledge of the surroundings, including several hours of observation over the border in Libya.

"We will meet you two in town in about an hour after you do a little snooping around. See how many know we are out here and if anyone is squawking over it. We don't need some squealer to announce our presence."

Chapter 17

They decided during dinner that Dirk and Maya would hide in some ruins overseeing the main road into the tombs where the crates were delivered on the past three missions. Just before midnight they arrive at the tombs. They scoured the area with their night visions goggles and spotted a pair of structures on opposite sides of the tombs just outside the path. Checking them out for stability they climb atop the massive, cool stones and lay down prone on the ledges to wait.

Shortly after midnight they observed a series of headlights slowly making their way towards their position. The small caravan of three farm trucks stop about a hundred fifty feet in front of them. The trucks' headlights are left on to aid in the digging; the light also provides clear viewing to Dirk and Maya to watch the operation.

Three large holes are dug where the smugglers, six of them, stacked six large crates, two on top of the other in each hole. They struggled a bit with the crates; they appeared to be heavy enough to be holding weapons. Suddenly a bright light is flashed around the nearby area as the men search to see if anyone has watched their work. Satisfied they are the only ones at the site, they cover the crates, climb into their trucks and leave.

"Did you get a good look at that those trucks?" I don't know about you, but I think I could pick them out in town," Maya said.

"I got a so-so look at them but could probably locate them in town as well. Just one question, for what purpose?" We ruled out removing just the smugglers who are bringing in the weapons."

"If for no other reason than to determine whether or not those guys are heavily armed," Maya said.

"When do you want to leave; now?"

"Why not?"

"Okay," Dirk says, "let's go. We're about three or four miles from town, so; what thirty minutes or so?"

"Sounds like a plan, let's go."

****

"About time you two got back. You took a lot longer than I expected. Did you encounter any problems?" Eddie asked.

"No," replied Dirk. We watched three farm trucks come in and get unloaded by six guys. Then we trailed them into town to examine the trucks to determine if they are heavily armed. We found they were carrying a few rifles, ammo clips, several hand grenades; nothing really major. What did you guys learn?"

"Our sources still indicated the other half of the operation will occur late tomorrow night," says Dave. "My best guess would be there will be three trucks coming in to pick up the stash. I would further guess that no more than three drivers would arrive, and together the nine of them would complete the operation."

"Sounds reasonable," Dirk responds. "The guys we watched certainly had no major trouble unloading the weapons and three more should simply speed up the process. Since they won't be expecting trouble at the site, I would see no reason for them to bring in extra firepower."

"Do you have a battle plan?" Eddie asked.

"When Maya and I examined the area we located several perches about a hundred feet above the ground and maybe two hundred yards away from the burial zone. Maya can pick her favorite spot and hide herself. After the trucks are on site she can take out the lights, rendering the area in darkness. The rest of us will swoop down, take out the smugglers and secure the weapons."

"Works for me," Eddie said. The others nodded in agreement.

****

The team spent an uneventful day divided between time in town, at their camp, and touring the ruins, including where they will trap the smugglers. They managed to talk with some travelers coming in from the east who reported knowledge of a small caravan headed towards Siwa. The talk is of three trucks moving in to pick up prized cargo to transport back across the desert.

At around nine pm Eddie makes a call for the latest satellite intel. He was told three small pickup trucks had been identified as headed in their direction. The estimated time of arrival is three to three and one-half hours.

The team left their camp at 11:30 pm and began their walk to the ruins. Once there they fanned across the area to take their positions at ground level while Maya positioned herself on a ledge about a hundred feet above the ruins' floor. The plan was to wait until after the men had left the trucks and had uncovered the weapons. Maya would determine when to start the action by shooting out the first light.

Shortly after midnight they listened as several vehicles approached the area. The drivers slowed their trucks and stopped about twenty-five feet away from where the weapons had been buried. The men exited the pickups, gathered in front of the trucks' headlights and laid their weapons on the ground near them. They laughed and jostled each other as they started excavating, totally unaware of the action that would soon be carried out.

Maya waited until they had been digging for a few minutes. She proceeded to line up her L96 Bolt Action Sniper Rifle and adjusted the night scope. She estimated she could shoot out most of the lights before anyone could scramble to the trucks to hide or retrieve other weapons they may have brought with them. Speaking into her throat mic she said she would take out the lights one-by-one in rapid fashion starting on the left.

She paused briefly for everyone to respond back then re-sighted the shot on the headlight on the first vehicle on the left. Maya counted down from ten and then started extinguishing the lights.

It wasn't until the second light went out that the smugglers realized they were being fired at. The men began reaching for their rifles at the same time as they started to scatter for cover. Some tried to return back to the vehicles while others headed for perceived safe areas among the ruins. Maya kept taking out the lights; at this point she had no interest at shooting people. Through their night-vision goggles the team was able to keep track of where the enemy had scattered.

When the lights were all snuffed out, Dave called out in Arabic, asking for them to surrender. The answer was a couple of shots fired in his general direction; wide right, sending rock chips flying. At least one had found a weapon to defend himself. Eddie announced over the mic to start eliminating enemy personnel; fire at will.

The team opened up and began picking off the smugglers. The return fire emanated from two angles in front of the team's general position. The sparsity of the defensive fire led the team to surmise that not everyone had been able to grab their weapons.

After a brief exchange of gunfire everything went silent. Scanning the area Maya picked up three men running in a low crouch headed towards the trucks. Maya got the first two but didn't deliver a kill shot to the last one, instead hitting him in the leg. She watched as he pulled himself into the truck. The lack of immediate noise from the vehicle led her to seek other targets hiding among the ruins. She found a person trying to flank Dave on his left and took him out.

The sound of an engine turning over, then kicking to life, drew fire from Maya's flanks. The amount of dirt that was kicked up meant the effort was focused on trying to blow the tires. "You got this, Maya?" Robbie asked.

"Just a second," she replied before sending a shot that pinned the driver into the seat. The truck stopped after crashing into a nearby pillar.

To her left Maya heard an explosion and watched as a fireball soared skyward from a burning truck. "What the hell caused that?" she heard Winter exclaim over the mic. Then, silence.

They waited in the dark for about five minutes; no return fire and nobody saw any movement. Eddie stood up and cautiously looked around. "It's over," he called out. "Is everyone alright?"

He waited as one-by-one they called back; no injuries. "Great, let's go see what they were transporting." He started to cautiously move forward from behind a pillar, slowly advancing toward the holes. The other guys also began to step out while Maya began to climb down from her perch.

Suddenly, a roar, an explosion and the burning truck now seemed to be emitting a fiercer red, orange glow mixed with black smoke; emitting a gasoline smell.

Everyone dropped to the ground in a reflexive action as they watched the roaring blaze. The truck, though lighting the night sky, was far enough away not to be a hinderance to finishing the excavation. Still, they wanted to get out as fast as they could. They didn't want to be present in case onlookers were attracted to the disaster.

It appeared the smugglers had completed about half of their task. It only took another five minutes of digging until they struck pay dirt. Allen and Eddie grabbed opposite ends of the first crate and lifted it out of the hole. They struggle to lift it out of the hole, the crate was heavier than they anticipated. Robbie helped to bring out the crate and set it on the ground. He then joined Allen and Eddie as they moved from hole to hole and brought everything to the surface. They each brought out the last three crates as they were lighter than the first three.

A couple of whacks with a shovel broke the lock on the first crate and they flipped open the lid. What they saw surprised them. It looked like bales of hay! "What the fuck," Eddie exclaimed, "we waylaid a bunch of farmers, for hay?"

Maya started sifting through the 'hay' and then sniffed it. "Au contraire," she said. "This is marijuana. I would be willing to bet a high quality product." As she continued to rummage through the crate, she counted six separate bales. "We have found maybe five hundred pounds of this stuff. It's no wonder you guys struggled to bring the crates out of the hole."

The second crate is busted open and contains five bales and ten bags of wind powder; cocaine. The third crate has thirty-five bags of the white stuff. Their curiosity heightened as they opened the fourth crate. Inside that box is money; stacks and stacks of clean, crisp one hundred dollar bills; like they were just delivered from a U.S. mint. The fifth crate is full of British fifty pound bank notes while the sixth crate is filled with French five hundred franc bank notes. Like the American bills they looked to be brand new, fresh off the printing presses. Finding these bills like this had to mean they most likely were freshly printed.

"Looks we have busted a major drug smuggling and counterfeiting ring," said Dirk. "This isn't some small time operation. Judging by the condition of the bank notes, the perpetrators had access to very sophisticated printing presses and plates. Those bills would fool anyone. I'll also bet that while the oasis is a great agricultural area marijuana isn't a local crop. Has anyone checked the corpses for ID? I'll guess these guys are nothing but mules."

"Just finished a quick search," Dave responds. "Found absolutely nothing; the best I can offer is they are Arabs. I agree Dirk, they just a bunch of mules who knew how to traverse the desert. Whoever sent them made sure they couldn't be identified if caught. What now, Eddie?"

"We'll load the booty into the trucks and head back to our camp. I will make a call once we secure the stash to learn what happens next."

****

A couple of hours later they arrived at their camp and files into the big tent. Eddie said to Maya and Dirk they will need to spend one more night with us and then you will be sent back to Cairo via a chopper.

Dave adds, "Hey, we can't let them go without a proper send off." I have several bottles of the locals' best stuff somewhere," as he begins to rummage around. "Ah ha..here it is. If this liquid doesn't kill them first, then they can leave."

"Absolutely," Robbie chimes in. "After all it's our duty to send them back with hangovers; just like the old days."

"One problem," says Dave. "I only have five bottles but plenty of cups. I'm not great at math so what I'll do is pour until someone just can't hold up their cup to be refilled. Or I pass out, whichever comes first."

With no complaints he begins filling cups, handing one to everyone.

Eddie had the first toast. "It's been great working with you guys. Maya, you more than held up your role; just like Dirk said you would. I would work with you anytime.

"And Dirk, it was like you never left. We functioned like a well-oiled machine, just like we always did. Thank you if your assistance with this operation."

The others offered their thanks as well. They agreed with Eddie that it was like Dirk had never left the team; everything still clicked.

They also toasted Maya. Although none of them really had any idea of what to expect from a female team member, they were still especially impressed with the first female operative they had ever met. She held her own, was very soldierly, and they would fight with her again if the opportunity ever presented itself.

"Gee, thanks guys," said Dirk. "But really, it's been great working with the team again."

Maya said, "I'm really at a loss for words. Thank you." Smiling broadly she adds, "I guess this makes me one of the guys."

Dave tried to make a toast but just slumped over; he was finished for the night. "Wimp," Eddie scoffed, "he's usually the first to go nite-nite. That's one area the kid can't match you in," he said to Dirk.

While no one was timing the event, it wasn't long before the rest of the team had their lights go out. Fortunately for Dirk and Maya the chopper didn't arrive until late afternoon the next day which allowed everyone time to recover from their headaches. Although no one was sure when they first started stirring from their slumber, the local liquor hadn't killed them, and they would live to fight another day.

Chapter 18

Cairo Base Camp

While somewhat bummed that they hadn't busted up an arms ring, they received plenty of kudos for taking a huge chunk out of one of the largest drug smuggling and counterfeiting operations the Green Beret had encountered. It was decided the best way to move the haul would be to send it back to Cairo with Dirk and Maya.

On the return flight the pilot joking asked them if they were sure they wanted to go back to Cairo."

"Where would we go?" Maya asked.

"Anywhere we wanted," said the pilot. "I got a look at some of the counterfeit bills. While I not an expert, I have hauled this type of cargo before. And, believe me, those are some of the finest forgeries I've ever seen."

"Well, there's just one major problem with any attempt to divert the cargo or ourselves. The Green Beret, along with Cent Com, knows we have this stuff. I don't believe there is enough money or drugs here to hide from them forever," said Dirk.

"Ah, you probably right," replied the pilot. "But, still..what a thought."

The chopper touched down late afternoon at the same spot they took off from four days earlier. Both Scott and Wilson were there to meet them along with two military trucks and about a dozen members of the military police (MP). Everyone was taking this transfer very seriously.

Scott jokingly said, "We were wondering if you would make it back with all of that money plus the drugs."

"Yes," Wilson chimed in. "That's easily a multi-million dollar bust."

"The subject was broached and discussed with the pilot, but we considered the work involved to hide out would be too exhausting," Maya said.

Dirk added, "I guess we're just too honest. Still, if we shoot the MPs, there one last chance."

Scott shakes his head as he watches the trucks take off. "Not any more there isn't."

Scott motions for Thernopolis, Winter and Wilson to follow him to his office. "I've been on the phone to London for most of the afternoon. They are highly impressed with you work out on the border. I know you would have preferred to have removed weapons from potential combat zones, however, the drug smuggling and counterfeiting bust was just as huge. The cash that was grabbed went have been used to purchase weapons, supplies and fighters by who knows who. Also, the drugs, if not convert to cash here, could have eventually made their way to U.S. or British shores to add to the legal drug trade in our respective countries. So, kudos from headquarters as well as from us.

"And now for some good news and some bad news," Wilson said. "I have been in communication with Cyprus where British commandos and American Navy Seals intercepted a boat in the Mediterranean Sea earlier today. The action was based on American intelligence on the ground that had been tracking activity at the Port of Limassol. They conducted a raid on a dock warehouse, similar to what you did at Port Said, and found documents identifying a ship carrying suspicious cargo. The intervention occurred in the open sea. The shipboard documents indicated the ship was headed for Lebanon and Hezbollah guerillas. The cargo was 100% military equipment."

Winter with a puzzled look on his face asked, "How does this pertain to us; is there more?"

"There is," said Wilson. "Analysis of other documents recovered from the ship indicated the same group behind the seized ship was planning more weapons movement. London and Washington are both looking for a very vigorous response. And, now for the bad news.

"Our participation in this venture will require the splitting apart of our team here. You and Thernopolis will be leaving us behind and flying to Cyprus late tomorrow morning. While I don't have all of the details, you will be tasked to engage in intelligence work to further enhance our capabilities to find out who's behind all of the weapons movement. You will be joining an operation already in place and being coordinated thorough MI-6. And don't worry; I've been told there is a lot of action right now; not the seat shining you were doing quite a bit of here."

"Good luck", said Scott as he rose to congratulate them after Wilson finished. "We will try to keep our heads out of our asses and not mess up the analysis work that Thernopolis organized."

Thernopolis and Winter, both caught off-guard with the news, just stared, not knowing what to say. An assignment like this never occurred to them; they figured they would remain in Cairo.

"One more thing. We will have a little soiree for your successful raid and for the fact that you'll be leaving us. And, while I don't want to name names but there has been a bit of an aromatic tinge in the air since we've gathered here; so, Winter, just remember to shower before you show up tonight," said Wilson.

"Gee sir, I always thought you like the earthy, rugged outdoors odors."

Wilson flipped him the bird as he walked out the door and headed across the compound.

After they leave Scott's office and stepped outside, Winter says to Thernopolis, "I didn't see that one coming. Cyprus, huh? I guess that means we a pretty good team."

"As long as I'm in charge and giving you directions, we a pretty damn good unit," she replies with a big smile. "And, I also haven't wanted to complain, here or while on task, but I agree with Wilson; you definitely need a shower." She quickly smells under one arm and proclaims: "I know you're too gentlemanly to complain, but so do I."

Winter started to reply but changed his mind. Sporting a sly mischievous look he said, "You know, we could shower together, save some water."

"It's a great idea, but there is a problem. If we did that, we wouldn't show up for at least two days, miss the feast, our plane, get court-martialed and so on. How would we explain that?"

Winter just shrugs his shoulders. With a big smile she says, "But I love your thinking and how our minds think alike on the subject. Besides, there always Cyprus."

With his head spinning with these revelations Winter can only give her a wink, then walks back to his quarters. Thernopolis heads in the other direction to her quarters. *I've befuddled the horny boy in him she thinks to herself. Still, it's a good idea, with or without the assistance of a nice shower. Then, whoa, what are thinking girl?? You hardly know him! But, so far he's been great to me, there is a spark, and, I don't know, I just trust him, okay.* She looks across the compound before she steps into her quarters; *I sure hope I was thinking to myself and not talking out; don't want people to think I'm goofy.* Fortunately, she was the only person going in her direction so nobody would have heard her if she was talking out loud.

****

It was quite the party and a terrific send-off. Although no one got teary-eyed, they were leaving their work family. It's really amazing how close you can get to people in a short time when you're dealing in life and death situations. Since they had endured a night of drinking, Thernopolis and Winter took things easy.

About two o'clock in the morning the group started to break up. Between Winter and Thernopolis, they were able to get Scott, who was singing very badly, back to his place. Before going inside, he shook Thernopolis's hand and planted a kiss on Winter's cheek. "Oh", he said, I think I got that backwards. Oh, well, goodnight everyone; maybe we will work together again someday."

After leaving Scott off they walked to Thernopolis's quarters. "Gee, kinda dark in here," she says. "Maybe you should help me inside." With that Winter leads her into the room. The open door allows the bright moonlight to enter the room; it disappears fast as the door closes behind them.

This time Winter is the aggressor as he pulls her close to him, smelling the fragrance of her shampoo as they hold each other tight. He briefly kisses her before deciding to shift his body; however, doing so causes him to lose his balance, tripping over his feet or her feet, or both. He lands on her bed which brings a soft chuckle from him; then he goes quiet and sits up. Bending down, Thernopolis starts to reach out in the air, searching for him. She bumps into something, hopefully it's him, then softly laughs as he drags her onto the bed, sitting beside him. Since she's the only female assigned to this unit, she was given the better quarters, including a better bed; however, while a larger size they won't be performing any bed flips on it.

They sit for a while before flopping down on the bed. They lay on their sides facing each other, slowly starting to kiss. They fumble with buttons on their shirts, beginning to undress each other naked to the waist. While not sure how it happened, Winter ended up on his back with Thernopolis astride him. Unable to see, he could only imagine what her breasts looked like. He reached up and with one in each hand, he started stroking them, gently rolling the nipples between his fingers. This elicited a low moan from her. She moved his hands around her chest as she reached down to kiss him even deeper. Reaching back with her hand she found something hard and gave it a gentle squeeze.

Suddenly a loud noise from outside brings them back to reality. They stop moving, waiting quietly in the dark. Everything returns to quiet; however, they simultaneously reach the conclusion to bring a halt to their fun. A little fumbling in the dark, along with kissing each other's chest, and they eventually get their shirts back on. Thernopolis turns on her nightlight; checks her watch, three thirty, and walks with Winter to her door. A quick kiss goodnight and out the door he strides. "Carefully who you wave at," she says, then closes the door. She's definitely sporting a big, dreamy smile as she turns out the light. As she undresses she happens to nonchalantly brush her hand between her thighs; her panties are damp. Damn, he's good!

Chapter 19

Winter raised his head, opened an eyelid and quickly shut it, slumping back onto his bed. He's not sure yet if he's alive after last night/ this morning's festivities. Even though he went easy last night, two nights in a row of drinking seems to have caught up with him. He counted to ten and tried to rise again. He lifted up his head and this time he opened his other eye; ugh, same disgusting view of a mess. He finally succeeded in sitting up, still trying to determine if it was worth the effort. Fumbling around he grasps a round object; its feels like his watch. He blinks a couple of times to focus on its face; ten o'clock.

Oh shit, nobody said last night what time is late morning. Better step it up, grab a quick shower, shave and be ready to go to the airport. Doesn't look like I'll have time for breakfast; tasting his cotton mouth; *on second thought that may not be a bad thing.*

Looking at his room with clear vision he smiled; guess this mess will just have to wait for the next guy. It really breaks my heart to leave it like this; oh well, hope he has no hard feelings. He picked up his shirt, it smelled like, oh yeah, it smelled like Thernopolis and puts it on. Searching his quarters, he finds one boot quickly, then mumbles to himself, *where the hell is my other boot?* He kicked a pile of clothes and a boot slides out. Uh, he exclaims as he grabbed it and pulled it on.

Fully dressed he sidestepped a boot as he headed outside for the shower. As he walks out the door, he squints, *muttering how the damn sun is always so bright,* though in reality this morning it's partly cloudy.

Forty-five minutes later he has completed his morning routine, thrown the least smelly shirts and pants he can find into a duffel bag and walks across the compound to headquarters. He looks around, finding no Jeep or other vehicle is in sight. *Damn, they wouldn't me behind, would they?*

While still pondering what to do Wilson bounds out of his office. Checking his watch, he says, "What are you doing here so early"?

"I thought I was catching a flight to Cyprus."

"You are. We couldn't put you guys on a military transport as planned so we had to book you on a commercial flight. Come back at three-thirty and there will be a Jeep here to drive you to the airport.

We send a guy over at seven to inform you; he came back saying instead of answering his knock you swore at him then threw a boot at the door. You know what they say, don't shoot the messenger."

Winter grunted as he turned around to leave. *So that's what that idiot wanted and why my boot ended up at the door. That's what you get for waking up the dead.* The first pangs of hunger hits. He checked his watch, eleven-fifteen. *Guess I'll go find Thernopolis, hope she's alive, and we can grab some grub.*

He takes a few steps toward Thernopolis' place when he hears a voice shout, "Hey, over here." He turns and sees her coming from the direction of his quarters. She's cleaned and shined and ready to roll. He grunts to himself before she's within earshot; *guess I'm the only one who died this morning.* He smiled; on the other hand, he hasn't seen Scott yet.

"I walked over to you place to see if you wanted a late breakfast." He smiled lewdly which was responded to with, "Get your mind out of the gutter."

"I didn't say anything," he responded in protest and dropped his duffel bag.

"You didn't have to, its written all over your face. You have no poker face when it comes to me."

Winter just shrugs his shoulders.

"To continue what I was saying, when you didn't answer my knock, I entered anyways. I took one step, nearly falling over a boot. I guess that was the cause of the thump someone heard coming from your place this morning. In addition to the misplaced boot there were clothes thrown everywhere. Immediately I thought, what a pig sty!"

"It's no worse than my college dorm room," he said as he tries to offer up a defense.

"Why am I not surprised. I figured after having a bite to eat there will be plenty of time to clean the place before leaving if we hustle."

"Will you help?" he asks.

"Nope. I'm not your mother or your maid. Nor have I been trained in hazardous waste disposal. Oh, in case you're thinking of just leaving it, Wilson happened to pop in and scanned the room also."

"Shit, what did he say?"

"He just shook his head and walked away, muttering to himself. Something about you could be replaced as my partner if need be. In addition to him being mad, I would also be very pissed if that happened. So, clean up the mess."

"Ah, Wilson wouldn't really replace me." Winter picks up his duffel bag as they start walking toward her place. "You can leave that here and after your place is cleaned we'll come back and retrieve my stuff as well," she says. He opens the door to drop his bag inside. It's the first time he's seen it in the daylight; of course, it's spotless.

A quick meal and back to his quarters. Thernopolis agreed to go with him, threatening to beat him with his dirty laundry if need be. Winter opens the door and peers in, his senses on full alert. In addition to the giant mess, it smells a little gamey.

Looking befuddled, Thernopolis starts giving him directions. After a few minutes of mumbling and general cleaning, he looks at Thernopolis and smiles to himself. Since it's daylight and there's no telling who might pop by or look in, there's no chance for tomfoolery going on. Still, she does look good.

An hour later, after throwing out garbage, making the bed and general straightening and rearranging things, he looks to Thernopolis, who's been yammering at him to hurry up, for approval.

Worse than any drill sarge he had ever encountered is his thought after she points out a couple of things he missed after she completes an inspection. Finally, she says it's good to go. They go back to her place, grab their gear and arrive five minutes before the Jeep does.

A short ride to the airport where the driver takes them around back for immediate boarding; the benefits and perks of being considered a VIP. They unload their bags, hand their papers to a security guard and board the plane. The best thing is it's a commercial flight and since no one knows them they cuddle a bit during the ninety minutes journey to Cyprus.

Chapter 20

Nicosia, Cyprus

A big, black sedan with the British flag attached to the front of the vehicle is waiting for Thernopolis and Winter as the plane lands. They are held on the plane until all of the other passengers have disembarked. After the plane is emptied a driver is waiting for them on the tarmac as they come down with the crew. He takes their papers, performs a quick scan of their ID cards and directs them into the car. After a quick call he departs for the British embassy.

It early evening as their vehicle was pulling into the far end of the underground parking lot. A quick walk through the back stairwell and into a key-coded elevator where the driver punched in the floor number. They disembarked from the car and strode into Sir Hillary's third floor office.

Sir Geoffrey Hillary, the head of MI-6 Special Operations in the Middle East, was waiting for Thernopolis and Winter as they entered. It's a big office but rather plain, both in color and in furnishings, actually the lack thereof. The main piece of décor was a huge, color picture behind Hillary's desk of him and the queen; probably he received an accommodation of some type.

Since Thernopolis has met Sir Hillary in the past, for her own commendation ceremony, she handled the introductions. Handshakes and smiles are followed by congratulations for their successful raid on the warehouse in Port Said and the busting of the multi-million dollar drug and counterfeiting ring in Siwa Oasis.

Sir Hilar's primary focus was on the raid at Port Said. Early reports from the analysts, said Sir Hillary, has confirmed several of their assumptions and provided important new data. Some of the encrypted writings will soon be deciphered by the interpreters. They patiently wait to be informed of their new assignment.

"On to current business and why the two of you are here," Hillary said. "There is an ongoing operation that has been established to track arms dealing activities in the Middle East. A rumor was making the rounds of a newly emerging player(s) wishing to enter the high stakes weapons arena. As of right now, the party and/or parties have not been identified."

"Another MI6 operative by the name of Whit Johnson, not sure if you know him Maya, has been working with gun runners in the Middle East for several years and has developed solid relationships with most of the dealers and wannabes. He's been directing the ones operating with our allies and trying to stop or thwart the undesirables. He's established a cover for you as Maya and Dirk Jackson, arms dealers from Ireland. You both had established your bonafides with the Irish Republican Army. You have stolen and/or procured the weapons needed to help keep the resistance alive. Two years ago, you began to branch out, running weapons for other "rebel" groups throughout Europe.

"Johnson has also arranged for the hotel that will be your official headquarters. It will be very discrete as they are one of our preferred establishments. Your true identity has been cleared with the consigliere service which is manned by our assets. They will be used at times to manage communications from my office. Also, you will be able to come and go without problems.

"There is a gathering of weapons procurement people here in Lefkosia tomorrow. Johnson will give you entrée into the meeting and vouch for your credentials. Initially you are just gathering information, trying to determine who is trying to move weapons and their destination. Our belief right now is the ultimate buyer is Iran; and since they are short on cash the payment will probably be some type of oil swap.

"You are at this point to simply identify key members in the buying and selling process; try to determine identities of the involved countries; arrangement for future meetings, and then report back here. We will run your information and compare it to the intel we have already collected. We will then plan our next course of action. Questions?"

Winter, "You said you established our new identities with the same last name. How are we playing this, husband and wife, brother and sister?"

Hillary, just a little hot under the collar, "You're kidding me, right? This is really your first concern? Nobody really gives a fuck how you handle your identities. You can be aunt and uncle for all I care. I'm quite confident the two of you will come to a reasonable accommodation. Thernopolis, are you concerned?"

She nods her head no. "I didn't think so. So, Mr. Winter, if you can't handle this assignment, speak up now."

Winter says nothing.

"Good," replies Hilary. "Besides, if you're an idiot, I'm quite sure she can handle you. I've seen her do so in the past with other morons. Now, are there any real questions?"

Thernopolis, "What do we know about the arms dealers that are expected to attend tomorrow's meeting?"

"An intelligent question," Hillary replies. "Pay attention to her Winter and you will learn why she's one of our top field officers. Johnson expects the usual crowd that he has worked with in the past. These players represent the sellers such as us, France, the US, etc. However, the unknown is China, yes/no, real or rumor? Johnson hasn't knowingly worked with any buyer or seller directly tied to them.

"If anyone has moved their weapons the transaction has been facilitated through a third party that hasn't self-identified with the Chinese. If there is an official representative of their government, it will be like their coming out party, their grand entrance with this group. Thus, the importance of learning names and affiliations."

Winter asks, "Do you have access to our databases?"

"Yes, yours, ours, the French, Israel, Interpol; the latest and greatest; and as I said there are no known Chinese arms dealers in any database that we have access too."

"What about Arabian buyers? There are stories of oil rich sheiks playing in the arena now," said Winter.

"The stories may very well be correct on that. The problem is none have been identified and entered into the intelligence databases.

Thernopolis, "Is it possible the USSR is involved?"

"Possible, but highly unlikely. Virtually their entire focus is on the mess in Afghanistan, so it isn't believed any of their government officials are involved. Anything else?"

Neither Thernopolis nor Winter responds.

"Good," says Hillary. He hands them a set of documents, "Here are your new identities, the address for your hotel and the address for tomorrow's meeting. Here is a picture of Johnson, he always carries a walking stick, very British you know. Now get out of here and good luck."

****

After leaving Sir Hillary, Winter offered, "I don't think he likes me too much; you know, that first question."

"You think?" she replied. "I was kind of taken aback myself."

"Well, I don't.. he stammered.

"Is it really that important to you? I thought, given the last several weeks we've spent together, we were past the awkward stage of our friendship." She was careful to avoid the relationship tag.

Silence.

"Would it be better if I changed the arrangements, to avoid embarrassing you?"

"No, nothing like that. It's just, it just happened out of the clear blue sky. It would have been nice if I had a heads up; had been asked my thoughts."

"But no changes?"

"No, none whatsoever," he smiled.

With that crisis solved, they wandered around the embassy's lobby for a bit. Thernopolis remarks how this lobby, the décor and the overall appearance is very similar to the one her mother worked at in Athens.

"Greece?", Winter asks.

"The only one", Thernopolis replies. Checking her watch and noticing it's eight o'clock, she says, "Let's go to dinner, and try to come up with a game plan of sorts. This type of assignment is new to me, what about you?"

It's all Greek to me, no pun intended," he replies. My work has been training fighters and conducting deep raids in enemy territory that have resulted in targeted takedowns, hostage recues and so forth. This type of infiltration work is new to me, I'm not sure if it's me."

"Does it bother you"?

"Not sure it bothers me;" he hesitated while searching for the right phrase, "it's just different. What about you?"

She smiled. "As long as you are my partner, I ready for a new adventure." Changing gears, she asks, "I've never been to Cyprus before, have you?"

"No, can't say I've ever had the pleasure."

"Alright then, let's find the hotel and eat at their restaurant. According to the directions I have it's about a mile from here. Are you up for a quick walk?"

Chapter 21

The walk was indeed a short stroll as they reached the hotel in about five minutes. They walked into the giant lobby and up to the registration desk. The lobby décor was a bit garish but unique, if not, perhaps a bit stylish in its own way. The desk's dark mahogany wood definitely stood out in contrast to the rest of the furnishings. Soon a clerk appeared to check them in. Addressing the gentleman in Greek, a tongue of which Dirk hadn't the foggiest notion of but was Maya's native tongue, she was able to complete the check-in process with Dirk simply smiling, nodding his head and signing where Maya told him.

As she grabbed the room key, she asked the clerk where the restaurant was located, and he pointed down a hallway to the left of where the registration counter was. Dirk hoisted the duffle bags and walked down the hallway to look for a nearby room to drop them in. Maya called after him and said the clerk would hold the bags. Dirk returned, left their duffel bags on the counter and headed down the semi-lighted corridor.

The restaurant at the hotel was on the fancy side and for a brief moment they thought they were underdressed. Maya, again speaking in her native language, explained to the maître d they had just arrived at the hotel. He smiled, nodded and took them to a table, handing them a menu and waved a waitress over who took their drink order.

The menu was printed entirely in Greek, leaving poor Dirk with a helpless look on his face. A quick glance showed a limited selection of cuisine however, Maya was able to find several of her favorite dishes were available. She asked Dirk what preferences he had for dinner and after a few minutes of discussion and explanation of his choices, she was ready with an order. The waitress returned with their drinks, took their order, Paidakia which is grilled lamb chops, and disappeared into the kitchen.

Looking around the restaurant they noted they had been seated in a somewhat cozy, comfortable location without a lot of foot traffic around them. "So, it's just the two of us now with no distractions. I feel there is a lot we don't know about each other; and it seems like we will have ample time to share. Do you have anything to talk about?" Maya asked.

A brief pause, an inquisitive look that says do I really have to go first? and then nothing. Dirk's doesn't want to blurt out, 'How do I get you naked', so he punts.

"Alright, I'll go first." She fumbles a bit as she is venturing outside of her own tight, controlled, comfort zone. "Let's get to know each other a bit more, our background and so forth," she begins. "As you know my first name is Maya. My father is Greek, my mother, English. My name, Maya, which among many interpretations, means daughter of Atlas. There's an interesting history behind it, but I won't delve into that now. Still, you should look it up someday. I had all of the usual childhood maladies, runny nose, chicken pox, and the such."

A bit of playfulness Winter thinks to himself.

"My father, an engineer, worked for British Petroleum (BP) and my mother worked for the British Embassy, performing background checks on Greek citizens seeking employment at the embassy. My father was transferred to BP headquarters in London during my senior year in high school. My mother and I joined him after I graduated. I went to the University of London and then my mother helped me get into MI6. I am single, never married and I have two younger sisters. What's your story?"

Someone is leaving out an important part of her history, thought Winter, like how did you become such a kick-ass operative. There's more than MI6 training involved. "Well, Winter replies, "my story isn't a whole lot different, except I'm not Greek or British, I didn't go to school in London, and I don't have a particularly cool name like you do. Other than that, pretty much the same."

There's that Yank humor again, Thernopolis says to herself, and I still don't understand it. Still, she was determined not to speak.

After a period of silence, which makes Winter a bit uncomfortable because he doesn't like silence when killing time, he adds, "I went to college, joined the military, became a specialist in unconventional combat, a combat weapons instructor and then joined the CIA. My father and my mother worked at the local college. Dad is a union plumber and mother a business professor. And I, too had all of the usual childhood illnesses. I've never been married, and I also am the oldest child in my family with both a younger sister and brother."

A pause in the conversation, the waitress brings more wine; and both realize they are being coy about disclosing too much personal information. Still.., it may be easier if someone expounds just a bit.

"You surely kicked ass back in Afghanistan," says Winter, "where did you learn to fight like that?"

"That was my father's idea. He wanted me to learn self-defense before I went to college, so I took some classes. I really
enjoyed it and expanded into the study of karate and Brazilian jiu-jitsu throughout my time at the university." The wine goes down easy and Maya wonders how much she's had; more than she usually consumes she thinks. "What about you?"

Winter also is wondering how much wine he's consumed, it definitely is good, and the waitress is quick to bring more. "Well, I played some hockey at college, wasn't good, and left the team and went looking for something else to do to occupy my spare time. I enrolled in the ROTC program my last two years at school and entered the army after graduation."

They spent the next two hours or so drinking wine; telling stories which revealed more details about themselves. The conversation was very easy and natural, with each making mental notes about how comfortable they were. This pairing could work out quite well.

Maya felt her mind starting to wander as she began to nod a bit. After a brief moment she blinks her eyes, regaining a full sense of her bearings. *Hope he hasn't been asking me a question as I totally zoned out, lost in my thoughts. Oh well, I'll just smile at him, make him wonder what I'm up to. Damn, suddenly I'm tired and my vision is a bit off; maybe too much wine.*

Winter was also starting to feel the effects of the wine and coupled with the long journeys the last week, he was feeling a bit beat. Around one-thirty he announced it was time to head up to their room. More wine and more chit-chat ensue as they seem to be developing some rapport. As a matter of fact, Winter notes, Thernopolis has a wicked sense of humor. *Hopefully it's not just the wine altering my senses.*

As the hour moves past two o'clock and the restaurant staff is being to close up, they both rise from their chairs to begin the journey to their room. Walking together and kind of holding each other up, they make their way to the elevator and punch in the floor number. After departing at their floor, they walked to their room where Thernopolis fumbles a bit with the key, giggling the whole time, before finally inserting into the lock and unlocking the door. Winter runs his hand over the wall, finds the light switch and turns on the light.

One king size bed stands in the middle of the room. They look at each other with the same 'now what look', neither one of them moving. Finally, they slide gingerly into the room, allowing the door to close behind them, and stop in front of the bed, frozen in time. Winter clears his throat and asks, "What did you tell the clerk when we checked in, as far as the type of room?"

"Nothing, remember I didn't make the reservation, Jackson did." To which Winter replied, "I'm Jackson, umm, your name is Jackson, uhm, we're both Jackson; remember?"

"Oh, whatever the fuck the other MI6 officer's name is," says Maya, slurring her words a bit. She surveys the room; the moonlight coming through the window luminating her jet-black hair. "Well, I not sleeping on the floor, Mr. ROTC guy."

"Neither am I," says Dirk, "besides the side chairs are too small for either one of us to sleep on."

With a sly smile she replies, "Just what are you proposing, Mr. ROTC?"

Dirk notices the smile lighting up her green eyes; and with his own sly grin says, "We will just have to share the bed."

"Ohhh, you think so, do you?" She pondered a moment. "Okay, here's the deal." Pointing to the side of the bed nearest the window she says, "This is my side of the bed, you can have the other side. You mind your Ps and Qs and I'll do the same."

Winter sheepishly replies, feigning a hurt look, "Okay."

Maya stepped over to the dresser and turned on the light. She spies a note on the top of it, picks it up and reads aloud. "Inside you will find a pair of shorts and a t-shirt; that should get you through the night. Tell Mr. Jackson he also has the same ensemble in his dresser. There are some toiletries in the bath. I will see you tomorrow morning and we will plan out the next few days. Cheerio."

"I'll go first" she announces as she takes the clothes out of the dresser and heads for the bathroom. After a few minutes she walked back in wearing a too small tee shirt, keeping her panties. She strides to her side of the bed, then turns off the light on the dresser, leaving only the light in the bathroom for Dirk to navigate by.

Winter's eyes follow her as she walks by, admiring her nice round, firm ass atop sexy, muscular long legs. He smiles to himself, says nothing, and heads into the bathroom.

A few minutes later he emerges, clad only in a pair of shorts, and climbs into bed. "I've been known to snore a bit when I've had too much wine," he announces. "If I do, I apologize now. Good night."

Did that action in Cairo really happen?

Chapter 22

Maya slowly begins to wake up in response to the sunshine filtering into the room. First one eye, then the other and then she quickly closes them. She tries again to open her eyes, this time keeping them open long enough to survey unfamiliar surroundings. She notices she is in a large bed, the askew blankets on the other side of the bed indicating she didn't sleep alone last night. *Where the hell am I* she wonders.

She turns her head in response to a noise, sounds like running water, coming from her left; a bathroom? She swings her legs out of bed and slowly, with a bit of a sway, makes her way to the light. Inside she finds Dirk, without a shirt on, in the process of shaving. *Oh yeah, she remembers, Cyprus, Winter, arms sales.*

"Good morning sunshine," he chirps; "did you sleep well?"

Taken aback for a brief minute she wonders, *Dirk is usually dead in the morning. Why is he so bright and cheery today?*

"Cat got your tongue?"

Did we have sex, and I forgot? Oh shit! She finally responded, "I slept well, how about you?"

Still sounding too damn chipper, Dirk answers, "Sure did. Are you alive?"

"Not sure, need a shower, then coffee. Why are you so damn chipper?"

"I've showered and in the process of shaving. I gotten rid of the morning fog."

"Uh," she grunts back. *Maybe we didn't have sex. It would be terrible not to recall the first time with him.*

As Dirk watches in the bathroom mirror, Maya reaches into the shower, turns it on and adjusts the water, strips down, does her business on the toilet, then steps under the hot water flow. From behind the shower curtain she says, "Better close your mouth before you miss your chin and cut off your tongue."

Dirk reflectively shuts his mouth and finishes shaving, asking himself did he really see what he thought he saw. *WOWWW!!!* Just amazing. Long, lanky, excellent muscle tone, nice breasts, ass. He had been wondering what she looked like without clothes for several weeks. Amazing!

Should I get in the shower with her? Except for the attempted romp in her room back in Cairo they had really done anything beyond some heavy kissing, a furtive grope here and there. He believed they both had enjoyed the touchy-feely stuff. But to just jump into the shower with her may be a bit too bold first thing in the morning. If I catch her by surprise she might kill me; still, not a bad way to die.

Nice chest is the admiring thought in the shower. Looked kind of cute in shaving cream. I wonder what he's thinking, no I don't, I know what's on his mind; Cairo, round two, in a real bed.

"And make sure there's no drool on the sink, it's disgusting," she shouts over the running water. Winter reflexively looks down at the sink. Ha ha, very funny. He puts on his t-shirt, walks back into the bedroom and makes a call.

A few minutes later Maya turns off the shower, grabs a towel and begins to dry off. She walks to the door and stops, listening. Hearing no noise, maybe he's left the room, she walks into the bedroom with a towel around her waist. Seeing she's alone she quickly puts on the panties and tee shirt she wore to bed. As she starts drying and brushing her hair there's a knock on the door. "Hope you're decent," calls Dirk.

As he enters, she inhales deeply, says "Coffee", drops the hairbrush and walks across the room. Before Dirk can shut the door she reaches for the room service cart and pours herself a cup. She savors the rich, nutty flavor, exclaiming, "What a dear you are" and gives him a peck on the cheek. After several sips she says, "I'm alive now, shall we go to breakfast?"

Seeing Maya in that tight t-shirt brings back his brightest smile. "Absolutely. When I called the front desk for room service I found out we have a guest waiting for us in the restaurant. Since the staff was busy I went down to the restaurant and grabbed a coffee cart."

"Smart boy." Maya opens a dresser drawer, rummages around a bit, finding a pair of shorts. She retreats back into the bathroom, emerging a few minutes later trying to loosen the t-shirt and hide the prominence of her nipples pushing against the cotton material. Satisfied she's done the best she can, given it's a bit of a tight fit, she tousles her ebony locks, refills her coffee cup, then reaches for the door.

"Must be what's his name, not Jackson, that's us, but, umm.. Johnson, yeah that's it, Johnson, is waiting for us. Let's go, I'm hungry." She stepped into the hallway, striding quickly for the elevator.

Dirk glanced around the room, closed the door, made sure it locks and hustled down the hall. He caught up with her as she reached the elevator.

****

Johnson is sitting at a table, impatiently waiting for them. "Took you guys long enough, I'm starved." Looking at his watch he frowns and says, "If we stretch it, we can call this brunch. I took the liberty of ordering the continental breakfast in addition to more of the same coffee that Winter had delivered to your room."

With a big shit eating grin, he says to Winter, "I see your in one piece so you must have behaved yourself last night." Winter just ignores him with a 'fuck you' look.

"Whit Johnson," he says, extending his right hand, formally introducing himself. "Winter, CIA," replies Dirk as he shakes his hand.

"Thernopolis" says Maya as she takes his extended hand. Johnson had some knowledge, all of it second hand, of Thernopolis, that she was a tough as nails operator. And good-looking, very good looking he notes. That fucking Winter may be one lucky bastard if he plays his cards right.

"Alright you two," Johnson begins. They helped themselves to the tray of food placed on the table. "We have to make you into Provisional Irish Republican Army members from Northern Ireland. A big part of that is to look the part. Thernopolis, your biggest problem is your physical appearance."

Maya starts to say something, but Johnson cuts her off. "Let me explain. There are very few, if any, Irish men or women with your dark hair and olive skin."

Thinking while talking and choosing his words carefully, Johnson continues. "We will pass you off as coming from the Middle East where you were engaged in revolutionary activities. You met Winter on a gun buying event and followed him to Ireland; things grew from there". Thernopolis nodded her head in agreement; not that her opinion really mattered.

To Winter Johnson says, "You look Irish, which is good. The problem is you look too damn military, like you would never break a fart let alone any rules."

Winter piped in, "I am proudly a former U.S. Green Beret."

Johnson dismissed him with a wave of the hand before responding. "It's all good actually. The aggrieved soldier watched his innocent buddies slaughtered by the Brits for something they didn't do. So, you join the Provisional IRA as a soldier and weapons instructor. Later on, you agree to procure arms for your brothers. And, your knowledge of weaponry makes it all work."

He pauses, evaluates his cover story, then proclaims, "I like it. The back-story works."

Handing them a sheet of paper he wraps up the meeting. "Go to any of these stores and tell them you are my associates. They will make sure you are dressed appropriately to look the part. They are our people so the costs will be paid accordingly."

He hands each of them $1,000. "Some walking around money. After you finish buying clothes the day is yours. Go sight-seeing, whatever, just don't get into trouble by drawing unwanted attention to yourselves.

"This part of the city will be crawling with spies, bad ass wannabes, etc. There is a gathering in the main ballroom here at nine tonight. It will be your coming out party. You will simply mingle and get your name out and what you are looking to accomplish. We'll meet up again tomorrow, here. Any questions?"

Silence.

"Good, get out of here and have some fun."

As they get up to leave Johnson has one more piece of wisdom. "Oh, Thernopolis, as a heads up. As far as I know you will be the only woman present tonight. A lot of these guys will be very, shall we say, handsy, you know, with a pair of roaming hands. If someone cops a feel or grabs your ass, roll with it. Don't be prissy. If it's too bad, remind them you're here with Winter and whatever he is, your husband, cousin, whatever works for you."

Thernopolis replies, "Gotcha." She gives Winter an embrace, "Let's go sweetheart."

Johnson watched as they walked out the door. Yep, he may be one lucky bastard.

****

They spend the afternoon shopping, sightseeing and enjoying a late lunch. They took their time buying clothes as each modeled their outfits for the other. They enjoyed ragging on each other as they engaged in exaggerated poses. Winter noticed that because of her model's height, Thernopolis looked great in the baggy clothes she tried on as everything just seem to cling to her body. They finally settled on several items and departed the shop.

The sightseeing included the Selimiye Mosque, a mosque in a 13th-century Catholic cathedral noted for its Gothic architecture; and the Cyprus Museum, which is home to the most extensive collection of Cypriot antiquities in the world. A nice late lunch capped off the afternoon. The conversation flows easily and effortlessly between them and they both had the feeling this assignment was going to be highly successful and they would work well together as a team.

Chapter 23

The "mixer" at the hotel hosted most of the major weapons and arms dealers from around the world, according to Johnson. Johnson made general introductions and then they separated to mingle. The alcohol and hors d'oeuvres flowed copiously to all guests.

Things were going good until a guy in a group of several men claimed he knew several IRA leaders. When Winter was unable to answer a few questions, he seemed to be in a bit of a jam. Winter brushed aside his inquisitor by saying he had a different recollection of an event and then launched into a vivid recitation of the weaponry used by the IRA in several battles he knew about. The men were impressed by his knowledge and moved on; street cred established.

Thernopolis was the biggest attraction in the room. As Johnson had surmised earlier, she was the only female present and she wowed everyone who came in contact with her. They were impressed not only by her looks but also by her story. She ran with the idea Johnson had presented about being a weapons specialist in the Middle East and how she ran off to Ireland with Winter when he came looking to steal weapons for his band of renegades. She also possessed the requisite knowledge of all things military and passed every inquiry thrown at her. She was a combination of beauty, brains and brawn.

Eventually she and Winter had lost eye contact with each other as they made their way around the rooms. Finally, in the wee hours of the morning she was able to extract herself from the main gathering. She swept through a couple of rooms; no Winter. She finally stopped looking and made her way back to their room.

On her way to the elevator she glanced back several times to make sure no one was following her as she was proposition for sex by several guys. Just before the elevator door closed three men joined her but they minded their own business. What a relief she felt as she had been rubbed, rubbed against and patted more than sufficiently to last a lifetime.

She exited the elevator one floor above where the room was and, when the elevator door closed, she walked down the stairs to her floor. After opening the door and noticing Winter hadn't returned, she flopped face first onto the big bed. After a brief moment face down, she rolled over onto her back and gathered her thoughts about the night's event.

She hadn't made any important contacts, as far as she knew, and seemed to have spent more time avoiding hand and/or bodily contact more than anything else. Since she was doing the majority of the talking she was able to minimize the amount of alcohol she drank. She was wondered how Winter had made out, did he make any contacts.

She changed position on the bed while thinking and wondering if she was successful or not. Slowly she could feel herself starting to drift off to sleep. She got up long enough to remove her clothes, then falls back onto the bed.

****

Winter wraps up his conversation and begins looking for Thernopolis. The crowd has thinned out quickly, so scanning the room isn't a problem. No Thernopolis. He checks the room where he last saw her; nothing. One last drink, another look around the nearly empty; no Thernopolis. He decided to head for their room.

He exited the elevator and walked down the semi-lighted hallway. Standing in front of the door he paused for a minute as he doesn't see any light coming from under the door. Maybe she asleep, he thinks and, as quietly as he can, he inserts the key and unlocks the door.

Initially he hears or sees nothing, then he notices a form on the bed. He sneaks over as softly as he can, standing for a moment to study the form in front of him. *Curb your lust he says to himself* as he tries to figure out how to wake her gently. He decides to shake her shoulder and begins to reach over her. Before he touches her, she sits up. "What's going on?" she asks sleepily.

"Maya, you need to get dressed. I received some actionable intelligence, but we need to act on it immediately." Mumbling to herself she rolls over to the nightstand by the bed and flips on the light. Finding her clothes, she begins dressing. "Where are you been?", she asks.

"I was talking with a group of guys, actually more listening than talking, when they asked if I would be interesting in examining an arms shipment that is in a warehouse across town. They gave me an address and told me to be there in 45 minutes. Hurry up!"

"I'm hurrying" she replies while pulling on a pair of sneakers.

Once outside the hotel they hail a cab and Winter gives the driver the address. After a short drive the cabbie says the warehouse is three blocks ahead, at the end of the street on the right. Winter tells the cabbie to pull over and let them out, they'll walk from here. They jog to within a block of the warehouse and Winter raises his hand; signaling Thernopolis to stop.

"Why are we stopping here?"

"I'm not sure," Winter replies, "but my instincts are telling me to approach cautiously."

They creep towards the side of the building and then climb up a fire escape to a catwalk at the top of the building. A large window in the roof is slightly open. With a slight tug Winter is able to open the window a bit wider and they both shimmy through, Thernopolis in front.

They observe several large shipping containers stacked along one side of the building. The giant cranes that unloaded the containers from the trucks looked exactly like the equipment on the docks at Port Said.

They watched as a group of men opened the containers and reached inside. They appeared to rummage around inside the box before lifting out their cargo. This container contained a large cache of rifles; from their vantage point they look like they could be AK47s or M16s. This might be the haul from the port in Lamaca.

They continued observing as another container is opened and the contents held aloft; shoulder launched RPGs. The third container held what could be anti-tank missiles. *The mother lode Thernopolis thought.* Winter checked his watch and whispered we need to leave.

A few minutes later they appeared at the front of the building where they encountered an armed lookout; a grungy looking, thick-set man wielding an automatic weapon. "It's Winter and his babe," he shouted.

"Let them in," Came the response. The lookout stepped back to allow them to enter. He leered at Thernopolis as she sauntered by.

They take a few steps when another man appears, one both Winter and Thernopolis recognize from earlier at the hotel, Dmetri.

"I didn't hear your vehicle drive up," he said. Winter, breathing a little hard as they had just climbed down from the roof, "We decide to walk over and enjoy the warm blowing breeze. So, what have you got here?" he says as they walk toward the containers.

"Only the best" he answers and proudly shows off the cache of weapons; all made in the USSR. Thernopolis was confused, Sir Hilary comments led her to believe no Russian weapons would be featured. Interesting!

Dmetri continues, "This is what I can offer you if you chose to buy weapons from me."

Winter and Thernopolis examined the merchandise and agreed it is high quality. Thernopolis also wondered if it's legit and if they represent the manufacturers. A more likely story is they stole the weapons. Some questions are best left unasked, she decided.

Winter asked, "What is the price of a haul like this?"

"Everything is negotiable," comes the response. "These weapons are headed for Iran to be used against the Americans and the Iraqis. But, for $2 million dollars I can say we were raided and the weapons were confiscated. I can blame the damn Brits with their MI6 and/or the American CIA. They are always on my ass, so the story is good. Then I can divert them to you."

No honor among thieves, Winter thinks. "I don't have access to that kind of cash as I wasn't planning on such a large buy. Give me forty-eight hours."

Dmetri shook his head and immediately responded. "Meet me here in twenty-four hours, or no deal," he said.

The negotiation, if that's what it was, is over. He pushed them forward and ushered them out the door, which is quickly closed.

About half-way back to the hotel Maya says, "There's no way you can rustle up that much cash in such a short time frame."

"You're probably right but I'll still check with Johnson tomorrow. It will give us something to talk about."

Chapter 24

They are both wide awake as they ride the elevator up to their room. They are excited they have made contact with a weapons dealer of some type; and, on their first attempt. They talk for a few minutes, trying to figure out what to tell Johnson. After a while Maya says she's going to shower before bed as she feels a little yucky from the night's festivities.

Dirk tells her to go ahead, he's good for now. *Like hell, he's thinking as she watches Maya go into the bathroom, I'm going to ambush her.*

Shortly, he hears the water begin to run. He waits a few minutes, strips down, then sneaks into the bathroom and pauses in front of the shower.

Maya stopped, trying to listen as she thought she heard a noise. When she hears nothing, she resumed washing her hair. Suddenly, she feels a bit of a chill as the shower curtain opened. She feels a hand on her shoulder, as Dirk says, "I'll wash your back."

She rinses the soap from her hair, looks at Dirk and smiles. She moved forward to allow him room to step in.

Admiring her gorgeous ass as he steps in, Dirk grabs a bar of soap and starts rubbing her back. Maya relaxes under Dirk strong hands kneading her shoulders. "Oh yeah," she says breathlessly. As she feels his strong arms engulf her, she leans back into him. Then she clears her throat and announces, "Those aren't on my back."

"So, call the front desk and make a complaint."

"Maybe later," she replies as her body begins responding to his massaging her breasts. Feeling something against her butt she turns and exclaims, "Oh look, a place to hang my washcloth," as she reaches over and slides her hand around it; nice and hard.

After several minutes of slipping, sliding, wild kisses and massages, the shower goes off. Dirk stepped out first, followed by Maya. They each grab a towel and quickly attempt to dry each other. Dirk steps over and opens the bathroom door. He turns back around, picks Maya up, walks to the bed and gently lays her down on her back. "So," she says laying back onto the pillows, "this act of chivalry makes everything official?"

"Works for me."

Pushing the bathroom door closed with his foot, Dirk slides onto the bed. They are both lying on their side facing each. The light from the partially closed bathroom door dances around the beautiful ballet on the bed. Not even the soft creaking of the bed springs completely drowns out the "Ooooos. Aahs and ummm yeahhh." Lucky bastard indeed! Actually, two lucky people!!

Chapter 25

It's shortly after noon when Thernopolis begins to stir. She smiles, remembering earlier that morning, then reaches across the bed. Finding nothing but empty space, she realizes that Winter has once again risen before her. Opening her eyes, she scans the room, noticing no light coming from the bathroom. *Where did he go? she wonders.*

She slowly rises to one arm, then gives up and plops back into the super comfortable bed. While debating what to do, she hears noise outside the door in the hallway. The door is slowly unlocked and Winter steps in, carrying a large bag. Setting the bag on the table he cheerily calls out, "Hey sunshine, you alive?" Sitting up and smiling, she suddenly realizes she is shirtless, and instinctively covers herself up with a sheet.

"Now we're shy?" Winter asks.

"Cold," she answers back, then, remembering this morning's activity, lets the sheet drop. Fighting the urge to jump her body, Winter turns his back to her and begins to unpack the food in the bag. "I brought over some things from the coffee shop around the corner; mostly sandwiches and beverages. I called Johnson; we're meeting him downstairs in about an hour. That should be enough time for you to get yourself ready."

Maya slips on a shirt and joins Dirk at the table. She says, "I plan on mostly listening to Johnson this afternoon. I don't know what your thoughts are, but I was a bit suspicious about this morning rendezvous. Maybe that's just how Dmetri operates, but I had an uneasy feeling. Not sure if he was playing us for idiots or what, but something just didn't ring true to me. Of course, I've never entered the world of weapon dealers before."

Winter is nodding his head as she speaks. "I had similar thoughts myself," he said. It just seemed strange that someone who we are meeting for the first time would be so trusting to bring us to his "place of business" and show his product. Then, he tells you he's willing to screw over his buyer if we pay more. He doesn't know us from a hill of beans; why so trusting? I just didn't understand the entire meet up. Of course, I understand there's no honor among thieves. Money is money and some people can never have enough in their mind."

He checked his watch, about thirty minutes before their scheduled meeting. He gives her a kiss on the forehead. "Go do your thing," he says as he gets up from the table and starts cleaning up. After about 30 minutes she emerges wearing a crop top and jeans, looking absolutely stunning. "Johnson called while you were in the shower; we're meeting him in his room."

****

Johnson listens intently as Thernopolis and Winter recount their impression of last night's gathering, engaging in an animated give and take with them while providing a thumbnail sketch of the players. It was definitely a gathering of an eclectic group of dealers and wannabes assembled in one location. One had to wonder just how many shooting conflicts they were keeping alive through their arms dealing. There were members from all of the major players in the international weapons market, with perhaps one notable exception. Again, no official Chinese presences. If they are trying to enter the marketplace, either overtly or through intermediaries, Johnson has been stumped. He knew everyone present and, with the exception of Winter and Thernopolis, there were no new representatives in attendance.

Johnson demeanor and facial expressions seem to change as he listens to the description of their meeting this morning at the warehouse with Dmetri. Johnson knows him well and has dealt with him and his henchmen on numerous past transactions. And, Dmetri took them to his main warehouse in Cyprus. What the fuck was that all about?

When Thernopolis asks him for his take on the situation, he paused briefly. *How do I explain this without revealing too much?* Thinking and choosing his words carefully, Johnson responds, "Dmetri Koloff, a man I know quite well. We have had a few tete a tetes over time."

Stalling a bit as he searches for the proper words, he continues: "What is the best way to describe him? He's a whore."

(Johnson catches a facial reaction by Thernopolis; she's probably never heard a man called a whore before).

"He would sell his mother's grave with her in it and not blink an eye. He will lie, cheat and steal without compunction, then laugh about over drinks. However, the person he actually deals with receives high quality merchandise, usually made in the USSR, and at the price agreed to. As I said, he's a whore, but an honorable one who never screws the people he ends up dealing with.

"However, he's had a few situations that have required the occasional killing to protect himself. While he will stick to his final deal, the others he has screwed over can get, shall we say, hostile. He has mean, vicious muscle nearby whenever I've dealt with him; in fact, I'm positive you saw them last night. That's how he always escapes, his, umm., shall we say, delicate circumstances. What surprises me is that he latched onto you two so quickly. He's usually slow to trust."

Without saying so, Johnson knows the reason why Koloff trusted them so fast is because of Thernopolis. Dmetri always fancied himself a ladies' man and he would have gone gaga over the sight of her, even from afar. He will have to give him hell the next time they meet.

"So," asks Winter, "is the guy legit?"

"Depends on what you mean by legit," Johnson answers with a little more confidence in his demeanor. "As I said, if you're the guy that he actually deals with, he delivers quality weapons, and you find him reasonable. Obviously, if you think he's screwed you in a deal that fell apart, your opinion of him is vastly different."

Winter: "I am more concerned about the weapons he pedals; is he a legitimate representative of a government or is he dealing in stolen goods?"

Johnson pauses for a bit and exhibits a pained expression before answering, he's always believed Koloff has no moral scruples and has probably dealt in stolen weapons. "I never really checked out the source of his weapons that closely. Remember, I not buying any merchandise. I just trying to keep weapons out of the hands of countries and/or groups that will use them against our country, our allies and others who are helping to see that our foreign policy initiatives are carried out. Koloff is a big asset to me out here."

Winter closely studies Johnson non-verbal behaviors, then decides to redirect the conversation in another direction. "How do we handle tonight's meeting? I never expected someone who would be so willing to attempt to sell you weapons based on a first meeting."

"Thernopolis is right, simply tell him you can't access that amount of cash that quickly. Leave him with the belief that you would be willing to reach out to him in the future. That way you keep your cover intact." *What a dumb fuck Koloff is*, as Johnson makes a mental note to rip him a new ass. *All because he can't control his dick's impulses.*

Johnson tells them of a shipment moving into the area in four nights. He gives them an address and tells them to go there tonight. The building overlooks the warehouse they will be watching, and the owner won't ask questions. He wants them to canvass the area so they can set themselves up to monitor activity including trying to determine who's running the operation. Use the back entrance, which is off street. I will have cameras delivered to your room around nine. He wants debriefs once every twenty-four hours. With that assignment the meeting breaks up.

After leaving Johnson's room they take the elevator to the lobby. Thernopolis checks her watch, they were with Johnson for over three hours. "Care to get a cold beverage?"

"Absolutely," comes the response.

As the elevator door opens and they depart Maya says, "The hotel bar, the restaurant we ate at yesterday or somewhere new?"

"Always up for something new. I have the address for a place about three blocks from here on the other side of the hotel."

A short walk leaves them in front of the new place. The aroma that hits them in the face signals to Thernopolis this place is old time Greek cooking. After settling into a booth at the back of the restaurant and ordering a local beer, Winter asks, "So, what do you think of Johnson's story?"

"Rather interesting to say the least," she responds. "At the worst you could say he was spinning a yarn to protect Koloff." "I agree with your assessment wholeheartedly. The problems as I see them; one, what, if anything, that Johnson told us was true and two, why is he lying about Koloff?"

Winter takes a swig of his beer as the waitress delivers their food; a hearty thick chicken gyro stuffed into pita bread for both of them. After chewing a bite of his gyro Winter continues. "There's something we're missing here but I just can't wrap my mind around it yet. Could Johnson be free lancing, you know, in business for himself?"

Thernopolis has been attacking her gyro while listening to Winter; she pauses to clear her month then adds, "He certainly wouldn't be the first MI6 agent to be a turncoat or go rogue; we've certainly had more than our fair share of those characters. Some agents have justified their actions by trying to maintain a balance on both sides of a war by providing arms to all combatants. Some turncoats are trying to damage the crown and her allies and still others are simply looking to enrich themselves.

However, before trying to make an absolute claim regarding Johnson, I'm willing to give him the benefit of the doubt. He may be looking out for an old friend who provides him with valuable information about weapons transactions and doesn't want us to mess up that relationship. Still, I agree that he was not completely telling us the full story on Koloff. The question is what do we do?"

"Our mission was to learn as much as we can about arms dealing, particularly to determine if the Chinese are attempting to enter the marketplace. We do have our second meeting with Koloff tonight; it seems reasonable to me we can try to surveil him as well as the other assignment Johnson gave us. Who knows what we will uncover? And, I still don't trust Johnson."

Winter looked at his watch; seven o'clock. "How about we take a run over to the place and start checking out the area of our new assignment. Maybe the camera equipment will be delivered a little early and we can set up there and still have plenty of time to meet again with Koloff".

****

At around seven-thirty, back at the hotel room, Dirk takes a call on the hotel phone, the caller telling them to come down to the front desk. Upon arriving at the front desk, they are directed to the bell hop station. After a short wait a 'bell hop' who is an MI6 asset, leads them down to the parking garage. He stops at a dark blue sedan and pops open the trunk.

Located inside the trunk are several cases which are opened one at a time. The contents contain the latest and greatest in surveillance equipment including several types of cameras, GPS trackers and listening bugs. They spend about an hour receiving a lesson on the equipment and how to best use it for optimal effect.

After their lesson is finished, they use the car to drive over to their post, turning into the building's rear entrance. Just inside the door a contact is waiting. After they are properly identified they are escorted to a large room on the second floor overlooking the warehouse across the street. Their vantage point provides an unobstructed view of the front entrance of the warehouse. The cameras would enable them to read license plates, decals and any other similar markings on vehicles. In addition, they would be able to enjoy clear facial details right down to a person's mole.

After calibrating the cameras, the three of them decide to cross over to the warehouse and plant several listening devices. They approach the building from the rear; finding a very simple lock on the back that Maya slips with ease. Once inside they hide listening bugs and a small camera in a room that looks like an office. They secrete another small camera over the back door they entered through; and in two light switches in the main loading/unloading area they install listening devices.

After they finish planting their devices, the contact leaves. Maya and Dirk conduct a quick check of the inside of the warehouse. The thick layer of dust on the floor in and around the loading dock tells them that whoever is going to be using the building hasn't made an appearance. They check the perimeter of the building, noting how the sight line from the main doors provides a perfect, nonobstructive view of their spy nest next door. Satisfied with the overall set up they slip out the back door, ensuring that it locked behind them.

Once they are out on the street Winter checks his watch, eleven o'clock. "Let head over to Dmetri's location and deliver the news to him," he says.

"What about the car?" asks Maya.

"We'll drive it back to our hotel and then walk over like we did early this morning."

Fifteen minutes later they emerged from the parking garage and begin the walk, following the same route from earlier. Before Maya can head toward the front of the building, Dirk grabs her by the arm, directing her to flank the building on their left. "What's up?" she asks.

"Just playing a hunch. I can't put my finger on it, but something still doesn't ring right with Johnson's conversation. I still have the feeling something is up between him and Dmetri. I want to survey the place before we walk in". Maya responds with a quizzical look while shrugging her shoulders. "Humor me," he says.

Weaving behind cars and other vehicles, they stealthily make their way to a semi-trailer truck about ten yards from the front of the building. Standing outside under a bright overhead light, with their backs to Dirk and Maya's position, are Johnson and Dmetri. The gesticulations from both parties indicates that are engaged in a passionate conversation.

"Maybe you've got something with your suspicions, Maya said."

"Yep."

After watching for a few minutes Dmetri makes a gesture waving off Johnson. He strode quickly into the building. Johnson hesitated, then followed him inside.

Dirk whispers to Maya, "Ok, let's walk in." They step from behind the shadows of the truck and walk to the building's entrance.

As they come closer to the building they can hear screaming coming from the inside. Before they are close enough to distinguish any words, Johnson comes storming outside, brushing Maya's shoulder. "What the hell are you two doing here?" he snarls.

"They are my guests," Demtri answers. "Ignore that bastard and do come in," as he waves them inside. With the dismissal Johnson disappears into the darkness.

Once inside they remember the same motley crew from their earlier visit, still surrounded by the same weaponry. "Well," says Dmtrie, "what's your answer?"

"I made several calls back home; I can't raise that much scratch so quickly," Dirk responds.

"Too bad, I was hoping we could do business." Smiling at Maya, he continued, "Tell you what, I don't know what it is, but I like you, hmmm, the two of you. I want to see you succeed and spread a little chaos wherever you go." He laughs an evil laugh while stroking his chin, thinking.

"Tell you what. I'm expecting another shipment to arrive right here in six weeks. Why don't you gather up your benefactors, do a song and dance pitch, then meet me here with some real money."

Winter pauses while appearing to be considering the offer. He says he would put it on his calendar.

When one of the men turns to talk to Dmtrie, Maya steps around him, quickly ducks down and slips a tracking device inside a crevice in the corner of the crate closest to her. She stands back up and looks around; no one was paying attention to her.

They spend a more few minutes watching Dmtrie's men repack the weapons into smaller crates for shipping, then Dmtrie shoos them out the door. As they walk out Dmtrie is leering at Maya's shapely ass and grinning. Turning to one of his men he tells him he can't wait to bed her. The guy just shakes his head, laughs and walks off.

As they walk outside in the direction of the hotel Dirk says, "That was kind of different, wasn't it?"

"You mean running into Johnson?"

"Of course."

"Well, yes and no. Just because Johnson was here doesn't necessarily mean anything is wrong or something illegal is happening. Remember it Johnson's job to know who is moving weapons and trying to ensure shipments are going to approved allies. Therefore, his appearance here isn't really unusual."

"Maybe, says Dirk, but I still have an uneasy feeling about him. As I've said, I can't explain it, it's just there."

They continue walking and after taking a right turn and crossing the street, they are standing in front of their hotel. "It's late and we've done our work. Let's call it a night and start again tomorrow. What do you say?"

Dirk looks his watch. "Well, I was thinking of maybe making a quick run by the other spot. But if insist on taking me to bed, I'm game."

Shooting him one of those looks that says we are a little presumptuous aren't we, Maya just smiles as she strides through the hotel lobby toward the elevators.

Chapter 26

The next day Dirk and Maya report back to Sir Hillary that, based on a tip from Johnson, they are watching a warehouse that is expecting receipt of an arms shipment with the next four to five days. They planted cameras and listening devices in an office and in several locations in the receiving area. They have a bird's eye view of the warehouse from a nest in a building across the street from the front entrance.

Hillary is familiar with their location; it has been used by his people for other surveillance work. The best part is no one will interrupt their work. He asked if they have any idea what country or group is participating in the operation. Dirk responded that Johnson's tipster didn't know.

As the meeting broke up Hillary wished them well and reminded them to keep him apprised of the situation; he wanted independent reports to compare and contrast with Johnson's work. Not that he had any reason to doubt the veracity of what Johnson was reporting; it's just always good to have another set of eyes involved whenever possible. He also was wondering about Winter and Thernopolis; their behavior seemed to give off certain vibes beyond being a well-oiled machine. Nah, probably just his imagination. After all they are adults. Still…

And speaking of the well-oiled machine; they were now experiencing the waiting game, just like back in Cairo. After meeting with Sir Hillary, they decided to casually stroll down the street where the warehouse was located to check for any action; nothing. Johnson's contact wasn't able to give him an exact date for the weapons to be delivered, so thumb twiddling was the order of the day. This left plenty of time for enjoying the city and all it had to offer.

However, after three days of checking with no results, boredom began to set in. The only saving grace was they were really getting to know each other quite well. They found out they had similar interests in music, movies, food and so forth. Though not daring to speak out loud about it, they both agreed there was some chemistry; a tight bond was developing between them. They both were career driven and had advanced rapidly in their respective agencies.

Neither of them had focused much time or effort on personal relationships or a love life and they liked what was happening in the here and now. Despite their growing ease with each other a lot of personal information had yet to be shared. They had both tapped danced around the issue, neither sure how to open up. During one of the endless watches Maya decided to tell the story of her most perilous venture.

She had been sent to infiltrate separatist groups in Greece, using her heritage to perfectly blend in. After a brief period of assimilating herself with various anarchists she learned of the group's leadership. She used this information to lead several raids which succeeded in reducing several mid-level leaders of the major terrorist group they were affiliated with. It was during one of these raids where she earned her reputation for fearlessness.

She had been outed by a turncoat and taken captive, being transported to Cyprus where was she held with several other Greeks fighting the separatists. She was subjected to enhanced interrogation techniques but didn't break. She escaped after three days of confinement, later meeting with up a special ops force sent to find her. Suffering from several injuries inflicted by her interrogators, she nonetheless led the rescue team on a counter raid to free her fellow captives.

She engaged in a nasty fight with her torturer who had mistakenly fancied himself an expert in the fighting arts. The problem was this Amazonian woman was no longer shackled and quite pissed. Blocking all pain from their prior encounter she inflicted a brutal beating on him but in the end refused to kill him. Instead he was taken prisoner by the commandos and she personally returned him to Greek authorities.

It was this episode which led her into intelligence analysis. She believed, as did other analysts, that the turncoat had dropped clues about their intentions and should have been apprehended before being assigned to that particular mission. She doesn't believe she flawless but simply has a bigger comfort level running her own show from analysis to action.

"That was quite an interesting story," Dirk said. Not sure if it was his turn to relate something similar to Maya, he went quiet for a few minutes. Just as he was about to speak, Maya said, "Over by the south corner of the building."

"Yeah, what"?

"Hold on," she responded. "See that black, delivery size van, driving slowly in front of the building; on your left."

Dirk refocused his binoculars, spotting the van which had stopped. "Got it." He watched, it drive around then said, "It looks harmless, what's you hunch?"

"That's the second time that van, moving slowly and deliberately, has passed by in the last ten minutes or so. It looks like someone may be casing the site." Then she said, "I can't get a good read on the license plates, can you?"

Dirk slides a few feet to his left, still focusing on the van. "If that even is a license plate and I'm not sure it is, I can't clearly see any markings."

Putting down his binoculars he walks to the back of the room and grabs a sat phone. He tells the person back in London what they have seen and asks for them to get a satellite read on the vehicle and tell him what they find.

He relayed to Maya what the call was about, which she had assumed that's what he was doing based on hearing his side of the conversation. "Stay up here, I'm going to go down to see if I can get a closer look at the van."

Before Maya can protest Dirk leaves the surveillance nest and starts down the back stairs. "Dipshit," she says. "Going out there with no backup may not be the best course of action. Oh well, I'll just stay here and watch the best that I can." Realizing she is only talking out-loud to herself she shuts up, returning her attention to the street.

She watches as Dirk hits the street from behind their building, sneaking along in the shadows to the right side of the van. Still in the shadows, Dirk gets within maybe thirty-five feet of the van when it suddenly takes off. As he watches it speed down the street and around a corner he lets loose with a "Damn" and turns to go back to their surveillance position. He slowly circles the block behind their position from the shadows. Seeing no other vehicles, foot traffic or even lights in other structures; eerie silence, he reenters their building.

As **he** walks into their "nest" he notices Maya is on the sat phone. She says "Yes", then "Ok" and disconnects. "That was our satellite guys; the news on the van isn't too promising. No satellite coverage was anywhere near our location. By the time they recalibrated a dish they saw three van/large trucks about five miles away that matched the general description I gave them. One or none of them may be the one we saw. If they learn anything else they will let us know."

Checking her watch, she says; "It's four thirty. Regular delivery traffic will soon start flowing. Let's close up, go grab a bite to eat and figure out our next move. By the way; you're a dumb ass. That stunt could have blown your cover and endangered the entire mission."

This was the first time he had encountered her wrath. She was right, it was a dumb move with no real thought put into it. "Sorry," he said.

****

The next three days proved rather fruitless as the action around the warehouse proved to be more of the normal daily traffic. It's possible that a vehicle or two could have been observing the area but there were no obvious clues like the van they had identified earlier as suspicious. And speaking of their report on the van, neither British nor American intelligence had scored any promising leads. Three possible hits turned up ordinary delivery vans used by local businesses. The companies maintained daily travel logs showing each of their vans to be on deliveries in other parts of the city during the time when Maya flagged the suspicious vehicle. Another dead end.

Chapter 27

Day four of the endless watching finally brought some action. Around eight-thirty that night, a small convoy of trucks approached the entrance to the warehouse. A passenger in the lead vehicle jumped out, inserted a key into a lock and entered the building. Light soon started to flow out the windows, followed by the raising of the large overhead door.

Six men disembarked from the lead truck; each man was carrying an automatic weapon. The truck they had been riding in left as they took up positions outside the front of the warehouse. One by one the other members of the convoy pulled into the loading dock. Several men exited their trucks and unloaded their cargo.

Dirk watched the action through a pair of binoculars from their perch across the street. He offered descriptions of everything he saw to Maya, who was relaying the information over the Sat phone while observing the movement of the men and trucks at the side of the building nearest their location. After about four hours the lights in the warehouse were turned off and the final truck departed, leaving two armed men still standing guard at the front entrance.

Maya ended the call and said to Dirk, "The intel guys want us to go into the warehouse for a little look-see. They want us to identify the material and find any documents inside that will indicate what will be the final destination of the cargo. And while we are there, we are to secure trackers to the boxes and pallets."

"Did you mention the two-armed men acting as guards?"

"Yes," she replied.

"And?"

"Use our discretion."

"That tells me a hell of a lot. Any ideas?"

Maya goes to the window, scanning the building with the binoculars. After a minute or two she responds, "Well, we could try one of two avenues."

"I'm listening."

"One, we could simply sweep one side of the building, stay in the shadows, and incapacitate the guards. Or, two, we could try to enter through the roof. We could ask Sir Hillary to find out if there is any roof top access. Since we found one in the building when he went to meet Dmtrie, I'm willing to bet this building will have one as well."

Dirk ponders for a minute before responding. "Well, option two is an attempt to avoid a direct confrontation with the guards, which is always a good idea. To accomplish that we will need to determine if they are walking a perimeter around the building, how frequently they walk it, and so on. Then we would have to scale the building at a time when they're not patrolling. And, we would need a plan in case they happened to enter the facility at the same time we arrive. That could get dicey."

"And that option would be time consuming, watching them as we try to determine patterns and times of movement," says Maya. "Since we have the advantage of knowing where they are, we could surprise the guards and take the direct approach; hitting them hard and fast before they figured out what was happening. After they are neutralized we would zip tie them."

"Then, what?" Dirk asks. Taking them prisoner does no good, nor does letting them go. Either way, once we make contact and take some kind of action against them, the rest of their larger group will know something happened. They will search the crates and the warehouse. And, as you know, a thorough search will find every device we planted, and we will be left without any intel."

"Hold on," says Maya who had resumed scanning across the street as Dirk was speaking. "A vehicle is approaching the warehouse, a small van."

Dirk spun around and grabbed his binoculars. The van pulls near the front entrance and two men depart from each side of the vehicle, walking toward the guards. "Those men look familiar, they sort of resemble, but who?" As they walk into the light his focus is clearer. "Is that Dmetri and …Johnson?"

Maya focuses her binoculars a bit, then lowers them. "I believe so."

Dirk continues watching as the door opens and the two new men, maybe Dmetri and Johnson, follow the guards inside. "What the hell is that all about?"

"Good question," she responds as lights come on in the front of the building. "It appears that Johnson is examining a crate of rifles and Dmetri is opening another crate a few feet away. He is lifting up a long cylinder type object that certainly resembles a Stinger missile."

Dirk is adjusting and focusing the camera to ensure the best view of the encounter is being filmed. Johnson is talking with the taller of the two guards; the conversation is getting heated as both men start waving their arms. Dmetri stops looking in the crate he was searching and hustles over to where Johnson and the other man are shouting at each other. Suddenly the guard shoves Johnson, knocking him off balance and levels his gun at him! "Are you watching this?"

He noticed some movement to his right and turned to see Maya bringing her sniper rifle to her shoulder, eying the scene across the street through the scope. After a few seconds she announced, "I have a shot lined up."

She watched the other guard push Dmetri towards Johnson, then starts to draw his weapon. As soon as she says, "I'm taking the shot," she squeezes the trigger and the first guard drops to the ground. Startled, the other guard whirls to look at his partner. Before he can turn back around Dmetri lunges at him, then falls to the ground, eating a bullet for his effort. Maya continued to watch the action through the rifle's scope.

As soon as Dmetri falls, she takes her second shot. The guard immediately falls, landing between Dmetri and the first dead guard. "We better hustle on over there," Maya said as she places the rifle on a nearby crate, then follows Dirk out of the room.

****

They arrive at the warehouse to find Johnson red-faced, the veins bulging in his neck as he stomps among the crates full of weapons. Startled as he hears a noise behind him, he draws his pistol. Turning as he brings his weapon up he finds himself looking at Dirk and Maya as they walk through the open door.

Screaming at them he says, "I should've known it was you two from across the street. What the fuck do you think you were doing?"

Taken aback by Johnson's overly aggressive stance Dirk responded, "Saving your fucking ass," as he inches forward toward Johnson.

Still screaming as he gets into Dirk's face, "And why in the hell did you think my ass needed saving?"

"From our vantage point you were knock flat on your back with two hostiles holding a gun on you and Dmetri," comes Dirk's response. He also red-faced as the volume of his voice has increased to match Johnson's.

Looking to de-escalate the situation Maya grabs Dirk, pulling him away. "Sir," she says, "It appeared to us that one of our assets was in immediate threat of deadly violence from a hostile. You were in a vulnerable position and.."

"I took the shots," Dirk said, jumping into the conversation as he brushes Maya back. Ignoring a 'what-the-fuck' look from Maya and staring back at her he continues, "I thought there was no other option available to us. Had we waited and tried to cross the street we may have engaged them in a shoot-out after they had killed you."

While not screaming and the color coming back into his face, he fumed, "Had you waited just a few minutes more the situation would have been resolved. Your stupidity just cost me three of my best assets here." Watching the quizzical looks on their faces, he continued.

"Yes, my field intelligence assets. Dmetri received a tip the warehouse had received a delivery. We came over and hid our truck in the shadows as they did their transfer. Waiting for a few minutes after they left, we came in to tag the crates. The guards, who had spent months working into their smuggling ring, and I had a slight disagreement over how to proceed with the tagging. They are, were, just a bit excitable and high strung. It's happened, like, a million times before. Until you two morons, playing cowboy, hero, whatever, decided to fuck up everything.

I understand Winter, the American idiot, who was raised on cowboy movies; but you, Thernopolis, I expected more of you. I was told I would be impressed with your intelligence and cool, calm decision-making under the toughest of conditions. That assessment was all bullshit. Now, get your ugly asses out of here while I figure out what to do."

****

As they slinked back across the street to their surveillance nest, tail between their legs, Maya is a stride behind Dirk. Highly pissed at him for jumping in on Johnson to take credit for the shooting, her face was flush with the steam just coming out of her ears. Not wanting to cause a scene in the middle of the street where Johnson might see them, she waits until they are secluded out of sight, and then lets loose.

Highly agitated, pissed and a lot of other emotions, she grabs Dirk by the arm and whirls him around until they are eye-to-eye. Yelling at him and wavering her arms about she demands, "What the fuck was that horseshit all about? Taking credit or blame for my decisions? I'm a big girl and fully responsible for my actions. I don't need or anyone else protecting me."

Dirk stands in place as she turns away and starts stomping around the room, holding back his return fire while trying to formulate a cool, level-headed response. He knows she's really mad as she never used the fuck word in a field situation since they started working together, no matter how justified that reaction would have been. Yep, pissed and other raw emotions are evident.

"God," she snarls, "I should just kick your ass for acting retarded." Continuing her journey around the room she asks, "Don't you have anything to say? God I'm so pissed at you. Why, why would you do that?"

Finally, he answers. "Are you finished?"

She stops walking and just glares at him, shooting a hundred daggers from her still flashing green eyes. Thrusting her chin out she stands with her arms folded in front of her, not saying a word.

Choosing his words carefully he says, "I wasn't trying to protect you, not intentionally, but I told Johnson what I did for a reason."

As Maya opens her mouth, he cuts her off. "Look, you're the golden girl here. If Johnson wants to think this was a cluster fuck, so be it. I'd rather he be angry with me than you. If the decision is made to split us up, it's better they remove me, believing me to be the screw up, than you. This is your command, so I can go but you need to remain to see this operation to its conclusion. Your skill as an analyst is greatly needed here and it's a skill I don't possess. Does that make sense?"

Taking a minute to collect her thoughts she responds in a calmer demeanor, "I guess. But still, I take responsibility, even when I screw up in a major, lethal fashion. I must be accountable for my decisions and actions."

"Agreed; however, I don't think you screwed up anything."

As a bit of frustration seeps back into her voice, she protests, "Stopping trying to protect me."

"I'm not."

"Of course, you are. I'm not a helpless little girl.

"I'm not trying to do any such thing," he protests. Besides, I never thought of you as helpless."

"Then why do you insist ..", as Dirk interrupts.

"Just listen. I don't care what Johnson said or thinks. From our vantage point he was in a bad way. We saw nothing to indicate that the situation was anything but desperate. I would have taken the shots if I was in your position."

"But.."

"No buts. What if we just did nothing and let events continue to unfold. And, what if we watched as Johnson was killed? How would that be explained; two assets conducting surveillance and not acting while their colleague was killed before their eyes? I would rather answer for the decision you made."

"But you told Johnson you fired the shots."

Grinning he says, "Don't worry, I'll tell everyone I was acting under your orders."

"Oh thanks, that will make things a lot better."

"Let's get out of here, go sack out and reevaluate the situation tomorrow."

"Should we first check on Johnson?"

"No, it's best to avoid him for a while. He looked to be as pissed at us as you were at me. Let him simmer for a while as he figures out what to do. Remember, this will also look bad on him as he forgot to inform us of what was going down.

Maya nodded in agreement.

Better communication from him may have prevented this whole mess; although I still insist, based on what we observed, you took the right course of action."

Chapter 28

Midway through the next day a shrill ring pierced the silence in their room. Frowning and hesitating a bit, Maya finally sat up and answered the phone after the third ring. As she dreaded, it was Sir Hilary. Instinctively she pulled up a sheet to her chin to cover her half-naked body.

He invited, maybe commanded is the better word, both of them to attend a lunch meeting tomorrow at his office concerning their assignment. Maya spent her time nodding her head as it was a quick call with no details provided and no chance to ask questions. After hanging up she told Dirk about the meeting.

"Well, it was nice working with you," said Dirk, as he walked over and sat beside her on the bed. Somewhat playfully and smiling he continued, "I enjoyed my time with you and everything we did. You're a remarkable woman and one hell of an operative. I have grown close to you and I…"

Maya's eyes are bright and she's smiling at where this discourse may lead.

"Oh, and in my book, you took the right action at the warehouse."

Oh, crap Maya thinks. Tight lipped and trying to maintain a neutral look, "I've enjoyed this whole adventure as well and I have also grown close to you during our time together. I.."

Dirk smiled at hearing that sentiment as she gives him a big embrace, losing the protective sheet in the process.

"With the ass-chewing I will probably receive tomorrow, I just hope my belly button doesn't cave-in. I wonder if I'll be brought up on charges and reassigned or worse, dismissed." She grimaced as she spoke those words.

"Let's not assume the worst-case scenario. The most is that this was simply an intelligence fuck up. Johnson didn't help by failing to communicate to us what he was doing." She smiled a bit.

"So, you don't think I will get my ass chewed"?

"Oh no, that's a given. I just don't see any major repercussions beyond a simple slap on the hand. Maybe a formal reprimand if it's real serious."

"Oh, it's real serious, remember I killed two assets." Dropping her chin, she thinks a moment before adding, "I've never had a mark in my file. This is new to me."

"You'll be fine, I have a positive feeling about the whole meeting."

She gives him a quick kiss, "Thanks, you're so sweet."

"Me, on the other hand, I could be sent back to the states if my partner is gone." He smiled, "I'm not ready for that."

"Let's stop at the 'nest' and review some tape; maybe we somehow happened to film the whole mess and it's been preserved. It would at least show what we were observing and help explain why I took the shots."

"It was a joint decision," Dirk interjected, "I didn't try to convince you not to shoot."

After about thirty minutes of searching and reviewing tape, it was clear that what they saw reinforced their thought process. Johnson was clearly engaged in a verbal altercation with two men he later identified as assets.

The situation devolved into a screaming match and appeared to be rapidly escalating out of control. The fact that Johnson had been knocked on his ass heighten the need to protect a known operative. They had no way to know the others were assets.

They reviewed the tapes one more time. They are biased to their position, but remained convinced the evidence would support their story in an official inquiry.

"Let's just hang out, do some sightseeing, then dinner; you know, regular tourist stuff," Maya offers after she watched the tape for the third time.

"I'm up for anything that will distract you for a while, maybe even putting your mind at ease for a bit. Being a tourist for the rest of the day should be fun."

As they walked out of the building Maya thinks, *Boy, he's cool; cause if he's the least bit worried he's not showing anything.* Then, *stop talking to yourself and enjoy the rest of the day.* She looked over and Dirk gave her a big reassuring smile.

****

The next day, at precisely noon, after a brief time in the waiting area, Maya and Dirk are escorted into Sir Hillary's conference room. The large, weathered, oak conference table, with six chairs surrounding it, dominated the sparely furnished room. Since the room is empty they stare out the window overlooking the asphalt surfaced parking lot as they continued to wait.

The silence is broken when Sir Hillary enters, accompanied by another man. After motioning everyone to be seated, he introduced the man as Captain Markopoulos, an official from the port at Larnaca, then began his presentation.

"Intelligence has been delivered to me which details the tracking of several boats making their journey across the Mediterranean Sea. They followed a haphazard route, very similar to what you, Maya, were tracking in Egypt. After three days one of the smaller ships broke away from the rest of the group and set its course towards the port at Larnaca."

"Here is my game plan," he continued. "Johnson stopped in this morning and we had a good conversation about your work at the warehouse. He told me about a shipment that was unloaded last night. He believes it is the overdue transfer his assets had told him about.

"When the unloading was completed, he was able to slip into the place and examined several crates. It appeared to him that two crates were carrying Silkworm missiles among other weapons. He electronically tagged several pallets of crates, removed the monitoring tape you had set up, then left the premises.

Before arriving here this morning he went to your building and pulled several of your tapes; bringing them here for analysis. Our analysts here reviewed all of the tapes and confirmed that what you had filmed showed the vehicles that went into the warehouse. They were also able to read license plate numbers. The insides tapes detailed all of the action of the unloading. Good work you two."

With her eyebrows arched, Maya takes a quick glance at Dirk who has an expressionless face. He looks at her and lowers his gaze. Maya takes this as a signal to change her expression.

Continuing, Hilary adds, "I have decided to split the two of you up for now. Thernopolis, I want you to stay here to run down the owners of the trucks and talk to them; find out where those trucks were going and who was driving. Be persistent but not threatening; we don't want them to think we are onto their dirty work.

"The analysts should have feedback from local authorities detailing the location of the business owning the trucks. After they close shop for the day slip into the building and gather documents that may tell us where the weapons are headed.

"Winter, you are to go with Markopoulos to the port. He will get you cleared as security for the docks, with access to all incoming loading documents. You are to work the night shift, watching truck traffic coming into the docks.

"Once Thernopolis confirms when the cargo is to be moved from the warehouse, she will contact you. You will match this information to your copies of the incoming cargo traffic. Once you have made a manifest match, we want you to work at that particular dock. You will verify the crates have been loaded onto a freighter; then return here. While we don't have an exact time of action, Johnson expects the move to the docks to occur in the next forty-eight to seventy-two hours. Any questions?"

No one responses.

"Good luck", he adds.

****

Once outside the embassy, Maya and Dirk hustled off to find a secluded spot. They see a park bench covered by trees across the street and, after waiting for traffic to clear, cross over.

"What the hell just happened," said Maya, taking a seat. "I was expecting a royal ass chewing at a minimum. And, Johnson, he said nothing about the shooting; or if he did, Sir Hillary decided to sit on the information."

"Not exactly," said Dirk. He started to stomp around in front of Maya.

"What do you mean?"

"We are being split up, maybe as a form of reprimand. I mean, do they really need me to watch for a truck full of weapons to arrive at the docks at Larnaca? And, what they assigned you to do, watching for a truck to load up at the warehouse and then call me when it leaves? Sounds like a bullshit assignment to me."

"I still think if Johnson had said anything derogatory then Sir Hillary would have at least mentioned something, just to get our side of the story."

"I sure they don't want our 'version' of events. In their mind we fucked up. Besides, Hillary said Johnson pulled our tapes; so I'm willing to bet they were destroyed. We have nothing that shows we were justified, not a damn thing."

He slammed his hands together loudly, then laughed sarcastically. "Maya, we are being punished by being assigned as glorified babysitters."

Not sure how to react, and shocked as Mr. Cool under fire has lost it, she responds, "So, what are you going to do, quit and go back to your unit.?"

Still speaking at a clipped rate and clearly agitated, "I'm going back to the 'nest' and report back the assignment; I'll let the big brass weigh in. If they think it's a good idea, then I will go to the port." Dirk walked to the curb to hail a cab.

As she hustled to catch up as he steps into the cab that stopped for him, she says, "I still think you're overreacting."

****

Dirk, still hot under the collar, is pacing back and forth in their surveillance room. He holds the Sat phone in his right hand while he swings his left arm as he talks. While a little calmer than before, his expression is not that of a happy person. To avoid any chance of contact, Maya is standing near the window, peering at the street below with binoculars while trying to piece together the conversation. After about forty-five minutes, Dirk expels a heavy breath, ends the call with "Ok, I'll keep you posted," and turns to address Maya.

Lowering her binoculars, and before he can say anything she blurts out, "Are you leaving me?"

As soon as she spoke the words she wondered if she made a mistake as Dirk's face showed surprise at the question. She read his surprised look and quickly corrects herself; "I mean leaving our assignment?"

"That's still undecided," he replied.

"What do you mean?"

"I was talking to Rob Wilson in Cairo and brought him up to speed with the change in the emphasis." Maya gives him a quizzical look. "No, I didn't tell him about the shooting."

Breathing a sigh of relief, she nods. "Good. Please continue."

"Well, Wilson understands my point of view and doesn't disagree with it. However, he would like me to stay on a while longer. Our intel agents are picking up chatter about a big movement of weapons to the Iranians on Al-Faw. The talk is they're trying to establish a site for launching missiles into the Strait of Hormuz and the larger Persian Gulf.

"If this effort is successful, all hell could break loose if they start lobbing missiles indiscriminately at the shipping traffic. The war between Iran and Iraq could turn into a bigger mess if the Iranians actually sink a tanker or two. The potential to set the entire middle east afire increases exponentially."

Pointing across the street at the warehouse she says, "We know there are weapons resembling Chinese Silkworm missiles in crates over there. If our assumptions are correct, this is the proof that China is entering the main weapons selling arena in a big way. Those crates have to be the prize."

"Precisely Wilson's point. If those weapons are bound for Al-Faw, and we tag them, we can intercept them and destroy them and/or the launch site before it's operational."

"But, if I want out, he completely understands. I can go state-side and see my parents and family for a few days. I haven't been home in over a year, and it's will be good to see everyone. It will give me a chance to recharge my batteries. After the time off I will be reassigned."

"I understand where you are coming from," she says softly. "I haven't seen my parents and sisters in close to a year. But one thing I have learned about you is that you don't like leaving a job unfinished. You'll hate yourself if you leave just before the fun starts and we break this operation. I also know a lot of American operatives would love to be in your place to strike a big blow against the Iranians."

Smiling ear-to-ear, she adds, "We also make a good, make that a great, team. So, I vote you get your butt up to that port, ASAP. And, you don't leave until we learn the final destination of that shipment."

Dirk takes a deep breath and smiles. "I didn't realize I had asked for a vote." Pausing for a moment, then, "You're right, I'll go home after the job is completed."

"Atta boy, good choice!"

****

Dirk spends the next two days watching the docks around Larnaca. He was hoping to flag any suspicious cargo arriving by truck to be loaded onto an outbound freighter. This effort proved fruitless as the only trucks coming into port carried agricultural products, manufacturing materials and construction equipment.

The time spent wasn't a total waste as on the second night he watched a boat unloading approximately twenty men carrying automatic weapons and ammunition into a military truck. He stopped the truck before it left the docks; flashing his port security badge. Since he was vastly outnumbered and outgunned, he simply hassled the driver over his paperwork. Pretending to examine the vehicle he slapped a small transponder behind the cabin, then waved it through. Once they were out of his sight he phoned ahead to the next roadblock and informed them of the fighters in the back of the truck. They called him back in twenty minutes and informed him they arrested everyone on the truck. A big thank you for the tip.

At around midnight on the third day Maya called; two vans had left for the port loaded with all of the weapon crates. She was standing in the warehouse office reading a manifest detailing everything aboard the vans, the freighter they would be leaving on, and their destination; a missile launch site being constructed on al-Faw.

After the conversation Dirk, dressed head-to-toe in black, headed to the dock Maya described. As he approached through the shadows, he noted a beehive of activity; preparations for something. He made his way to the front of the building where he was meant by a heavy set, armed guard who point his weapon at him. *Yep, something is definitely going down.* He raised his hands, explaining the best he could that he wanted to show his identification. After several minutes of back and forth with the guard speaking in broken English, he flashed his port badge.

The man, who had almost no neck and a shaved head, nodded and lowered his weapon. Walking around to where the freighter was docked, Dick used his flashlight to locate the ship's numbers; they matched perfectly to the information Maya had provided. Another man, not as menacing in appearance as the guard, at least he had a neck and spoke much better English, approached him coming through the light, and asked if he could identify himself.

Once again he displayed his badge. "Just checking to see if this freighter is the same one I was told would be leaving port later this morning," he lied. This exchange prompts a puzzled look from the other man. Playing it to the hilt, he walks arounds, then announces, "Everything looks fine to me. Al-Faw, hey?"

"I don't really care, I just do what I'm told," is the reply.

"Just doing my job too," Dirk says.

"And if you're done then I will get back to mine."

Dirk nods and the man turns and leaves. After several steps he turns back to see where Dirk is. Dirk took this as a signal to move along and after one final glance at the freighter, started to walk away. Slipping back into the shadows he carefully slides through the darkness.

Dodging the guard he had met earlier, he slipped into the pitch black warehouse. He drops down and scoots to an object that appears to be a desk. Slowly pulling himself up, he sees several documents that are luminated by the moonlight. A shipping manifest is printed on the front page. Bingo! He scans the first few pages, finds the destination, returns the papers to the desk and sneaks back out.

Dirk calls Maya back at three o'clock. "The freighter is loaded and headed out to sea, having left the port about fifteen minutes ago. I checked the identification numbers you provided me, everything matched. I slipped into the office and reviewed the paperwork. The weapons aboard were listed, including Silkworm missiles, and after two in-between stops, the final destination is al-Faw. I believe something heavy is being planned."

Chapter 29

Sir Hilary and Maya were waiting for Dirk in the big conference room, surrounded by maps on the walls and numerous documents on the table.

"This will be a very short meeting," Sir Hilary begins. "Maya has briefed me on what you told her. I called Rob Wilson in Cairo and together we have compared and contrasted what you learned in conjunction with our other intelligence.

"Your report confirms what our satellite photos have picked up in the Strait of Hormuz. Iran is constructing missile launching platforms on the al-Faw Peninsula." Walking across the room to where several large photos are displayed, he begins drawing several circles in red.

Pointing at the first circle, he says, "This area here.." His desk phone begins to ring, interrupting his presentation.

"Yes," he says into the phone. He nods his head, responding, "His timing is perfect, send the call through and I will put it on the speaker." A brief pause; "Go ahead, you are on the speaker."

"Dirk, Maya?" comes the voice over the phone. "Rob Wilson here. I'm sure Sir Hilary has been bringing up to speed on our conversations."

"I was just beginning when your call came in," says Sir Hilary.

"Good, good," Wilson replied. "I've confirmed Dirk's work with our assets and a ground commander in Saudi Arabia. The intelligence has been confirmed. I have new a mission for you Dirk if you're willing to move ahead."

Dirk answers, "Go ahead sir."

Wilson, "I know you and Maya have been a bit stir crazy performing all of that surveillance work. Just wanted to let know your analysis has been very positive to several operations at our end. Moving forward, we would like you to lead a strike team into al-Faw. We want you to take out the missile launch site that is at the most advanced stage of construction. We want that sucker totally destroyed."

Still at the photos, Sir Hilary resumes pointing at the circles drawn in red. Speaking to Wilson, "I'm showing them locations on several photos of suspected construction sites on al-Faw. The northern most location appears to have more vehicles coming and going than the other sites. At this time, we believe this to be the scene of the most activity. This information will later be confirmed by our Iraqi assets before we send you in."

"How about it, Dirk, are you on board with leading the team?" Wilson asks.

Finally, some real action, Dirk thinks. "Yes sir," he responds.

"Great. Sir Hilary?"

"I concur, great to hear. Now, I will be assigning Maya, along with Rick Williams and two members of his commando team to this mission. Wilson?"

"I have three operators that Dirk has worked with in the past that are ready to go. That's an eight man team. Anything else to add?"

The conference room is silent.

"Okay, we will be delivering intelligence to you once you're in position to go. Good luck everyone." With that, Wilson hangs up.

"Alright," said Sir Hilary. "you two will be taking a flight out of here tonight for Basra, Iraq. You will be met by British MI-6 and taken to your temporary quarters. In coordination with all of our assets, the mission will be planned and executed. Questions?"

"No sir," comes the joint reply.

"Good luck. One more thing, don't worry about breaking down your surveillance post. We plan to leave some equipment there to monitor future activity at that warehouse."

****

At their hotel room as they are throwing together some clothes and other items, Maya asks, "This mission looks to be much more action oriented, which should be to your liking. Are you glad you decided to hang around?" She grabs the ringing phone.

Dirk is slowly going through his half of the room; for some reason it doesn't seem any different than his quarters back in Cairo, or anywhere else for that matter. Some people are neatness challenged.

He performs the smell routine on some shirts, trying to determine if they are semi-clean. He decides to dump them in a growing pile of smelly items.

""Yes," he says in response to Maya's question. "You do realize that my boredom had nothing to do with you. I just get antsy from time to time; especially when I not sure exactly why I'm in a certain situation. I'm looking forward to this trek."

Maya, with a look of amusement on her face, tries not to laugh as she watches him sort his laundry. She was finished in less ten minutes with everything in neat piles, folded and placed in a soft pack, ready to go.

"Glad to hear you're not bored with me," she says in a soft voice.

"Who was on the horn?"

"Front desk telling us not to worry about what we leave behind. Anything of value will be returned to the embassy."

"They better wash most of my clothes first," as that last whiff nearly crossed his eyes. "I'm definitely ready to rock and roll," he says as he heads for the door.

"Me too," she says. Before closing the door, she takes one last look at his mess. "It was fun, wasn't it?"

"Yes, it was," and he turns around, giving her a big hug and a quick kiss. "Onto the next adventure."

Chapter 30

Near the Sunehri Mosque
Peshawar, Pakistan

The leadership of the shadowy group monitoring events under their influence, if not outright direction, in Afghanistan, was holding a strategy session to provide updates on future operations. Although the group's driving forces were the clergy from the Sunehri Mosque, they preferred to maintain a facade that they were separate, and indeed, had little connection to the mujahideen. Hence, they continued to gather in a building down an alley from the mosque. In fact, to maintain their charade they went to the ridiculous ritual of exiting from the back of the mosque and would reenter through the same entrance at the conclusion of their gatherings.

Today's work had the leadership particularly ecstatic, maybe even downright giddy. They were going to accomplish a coup, if you will. No, they weren't plotting to overthrow the government of Pakistan, although that idea was always a delicious thought. No, in this instance, this type of coup, would establish them as brilliant military strategists and tacticians. And, the fact their action was fraught with extreme risk, would make the rewards all the more satisfying.

The attendees are the same general cast of characters as before. The makeup of the commanders depended on who was available to be rotated in from their field duties. And of, course, the tall one.

Some of the clerics watched with envy and disdain as the tall bearded guest has risen in prominence; one trait that stands out amongst the holy men is the sin of being jealous.

Although not a warrior, his money, which allows him to buy needed supplies, food, and so forth, has resulted in garnering him respect and loyalty. Some of the commanders, in fact, referred to him as a Sheik, a title the tall one likes. Thus, the increased importance on the clerics plan to rebolster their standing among the faithful.

The assemblage listened intently as the senior cleric launched into his presentation. He started by updating the group on battlefield achievements, exaggerated of course, and spoke of territory gained. The infidels from the USSR are definitely on the run, their resolve growing weaker with each agonizing defeat on the ground. Final victory is within our grasp.

"The increase in military confrontation has led to an increased need for more weapons, new weapons that are more powerful than the older ones we currently use," he said.

Here it comes thinks the Sheik, how big will the financial hit be to me.

"Our master weapons procurer has arranged for us to secure a massive new trove of weaponry to allow us to continue to pursue our victory. This delivery will bring the finest and latest versions in automatic rifles, RPGs and, a new toy for us, the Stinger missile," said the senior cleric.

An audible gasp swept through the audience, many of them had heard about this missile with the potential to alter battlefield techniques, yet none of them had ever dreamed they would be able to use one.

Correctly gauging the impact of such a statement, the cleric, speaking with ever greater aplomb, ventured on. "For those of you unfamiliar with this new weapon, it is a shoulder mounted device that has proven to be quite adept at bringing down Soviet helicopters. It is proving to be a game changer in negating the vast air superiority of our enemy. It is definitely changing the effectiveness of our fighters while helping to take the fight out of the godless foe."

Before the cleric could continue, the Sheik, sensing the hypnotic effect the news had on the group, rose to speak. "All of these fancy weapons are nice, but bottom line, how much is this endeavor going to cost me?"

An angry buzz encircled the crowd with harsh stares fixed on him. They openly whispered among themselves, wondering if our Sheik would be considering to hamper our brilliant warfare, over what, money? Especially, according to him, he possesses so much of it; what gives?

The cleric, reveling in the poor timing of the Sheik's question, raises his hands as a gesture to calm everyone down. Smiling, he responds, "Not a penny, my brother."

"Come again," said the Sheik.

"The cost of our bonanza has been taken care of, at no cost to us."

The Sheiks scoffs at that answer. "Come on, who would willingly provide us with such charity?"

"Precisely my brother," *how the cleric had grown to hate referring to him with that term, brother.* "Willingly is the key word. Let me explain."

With a bit of vitriol now evident in his voice the Sheik booms, "Please do, I am very curious to learn what mess you may have gotten us into".

Glaring back at him, the direct challenge has made everything personal, the cleric continued.

"As I was saying before I was so rudely interrupted, our weapons procurer is responsible for our windfall. His contacts in the weapons smuggling arena have been working with a wanna be player in weapons selling, the country of China." He paused for effect.

"The Iranians are looking to change the balance in their eternal war with their sworn Iraqi enemy. Our middleman has been able to arrange an introduction with the Chinese and the Iranians through him. The cost of admission to the Chinese, a vast order of weapons for us; while they sell Silkworm missiles to the Persian dogs."

"So now you have us in bed with the Iranians? How can you, a Sunni senior cleric, allow yourself to get into bed with the Shia bastards?", screams the Sheik.

Grumbling of disgust emits from the crowd. The cleric raises his hand to once again seek silence.

"I've done so such thing," the cleric calmly replies. Taking a shot at the Sheik he says, "Let me make this simple enough for even you to understand."

The Sheik scowls to cover clenched teeth while shooting him an angry look.

"This exchange is being done as a favor to us. Our brother is buying the missiles from China and selling them at an astronomical price to the Iranians. After taking his outrageous share of the money, he will pretend to help the thieves who grabbed U.S. weapons that are too hot to move otherwise.

"However, instead of moving the weapons he will hijack their trucks and divert the arms to us. For good measure he will report the thieves to the U.S. government.

"So, the Iranians don't know we exist, and you only know they exist because I trusted to share that information with you. We are clearly winners with our trusted friend."

With nothing else to say the Sheik spits out through teeth clenched so tight his jaw aches. "Well done. By the way, did you happen to hear where the Silkworm missiles were going?"

Basking in the glow of the commanders, they would forever regard him as a brilliant, mystical, god-like leader, the cleric responds over his shoulder, so he doesn't have to look at the chastened Sheik. "Not that I really give a damn, but I believe al-Faw was mentioned as the final destination."

Chapter 31

Basra Iraq

Everyone knows there is a hatred of Iran within the ranks of the CIA, and sometimes such a strong emotion can lead to mistakes in decision making. The United States, through the efforts of the CIA and aided by British intelligence, had a long involvement in determining the ruling of Iran for over a twenty-five-year period. Beginning with the 1953 coup in which the U.S., under the administration of President Dwight Eisenhower, played a significant role in orchestrating the overthrow of Iran's then popular prime minister and the installation of the Shah of Iran as their leader.

They continued to work closely with the shah to maintain his rule. This relationship allowed the CIA to stage many of its Middle Eastern operations from Iran. The justification of their actions was explained away with the caveat they were ensuring the flow of cheap oil to the world, especially the US.

This arrangement came crashing down when the Iranian despot was over-thrown in a coup in early 1979. The revolutionnaires seizure of the U.S. embassy in Tehran and the hostage taking crisis in late 1979, had a major impact on the American psyche. This action caught the CIA operatives off guard and was a major embarrassment to them. The embassy staff believed they had destroyed sensitive documents but later learned many of the supposedly shredded documents had been reconstructed. Thus, it was with relish when Winter and others were finally allowed to be involved with direct action against Iran.

****

Winter and his group were working out of Basra, not far from the north end of the Persian Gulf. Basra is known for its suffocating, hot desert climate, especially in the summer months. The humidity can reach 90% with temperatures exceeding one hundred degrees, and at times it seems almost impossible to draw a breath of fresh air. And when you draw a deep breath of air, you'd swear your lungs were on fire. The conditions are just plain nasty. But that is manageable, Winter reasons, as long as we can strike back at Iran.

Their target was on the al-Faw peninsula near the Persian Gulf. The peninsula is located in the extreme southeast of Iraq. The marshy peninsula is twelve miles southeast of their position in Basra and is part of a delta for the Shatt al-Arab river, formed by the confluence of the major Euphrates and Tigris rivers. Al-Faw is the only significant town on the peninsula and its namesake. It is a fishing town, marshland, port and more marshland which features the main naval base of the Iraqi Navy.

The remainder of the al-Faw Peninsula is otherwise lightly inhabited, with few civilian buildings or settlements and most of its few residents involved in the fishing, oil, or shipping industries. It is the site of a number of important oil installations, most notably Iraq's two main oil tanker terminals; Khor al-Amaya and Mina al-Bakr. Hence, its main importance is due its strategic location controlling access to the Shatt al-Arab waterway and thus access to the port of Basra.

During the Iran-Iraq War al-Faw was the site of many large-scale battles. In early 1986 the Iranians capitalized on the weakness of the Iraqi defenses located at the southernmost tip of the peninsula by launching a surprise attack against Iraqi troops defending al-Faw; capturing control of the peninsula. The attack was sudden and intense, with the Iranians routing the poorly trained Iraqi defenders. It marked the first time that the Iranians had successfully invaded and occupied Iraqi territory. The Iranians defeated several subsequent Iraqi Republican Guard counter-offensives; managing to hang on to their foothold.

The occupation of al-Faw put forth two possible outcomes. One, Basra, the Iraqi capital, was now at risk of being attacked. The second outcome, as confirmed by U.S. spy satellites, showed the Iranians would be using the peninsula as a launch pad for Chinese developed Silkworm missiles to be deployed against shipping and oil terminals in the Persian Gulf, and also against Kuwait, which supported Iraq throughout the war. Thus, the importance of the mission of Winter and his group; slip onto the peninsula and create as much damage as possible to the missile installations.

Winter would be leading a team of eight operatives; an equal mix of American and British forces. As he was examining close up photos of the launch site with Williams and Thernopolis, he felt a slight bit of apprehension as he considered the makeup of his squad. Although he had prior mission experience with his operatives and Maya, he had never worked with Williams and the two British commandos. In this type of an operation precise, coordinated teamwork is required to be successful. He would feel better with a practice takedown; really any type of action, just to get to see if they can develop a rhythm.

In the middle of formulating their plan of attack he received a message from British intel informing him of a raid on the outskirts of Basra that went sideways. He read the message aloud: "Iraqi soldiers were chasing an infiltration squad of Iranians spies when they stumbled onto a large operations facility occupied by Irani soldiers. The Iraqi troops came under heavy fire; losing the spies in the process. Intel wasn't aware of how many Iraqis were alive and how many had been killed. Winter and his group were the closest operatives and were requested to intercede if they were ready."

The other two nodded in agreement and left to round up the team. Winter grabbed a Sat phone and placed a call to the British telling them they would lead an assault on the facility. They gathered up some equipment, including explosives and headed out. An Iraqi asset accompanied the team on the fifteen- minute ride. He knew the area quite well and filled in the team on the general grounds and the facility they would encounter.

The weapons fire ceased as they stopped their Jeeps about a mile away from the location for a quick meeting. The road into the grounds was from the north; they expected the heavy defense to be located there. Rather than using head-on blunt force, three members of the team would approach from the east and from the west, setting up sniper positions to take out the guards from the unexpected position. The other two members would maintain position in the front.

Before they divided the assignments, Williams noticed movement in the dark, figures slowly moving toward them. The Iraqi accompanying them spoke in whispered tones, receiving acceptable answers. Two men revealed themselves as the asset explained these men survived the Iranian attack. The men believed there was between fifteen and twenty Iranians, heavily armed with light weapons, barricaded inside.

Under the cover of darkness they split up. Winter took two of the British commandos and one Iraqi, and flanked to the east. Williams moved to the west with two Americans and another Iraqi. Thernopolis, with an American and an Iraqi took positions in the front. Winter gave everyone five minutes to get set; he would take out the first defender he saw inside, signaling the others to commence firing.

Winter's team was in superior sniping position and with the use of night vision googles, they sighted their targets and methodically took out the defenders. After several minutes of quiet Winter contacted the team to storm the building. The facility was assaulted from three sides, drawing no return fire. The team entered through the front of the building and heard what sound like a heavy door slamming shut. They found what appeared to be a near impenetrable, concrete bunker. The attack was at a temporary standstill. Winter decided that anything of value was inside the bunker. After looking over the bunker Williams asked, "What's the prognosis"?

"Looks like we going to have to blow it," Thernopolis responds. "However, it's beyond my expertise. Should I assume both of you guys like to blow things up?"

"Absolutely," they respond in unison. "That's why I brought along some explosives, you know, just in case," added Winter.

Winter takes a quick jaunt back to his vehicle and returned with some C-4 plastic explosives. "Just one potential problem, I can't guarantee the condition of the people inside as I don't know where they are in the box. And guess what? I don't really care."

Williams and Thernopolis both watched as he placed a small amount of the explosive around the edges of the heavy steel door. He tells them to move about fifteen feet way, then tells Williams to fire at the explosives. Williams hit one explosive which was enough to ignite all three charges, blowing open the door. As the first person in by a step, Thernopolis took out a guard with Williams getting the second one. Winter, who charged in with Williams, disarmed the last remaining guard and grabbed the commander by the throat.

The so-called tough guy who had urged his men to fight to the death in the fierce fire fight, cried like a little girl when Winter throttled him. Even as he was being tied to a chair he was surrendering a trove of information, begging them not to kill him. All he wanted in return was to be hidden deep in a British prison where the Iranians couldn't find him.

Two months later, after weeks of double and triple checking and cross referencing the information from the captured soldier, it turned out most of the data gathered proved to be actionable intelligence. The biggest coup de grace was the decision to send a U.S. Navy Seal Team to takedown a Norwegian-flagged container ship. Satellite imagery showed the ship to be tightly hugging the Red Sea coastland and into the Gulf of Aden; moving mostly at night and resting in small ports in the daytime. The intercept occurred shortly after the ship had reentered the Gulf, near the Yemen border with Oman. The Navy Seals found the ship to be Iranian manned and loaded with light and heavy weapons headed to Iran. The possibility also existed the ship was one of the group that Thernopolis had been tracking back in Eqypt.

****

Having returned to their Basra base, Winter and the team meet for a brief recap of the night's action. All agreed that the operation was a success; they achieved their objective and gathered important information that would be valuable in future operations. The final count was seventeen dead Iranians and two captured, while they suffered no casualties. Overall, they worked well together.

Later that morning Winter resumed planning their mission on al-Faw. He had the latest CIA spy satellite photos of the peninsula and was reviewing them with Thernopolis. The latest photos showed the current status of the Silkworm launch sites they were to eliminate and/or damage. The time lapse photos showed test firing had occurred at the largest pad with a possibility the Iranians had engaged in live fire yesterday at shipping vessels in the Persian Gulf. No information was provided on whether or not any targets had been hit. However, the notes and summaries provided indicated the mission was still a high priority for the CIA; render that place inoperable.

Winter and Thernopolis agreed that the site would be heavily guarded. Winter was wondering if they had sufficient firepower to succeed in a what may be a drawn-out firefight and still be able to damage the launch sites. Just as he blurted out, "Where the hell is Williams", he walked in as if on cue. He was carrying the latest reconnaissance data gathered by several Iraqi operatives already on the peninsula.

"Your timing is perfect. What is the status of Iranian military personnel protecting the missile sites?"

Williams replied, "Since the initial defeat of the Iraqi defense forces and the subsequent fleeing of those not killed in the battle, the sites have had minimal security; no more than two or three men patrolling at each site. We should be able to take them by surprise and eliminate them rather easily."

Winter asked Williams if he knew how old this information was. He replied it was based on observations from last night and this morning while we were on our mission.

Winter, "It just seems counter-intuitive. I would have thought the place would be more heavily guarded; in case of a raid."

Williams, "These guys have been to this site several times over the last week with the same results, no more than two to three guards at night."

Thernopolis chimed in, "Maybe the Iranians don't foresee any actions here. They have defeated several Iraqi attempts to recapture al-Faw and maybe they feel a bit invincible. I'm guessing they have no clue our side is operating this close to the Persian Gulf, thus no reason to have large patrols at night. And, with our ability to attack at night I would say the odds would be in our favor."

Winter listens intently and finally nods in agreement. "It sounds reasonable and makes sense." To Williams, "What other info have you got?"

Williams responded, "Our operatives, with the help of Iraqi soldiers, have been able to move and hide a stockpile of explosives and ammunition in a secured location. This material should be sufficient enough for us to blow the site and the launch pads. Also, it enables us to travel with fewer supplies, giving us more flexibility and speed while traversing the swamps."

In consultation with their Iraqi operatives Winter, Thernopolis and Williams decided to move out from Basra under the cover of darkness. They had received a good weather report; no rain is expected, and the temperature should be under one hundred degrees that day. The operatives, using three Jeeps, would act as guides, driving them across the marshes to a point near the middle of the peninsula. They would silently cover the final three miles to the Chinese Silkworm missile installations by foot.

The explosives were buried about a thousand yards from the launch pads. Once they reached that point, four members of the team would stay and uncover the munitions. The other four members would proceed to the missile sites. They would take up positions around the front of the buildings and attack the building. They would eliminate the defenders and enter the facility. By this time the men should arrive with the supplies. They would lay explosives around the missiles, the building and the launch installations then remote detonate. With success they will destroy the missile stockpile and render the sites inoperable.

The Iraqi operatives would remain at the drop off site to take them back to Basra after completion of a successful mission. If they don't hear the explosions from the detonation after one hour, they are to go to the launch pad to provide any assistance needed to complete the assault. If the plans went to shit, they would proceed with an extraction operation. Hopefully, there wouldn't be a total fuckup as they were totally on their own with no official help available to bail them out. Even if the CIA and MI-6 knew where they were located, they would be disavowed; left to figure things out on their own.

Chapter 32

Nightfall is rapidly approaching, signaling the time is near to prepare to leave. It's a moonless night as the squad readies to move out. This situation proves to be a perfect cover as each member is wearing the latest in night vision googles. They load the three Jeeps with their light weapons and, of course, Winter's favorite explosive, C 4. He always carries it on this type of mission, you know, just in case.

Williams introduced the team to the three Iraqi soldiers who will drive them through the marshes and onto the peninsula. When Winters asked if they can be trusted Williams said not to worry; they have been thoroughly vetted and have worked with other British excursions. Remember, they hate the Iranians as much as the CIA does and would love to accompany us straight into the action. They will wait to ferry us off the peninsula and back to Basra. And, they will be ready in case the 'shit hits the fan' and everything goes to hell. They can handle themselves in a fight.

After they finished loading the Jeeps, checking and rechecking for the umpteenth time to ensure noting is left behind, Winter has a quick conversation with the Iraqis. The decision is made to leave in thirty minutes.

Winter and Williams head back inside where they find Thernopolis has returned to the latest photos and reconnaissance reports. Winters asks, "Anything new to report on?"

"Not really. The last report was based on observations from earlier this afternoon. An Iraqi soldier was able to get within one thousand yards of the missile site. They are definitely operational.

"Shortly before he positioned himself he heard a noise that lead him to believe a missile was fired into the gulf. The spy photos didn't show any ships being hit.

"The question is are they still learning the firing protocols or are they just bad shots? Regardless, we can't wait for the answer. Fire enough missiles and at least one will hit a ship, even if by accident. Then all hell will erupt."

"Then, tonight we do our best to destroy everything we find at the site." Checking his watch, Winter announced, "we're leaving in about twenty-five minutes."

Turning back to her maps and photos, Thernopolis continues. "The site is about 20 kilometers or twelve miles for you Americans, from where we are now." Pointing to the big photo, "Any guards are expected to be on the north side of the site, in this area. Our latest recon work still shows heavy activity in the daytime. Nothing has been observed to contradict that the majority of people leave at dark. The results are similar, whether by satellite or by human intel."

Pausing, she looks at Winter and Williams for any questions or comments. They are silent so she continues.

"Obviously if there are guards, we will take them out." Pointing to the photo, "we will lay explosives here, here, here, and here in the approach; and then around the three launch pads".

Pointing to another photograph, she adds, "Also, we have found a building, here, which is where we believe the missiles are being stored. We will take down this facility as well. After we detonate the explosives we will come back here, gather any leftover gear and hike back to the rendezvous point where we were dropped off. The Iraqis will drive us back across the marshes into Basra." To no one in particular she asks, "What do you think of our mission?"

Williams, "If we are successful, our work will render these sites temporary unusable. Since the Iranians still control this territory, they will repair and rebuild. However, anything that slows down the missile launching, the safer it will be for shipping in the Gulf. Winter, anything to add?"

"Not really," he responds. "It sounds like a good plan and as long as the intel is somewhat accurate, we should be able to execute it.

"But, if there's one thing I've learned in field operations is the best laid plans of mice and men often go awry. So, if something can be fucked up, it will. In my book, the best course for success is having the ability to adapt on the fly and get out with our collective asses intact. We are all experienced operators and know what the goal is. As long as nobody panics, we'll be fine."

Before he can add anything else, he hears talking outside. He leads them outside and walks over to the Jeeps. He walks the perimeter quickly to look over the terrain while Thernopolis and Williams stay with the remainder of the team. Everyone is dressed in desert camouflage, holding their helmets with night vision goggles attached, and ready to go.

He finished up in front of the Jeeps and said, "Ok, it's show time."

****

The winding, near lightless trip through the marshes goes without incidence. Williams is in the lead Jeep, and according to the information he has the rendezvous point with the buried explosives pretty much straight ahead. Moments later he signals his driver to stop. The convoy halts; everyone piles out of the Jeeps and begins to unload them.

Winter goes over the plan of attack one more time. "Once at the front of the building, Thernopolis will take her two guys and go about fifty feet to the east, behind those trees or overgrowth or whatever they call that vegetation that appeared on the photos. That should provide some cover for your position. Watch me for signals," Winter adds.

"Williams and his two commandos will dig up the explosives. When they meet with the rest of the group, Williams will take his two men and circle west, hitting the facility from that side. I and the remaining operator will remain at the front, the north end, of the site. We will attack from that position."

"With three to four minutes to get everyone in position and a few minutes to establish firing angles, we should be ready to take action after about ten minutes, tops. If there are guards that need to be neutralized, so be it.

"We will then lay the explosives at the pads and meet up at the storage building. We will quickly check its contents and then prepare to denotate it. After our work is done we'll meet back here to be driven back to Basra by the Iraqi soldiers. Everyone good?"

No one responds.

"Ok, let's move out."

They each grab their night vision googles, rifles and ammo while Winter slings a small bag with C 4 inside it, you know, just in case. Looking skyward, Winter noticed the inky darkness has fully enveloped them. The witching hour has arrived. Fully armed and ready, they start their journey.

The brutal temperature of the afternoon has dropped from oppressive to merely highly uncomfortable. The air is stale and disgusting, but at least Winter's lungs don't feel like they are on fire as he ratchets down his breathing to a measured pace.

Deliberately, and with a steady stride, he leads his operatives forward. The steady pace is to ensure they are as quiet as possible; in addition, it allows everyone to be alert for any signs of snipers or other surprises, weird creatures come to mind; which may be waiting for them.

Three minutes in; so far, no problems. The Iranians must be supremely confident that there are no Iraqi soldiers on the peninsula to interfere with their plans. They are partly correct, there are no Iraqis involved in this mission; at least not yet.

Cautiously they crept ahead, trying not to talk or make any noise themselves that will give away their location. After walking for about five minutes, Winter raised his right hand to signal a stop. Two hundred yards ahead, give or take a few yards, they see the launch pads. Thernopolis slides next to Winter, pauses, then whispers, "The silence is deafening. Plus, I don't see, or sense, any activity in the area."

"You're right," he whispers back. "Not sure if that's a good sign or a bad one. He looks over the terrain, then instructs one of the guys to sneak to the right through the heavy vegetation. You should be able to get within fifty to seventy-five feet of the building. Perform a quick observation and report back here." The guy takes off.

"So, what now, just wait?" asks Thernopolis.

"Yep. I think we are out of the sight of whoever is guarding the building and we should be safe for now.

The scout returns in about five minutes. He saw four men at the site; outside the building. They don't appear to be guards patrolling the grounds but rather it looks like they are planning preparations of some type. They seemed to be measuring distances by scanning the night sky and then sighting through some type of equipment towards the water. The Iranians may be readying the site for another launch.

"Did you notice any guards?"

"Not from my location. I will hazard a guess those guys are engineers. Regardless of who they are, I also don't believe they are out there alone. The only question is how many guards are out there with them."

"As I stated earlier, the best laid plans of mice and men." "You know the plan," he said to Thernopolis. "Any last minute questions?"

"Nope, we're ready to go."

"Alright. You may as well leave and get set up. Contact me when everyone is set."

With that she informs her men of the plan, and they set out in a low crouch, heading east.

Winters watches as they sneak into position, then Thernopolis calls in on the mic. *Good, they are set and well secluded. Now, I just need Williams to show.*

No sooner than he turns around to look for Williams, he appears, as if on cue again. He noticed each man is carrying a small crate. Williams sees Winter at nearly the same time, he sets his crate down and signals his guys to do the same. Cautiously he looks arounds, then glides quietly toward Winter.

Winter brings him up to date on the live intel the guy who did the scouting mission found. He listened attentively, then slowly walked back toward his group. He advanced about ten feet when a single *crack* rings out. Williams reflexively ducks at the sound of the shot, hearing the bullet buzzing past his head. *Oh Shit,* he thinks.

Chapter 33

Winter reacts in the same manner as Williams, dropping to the ground. He looks around, watching as the others scrambled into the nearest vegetation. Signaling Williams to not utter a sound, he listens carefully. Silence. It's been about two minutes with no additional shots. He sits up and looks at Williams.

"Someone sure as hell knows we're here," he says. "Based on where you were standing, I believe the shot came from the north, straight from the front."

"Agreed," Williams answered. "Think someone was waiting for us?"

"Damn good question. Thernopolis and her men are already in position to the east. The good thing is they didn't panic and return fire."

Crab walking toward his left he finds a tree to hide behind. He whistles and waits for a response. Another shot rings out. *Are the defenders simply responding to sounds or can they see my people?* He hears a return whistle. Looking toward the area where Thernopolis should be, he finally locates them.

In the meantime, Williams and his guys scramble to the west, hiding within some overgrowth. He also whistles, and Winter locates them quickly. *Interesting, no shot after that whistle. So, they either didn't hear that whistle or they are firing indiscriminately.*

The brief silence is broken by the staccato sound of a machine gun burst, then another and another. Winter reaches Thernopolis and Williams via their mics. He tells them the fire has all been high, so the defenders haven't been able to pinpoint their positions; they are firing blind. Pick your targets and return fire when you are ready.

Winter sights at least five men, a hell of a lot more than the two or three defenders they were told to expect. He begins returning fire, starting his team's assault on the building.

Winter watches as two defenders in front of the building fall. As he begins to look to the right, the machine gun starts again, causing him to drop on his butt. After the burst he looked up; the bullets stripped the trees above him of their leaves. They seem to have a better idea of where his team is, but it's still blind firing. However, that can be just as dangerous as pinpoint firing since one never knows when their accuracy may improve. Even worse, you can inadvertently walk into the bullets.

Winter's hears a single shot from his left, Thernopolis's position. He watches as another defender falls, that at least three, then quiet. He radios each team to tell them to begin to move forward and start to close in on the building. As he readies with his guy to move out, there is an unexpected whump and a loud boom. *What the fuck, a mortar round? Who the hell has a mortar?* He radios back looking to get a status report from each team.

"Thernopolis, what's your situation?" he asks. After a brief period of no response, a voice crackles, "Same as yours. Just talked to Williams, we are taking return fire that seems to be coming from the building that we believe houses the missiles. Apparently, it is housing some additional weapons and troops."

Winter, "Was that a mortar round I just heard?"

"Certainly sounded like one to me," she responded.

"A machine gun nest and a mortar? We are definitely outgunned and probably outnumbered, too." Winter pauses a moment, trying to formulate a plan "on the fly' as he likes to call it.

"We need to back off, regroup and quickly come up with a new plan," Winter said. "Not too far from where Williams is secluded there is an area where we can meet and be partially secluded. Make you way there as soon as you can. I'll let Williams know we coming to his position."

"Stay down," he adds before switching to Williams.

"Right, we're on our way. See you there in about three minutes."

A round of fire is loosened in their general direction followed by a loud boom, emphasizing the need to stay low. Also, the general fire wasn't the staccato burst of a machine gun; Winter believes he may have killed the gunner. However, even if no one jumps in behind it, they still have the mortar. And, he expects someone to man the machine gun.

In short order Winter and Myers, along with Thernopolis and her guys rendezvous with Williams and his group. Winter does a quick head count and arrives at eight. "Good," he said, 'no casualties. Well, as you have probably guessed, Plan A is fucked. What have we got?"

Williams, "I'm going to assume each of you had no troubles taking out the several guys hovering around the launch site?"

Everyone nods in agreement. Williams continues, "I count least seven dead, obviously way more than the two or three guards that our intel was projecting. I'm guessing the Iranians were preparing to launch more missiles and brought in extra defenders, just in case, and had them inside the building. Well, we are their just in case nightmare. Did anyone get a good visual on what we are facing?"

Winter, "Not really, but I agree with your assessment. The return fire was scattered and fired blindly; I don't believe they can see us but obviously know a bunch of somebodies are out there. In addition to automatic weapons they have some type of mortar as well. Anyone have any ideas?"

Winter's guy, Myers, responds, "We can take a team and circle behind the building. The others will stay out front and keep assaulting the building. That should keep the defenders busy long enough for us to plant your C 4 explosives and blow the back of the building. We then hit them from the front and back at the same time and neutralize their position. We replace any explosives we use by grabbing some missiles."

"Come again on that one?" Winter says. "If we find ourselves short on explosives, we'll simply wire up a few missiles? You can do that?"

Myers repeated his line of reasoning.

Winter thinks for a minute. "As long as we can successfully detonate them I'm quite sure they will cause more damage than everything else we have available." He nods, "I like it. And, you and I will do it. "Any objections?"

Looking skyward, Williams says, "This can't be a long firefight, we have at best two or three hours before the sun starts to roll across the sky. Plus, we don't know if they been able to contact anyone for reinforcements."

"We only have three guys in reserve, he adds. "So, the faster we move the faster we can get out with our asses intact."

"Just a minute, I'm not sure I can buy into your revised plan," Thernopolis said.

A brief burst of staccato fire interrupts her objection. Someone did man the machine gun.

"Notice the silence, they are still flying blindly, not knowing if they have repelled the attack or not," she explained. "So, we still have an advantage of the night vision goggles allowing us to see them from our side. We can continue to use the vegetation for cover; stealthily move closer to the building; then launch a full-scale assault."

Williams, "I tend to agree with Thernopolis. We also have grenades and an RPG. I think hitting them with everything we have will increase the odds in our favor. Remember, we can see their every move while they can't see us. I like those odds better."

"Plus," adds Thernopolis, "we don't know where the missiles are located inside. If they are near the back of the building you may create a bigger bang than you are expecting when you blow your way in."

"I hear what you're saying but as you know we don't have a lot of time to complete this mission," Winter answered. "Remember, we are out-numbered, they have heavy weapons and, they could have back up coming. If we haven't eliminated the defenders in thirty minutes, I'm blowing my way in. Let's rearm and commence again."

A battle rages for thirty-five minutes without much change in the outcome. The Iranians, or whoever the hell they are, have also regrouped. Their aim, especially with the machine gun, has gotten better. In addition to stripping away a lot of vegetation, they also have killed a British commando and seriously wounded a second one who is now unable to continue fighting.

While Winter and the team have killed another ten or twelve defenders; they still keep returning fire. There must be thirty or more of them, and they're well-armed. And the damned RPG didn't work.

Winter radios each team and they meet again. "This isn't working, and we are pretty much in a stale mate. And, the longer we screw around, the more the odds favor them."

"We're already down two men. Somewhere, the intel was really a pipe dream; this place is heavily defended."

He looked his watch, "Give us fifteen minutes and Myers and I will take off the back of the building. Just remember to keep them busy out front."

Resigned to the current futility of the current situation, Thernopolis and Williams solemnly agree. Before Winter can leave Thernopolis wraps her arms over his shoulders and whispers something. With a big grin he answers, "Don't worry, we'll be careful." With that Winter and his Myers depart.

Williams, "What was that all about?"

"I kind of feel responsible for this mess," she says.

"How so, Joan of Arc?"

"I ran the intelligence end of this operation and it was 100% wrong."

"Maybe or maybe not; you know how things can change at the last minute, especially in a combat situation. Even so, you can't blame yourself if you are given bad information. As the man said, you have to adapt on the fly when the original plan goes to shit. That's what he's doing."

Thernopolis, with great trepidation, said, "You heard the man, let's go make some noise and give them time to do their thing. We'll position up on either side of the front of the building. In five minutes, we hit 'em with everything we've got."

A burst of fire from the building causes them to stop in their tracks just as they begin to take up their positions. Again, the shots don't appear to be well aimed at them, just the Iranians reminding whoever may be out there they are still ready to defend their turf.

After they waste a couple of minutes, they reposition themselves and then let loose with a heavy volley, aiming at the doors and a window at the building's right corner.

Winter and Myers hear the exchange of gunfire and sneak up to the back of the building; no windows, no doors and no one knows they're there. They begin laying the explosives on the pattern of a doorway along the bottom edge and up the building. After taking cover and five minutes after the mark time, Winter fired the shot that set off the explosion. A nice hole is blown through the back of the building large enough for Winter and Myers to enter through.

Winter counts to thirty, then looks over at Myers and nods. Just as they stand up to move forward another explosion goes off, blowing a tremendous portion of the concrete building back towards them.

"Shit," says Thernopolis to no one in particular. "That last explosion wasn't part of the plan."

Suppressing the urge to sprint to the back of the building to rescue Winter, she just knows he alive; she can feel it, she remains secluded. Dead, eerie, silence. She looks at her watch; three minutes have passed with no defensive fire. She radios Williams and they talk for two minutes. She cautiously stands up, surveying the leveled building in front of her.

At the same moment Williams has done the same thing. With their weapons at the ready, the four of them, the other casualty died of his wounds, slowly make their way forward towards the huge pile of rubble which was once a building.

Arriving together at the site, they inspect the damage. The pad is ripped apart; they spot remnants of a mortar which are scattered across the ground; but no signs of the machine gun. They roll over two of the dead; they are wearing Iranian military uniforms; confirming who the defenders were. They count eighteen dead outside and who knows how many more inside. Two or three guards my ass.

Thernopolis noticed Williams was on the phone. She heads for where the back of the building should have been and suddenly stops. Her heart skips a beat as she drops her weapon; staring at what is now just a large pile of rubble. *Winter is here someplace!* She finds it hard to breathe as she stepped gingerly around the mess.

Not finding any bodies she starts to run toward the vegetation in front of her; stopping suddenly as Williams grabs her by the arm. Twisting and turning, tears flowing down her face, she tries to break free of his vise-like grip. "Let me go, or help me God, I will shoot you Rick."

"Maya, stop it, you don't even have your weapon," he says. "I know how badly you want to keep searching for the bodies and there's no reason to do so. The double blast was too intense; you know they're both dead. Why put yourself through the horror?"

Finally looking at Williams with her tear streaked face, and watery eyes, she wails, "Oh God, it's all my fault." Through her sobs and shaking body, she tries to steady her breathing. "Why wouldn't he listen! I knew something bad could happen and it did. Why do you stupid men never listen? You all think your supermen."

Williams pulls her shaking body to him. "Let it out," he says softly. After a couple of minutes her sobbing lessens. "This isn't your fault. He knew the risk he was taking, and he selflessly took it so we could finish the mission. He's a hero!"

Maya is softly crying as her body slowly stops shaking as she holds to Williams.

"I just took a call from Basra," he says in a firm voice. "Our little fracas and the explosions have alerted Iranian troops that something happened at this launch site. The chatter says a group of eight to ten soldiers are moving out in thirty minutes; destination, here. We need to make our way back to the pick-up point and get the hell out of here. Now!"

"What about their bodies?"

"I saw the back of the building, or at least what was the back of the building. I'm not sure anyone could find any bodies in that mess. Besides, any retrieval effort would require heavy equipment, which, as you can see, there is none in sight."

"Look," he continues. "I know you some have feelings of deep friendship with Winter, you guys worked closely together over the last several months. But he's gone now, and, I know that he would want you to complete your work."

"You're right; let's get back to Basra," she said through sniffles.

As they walked back to the waiting Iraqis, Maya can't stop thinking about Dirk. They were very close, lovers in fact, and who knows what else might have developed. And now, he's gone. Who will tell his parents? Who will tell Rob Wilson; he also lost a great operative and he sent us on this mission? The tears start again. Will my heart ever stop breaking and will I ever stop crying?

"Maya?"

She realizes Rick is talking and stops sobbing for a minute, wiping her eyes with her sleeve. In a halting voice, "What is it Rick?"

"You ask why us stupid men never listen to you females. It is because we do believe we are supermen and are invincible; especially those of us like Winter who serve their country in combat.

"But also know, at some point we learn to listen to women like you. And, sometimes, we find a special one, like you, to help guide us through life. I can only imagine how you feel, how much you hurt. But remember, Megan, (Rick's wife), and I love you and we will be there to help you every step of the way."

"Thank you," she sobs.

Chapter 34

Grabbing only the weapons they came in with the survivors trekked in silence back to the drop-off point. Thernopolis was in a daze as she plodded along in step with the others; her mind racing over what seemed like a thousand different thoughts and feelings. She even initially walked past the Iraqi soldiers before she stopped when she heard Williams speaking to them. At least that's what she thought she heard; maybe she stopped just to stop; she didn't know. She wasn't really sure if she wanted to continue walking, talking, anything. In fact, an American operative had stopped her and turned her around.

Regardless, she just stood and stared. Her eyes burned from the tears and her vision wasn't clear. Her face showed a pained expression, shocked, traumatized, with a blank look in her eyes. She closed her eyes and slowly opened them, hoping somehow, she could return everything to normal and end the nightmare.

Williams did stop long enough to engage in a few minutes of conversation. Their guides were eager for details as they saw that only four men returned while they had transported eight. Williams hurriedly informed them of what had happened, how the mission had gone awry, the breach of the building and the bloody conclusion to the firefight.

While not close enough to have heard the gun battle, they heard a noise that sounded like a mortar round exploding; then later they heard the other two explosions. At that point they had considered moving forward to provide additional fire power. However, the agreement was for them to remain in their position unless they received radio communications telling them to proceed in a different method. The situation became very eerie when everything went silent after the second blast. Again, they overcame the urge to move forward to render assistance.

Williams told them they made the right decision to stay put as the battle was over after the explosions leveled everything.

They asked Williams if they would be returning to the area to attempt to retrieve the dead. Williams explained that he had been informed an Iranian force was primed to move from southern Iran onto al-Faw. They needed to leave now to avoid further trouble.

Although the Iraqi's had more questions, they quickly loaded the three Jeeps in silence. They kept the lights off to make it more difficult for anyone to track their position. They arrived back in Basra just as the sun began to shoot out its initial probing rays, signaling that dawn would soon be arriving.

As the Jeeps were unloaded the men still observed the decorum of silence; in deference to their fallen comrades. Thernopolis was still operating on autopilot, robotic like; as she assisted unloading the Jeep she rode in. After some sleep everyone knew an official inquiry would be called in an effort to answer questions; especially the big one, 'What the Fuck went wrong?'

****

Thernopolis and Williams stayed in Basra for the initial portion of the inquest. Maya spent the first day reacting to, in her mind, a series of disjointed events. She would close her eyes and the surreal dream repeated itself over and over. How could she have possibly lost her comrade, her friend, her lover, in such a manner?

The mission faced danger, every field assignment did, but everyone believed they had taken the necessary steps to reduce that risk to a manageable level. Everyone felt comfortable with the final plan; that the odds were in their favor. And, even when Winter decided to blow the building? While Maya was against the idea, it was Winter's specialty, right?

Why did he have to blow the building? Because Plan A went to shit, and he had to improvise on the fly. Why did the plan go to shit? She didn't know. That was the real question to be addressed and answered. Why??

Having watched Thernopolis' reaction to the final outcome and, in particular, Winter's death, Williams wasn't sure how engaged she would be during the investigation. He has known her for five years and never saw anything rattle her like the events on al-Faw did; not even when she was captured and held as a prisoner.

He was worried about her mental health. He surmised she and Winter had grown close during their time together; yet he had no idea how close they had become. He had tried to talk with Maya on the way back to Basra, and later after they had grabbed some chow and were trying to relax. Both efforts were met with silence; the far-away look in her eyes telling of the pain she was confronting.

On the afternoon of day two in Basra the investigation began. Thernopolis and Williams were debriefed by both American and British intelligence investigators. They were told that no one was being accused of doing anything wrong; nor were they being held responsible for the death of their four comrades.

This series of meetings was to try and piece together what had occurred and why. Could the outcome have been different with different decisions, different actions, was anything overlooked, ignored, and so on. They hoped to find out why the initial plan broke down.

The investigation began with the review of the decision to develop and assign a mission. The request came from Rob Wilson, CIA station chief in Cairo, Egypt. The impetus was based on satellite photographic documentation that Thernopolis worked on while she was stationed in Cairo earlier this year. Her analysis identified suspicious shipping activity in the Mediterranean Sea. This led to a takedown of a ship by a U.S. Navy Seal team.

Among the information discovered was a detailed plan to introduce Chinese Silkworm missiles by Iran into captured al-Faw. This information was vetted by British MI 6 intelligence assets in Iraq; leading to the decision to take action.

They moved onto why the team Wilson chosen was selected. The assignment was to assault a launch site that was under construction and could be operable in a short time frame. The objective; render the storage building and launch site inoperable. The eight individuals selected had previous successful experience with similar operations. The team leader, Dirk Winter, was an experienced CIA paramilitary operator who had led teams on facilities assaults in the past.

The first glitch in their plan was the site that was selected turned out to be operable. Reports were written that indicated missiles had been launched the day they went live.

From there, they walked through the planning, the human intelligence reports, the analysis of the satellite photos, the decisions made before leaving, the Iraqi escorts, the decisions made during the fire fight, who did what, who decided to blow the building, did everyone agree to that action plan, and on and on. A mind-numbing exercise, to be sure, but vitally important to the review.

Much to Williams' relief, Thernopolis was clearly engaged in the entire process, both asking and answering questions, recalling precise details and decisions; acting like herself. She was definitely interested in determining what went wrong and why. She even corrected some of the investigators assumptions when they went astray.

After four straight days of debriefing and questioning the sessions concluded. They had answered questions and repeated stories so many times they wondered if their minds would be permanently numb. While they were anxious to participate in the process to try and determine what went wrong, they both also wanted the questioning to end so they could stop reliving the nightmare. They had lost fellow operatives and felt some degree of responsibility; especially over the fact they had to make the decision to leave their team members' bodies behind on al-Faw.

The investigators had meticulously gathered, categorized, and indexed the information they needed to allow them to make findings of facts, initial determinations and conclusions, and recommendations for the formal inquest. The final count; the investigators had reviewed over one hundred documents, including satellite intelligence photos. They had written numerous pages of notes and statements; and had compiled and recorded over thirty-seven hours of questions and responses. They examined and reexamined, over and over, and over again, trying to ensure no small detail had been overlooked.

When the inquiry was finally concluded, the talked out, mind numbed, exhausted duo knew that this was only the end of step one. Now, they wondered how long before the formal inquest would begin. That evening's dinner capped their final night in Basra.

The following day was shaping up to be another typical hot Basra day; even in October the temperatures can still threaten the hundred-degree mark. Williams and Thernopolis had just returned from breakfast and were wondering what the day ahead would hold. They were tired of this place; just plain tired period, from all that had transpired over the last two weeks. Just as they were about to go back to their quarters, a person, waving a sheet of paper, approached them. He was carrying the official notice of orders, which read; be prepared to leave later this afternoon to be flown to the British embassy in Nicosia, Cyprus.

They looked at each other and shrugged. They knew the orders would be arriving, they just had no idea how long it would take. Perhaps it was best they arrived quickly rather than having to hang out here for several more days. They briefly met with the other two members of their team as all of them were wasting time. It was their turn to be interviewed, starting this afternoon.

Thernopolis and Williams stayed long enough to grab lunch. Packing was light as they only had their camouflage gear and fatigues, as civilian clothes weren't required for the mission. They were driven to the airport in a Jeep where they boarded a commercial flight for the five hour and thirty-minute flight to Nicosia.

Chapter 35

It was around nine o'clock in the evening when they got off the plane and started making their way through the airport. Slowly winding across their way around the facility, neither of them was in any particular hurry to go anywhere. They finally exited out the main terminal where they spotted a car with official British government plates on it. The driver, who was standing outside the car with the trunk opened, let them toss their duffle bags in, then closed the lid. He informed them that since the hour was late they would be taken directly to their hotel.

As the vehicle made the journey along the main streets many of the sights looked familiar to Thernopolis. She wasn't 100 percent sure but believed she recognized the streets as leading to the hotel where she and Winter had stayed. Five minutes later her belief was confirmed.

She briefly closed her eyes as the memories came flooding back. It was still surreal to her; it seemed like another lifetime ago. It was, it was Winter's lifetime. She sighed as she opened her eyes and wipe a tear or two from them. God, how it hurt and how emptied she still felt. She looked over at Williams; if he had seen her reaction he didn't comment.

After checking in, at least she was given a different room, she met Williams in the restaurant for a late-night dinner. The time spent eating the meal passed with little conversation. She mostly picked at her food, eating here and there; her appetite hadn't completely returned. Forty minutes had passed when she smiled, said she was tired, and went back to her room. Williams understood and left after he finished his glass of wine.

Tossing and turning for what seemed like forever she finally fell asleep. She was awaken the next morning by a droning, annoying, ringing phone. The call came from the embassy from someone who spoke so fast she barely comprehended what was said. The message, she believed, was be down in the lobby in forty-five minutes ready to go to the embassy. The hour of decision was here.

When she got down to the lobby she found Williams and Rob Wilson, the CIA's station chief from Cairo. Wilson waved her over to a table where he had steaming coffee and pastries waiting. She wasn't sure which smelled better, the hearty, nutty flavored aroma of the coffee or the sweet, lemony smell of the filling oozing from the piping hot baked goods. Yum!!

They engaged in small talk while enjoying the continental breakfast. Recognizing Williams and Wilson had never met before, Thernopolis provides the introduction, praising both men for their leadership qualities. Wilson said he was aware of Williams reputation as a top notch operative, even sharing anecdotal knowledge of one of Williams' operations.

Although sad to reconnect with Thernopolis under the current circumstances, Wilson was nevertheless pleased to see her again. He shared a couple of stories of their time in Cairo, including the raucous reassignment party.

Maya is only half listening as she is devouring the pastries. She takes this as good sign since she had no appetite last night and was a little nauseous while showering earlier. Probably from nerves and not eating much the last several days.

Wilson looked up at a clock and saw that over an hour had lapsed since they gathered. As much as they tried to dance around the true purpose of their meeting, and how they each enjoyed the story sharing, it was time to address the serious, though sad, business at hand. After another thirty minutes or so of what was stories turning into a touch of bravado, Wilson started the real conversation.

"First of all, thank you, both of you, for agreeing to come here and appear before the inquest."

Yeah, like we had a choice, Williams thought.

"We know this is a very difficult moment, as you not only lost comrades in the battle, but the fact that you were also unable to retrieve their bodies for proper burial," Wilson said.

"And, while both conditions are horrible, the incident of leaving behind others is probably the hardest thing to do and the hardest set of emotions to deal with. While we are taught to accept the consequences of severe risk, we are also taught to return with our fallen.

"Sometimes people perceive the inability to complete this portion of their mission as a failure. It is not a failure as in some combat operations other factors arise that renders the retrieval of fallen comrades an impossibility. That was the case with this mission.

"Second, despite the personal loses we suffered, the mission was rated as successful from a military standpoint. The missile site was rendered completely inoperable, and as a result of the damage incurred, it may never be operable again. Kudos for a job well done."

Williams and Thernopolis, her eyes a bit damp in the corners, nodded silently at the acknowledgement.

"Now, for today's business," Wilson continued. "As I mentioned, the official reason for your presence here is to appear before the inquest that is already underway. The purpose of the inquest is to examine what happened regarding the conduct of the mission starting with the planning stage, the execution phase of the operation, and the aftermath. The panel wants to determine cause and effect so procedures can be developed to further minimize, if possible, the risk of future operations of this type.

"Our preliminary work leads us to believe no member of your team committed a major error, yet we did suffer four KIA (Killed In Action). We hope to find out why. Any questions about the purpose of this inquest?"

Silence.

"Okay, good so far. While the inquest is underway, the panel at this time isn't ready for your appearance; they don't anticipate needing you for several days. They are anxious to review the investigators report before meeting with you."

With a puzzled look, Williams asked, "then why are we here now?"

"Because we wanted to get the both of you out of Basra as soon as possible. While we recognized the burden placed on your team's members and the loss they are dealing with, in many cases the leaders of an operation, in their mind, bear greater responsibilities. They tend to continually rehash their command decisions. In some cases, this kind of thinking and repeated self-doubt can lead to depression and feelings of hopelessness. We hope to prevent that cycle from happening, or help to mitigate the behavior, if it is already present in your personal thoughts.

"The next four days to five days are yours for whatever purpose you desire. If you need to talk to someone you can reach out for assistance. Maya, I know you and Dirk had worked closely together for the last seven months, including on an assignment with me in Egypt. I know that in that time frame people can get very close with each other, even to the point of thinking of them as family. So please, if you are feeling despondent, having trouble sleeping, and so on, let us know. We can arrange for you to talk to our experts to assist you in sorting out your feelings and how to address them. It's not a sign of weakness and nothing is ever recorded or reported, it stays confidential with the person you speak to. That's goes as well for you Williams. Any questions?"

Maya shifted in her seat, looking and acting like she wanted to speak but doesn't say a word. Williams remained stoic in his seat throughout the entire presentation.

"Alright," said Wilson. "We will contact you when the panel is ready. Reaching into the inside breast pocket of his jacket he withdraws a business card, handing it to Maya. "The embassy has an account at this clothing store. Since you will be here for several days and only have military gear with you, I encourage both of you to update your wardrobe."

Once they are outside the embassy Williams speaks to Thernopolis. "What Wilson said about talking to someone; I'm here if you want to talk to someone you know."

"Thanks, I'm good."

The sun is high and bright in the midday blue sunny sky. A check of her watch reveals it's one o'clock, time to consider lunch. Wanting to eat two meals today; not bad for someone who had no desire for food last night.

"Suddenly, I'm starving," she says. How about we grab some chow and just hang out; you know, the tourist thing."

"I can do that," he replies and veers across the street towards a small café.

Chapter 36

After lunch and over the next four days, the tourist thing is what they do. They generally dined together, which is much more fun than dining alone and moping. The type of eatery was totally dependent on Maya's wants in that area. Usually after they ate, they walked around, occasionally popping into a store or two to browse. Other times, they watched other tourists scurrying around, trying to determine what local attraction to visit next.

On the second day they decided to stop at the embassy just to hang out and hear what they could possibly hear; snooping, as it were. However, the secretaries had all been placed on high alert to watch out for them. Since they had no official business with embassy personnel, they were shooed away with the suggestion of visiting an art gallery, such as the Gloria Gallery.

On the morning of the fourth day they received a package with investigative information to review and a series of questions to answer. Since it was due back to the embassy by the end of the day their strolling around the city was eliminated.

There was also a lot of alone time, usually at Maya's insistence, and sometimes after Williams's was attempting to engage in conversation. She would listen a bit and then politely shut him down after a few brief exchanges. He didn't think she had reached out for professional help; hopefully she was working though things on her own.

When alone, she would sometimes workout at the hotel's gym or just wander around the city. She purposefully avoided most places she and Dirk frequented. The hurt was still very strong; at times it felt like a fist was pounding her in the stomach.

On one of her journeys around the city she happened to end up at their 'spy nest'. It was quite by accident in her mind, but when she realized where she was, she immediately turned around and left the area.

Upon arriving at the hotel after having dinner on day five, quite sure they had seen every site they had an interest in seeing, the desk clerk handed them a message. They were requested to be at the embassy the next morning at eight o'clock. A request; like they had a real choice to refuse. Anyways, the summons was good; they were both tired of waiting and sick of sight-seeing.

****

Thernopolis had a rough night and tossed and turned repeatedly. Anticipating she would be testifying for a long time before the panel she was reliving the battle. During the night she experienced a series of flashbacks to the night of the raid. The horrific happenings finally caused her to awaken in a cold sweat, triggered when the second explosion at the building occurred.

It had felt so real that she bolted upright in her bed, screaming out Winter's name, clearly shaken. She got out of bed, wandering around the room in a bit of a haze. She finally made her way to the bathroom where she promptly threw up. Nerves, she mumbled to herself. She splashed some cold water on her face, rinsed her mouth out with the cold water, and with great trepidation, warily climbed back into her bed.

A loud ringing banging in her head caused her to wake up a second time. The sunlight was slowly slithering into the room. The sunshine was the hint; morning; she had survived the nightmares.

That damn inferno ringing again. Reaching out with her hand she searched for the phone. That damn ring again, someone is sure as hell persistent. Her hand felt the phone, she took it from the cradle, mumbled something and dropped it back down. It's the damn front desk with her wake up call.

She staggered into the bathroom, pausing long enough to look in the mirror. *Ugh!! I look like hell. If it was a hangover at least there would be a logical explanation. Maybe a hot shower will fix everything.*

Thirty minutes later she walks into the hotel lobby where she finds Williams over at the coffee bar. Although the menu was pretty the same each day, this morning everything smelled particularly nauseating.

"Rough night?"

She nods in response. "A real bad one."

"The raid, the building blowing up again?"

"Yep."

"You should really talk to someone about this Maya. It's still happening."

She shakes her head no, "Really Rick, it been better. I hadn't had a nightmare in close to a week." She follows him out to the waiting car. "It only happened last night because of having to rehash everything in front of the panel this morning. When this ordeal is over I'll be fine."

Williams shrugged his shoulders and frowned. "Hope you're right about this, you stubborn…whatever," as he enters the car. At least he tried again. Maya just smiles back as she climbs onto the seat beside him.

****

When they were escorted into Sir Hillary's conference room Thernopolis recognized many of those in attendance. In addition to Sir Hillary also present were Charles Scott, the chief MI6 Officer in Cairo; Rob Wilson, and Ed Jeffers, the CIA station chief in Afghanistan. She nodded at everyone she knew, then paced around the room a bit, pretending to look for a chair. Finishing the charade, she finally landed in one of the two chairs in front of the panel table.

Since Williams knew none of the assembled. he was introduced to the panel; then took a seat next to Thernopolis. They were both on edge, not sure what to expect or how long they would be here.

This was Sir Hillary's show, so he ran the proceedings. "We, this assembled inquest panel, has brought the two of you here to formally notify you of the findings of our inquest. Let me first express our condolences for the loss of your team members. There is nothing harder than dealing with the death of individuals who died during combat carrying out your command decisions."

Great thinks Thernopolis. Guilty before we have a chance to defend ourselves. Better keep listening to find out how long we will be locked up for after the court martial.

"I also commend the tireless work of our investigators. They conducted over one hundred hours of interviews and examined more than one hundred documents. They put forth tremendous effort to expedite this investigation so we could address this situation promptly and implement the corrective actions they recommended.

"The biggest question to be answered by this panel was; when the original site was identified as having gone live, should an alternative site have been chosen?

"We have reviewed all of the evidence gathered by our investigators in Basra. This group is some of the best in the business and were from both British and American intelligence agencies.

"The good news is their conclusions, which we concurred with, did not find any errors from the three individuals responsible for command decisions. We agreed with their fact finding.

"In fluid, fast moving combat action, decisions must be made quickly based on the information available. In answer to the major question, the answer was the latest intel still indicated the site was sparsely guarded. The choice was to proceed with the raid.

"When in the heat of combat, it became obvious the intel reports were wrong, Mr. Winter reacted according to the new realities and adjusted his action to the new reality.

"While Mr. Winter's decision to blow the building resulted in the loss of his life and his fellow operative; we believe he made the correct choice. Unfortunately, luck wasn't on his side; and while your objections, officer Thernopolis, turned out to be correct, Winter's course of action resulted in the total destruction of that launch site. We do not believe that site will ever be returned to operational status.

"The investigators thoroughly reviewed your planning process and the initial operational plan that was developed. We agreed with their conclusion that nothing was ignored from the information made available to you. You properly identified the operational risks involved and developed procedures to eliminate and/or minimize those risks.

"So, what happened and why did your mission encounter the problems it did? Human intelligence gleaned over several days including the afternoon before your team departed, indicated the site was minimally guarded at night. The three of you carefully, and correctly, planned your attack based on that information. The conclusion reached by the investigators was the leaders followed proper procedures and that a very late decision was made to increase the numbers of guards in the rotation assigned to that site.

"We agreed with that conclusion. We were able to review satellite photos taken just two hours before you moved onto al-Faw. The number of guards on site at that time was five; a number that wouldn't have caused any changes to your plan of attack. Yet, somewhere, somehow, and for reasons we may never determine, the Iranians made a command decision to alter their rotation at that site at the last minute.

"The position was actually heavily guarded, we believe the final number was thirty men reinforced with heavy weapons, including a machine gun and mortar set up. Given the fact you were armed only with rifles and some explosives for a fast attack, you likely would have never survived a protracted firefight. You essentially walked into a death trap.

"It is our conclusion that Winter's decision to blow the building saved the lives of the four survivors. He was a hero and will be remembered as such.

"This presentation of the investigators' work has completed the requirements of this inquest. We have unanimously adopted their report. This hearing has concluded, and the panel is dismissed. Thank you everyone for your participation in examining this tragedy."

As the meeting breaks, Sir Hillary signals Thernopolis and Williams to remain behind. They chatted briefly with the panel's members as they were leaving the room; most of the conversion consisted of the panel members extending their condolences for the loss of their team members.

Once the room was cleared, Sir Hillary informs them they will be flown back to London for much needed rest and relaxation. He also ordered Thernopolis to see a doctor upon returning. She looked run down, exhausted actually, and the chance to recharge her batteries would be beneficial. To enforce his wishes Sir Hillary had said she wasn't allowed back on active duty until she was cleared by a doctor and the paperwork was reviewed by command staff at headquarters.

"I wish once again to express my sincerest condolences for the loss of your team members. And, to thank you for your service. It is through the efforts of outstanding people like yourselves and your team that helps keep the world a safer place. Now, if neither of you have no questions or comments, your flight back to London leaves in ninety minutes."

They both thanked Sir Hilary for his kind comments and also for the swift action of the inquest panel. To say they had gone through several tense days would be an understatement. All in all, they were proud to serve.

Before departing, Thernopolis asked what would happen to the bodies left behind on al-Faw. Sir Hillary explained that unknown to him, an American Navy Seal team was already aboard a ship operating in the Persian Gulf off of Kuwait as your backup. When the ship-board satellite picked up your explosion, they fast boated to al-Faw. They pretty much landed simultaneously with the Iranian reinforcements, who were members of their elite Quds force. After a brief battle eliminated the enemy, they recovered the bodies, with the two British members being turned over to MI 6 in London.

At least Dirk and the others will be returned to their families for proper burial, she thought.

****

A car was waiting for them in front of the embassy when they walked out of the building. A short fifteen-minute ride took them to the airport where the driver checked them in as VIPs. They had a few minutes before they had to board so they stopped at a restaurant inside the depot for a quick lunch. Maya was famished; her appetite had returned once her nerves calmed down.

In between bites, she said to Williams, "Boy, just when you think you know all of the answers someone goes and changes all of the questions. I thought for sure we would be testifying before the inquest panel and that it would be hours and hours; a complete rehash of the investigation interviews."

"So did I. I was prepared to go brain numb again."

"Oh yes, me too. Now I can go home, relax, breathe easier and return to my normal self." *That last sentence was to convince herself as much as it was Williams that she would be fine.*

"Looking forward to some R&R myself." He watched Thernopolis as she ate, trying hard not to stare. It was good to see her eating again; maybe she's right; the reduction in stress levels can do wonders for the body. Still, she looks haggard. He feels better knowing she will be going to a doctor and has to be cleared before returning to work. No more bull shit allowed. Also, no need to for her to rush back, she's been through much more than I have.

Soon, they board the plane for the flight back home.

PART TWO

Chapter 1

Port of Beirut
Beirut Lebanon 2007

A small contingent of U.S. Green Beret operatives, hidden among stacks of containers, are watching as a beehive of activity unfolds dockside. They have assembled a series of lookouts and nests from different vantage points to give them an unobstructed view down to the water. They have set up a host of cameras and scopes with special lenses to enhance their ability to see and take pictures in the night.

The night was cloudy, not even the moon was emitting light, and in contrast to most of the day, which was sunny and humid. The darkness provided great cover for the operatives who were dressed in black clothes. Their cameras and scopes, along with their night visions gear, was suited for the dark work. A more perfect night for a little observance couldn't have been ordered any better.

The CIA had been tracking a ship that had left Iran under similar nighttime conditions. They followed the ship directly to the port of Beirut. Their estimate was the cargo, weapons, would be unloaded clandestinely, taken to a warehouse about ten miles from the docks. The building was listed as owned by an offshore shell corporation controlled by the Iranian Islamic Revolutionary Guards Corps. From there the belief was the cargo would be diverted to the battlefield in Afghanistan. This line of reasoning supported theory that Tehran viewed the Taliban as somewhat useful to their cause if they could keep the U.S. busy on the battlefield. Therefore, providing them with some weapons could achieve this goal.

Despite the protestation from the Lebanese government there was no question this port was being used for weapons shipments, storage and distribution; the filming of tonight's activity will provide irrefutable evidence. The best defense Lebanese government officials could offer would be that the loading and unloading of ships wasn't being completed with official approval. Perhaps one could give them the benefit of the doubt as the operatives watched a ship being unloaded in the middle of the night. The use of portable lighting structures would, arguably, be exhibit one in saying the operations are being conducted by rogue groups. True enough, except all of the prior events also happened under the cloak of darkness. How could the owners of this port not know what was occurring at their docks? As they say, money talks, especially when there are many corrupt players involved.

Brian Stone, who is leading the Special Forces effort, has an asset working at the docks. Although there was plenty of chatter this morning of a major unloading very early tomorrow morning, no manifest or other paperwork existed. This is the first sign the operation's purpose is dubious at best. In addition, as they focused in on the dock workers, they are carrying what appear to be automatic weapons; which just don't happen to be standard equipment for the average local dock employee; even in Lebanon.

****

The unloading takes three hours to complete. The crane operators are quite skilled, efficiently taking the containers from the ships. More importantly, Stone noted, the operators aren't carrying weapons; odds are they are legit. The armed men loaded three trucks in the same efficient manner. They kibitzed with the crane guys for a while, then handed several envelopes to one of them. Shortly after that exchange, the crane operators departed the docks. After the lights are extinguished and loaded onto the trucks, the remaining men drive away from the dock area.

Stone and his men, seven in all, waited until the lights from the trucks vanished, then gathered together for a brief powwow. One of his guys was able to locate and jot down the ship's International Maritime Organization number. Bingo, it was a perfect match to the number intel provided to them; no question they had the right ship. They also counted fourteen heavily armed men board the trucks that left the port.

Stone called ahead to the interception group. "The ship's identity was matched to the CIA info. Three trucks were loaded with weapons; they have been picked up by the satellites and are headed in your direction. They won't be able to generate a lot of speed in those vehicles so you should see them in about fifteen to twenty minutes. In addition to the weapons the trucks are carrying fourteen heavily armed men."

A brief pause as they climb into their Hummers then, "Right, we are on our way. We will follow behind and use our vehicles to set up a roadblock to stop any attempted retreat back the way they came in."

Stone waits for a response and answers; "There are seven of us."

Pause.

"And one more thing, will you be using a sniper?"

Pause.

"Ok, just let them know to be very careful firing back up the road, we would hate to be the victims of friendly fire."

At the other end of the conversation, Staff Sergeant Rick Williams speaks into his throat mic. "Listen up everyone. The transport vehicles have left the port and should arrive in about fifteen minutes. There are fourteen heavily armed combatants arriving with the weapons. They are being followed by a team of seven U.S. Green Beret soldiers. They will set up a roadblock about a mile up the road to prevent any retreat. They will also provide backup if required. Let's get ready.

****

At the end of a road, roughly three miles in length, stood a series of buildings that resembled a warehouse complex. The relative smoothness of the dirt road gives the impression the site doesn't see a lot of traffic; in fact, it may even be abandoned the majority of the time.

However, what counts now is the front building has sprung to life. The site is flooded with lights with the front and east side of the site bathed in a bright yellow light. Four mid-size forklift trucks are rumbling all around the place moving small crates and other objects. The overhead front doors have been raised and you can see men hustling inside, outside and back inside. No question preparations are being made to accommodate someone.

Williams and his eight men have been on site for forty minutes or so. They parked their Hummers about two miles off the beaten path and hiked through some wooded area behind the buildings on the right side.

During their hike in they found a tall, narrow rectangular building five hundred to six hundred meters from the main warehouse. The sniper quickly cased the building, finding a relatively easy climb from the back to the top floor. Inside the large room was several old desks and filing cabinets; probably a warehouse office during its useful life. Across the room to the side facing the warehouse was a glassless window. Taking a few minutes, a nest was constructed with an unobstructed view of the warehouse on the other side of the road. The filing cabinets, which were empty, were moved into position to provide cover in case of return fire. One was turned over so the sniper could sight and fire from a prone position. Perfect.

Williams and the rest of the team remained at ground level. As they made their approach to the warehouse the grounds jumped to life. Splitting into two groups of four they fanned around each side of the building. The shadows and cubby holes provided by the other buildings enabled them to hide out of sight. Just as Williams eased himself behind a small storage shed, he heard the roar of the heavy-duty truck engines strain down the roadway. He watched as two trucks pulled to a stop beside the building. *Hmm, interesting; I'm pretty sure Stone said there would be three trucks in this convoy.*

Continuing his silent observation, he sees two men talking with one pointing and gesturing back at the roadway. Must be one of the trucks lagged behind and would arrive soon, was his guess at their conversation. Speaking softly into his mic he checked with the sniper and one of the guys on the opposite side of his position. The agreement is there are at least fifteen armed men on the grounds across the way. Plus, however many more are on the delayed transport. Since he is one of nine on his side the action could get very interesting. His sniper had better be very accurate for this mission to be successful.

The rear doors on both trucks are opened as men attach ramps to the trailers and clamor aboard the trailers. A few minutes later crates are being slid down the ramps, guided by a man on each side of the ramp. Williams checks with his sniper who reports a series of targets have been picked out for rapid extinguishment. Just seconds before he can give the order to start shooting, the din of the unloading operation is drowned out by the unmistakable sounds of automatic weapons fire. He waits and listens; the noise is definitely coming from up the road the trucks just traveled down. "What the fuck is going on?" he says into his mic. Then, "That firefight must be the Americans," Williams shouted. "Everyone open fire and let's neutralize these bastards."

Then all hell breaks loose as bullets begin flying toward the scene in front of them. The men at the warehouse dropped several crates and started to scramble for their weapons. The sniper quickly takes out the lights, plunging the area into darkness. Advantage, good guys as they are taking advantage of the IR laser mounted to their rifles.

Watching their lights disappearing in rapid fashion, the men at the warehouse realize the firing is coming from in front of them, not from the roadway. They begin returning fire into the darkness, hoping to get lucky. If their straggling comrades up the road are in a mess, that's their problem.

A major battle was waged at two different locations; at the warehouse and somewhere back up the road leading into the complex. After about five minutes of receiving no return fire, Williams told the sniper to remain vigilant while he led his ground group forward. A brief conversation after everyone gathered revealed no casualties; one man had rolled his ankle while changing his location after a bullet whizzed by him too closely. He assured Williams he could walk with no problems. He somewhat gingerly followed the others as they crossed over to the building; six of them entered the building while the other two remained outside.

Once inside three guys began searching the place looking for any documents, computers, and so forth that may contain intelligence. Williams joins two others as they opened the containers with the weapons to determine what they found. The last two guys stayed outside to search the bodies. They were looking for similar papers in addition to noting anything which may reveal identities of the enemy.

While still searching the premises, the sniper heard two trucks start up. A call downs to Williams results in him telling his men to hide and be alert. A couple of minutes later the sniper is able to identify two American Hummers. The call is made to Williams to stand down; friendlies are approaching.

The lead Hummer veers across the road and stops next to the transports where the weapons were unloaded. The headlights from the vehicle illuminates the ground and surrounding area. It's the first light since the shooting started and it reveals dead bodies and dumped containers that should be full of weapons. No matter how noble the cause may be, carnage is still carnage.

A Green Beret called out, "I'm looking for Staff Sergeant Williams."

"Over here," replied Williams as he emerged from the warehouse and strides towards the man.

Extending his hand to Williams he says, "Staff Sergeant Williams, I am Team Leader Brian Stone." Surveying the scene he adds, "It looks like you also had yourself a bit of tussle here. No casualties, I hope."

The rest of Stone's men disembark from their Hummers as Stone and Williams continued talking. They fanned out around the premises of the building, introducing themselves to the British commandos. They briefly look over the grounds outside the warehouse then the two groups headed inside.

Williams said, "Nothing major, one guy rolled an ankle. So, that was your fight back up the road?

Stone nodded in the affirmative.

Williams, "What happened?"

"Well, said Stone, "As I explained on the phone, we followed the three trucks towards your position, trailing about a half mile behind them. As we rounded a curve in the road, we saw a truck stopped like four or five hundred feet ahead of us, with fighters scurrying around. We guessed the truck broke down and that they were far enough behind the others that no one noticed they were missing. We immediately killed our lights, pulled off the road and took up positions behind several trees and rocks to watch the proceedings. A couple of their guys attempted to try to restart their ride. After five minutes or so they began to gather up their weapons; that's when we opened fire.

"Shortly after we started the fireworks we heard your guys attack begin. There were ten enemy fighters in our group. We took out eight rather quick and had to hustle a bit to get the other two who we found hiding among the rocks. When we had finished we could still hear your battle going on. I told my guys to stay put until the shooting stopped, then we would advance. While we believed you team would control the situation the guys remained on high alert just in case we needed to take out the winners. Fortunately, we didn't. Also, my thanks to you sniper for good spotting. It prevented a whole lot of problems by recognizing we weren't arriving in trucks."

Williams, "When we heard your vehicles approaching, we were hoping, like you were, that the good guys had prevailed." Looking past Stone, he sees a familiar tall, lean figure approaching. "As a matter of fact," he adds, "You can thank our sniper yourself." To the approaching figure: "Maya, come on over; got someone here who would like to meet you."

Maya..Maya, Smith pondered, why do I recognize that name?

"Maya, this is Brian Stone, Team Leader of this Green Beret Unit," said Williams.

Extending his hand while racking his brain, Smith says, "Please to meet you, and, thanks for identifying us as the good guys so quickly."

"You're welcome," she says while shaking his hand. She notices Stone, who has gone quiet, seems to be staring a bit at her.

Still searching his mind, he says, "Excuse my intent look ma'am, it's nothing sinister, I assure you. Is your name Maya Thernopolis?"

"Yes, it is," she replied. "I'm sorry but I don't recognize your name; have we met before?"

Before Stone can answer Williams says, "If I'm not needed here, I going back into the warehouse and see what the guys have found."

"Please, let me explain," Stone offered. "We don't know each other but I know about you."

Puzzled but curious, she responds, "Please continue, I'm interested in your story."

Chapter 2

Thernopolis followed Stone to a weapons container where they both sit down.

Stone: "Do you remember a mission you were on about twenty years ago in Egypt?"

Thinking for a minute she responds, "I believe so."

"You and an American CIA operator, Dirk Winter, worked with a small Green Beret unit. Do the names Eddie Fallon or Rob Smith ring a bell?"

Nodding her head as the memories start rushing back she said, "Yes, yes I remember." Looking at him quizzically she added, "You're too young to have been one of them." Placing a hand over her month, "Oh my god, are you going to tell me one of those soldiers is your father?"

"Oh no," Stone replied. "This team I'm leading now is part of that unit. There are two guys from the group you worked with who are still active. They were working on another mission, so they stayed behind at the base."

Not exactly sure what to say she simply said, "Sorry to have missed them. Well, thanks for the trip down memory lane. Now if you will excuse me, I'll get back to work." She starts to stand up to leave.

With a pained expression on his face Stone continues, "Please, before you leave, ma'am there is one more thing to tell you; the real reason I wanted to talk to you in private."

Noticing the change in his facial expression Maya sits back down. "Is there something difficult you want to talk about?" she asks. "Oh, you don't have to keep calling ma'am, Maya is fine."

He shakes his head, "Yes ma'am; um, sorry, Maya. As I said, I lead Dirk's old Green Beret unit. I didn't join until about fifteen years ago, after he left, so I only know about Dirk through stories told by the other guys about what a great soldier he was. They also spoke of one mission where they worked with a female MI6 operative, Thernopolis, which would be you of course."

Stone leaned toward her and looked her directly in the eye. "This is the hard part Maya. The guys who worked with Dirk, especially Eddie, never believed the official story released about the aftermath of your raid on Al-Faw."

Attentively listening now Maya asked, "What do you mean, what don't they believe?"

"They don't believe Dirk was killed in that raid."

Maya gasped at that statement; her chest tightens, and it feels like she can't catch her breath.

Noticing the change in her demeanor, Stone said, "I sorry, I didn't mean to upset you. Let me explain. Eddie, after hearing about Dirk's death, tried to get information about what happened beyond the official story that he died blowing a building. He and Dirk had worked together on many building breaches, including with hostages inside. He claimed he would have been extra careful knowing the potential for missiles being stored in that building, regardless of what the intel said."

He stopped his story for a minute to check Maya's expression. She was still gasping a bit; trying hard not to shed tears.

"Anyways," Stone continued, "Eddie pestered our command for a long time. His intent was to recreate the breach to try and determine what really happened. The Green Beret have always worked very closely with the CIA and our commander had a good rapport with his CIA counterpart; however, on this issue there was nothing but silence. They won't even budge on a request for this information as being paramount for learning requirements for future missions. Strike one, in Eddie's book.

"On his own, and working with limited official information, Eddie constructed his own forensic examination of the events. He created a training exercise where the team breached a warehouse just like the one Dirk encountered.

"Based on his knowledge of how he and Dirk had done this work in the past, he concocted several takedown scenarios with him playing Dirk's role and using a different guy each time to assist him. His conclusion; someone would have needed to have the ability to remotely denote explosives inside that building in mere seconds after the moment of his breach blast. Since two explosions were reported, that event was possible; however, Dirk always incorporated sufficient wait time, distance and a barricade of some type to shelter behind. This extra precaution was designed to allow for a booby trap to detonate.

The official claim was that Dirk and his partner, who was also trained in building breach protocols, both of them somehow mistimed the standard wait period. While possible but highly unlikely, the other protocols followed would have shielded them from the brunt of the blast; that blast would not have killed him or his partner. The worst that would have happened is they may have been injured but not killed. Strike two in Eddie book.

"Eddie tried reaching out to you to determine what had happened and to express his concerns. He remembered you were with MI6 but had no idea where you were assigned. The initial result was that you had been severely injured and had left the agency. Not believing that line of crap he tried reaching out to other friends who tried to locate you. He finally received a warning from our command to drop all efforts into trying to talk to you. When he asked why he was told you had died and that unless he knew how to conduct a séance, to forget it. Bullshit, and strike three.

"Over the years Eddie and our team continued to work closely with the CIA. He developed close contacts with intel agents with whom he shared his story. The team even went as far as to breach an office in an attempt to find any records. What they found followed the official story was that he died in action. That still didn't change any opinions. Dirk's breach protocol said otherwise.

"Eddie watched, noting in particular operations involving breach actions. He read voluminous records that described the procedures involved. In particular he catalogued several that resembled the methods he and Dirk had used. While acknowledging the possibility that other operatives could have copied Dirk procedures, he never believed that anyone other than Dirk could have successfully completed the extremely complex missions."

Stone paused to catch his breath and to further gauge Maya feelings. He had watched her expression change several times from shock to what appeared to be anger. He didn't think it was directed at him but rather over the fact of how she may have been lied to and played for a fool.

Taking a couple of minutes to regain her composure. Maya drew in a deep breath and let it out. There was moisture at the corners of her eyes. She winced a bit, then finally spoke. "I have taken similar actions myself over the years and came up with the same results as Eddie did; the official story was final. I never believed the lie that was told; however, I was also stymied at every step. I also watched different operations that seemed similar to the al-Faw raid. I had no idea of the protocols that Dirk observed, I just knew that he had specific plans for breaching a structure. In addition, he always had a plan for just in case, as he called, to be triggered if everything went to hell during a mission. His work was meticulous."

One of Stone's men popped over; their work was done here, and it was time to leave. Stone nodded and stood up to go.

"Whatever you do Maya, if you still want the truth, don't quit. Eddie convinced me, I believe Dirk is alive, well and still in action. I will continue to believe this until I see unfiltered direct evidence to the contrary. Good luck with your search." He shook hands with Maya and walked away.

****

Williams is walking out of the warehouse as Maya starts to walk towards it. He said, "You and Stone seemed to be deep in conversation."

"That we were," came the reply.

"Anything you want to share, or is it private?"

"If I did you'd probably think I either had a screw loose or was crazy; maybe even both," she said.

"Maybe," he grinned. "Wanna give me an opportunity so you can know for sure?"

"Ok, but this may knock you helmet off."

He firmly plants his feet and puts his hands on his helmet. "Alright, I'm ready. Hit me with the nastiest information you've got."

Maya relates hers and Stone's conversation in a shortened version. "Bottom line, both Stone and the prior team leader believe Dirk is still alive and working with the CIA."

Williams lets out a whistle, says "You're right, I never expected that," and then goes silent. He helps the rest of the team load their vehicles then beckons Maya into the back seat to begin the trip back. The return journey to the safe house, while only a fifteen-minute drive, is completed in silence. After they arrive they go inside and sit in a corner by themselves. "So, with no concrete evidence, just a hunch.."

She interrupts, "An educated one."

"Ok, but regardless of the analysis Dirk former teammates conducted, and, perhaps they have a strong conviction, it's still just a hunch." He strokes his chin as he searches for the proper words. "Do you believe it's possible they're right?" *Silly question, of course she does, otherwise we wouldn't be having this conversation*, he thinks.

"If you remember, after that explosion I wanted to go search for them but you said no because you wanted to protect me from what you believed was a grisly truth. But I always believed somehow, some way, they survived."

"I remember. But what about Sir Hilary and the inquest, and the fact he said a team of U.S. Navy Seals recovered and returned the bodies?"

"Once thing that always drove me," she says, "was that Sir Hilary only mentioned the return of the bodies of the two British soldiers. He never said anything about Dirk and the other American operative."

"Quite true but I believed it was assumed the Seals delivered the Americans' remains back to the United States."

"Ahha," she answers. "Assumed but never clearly stated. And you know what happens when you assume."

Williams sits with his left elbow resting on his knee, his hand supporting his chin. A loud explosion erupts that lights up the early morning sky. "What the fuck is going on?" Maya blurted.

Before he can respond the phone rings while an explosion is heard. It's definitely heavy artillery and it's getting closer. Grabbing the ringing phone, "This is Williams." "I sure as hell did." "What..?" An explosion, closer yet. "Yes sir, we're moving now."

He dropped the phone as the others enter the room. "We're under attack; this safe house has been compromised. The premises have been marked for bombardment by our enemies. We need to get out, remote detonate and go to our rendezvous point for an emergency evacuation. Now."

Everyone grabs their rifles and some ammo clips. They sprint about a hundred yards away, ready to set off their explosives. Just as Williams does that an artillery shell hits their Hummers. They watch for a few seconds as the flames light up the early morning sky, the fire's glowing fingers reaching skyward.

Williams detonated his charges, adding to the noise and flames of the last blast. At a fast-paced lope, they head away from the shelling. After a mile or so they spot a quick flashing of lights around seventy-five yards ahead of them. They sprinted for the lights, finding a waiting escort outside two Jeeps. They jumped in as the vehicles speed away. The driver of William's Jeep tells him that they don't know how, but the location was found out. We can hide your team in an underground area for the next eighteen hours, then you will be flown out of here by a chopper.

****

Once they are at the new safe location Maya continued on with her thoughts to Rick regarding her conversation with Stone. "I've had the same thoughts as Stone, Eddie Fallon and others who don't believe the official version…"

"I was there," Rick interrupted. "I still believe to this day that no one would have survived that last explosion."

"I know," she said. "Just hear me out. "Forget everything about survival or not. Just think about this. Why do our CIA contacts refuse to acknowledge any details or answer any questions about Dirk or Myers other than the fact they died?

"Or that I had several personal items of Dirk's that the CIA told me to dump them; including a picture of his parents?

"And why were my letters to his parents returned unopened; marked address unknown, yet without postal markings anywhere on the envelopes?"

"I never knew that," Rick replied.

"I never told anyone for about two years until I told Megan. I swore her to secrecy and she never told you. That's why she's my best friend."

Rick sat stoned face and just nodded.

"This whole thing stunk twenty years ago, it still stinks today, and it will stink tomorrow. That mail was grabbed by the CIA for one reason and one reason only…"

Rick braced himself and grimaced.

Her voice rising, she continued, "Dirk is alive and has been hidden off the official intelligence grid all these years. And I plan on finding him and I won't quit this time until I do." When she finally finished she was really on a roll. Her jaw was jutted, and her green eyes were flashing. She was mad, defiant and ready to take on whoever thought they were going to stop her.

"Okay," said Rick. "Just lower your voice a bit, people are starting to stare."

Maya looked around and saw he was right. "Sorry," she said. "Private conversation."

Rick said, "You make several exceptionally strong points." He brings his left fist to his mouth, almost like he wanted to bite it; trying to choose the right words. After a moment he responded; "Tell you what, when we get back to London, we can look deeper into this. Just one thing; we can't allow this to interfere with our official work. Deal?"

"Deal."

Chapter 3

London

It's mid-afternoon as Maya enters her office. It was a two hour debrief for her and Williams as the senior leaders of the just completed Beirut operation. The mission, while it got a little wild at the end, was a success. The weapons were destroyed in what turned out to be a joint effort by the British commandos and the advancing Hezbollah fighters. They were able to escape the attack on the safehouse and the team was flown out of the outskirts of the city after lying low for about eighteen hours.

The biggest question, at least in her mind; how was the safehouse located by the enemy shortly after their arrival? That location, which she found and established with MI6 resources, had been used for several years with no problems. It had a strong cover punctuated by the fact that several locals had utilized the facility for many legitimate purposes as well as semi-military operations. In addition to several local businessmen gathering there, they also had a guerilla group meet there for several days.

Whatever may have been the case, in this type of operation sometimes the enemy is just lucky. Perhaps someone had a hunch and happen to stumble upon the place while they were prepping for an operation and were watching the place. Yeah, right. When you assume.. it can come back to bite you in the ass and sometimes it's a big bite.

Rick wasn't able to join her, so this left her plenty of time to reflect and recall as she puttered around her office. She quickly scanned several intel reports. She saw nothing to catch her attention so she continued walking around before settling into a nice side chair.

She's been leery and suspicious of coincidences since the disaster early on in her career and it played right into the al-Faw mess. She always believed that someway, somehow, on that fateful night they walked into a pre-arranged death trap. Someone ratted them out, and in spite of her best efforts she was never able to pinpoint definitively the guilty party. Yes, party. No evidence was ever found to dissuade her belied that more than one person directed the counter offensive. The plan was so intricate that while one maestro may have planned it, it took the involvement of others to have successfully pull it off.

Her own investigation was sweeping with everyone in the chain of command, both Great Britain and American leaders, initial suspects until they were cleared one by one. A leak here or there, careless or purposeful. A compromised officer, a double agent. It would have most assuredly happened within MI6 and/or the CIA, but no real hard leads materialized.

At one point she held a strong belief a clerk or an analyst might have been turned. Her interest peaked when a London analyst went missing; he was later found dead behind an off-base bar. He was drunk and found with no ID or money. A robbery gone bad was the conclusion. Maybe, but he was killed because he knew too much? Again, no concrete evidence ever emerged to cast doubt on the reported assumption.

She even went so far as to suspect Whit Johnson even though he wasn't in the chain of command. Both her and Dirk, especially Dirk, believed it was possible he was dealing in more ways than for the MI6 operation. The incidence at the warehouse, where she killed two of his assets, certainly provided motive; a perfect way to gain revenge. However, Sir Hillary vouched for him; saying he was cleared by the formal inquest. Perhaps a loose string, perhaps not.

****

Headquarters, London. It is where Maya has been based for most of the past twenty years; sometimes it's been liberating other times confining. God, has it really been that long, twenty years? It doesn't seem possible. She was a young, idealistic officer and now, a wise veteran of twenty-fours experience; a Supervising Agent attached to the Intelligence Department. Suddenly her thoughts are interrupted by a voice in the doorway.

"Awful quiet in here Maya, did you come into sleep or did you just die? If you died, say something so I can remove your old carcass before it starts to stink up the joint."

Maya looks up to see her number two, Kate Jackson, slouched against the doorway with her right hand on her jutted hip, defiant and self-assured. Kate sports a lean, somewhat lanky build, tall but not as tall as Maya, as blonde and light skinned as Maya is dark. Captivating brown eyes, a pretty smile and a quick wit; they shared several common traits. They have proven to be a spectacular team with numerous takedowns and recoveries to their credit.

"Just thinking," Maya replied.

"I thought I smelled something burning in here. I just didn't realize you were using the gray matter. Did you read the reports I left you?"

"I did, nothing interesting caught my attention," said Maya.

Kate sauntered in and takes a seat at Maya's desk. "I was kind of hiding this one from you," as she searched Maya's worktable. She gathers the report and hands it to her. "Read this, it will knock your socks off."

Maya started reading the papers. It's about an intelligence operation against a black-market weapons dealer in Afghanistan located along the Pakistani border. A reported operation run by the Taliban; perhaps with the implicit consent of Pakistani intelligence, certainly right under their nose. The small compound had been raided by a US Navy Seal team and CIA personnel; in an overnight operation. The takedown was accomplished when the main storage building was breached from the rear using precise location of C4 or a similar explosive. According to sources in the field it was a very concise, professional operation. The building would have been solid until suddenly a rectangular section of the building would have just been blown away. The explosives would have needed to be placed in such a fashion to have avoided any weapons which may have been stored in the back of the building.

"This action occurred three weeks ago and is the tenth similar operation in the last nineteen months in the mid-east/north Africa territory; and the third raid in the last seven months in Afghanistan," Kate said.

Clearly interested now, Maya finished reading the report and then reads it a second time.

When she finished Kate said, "Step into my office, I've put together a little presentation."

Maya followed her to the several giant computer screens which are tracking general troop locations. Pointing at a map she said, "Is this the general location where Dirk trained Afghani fighters and where you and Rick conducted your rescue mission twenty years ago?"

"It sure looks like it," Maya replied.

Kate asked. "And, if anyone knew that area exceptionally well it would be Dirk, correct?"

Maya, with an intense look on her face answered, "Agreed."

Kate winced, not sure how to continue. Before she could go on, Maya interrupted. "Alright," she said, "it's time to tell you about the action in Beirut the other night."

Maya tells Kate about the action with the U.S. Green Beret and her conversation with the team leader after the action concluded.

"Damn Maya," said Kate. "How come you never told me you were conducting this type of work again?"

"It's only the second time I been on an operation like this. The other types I have left a secure base have been when you and I have performed a little espionage. Besides, that's not the point I trying to make."

"I know where you are going with this story," Kate said. "It's just, it's just; he's been missing for the last twenty years, and you have been told both officially and unofficially that he was killed during your operation in Iraq. And, how long had you spent a lot of time searching for him, only to come up empty handed?"

"Seven long years, then sporadically since. But I never fully accepted what I was told at any point back then. And then, off and on over the last ten years."

"You know I love you like a sister," Kate said, then paused. "So, I ask, are you sure you ready to do this one more time, perhaps to only meet heartbreak again?"

"Yes. I'm even more certain because Dirk's old Green Beret team also believed he somehow survived. If anyone had a strong intuition about the situation, it would be those guys. Plus, the song and dance they also received from official U.S. government sources only strengthens my belief."

Silence. Kate saw the look of determination in Maya's face and noted how she clenched her jaw and neck muscles; nothing was going to sway her away from this inquest. "Okay, I'm in for whatever you need."

"We'll work out a plan together, like we always have," Maya said. "And, promise me that no matter how hard I try to convince you otherwise, whatever you do, don't surrender your skepticism to me. I am really going to need you to keep me focused, balanced, and centered."

Silently wondering what she has gotten herself into, she nodded her head. "I've got your back."

Chapter 4

After Kate left Maya returned to contemplating. Twenty years. Where has it gone. So much has changed, so much has remained the same. The new, she directs a staff now, Kate and three other analysts. The new responsibilities keep her mostly chained to a desk. Maya wasn't sure initially how well she would adopt to being tied to a desk. However, her superiors, some say on orders from Sir Hilary, wouldn't let her stray far from headquarters; therefore, it was adapt or leave. Since she wouldn't think of leaving, she was stuck behind a desk.

Although it was never stated, she understood why she was being 'protected' and as long as she filled a very valuable role as one of MI6 best analysts, no one complained.

Resigned, she attacked her new assignment with her typical aplomb; rising to the rank of Supervising Agent with her own group of analysts. This part of the job she really enjoyed as she was responsible for hiring her own staff and overseeing their development. Since her did a great job with her people, her ranks were often raided for the talented staff. Although somewhat miffed, in fact one time she had to stop a transfer as it would have left a staff too green and inexperienced; she was also appreciative that other supervisors valued her people. She was a talented evaluator of people and trained them well.

She is a mother now; a single mom; never married, raised a son on her own with outside assistance.

First there was her family. Her parents who were a just magnificent; in her opinion they went above and beyond the normal grandparent role. There were never any questions about who the father was and why isn't he available to perform his duties; they helped with no questions asked.

Her father also played the role of father to her son in fact, they became good buddies. And, her mother provided a lot of help and direction; she was always available. Plus, her sisters relished the role of being aunts; providing babysitting and other activities.

Then there was uncle Rick and aunt Megan. Nicky spent a lot of time with their two boys, one a year older than him and the other two years younger. Rick became a father figure and took Nicky along with his sons whenever he could; in fact, the boys referred to themselves as brothers. And, it made life a lot easier for Maya. It really does take a village to raise a child and she was grateful for everyone's assistance.

She never talked much to Nicky about his father. When he was three, he noticed other boys with their fathers, including Rick boys. He wanted to know, where was my daddy? She told him he was unable to come home because he had been badly injured. Later, shortly after he turned ten, Maya grandfather died. While Nicky understood what had happened to pop-pop, he asked his mother; is this what happened to my dad? She responded that his daddy was injured in a battle and died as a result of those injuries. He was a hero, and saved many lives including my own. That seemed to satisfy his curiosity.

As for her own life, Maya dated a few times but nothing serious ever developed. Initially, she thought perhaps it was because of how her relationship ended with Dirk and the lack of true closure. Maybe so. But as Nicky got older his wants became paramount, so she had another excuse. Plus, with Nicky fitting in with Rick and his sons, she didn't want to upset his life when it was working so well. Her own personal life could wait.

****

With a minimal love life, Maya focused intently on work, much like she had always done. She maintained her superior shooting skills and won nearly every skill contest she entered. To satisfy her need for action, she was allowed to instruct new recruits on basic rifle skills while for the advanced riflemen she taught sniper skills.

Her physical appearance had undergone subtle changes. She wore her hair a little longer than in the past; it was still jet black as she attacked the few foreign invading colors with a vengeance. And those green eyes still smiled or flashed depending on what the situation called for. Both Nicky and Rick's boys knew what it meant when Maya gave that laser eyed, glare; they froze in place; with a total change in behavior resulting.

She also worked hard with her physical training; in fact, she was in great shape for someone in their late forties. She could still keep pace with some of the new guys on the obstacle course. Only the elite guys could smoke her, and once in a while she could beat some of the slower guys. Tip top physical condition because; as a friend once said, to be ready, you know, when just in case happens, like with Beirut.

Finally, after Nicky had turned twelve, she was on occasion allowed, under certain conditions, to follow the commandos into the field to direct live action from a secured location. The conditions were to ensure there would be no more combat roles like with al-Faw, at least not on purpose. She accepted the restrictions as it got her out of the office from time to time. And, she still liked the adrenaline rush from being out, even though she was nowhere near the real action. Plus, she got to work with an analyst from the commandos since no one on her staff liked venturing from the office.

When she asked her parents to watch Nicky for an extended period of time on first assignment, her mother was horrified when Maya explained what she was going to do and where. While her mother knew better than to try the guilty trip of how could-a-mother abandon her only child, Maya still had a lot of explaining to do. She worked very persuasively to convey that the work would be performed at a well secured military base in Germany. She would never leave the base while she coordinated commando raids in real time on a computer screen. When she finished her father totally understood which helped soothe her mother. When Maya returned home alive without a scratch on her, mom was extremely happy.

Her forays into the field where the real action happened, had been greatly diminished. Again, she was confined to highly secured field bases. And, no operation had ended as Beirut did. Never, under any conditions ever; did she have to flee a breached safe house. Events moved so quickly she never had the time to consider if she was scared. However, she had to admit she that liked, no, loved the exhilaration, the blood pumping, the adrenaline flowing. Still a bit of a thrill seeker. And she liked how she still had it, how she could dig down deep and rev up the body, the old senses kicking in. But, yeah, that type of excitement was in the past, perhaps for the better. That is, until she hired Kate Jackson and new ventures began.

****

Kate was a Royal Navy diver, trained to plant explosives to clear underwater obstacles blocking harbors and ports. In just a short time she had shown herself to be very skilled, including a letter of commendation from her commander. When Maya finished reading her file, she was a bit confused why Kate was sent for an interview for an analyst position. Nevertheless, she decided not to reject her for an insufficient background; she wanted to listen to the woman's story.

When Maya interviewed Kate, she encountered a bright individual looking for a career change. She enjoyed her time in the water but didn't view diving as a long-term career option. The analyst work, she believed, would provide her that permanent position. Maya didn't pry too deeply into her story; Kate confirmed what was in the personnel file; she was simply looking for a new line of work. Overall, Maya was impressed with her background and how she presented herself. She hired her without hesitation.

Given her background it was obvious that Kate was a thrill seeker, just like Maya. And, like Maya, she also struggled a bit at first while adapting to the office routine. When one of the other analyst's mentioned to Maya that Kate seemed distracted and was having trouble with simple assignments, Maya decided to offer her some extra attention. She believed it was time to learn the true reason why Kate stopped diving.

During a casual conversation after the office had emptied for the day, Maya told Kate how she encountered some difficulties with a major career change. She highlighted her experience at al-Faw that led her into the inside position. It was a major culture shock and she floundered for a while as she lacked her normal physical outlet. Understanding how difficult it must have been for Maya to relate her story, Kate in turn opened up as well.

She told a surprised Maya why she had migrated into the intelligence services after she was almost killed and her partner died during a training accident. The official investigation disclosed the incident was an unfortunate accident that resulted from defective equipment. Since that incident it has been impossible for her to go into any body of water. All of her work since returning to active duty had been strictly above water.

When she finished, although Kate didn't provide details about what happened; Maya completely understood. She recognized the pained expression on her face, it was probably the same look she had in the aftermath of al-Faw. She now fully understood how Kate's life was dramatically altered through fate; her situation in many respects mirrored her own. Since Kate was an outstanding recruit the Navy did their best to save her career. They created a non-existent position in their intelligence unit and kept her there while she worked her way back from her trauma. Eventually an analyst position opened up in MI6 and she was transferred over.

Kate drew inspiration and renewed confidence from Maya's story. She threw herself totally into learning the job and proving her worth. In fact, to her own surprise and Maya's; she volunteered to accompany her to a military base to provide real time guidance on a commando rescue of British aid workers. Maybe if it had been an underwater assignment, things might have been different in her mind. Still, the decisions came with life and death implications and Kate didn't falter. She proved to herself she could still excel under duress.

When Kate had been with her for five years, Maya thought Kate had gained sufficient knowledge and showed great decision-making skills. While they were working in Ankara Turkey, Maya decided to hit her with the big request. "Would you like to work off-base missions with me?"

Since she had some knowledge of Maya's prior work history, she responded, "Before I can answer I need you to clarify what you are proposing; I have no interest in exchanging gunfire with anyone."

Maya chuckled a bit at that question before she answered. "I occasionally conduct clandestine operations into the surrounding area outside of the base of operation. The work has strictly been espionage missions; watching, observing, passing false information to disrupt the bad guys; perhaps some breaking and entering to steal stuff, but never any gun play. If I had a partner the amount of work could be increased."

"Was it safe?" Kate wanted to know.

"I've been doing it for two years now without a problem; in fact, I've never encountered another person while off-site," Maya said.

To make a long story short, Kate agreed and they became a phenomenal team. The extracurricular events provided enough pulse raising action to satisfy the thrill seeker in each of them.

****

Wow, ten years. They had developed a strong bond over that time; an ability to read each other's moods and thoughts. They evolved into elite analysts and developed an outstanding team that supported their work. The team had accomplished a wide variety of missions that ranged from tracking black market weapons dealers, to raiding smuggling rings to hunting for terrorists, including their assistance early on in the search for Osama Bin-Laden. They were the first team who tracked him to his hide-out at Tora-Bora mountain and shared this information with the CIA. They were among those who watched in stunned disbelief at the dilly-dallying the Americans engaged in. That fuck up, official protocol they called it, allowed the Afghanis to lead the final assault, that ultimately led to Bin Laden's escape into Pakistan. All this means they had been through a lot together and a strong bond had grown between them. So, when Kate said she had her back, Maya knew she was fully committed. And to succeed she knew she needed someone she could trust with her life.

Chapter 5

Three different times over the first seven years Maya had investigated reported identification of men who looked like Winter. The first time, and perhaps the most promising was eighteen months after the al-Faw action. The man in question was photographed by an MI6 officer leaving a meeting the officer had attended concerning a warehouse take down in Cairo, Egypt. The man in question sported a red beard and bore a strong resemblance to Winter physically. The capper for Maya was when the warehouse was breached two days later using the same technique Winter developed to be used when dealing with near impenetrable structures. The laying of the explosives was very precise. The building was opened and the hostages were rescued; alive and unharmed.

Maya did her best to track the mystery man through her MI6 friends in field operations. After three months the man just suddenly disappeared somewhere in Germany. Later a message came through official channels asking why MI6 was trailing a CIA asset. At least he worked for the Americans.

Sir Hilary's himself denied the action and said there was no official effort being engaged to intercept any asset being used by a friendly agency. Through unofficial channels a warning was issued to halt any attempts to surveil CIA assets or officers. When Maya received the communication she simply shrugged and professed her ignorance of the incident. After receiving the message she put her efforts on hold. She gathered the file she had put together and took it home.

Three years passed before another potential hit occurred. The genesis of this action was based off an oral report of a similar breach of a warehouse where smuggled weapons were stored. The action was a fast raid, the building was breached, and the weapons recovered. Maya spent close to six months tracking down leads before concluding the raid was a U.S. Special Forces operation; perhaps Dirk's old team that she worked with in Egypt. Another false alarm.

The third possibility centered on an individual who, from facial pictures, could have passed for Winter's twin according to Maya aging analysis. Again, close to a year was expended with Maya actually convinced by photographic evidence that this time was for real and her hopes were high. Finally, the man was located right in London.

She thought it odd that Winter, being a CIA paramilitary officer, would be assigned to London. That was usually a posting of a different nature from someone with Winter's specialized talents. Nevertheless, she was too invested not to find out for sure. She was able to arrange for an 'accidental meetup' at a restaurant coordinated through a mutual acquaintance. As she entered the place her heart sped up as she spied a man with a profile matching Dirk's sitting at the bar. As she approached, the man turned and faced her. His hair was darker, a dye job perhaps to hide his true identity. He smiled at her as she took the barstool next to him, and they exchanged greetings; Maya Thernopolis meet George Brown. Hmm.., could be a fake name as well if Dirk was in hiding.

After some brief small talk the man's name was called and he rose to lead her to a table the waiter waved them to. When George stood she immediately knew he wasn't Dirk. The clinching clue was the guy was sporting a small paunch over his belt. Dirk would never let himself get out of shape as she believed him to still be an active officer who was blowing buildings and leading raids. No way, impossible.

Over dinner she learned he was a civilian, a British bloke. He turned out to be a real sweet guy. He was single, battling hard to raise a daughter. He and his daughter were left alone after his wife was killed in a car accident. Tragic, thought Maya; his status not too different from her own.

Still Maya was intrigued, and she even went out on a few dates with him. The relationship ended after an incident when he arrived to pick her up for a date. He admitted to having had a few, she could smell it on his breath, before coming over. She turned to reach for a light jacket when he grabbed her and spun her around. His hands immediately went to her breasts which he squeezed hard. Totally stunned at first, she pulled away, shifted her weight, then pushed him back. He reacted my making a big mistake; he slapped her and smiled. He definitely had her by a good fifty pounds, but she had handled bigger men than him before. In what seemed to have occurred in the blink of an eye, George ended up on the floor, blood pouring through his hand which was covering his nose. She opened the door, yanked him to his feet and shoved him through. She watched as stumbled down the steps and fell on his face.

And, wouldn't you know, about an hour later the bastard came back with the police to have her arrested for assault. The bobby listened to both parties; not believing for a minute Maya had caused the damage; a broken nose; which had managed to stop bleeding. When Maya produced her MI6 ID, the bobby asked if she wished to press charges. He dragged the cursing lout out of the house and stood on the sidewalk. He told the guy that if he was smart, he would never return here, the next time the result could be worse. When the guy threatened to return with a gun, he was hauled down to the station. No reason to let things escalate to the point where Maya would have to shoot the dumb bastard in self-defense.

That whole debacle was a tough one. While it was impossible to determine if a true relationship would have blossomed, Maya had genuinely liked him. She had invested four months with the guy, even opened up to him which was always difficult for her to do. A few days after the incident a police sergeant returned and told her Brown had two prior arrests for drunkenly assaulting women; couldn't handle his booze. It was also the first time he took the brunt of an assault; he had been slapped before but never knocked on his ass with a bloody nose.

That was an explanation, but the episode still hurt. She wasn't sure if she would trust again, giving her further reason to shut off that part of her life. The fallout affected Maya for several weeks.

Chapter 6

The next day in the office Maya was beginning to lay out and process the latest intelligence information. She had to determine how to move forward and formulate a course of action. Over the ensuing years potential events transpired during her on again, off again search. Only reports that fit the general criteria Maya had established; namely an individual who employed similar operating procedures that matched Winter's work, would elicit a look-see from her. She decided actual sightings proved to be too unreliable; besides, had anyone allowed for his look to age? It's possible a person could have swapped beers with him and not even be aware of that if they focused on the appearance of the younger Winter.

She paced, thinking, asking herself why would this time be any different? The rumors had actually dried up with nothing coming in over the last five years. Why should one expect a positive outcome after twenty years of nothing but swings and misses?

Because this time I didn't actually instigate this quest, she reasoned; rather it came from Dirk's former Green Beret comrades. She realized now she was speaking out loud. She looked up, wondering if anyone had heard her. The office was still empty; besides it didn't matter.

The former Green Beret team knew Dirk's operational tactics extremely well, maybe even better than Maya, and they were convinced he was still an active operator. And, the runaround they encountered when they tried to investigate, was the exact same stonewalling Maya ran into. No definitive proof but.., she was just convinced.

Kate came into the office, peeked into Maya room and said good morning. No response; Maya was lost in her own world and thoughts. Kate turned around and went to the coffee pot; empty. She whipped together the ingredients and inhaled as the pot started to brew. There's nothing like the smell of percolating java in the morning.

The more she paced around the office, the more revved she became, even ignoring the aroma coming from the other office. The premises and ideas were coming fast and furious. Her chest was pounding a bit and her pulse quickened, she was hyped and ready to restoke the hunt.

The Afghan provinces of Badakhshan, Nurestan, Konar, Nangarhar, Paktiya, Khost, Paktika, Zabul, Kandahar, Helmand, and Nimruz; located along the Pakistani border, she knew they were Dirk's old haunts. Taking the position that he is still an active operator, it would make perfect sense for the CIA to assign him to territory he has knowledge about.

Maya stopped and sat down at her computer. Tapping her fingers on her chin, she suddenly snapped her fingers and typed into a search field. A few minutes of searching, then select and print. She waited for a few minutes, then the office printer sputtered to life. Was that a wheezing noise? That sucker needed to be replaced before it stopped working in the middle of printing an important report. She made a note to place another order this afternoon; the prior two had been ignored. Silence. She got out of her chair and walked over to the desk that printer sat on. She picked up the papers and flipped to the end; it looks like the report is intact. Whew!

"Hey Kate, we need to order another printer," she called out, then, "Is that coffee I smell?"

"This will be the fourth try for a new printer," came the reply. "Yes, the coffee is ready; has been for ten minutes. I wondered when you would come back to earth."

Maya got up and walked over to pour a cup. She inhaled, hmm. "I thought this would be the third request," she said.

"Whatever."

"And, call your friend, what's his name."

"It's Steve in IT," Kate replied. "I've called him so many times he may start to think I want to go on a date with him."

"At least one of us may find some action. Now stop your chattering, I've got a report to read."

"I didn't," said Kate, but she stopped herself, deciding it was better to quit.

It was a report of another raid. Maya eyes opened wide when she read the date; this morning; it was fresh. The information was developed by an MI6 analyst running an op in North Africa. MI6 was swapping satellite information with the CIA and Mossad forces that were tracking a Muslim oil smuggling operation.

Maya looked up to see Kate has wandered into the doorway of her office. "Do we have an analyst in North Africa right now?"

"Yeah, I forgot to tell you. I sent Ray Scott over there while you were in Beirut. They are tracking an oil smuggling ring that is supplying Taliban forces with money. Why?"

"I just finished reading his report concerning a raid in Afghanistan that happened last night," Maya said. She paused while she drummed a pen on her desk, thinking. She finally said, "I need your help."

"Of course, what do you need?"

"What information can you access regarding the raid last night?" Maya asked.

"Wait, what?" Kate replied, a bit defensively. "I won't be helping you do anything illegal."

"I not asking you to do any other than a little detective work; strictly legit. Please."

Kate turned her head away from Maya and rolled her eyes. She walked back into her office and sat down in front of her computer keyboard and started entering data. "Alright," she says after a few minutes of waiting, "That wasn't a joint action last night, it was strictly a CIA operation. It was a quick raid conducted on a weapons depot used by the Taliban to transfer weapons back and forth between Pakistan and Afghanistan."

A few more keystrokes then Kate said, "Some intelligence was grabbed from hard copies of documents and computer disks located on site. In addition, two men were captured in the process of destroying evidence. They were transported to Kandahar for interrogation."

"Was the building blown?"

Kate read a little more then answered; "Nope, the door was kicked down."

"Do you know the names of the CIA field officers involved, are they listed in the report.?

"Maya, how many times have we gone down this road?"

Silence.

"Exactly, too many to count." She reads on. "There is no listing of any operative by the name of Dirk Winter, and none of the people we have contacted in the past have run across anyone with that name or any name remotely resembling that name. There are no reports of Dirk Somebody or Somebody Winter. If Winter does indeed exist, he's using a different name."

As soon as she says that Kate put her hand over her month; "Damn, I was just thinking out loud."

"Aha," exclaims Maya, "Exactly as I've thought, we believe in the same thing."

An exasperated Kate; "Maya!" she exclaimed. "Remember what you told me, I need to keep you centered? Well, here's that time. It hasn't been proven that he's alive. Besides, the building wasn't opened with explosives of any type; it doesn't fit your pattern."

Ignoring her pleas Maya continued to rattle on. "He had to change his name because somehow before our last operation in al-Faw we were outed by a double agent. He was found alive and the CIA returned him to action under a new identity. You never get rid of a great field officer. Besides, he had kicked in doors before and this was his old stomping grounds."

"Oh shit!"

"What have you got Kate?"

"Nothing," she said while trying to determine her next move. "Alright, I may have several grainy photos."

"Pictures of what or who?"

"Who."

"Come again?" Maya asked. "Who what or what who? What did you do, tell me now?" she demanded with a sharp, semi-threatening tone.

"I did nothing more than scroll on attached photos from the raid. There are several grainy photos of what appears to be the lead operator."

Maya walked into Kate office. Elbowing her aside she said, "Let me see."

"Now remember;" Kate interjected. "1) the quality of the photos are suspect at best, and 2) It is a current picture of someone we have no idea to his identity. We have no idea of what Dirk may look like today."

Maya ignored her commentary and squinted to examine the computer screen. After a few minutes she shook her head and said, "You're right on both points." She began to pace around Kate's office. "Facial recognition," she blurted.

"What about it?"

"You can access it right?"

Kate nodded in the affirmative.

"Let's create a sketch of Dirk, run it through an aging app and then take that final product and run it thorough the facial recognition software to see if anything matches."

Kate ponders for a moment. "It might work," she said. She sits at the computer and together they create a facial profile of Dirk. Maya can still see his face; remembering nearly every feature on it. They then start using the aging component. They came to an agreement on what they believed to be two possible future looks for Dirk and ran them through the facial recognition software. A hit; Jason Cameron.

Maya is visibly excited as she thrusted her arms in the air and shouted "Yes, I've have found him."

"Whoa, time out," said Kate to the cheering Maya. "Centering time again. This is highly speculative at best and the odds it isn't him are probably greater than the odds it is him."

"No, I finally have something, no someone, to track. It's a real live person and the best chance I've ever had to solving this mystery."

Kate, recognizing she's losing the centering battle, admits to herself she also excited. "Okay, what's next? You know absolutely nothing about this person; like who does he work for, where is he right now; and so on."

Dropping back down to earth from her emotional high, Maya acknowledged what Kate has said. "You're right, I really know nothing." Back to pacing, then, "How about this, let's try to find out what we can about Jason Cameron. We will learn this by finding out who he works for."

"And, how will you accomplish this?"

"We will do this by the process of elimination."

"What, exactly, does that mean?" Kate asked.

"I'm betting Jason Cameron either works as an intelligence officer or is a soldier. I say we start with searching through the British personnel data bases first. If we strike out, we move on to the next most likely source, The United States."

"By we you mean you and I, right?"

"Of course, what else are best friends for if not partners in crime?"

Kate's eyes opened wide in a 'You must be crazy look' before Maya added, "Besides, if we're caught and locked away, I'll ask for you to be my roomie."

"I'm not sure I like you that much Maya. How do you know I wouldn't smother you in your sleep?"

Maya sticks out her lower lip in a pouty face. "Aww, you would hurt your best friend?"

"No, not really." Then, "Alright, what the hell. The sad part is I have nothing else going on in my life. And stop the face, you look ridiculous."

Maya answered with smile, "This has to be done in our spare time and on the QT."

****

Over the next several weeks they slowly began their adventure. The troop action was hot and furious in Afghanistan and Iraq as the British stood tall with their American counterparts in the fight against terrorism. Planning and coordinating with the troop commanders to ensure pinpoint sighting for bombing campaigns, piloting drones, tracking the movement of enemy troops and directing raids, among other duties, keep their unit busy nearly nonstop.

Finally, after five weeks of near round the clock work for the team, Maya found an opportunity to contact the central personnel office. She said she was looking for information on an applicant, she believed the name was Jason Cameron (just s small lie). She had received a file on him that stated he was seeking an analyst's position. She would like to contact him for an interview; however, I seemed to have misplaced the paperwork. She further explained they were short-handed and really needed another top-notch person. A personnel clerk said she would get back to her in a day or two with an answer. Great, Maya thought, that's probably a week minimum.

Four days had passed when Kate fielded a call from personnel regarding their urgent need for a new analyst. Since she had no knowledge of Maya's scheme, she told the caller that she was mistaken, they were fully staffed. After a few minutes of back and forth, each of them insisted they were right, she rang into Maya. "I've got this lady from personnel on the phone, blathering on and on about a new analyst position we urgently need to fill. I said we were fully staffed and that no one would have called. She insisted that her supervisor told her to respond to us. It's your turn with her. She's on line two, good luck!"

Wracking her brain for a reason why personnel would be calling them, Maya warily answered the phone and listened, still trying to come up with an answer. The woman identified herself as a supervisor. The personnel clerk who called was responding to a request for a file on a Jason Cameron.

When the lady mentioned Maya came to life. "I apologize for zoning out for a moment, we've been extremely busy. What did you find out about my job candidate?"

Kate walked into Maya's office and took a seat and wondered what was going on. Maya flipped on the speaker.

"My department searched our internal records and came up with nothing," said the personnel supervisor. "This individual, who name is spelled J-a-s-o-n C-a-m-e-r-o-n, doesn't work for either British intelligence or the British military. Are you sure of the name and it's spelling?"

"The name, yes, on the spelling I'm not sure," said Maya. "When I called in I said I had lost the file and was guessing on the spelling. If I do a better job of remembering I will contact you again. Thank you for your help."

After she hung up she said to Kate, "Well, at least we know he's not in the employment of our government."

"Now what?"

"Well, I'm going to assume he's an American. My conversation with his old Green Beret unit leader indicated he's didn't rejoin special forces. Therefore, I going to conclude he's still with the CIA. Any way we could tap CIA records?"

Kate just stares with a horrified look like are you crazy?

"Just kidding. Relax your face before it freezes like that. You could scare rats away with that look."

Kate gave her the bird, got up and walked back to her office.

What now indeed, she thinks as she begins tapping a pencil on her desk. Before she can get too lost in her thoughts, the phone rings. Back to the war and the real world.

****

Two days later, the push in Afghanistan has subsided leaving Maya with a chance to work on her other project. Chatting with Kate she said, "So, if we accept the premise that Dirk is alive and still works for the CIA, where would he be stationed?"

"Still we, huh."

"Of course, it is. Now, are you going to help me think this through or not?"

Kate hemmed and hawed, then chimed in. "Well, if we believe he led the raid near the Pakistani border that happened about a week ago my guess is he is somewhere near Kandahar."

"I tend to agree. There is also a chance he could be working from the Pakistan side of the border, but regardless, he should be somewhere in that general vicinity."

"Right," said Kate. "In addition to our MI6 location, the CIA still has a station over there. Maybe one of our guys can give you some help." She walked over to the window and stared outside, it late June and summer has just started. She stepped away and checked her watch; noon, no wonder her stomach is talking.

"Hey, I'm hungry. It's a beautiful, warm sunny day, so I'm going to go out and grab a bite. Want to join me?"

"Nah, but if you could bring back a sandwich for me that would be great."

"You know Maya, you need to get out of the office every so often, otherwise you brain will turn to mush."

"Not today, too busy."

"Sure. Same order as usual I suppose?" Kate said as she heads toward the door.

"Absolutely, when something is good why change."

"Got it Ms. Predictable," said Kate as she closed Maya's office door. "See you in a few."

****

Shortly after one Kate strolled back into Maya's office and dropped a brown paper bag on her desk. "Per your request," she said.

Maya opened up the bag and took out the sandwich. "Gyro with chicken, from our favorite place Greek place?"

"Of course."

Maya takes a bite, hmm., tasty as usual. "What do I owe you?" she said between bites.

Kate wavers off the request, "You buy the next time. Accomplish anything while I was gone?"

"I never stop working when on the hunt. I called Rick Williams and found out his unit is deploying to Kandahar in two weeks."

Kate raises her left eyebrow and tilts her head as she hesitatingly inquired, "Okay, I guess; but what has his deployment have to do with us?"

Maya smiles.

"Oh no, tell me, you didn't." She started to pace. "No, you didn't, did you?"

"No, I didn't, headquarters reached out to me." Maya said. "After I finished my call to Rick, I fielded a call from the director's office. We are rotating to Afghanistan next Tuesday. We will be in Kandahar to coordinate and provide logistical support to clandestine and non-clandestine operations originating from our joint base with the Americans and our other allies. So, Rick's unit won't be the only group we will be working with when we go on-site."

"At least you didn't volunteer our services, Kate said."

"Would it have made a difference?" asked Maya.

Kate stopped pacing Maya's office and thought about the prospect for a minute, then replied, "No, not really. It's the job I signed up for."

"Besides," said Maya. "It should be easier to determine if Winter is alive and operating from the main base there. That will increase the odds of finding him."

Kate grimaced a bit.

"Look, I need to find closure one way or the other," she continued.

"I didn't say anything,"

"It was the look on your face. Look, if I do the work, with your assistance, it will be for real. There will be no misunderstood communications like those that can occur with other parties involved. And if he's truly gone, it will be hard, but I'll be able to accept it and move on."

"Okay, let's say you succeed and, let's make this a happy ending, and you find he's alive, well, and roaming around back and forth between Afghanistan and Pakistan. Then what? He's been avoiding you for the last twenty years, do you really want to rush to him?"

Maya thinks for a moment, she hadn't really thought that far ahead of that possibility. She just wanted some kind of finality to everything, to know for certain that he did or didn't survive that raid on Al-Faw. Yet, deep in her heart, if she's still pursing every potential scrap of information to locate him after all these years, deep down she's still clinging to something; hope, or maybe an unwillingness to deal with the truth. But something still drives her to continue reach out, and that reason is the faintest hope that he's somehow, somewhere, still alive. Besides, who says he hasn't tried to find me. And maybe after running into the same obstacles I have, he found it impossible to keep looking.

She looks at Kate who's still waiting for an answer. In a concise, unemotional response she replied, "I'll cross that bridge when I get to it."

Chapter 7

Kandahar, Afghanistan

In the early evening on a hot, Wednesday in early July a British transport plane arrives at Kandahar loaded with troops, supplies and two passengers from MI-6 rotating in to provide logistical support for MI6 and CIA missions. After disembarking from the plane, a British airman hands each of them a cold bottle of water, even though it's evening the thermometer still reads a robust ninety-five degrees. It quite a difference from the low to mid seventy-degree temps back in London.

After the passengers grabbed their bags, they followed the airman across the tarmac, taking long swallows from the bottles. He walked them to a parked car with British insignias on it. He leaned in and told the driver where to take them. The driver salutes and takes off.

The car stopped in front the base's main operations facility for British personnel. The driver gave them directions, telling them to hang a left once inside the building, they will be taken care of from there. A burly individual arises to greet them as they walked through the door.

"Ladies, welcome to Afghanistan, the hottest spot for clandestine operations in the world." Noting the water each one is carrying, he continues, "And today was a cooler day. Just a bit warmer than London, wouldn't you agree?"

They both wiped sweat from their brows and nodded in agreement.

The man watched Kate's facial expression change as a fighter jet roared off; must be a rookie. "Don't worry," he said, "you'll get used to it."

As the ladies removed their shades, his gaze is fixated on the taller of the two women. While her partner is tall for a woman, this one's height dominates every other woman at the base, including her partner. In fact, he believes, she's taller than some of the men on site. All eyes are on her as she strode across the room.

Their greeter thinks the tall woman looks somewhat familiar; I think I know her from another time. Hmm…maybe not; but then, it could be. The tall woman squints to adjust her vision, looks the man over and has the same thoughts. I believe I know him. Kate extends her right hand.

"Kate Jackson, MI6 analyst," she said, breaking the awkward silence.

The other woman follows suit, "Maya Thernopolis," she said, "and you are?"

"Whit Johnson," the man says as he shakes their hands. "Welcome."

Simultaneously, Johnson and Thernopolis think, yes, twenty, maybe twenty-one years ago on an assignment in Cypress. Jackson handed him some paperwork that Johnson quickly scans. "So, ladies, I see you've spent the last fifteen months in London, why are you coming to hell? As you can tell it's extremely hot, dirty, dusty and you're in the middle of a war zone, no place for a vacation.

"Just doing our duty," answered Thernopolis. She clearly wasn't happy being slammed with the vacation comment.

Interesting, Johnson says to himself. The last person I expected to run into out here is Maya Thernopolis. She's kept herself up over the years, still looks good. What ever happened to that asshole she was with? Oh yeah, now I remember, something like shit for brains. He stops his recalling to return back to the moment as everyone is staring at him.

"Hannity here," pointing to the woman on his left, "will show you around and help you get oriented to this paradise. There will be a meeting tomorrow morning at 8:00 to start bringing you two up to date on our active missions. See you then."

As Johnson walks off, Hannity rose to greet the women. "Linda," she says with an edge to her tone. "Don't worry about Johnson; he's an asshole, but he's our asshole."

Kate, unsure about what was occurring, forced a weak smile while Maya beamed a bit at the comment.

"Now," Hannity continued, "He is right about one thing. If you are used to an office in London, this will be a bit of a culture shock. Every mission is guiding operators through combat activities on a regular basis. People will get killed; the goal is to ensure it not our men. That makes this a high stress work environment."

"That alright, Linda," Maya replied. Both of us have been in field assignments in the past. No, they weren't in Afghanistan, but the stress of combat is the same regardless of where the action is taking place."

Kate nodded in agreement as she noted how Maya left out they weren't located in a country where an active war was being fought.

Taking the edge off her voice, with a slight smile, Linda went on, "Good to know. Since you are both experienced analysts, you should adapt to the place rather quickly. You will report directly to me and I will do my best to orient you to this place." Walking to the door she said, "Come on, I'll show you to your quarters. Hope you don't mind being bunkies."

As they followed Linda across the compound to their quarters, an explosion roars through the air that sounds like it's right outside the base. Kate is thinking maybe I'll just kill Maya for getting me into this mess. Nah... there would be too much paperwork to fill out, plus the extra effort to hide the body.

After two days of briefings that covered current field operations under their purview, they watched the direction of a nighttime raid by another analyst. The work would be no different than the other work they had performed when in the field. They soon fell into the routine.

Kate, however, wasn't quite sure if she liked this assignment. She was thrust into an experience she hadn't been in since she gave up her prior life as a navy diver. She wasn't prepared for the occasional gunfire or small mortar fire that was directed at the base. Most of her overseas work for MI6 was in places such as Germany, which was safe, and Spain and Turkey, which were considered relatively safe.

The craziest action she and Maya had engaged in was to scale buildings to carry out some breaking and entering operations. They had either stolen information or planted misleading documents to screw up foreign operators. Maya always led the way, and there was no gunfire or shells bursting nearby. Besides, now she was strictly a computer geek and analyst. Her need for adrenaline spikes were satisfied by being a high-class cat burglar, not a shoot'em up operator. Nor was working in a place where the 'hot action' was so close her idea of fun. Once again, she contemplated killing Maya; paperwork be damned.

Maya, on the other hand, slipped into the routine with no problem, not at all bothered by the sounds of war, even if it sounded like it was right outside the base.

Chapter 8

They had been at the base for ten days when Maya caught up with Rick Williams as he popped into her office to say hello. After the usual small talk of how are you and Kate adjusting to the environment and so on, Maya got down to her other business. She hadn't had the opportunity to talk with him regarding the progress in locating Dirk in several weeks. She took several minutes to explain to him the CIA raid near the Pakistani border, Dirk's old stomping grounds, how she believed she found his cover name, Jason Cameron; and why she believed he was operating from here.

After she finished, Rick formulated his response. He could tell from the determined look on her face that arguing would be a waste of time. "So, let look at this from the position that Dirk miraculously survived al-Faw."

Maya, caught off guard by as he readily accepted her thesis, nodded her head in agreement.

"Given all that," he continued while thinking, "it does makes sense. The border with Pakistan was an area he would know very well."

"It's where we first saved his ass twenty years ago," Maya interjected.

"Right, I remember that," Rick said. "So it would make sense that the CIA would assign an operator to territory he knew well. That assumption was paid off with the successful raid conducted several weeks ago. The question to you would be given how he slipped back and forth between the two countries border, why do you think he would be here in Afghanistan as opposed to Pakistan?"

Before Maya could answer Kate popped into the room. Rick stood to leave but Maya waved him down. "It's alright, Kate knows, she been helping me."

"I see," Rick said. Since he wasn't sure of Kate's stance on this quest, he decided to be careful with his words to avoid crossing swords with them. Finally he said, "Welcome aboard Kate."

"Glad to see there's another voice to this exercise," she said. "If I remember correctly Maya said you knew Dirk prior to the action on al-Faw. Well, what did think of our idea so far?"

"If we accept all the assumption as being correct, then I agree, it makes sense. But, as I was asking, what makes you think he's operating out of this base?"

"I don't think it really matters," said Maya. "He could be operating in Pakistan and crossing between the two countries as he sees fit, it doesn't matter. The key is he's here; not in North Africa, Venezuela, or Lebanon. And, soon or later, he will conduct an operation that will identify him."

"You make a good point," said Rick. Again, careful with his choice of words he asks, "What role do you want me to play, if anything?"

Maya, "For right now be alert."

"Come again?" Rick said.

"I now you operatives run joint missions, sometimes if even as a back-up, if you are in the operational area. I know you guys talk, especially over a few cold ones. Keep your eyes and ears open, you're bound to learn something."

"Hopefully I learn something before I return back to London," he replied. Turning to Kate, who has remained silent since entering the conversation, he asked, "What do you think?"

"This is the most detail that Maya has shared so far," Kate said. "It sounds like she been planning without my input. Seriously, I think she makes a good point, that somewhere Dirk will take on a mission that clearly signals his own unique style. As a result, hopefully, we can find him."

As the meeting breaks up, Maya opined, "This will work, it's just a matter of when, not if. Everyone, you in particular Rick, stay in touch, especially when you're in the field. That's where we will locate him."

****

A week had passed with no information from the field. Maya and Kate's work ebbed and flowed in response to their combat groups' needs. Rick's team had been randomly assigned to their oversight, a fortunate event in Maya's thinking as she would know where they would be deployed; in case of a meetup. Speaking of deployment, Rick had left on a mission three days ago to track down the source of incoming fire directed at the base. The goal was to locate the source and take it out.

Kate was in charge of running the logistics for this foray. The drone she tracked displayed images of several fighters as they dragged what appeared to be a mortar over mountainous terrain. She watched as they darted around boulders and other formations as they advanced up the mountain. About a third of the way up they entered a cave and took up positions. They had sensed they were being followed and were looking to ambush their pursuers.

Rick's called in and said the team was having trouble keeping track of the enemy. Kate told him no problem; she was seeing everything in real time. She told him to slow their pace. They were about 2 klicks ahead of you and you are closing ground too fast. The enemy has taken refuge in a cave about a third of the way up the mountain in front of you and are taking positions to attack.

You're cleared for a click, working around the formations. Even if they spot your movement, you're out of their firing range. At that point you will need to determine if you can safely work your way into firing range; otherwise fall back to a position you can hold and wait for them to move.

Ten minutes later Rick calls back. "It looks like there is a lot of open space about two hundred feet ahead of us. If we tried to move to that position the enemy would still be out of range and the natural vegetation cover we have here starts to thin out at that elevation. I think it's in our best interest to stay here for the time being."

"I agree with that assessment," said Kate. "Maya has also reviewed some satellite photos, looking for any differences from what the drone is showing; everything concurs with the images. If anything changes on the ground let us know, and we will also update you with any new information we gather. Stay covered and stay safe."

"Will do."

Rick calls his patrol, seven other men, to tell them they are hanging out for now. The fighters they have been chasing have retreated into a cave up ahead and have taken positions to attack if they come too close.

It's a message that was understood but still not well received. It's mid-July, hotter than hell as you breathe in the searing heat and dust. At least there is some shelter out of the sun behind the rock formations. He figured they would be good for maybe ninety minutes, two hours tops, then they will need to change tactics, or at least find more shaded locations. Afghanistan, fun in the summer.

One hour later Kate called back to Rick. "We have picked out activity on the far left side of the mountain. At this time we are confident this group has no idea of your team's existence. We also have no knowledge of their identity, foe or friend. Stay tight for now until we can gather more information. If it is determined you will need to leave your location we will guide your movement out."

"Roger that, we'll hold tight," Rick replied.

Twenty minutes later Rick received another call. "Maya here. We have additional information to our earlier report. Satellite photos found a group of fifteen to twenty fighters moving toward the mountain where your team is located. The drone feed shows them moving quickly along their path towards the mountain. The ease they are navigating the terrain leads us to believe they are Taliban fighters. This cave may be a major staging area, maybe a weapons storage depot, that they are interested in defending."

"You are full of such good news," said Rick. "It sounds like we need to scoot as fast as possible."

Kate walked into the room and flipped the phone on speaker. "I have another update. We are positive there is another group three klicks behind the supposed group of Taliban fighters making their way up the mountain.

At this time we believe they are our allies and are chasing the second group of fighters. We used the same technique to identify them as we did the other groups, that they are searching their way over the terrain, much as you guys did, which demonstrates unfamiliarity of the area. To confirm our guess we are contacting U.S. intelligence to see if they are running an operation similar to ours. Be ready to move quickly."

Hurry up and wait, the story of a commando's life Rick muttered to himself, before he replied. "If there's another operation being run by the Americans, it would be nice to hook up with them, find out what they are trying to accomplish." Getting impatient, he follows with the demand. "I'm tired of waiting. Guide me to their position."

Rick told his men what he was doing and to stay put. He walked down the mountain about a klick, then headed to his left. He walked another four hundred yards, saw a group of men ahead of him and called out, his heavy British accent. "Staff Sergeant Rick Williams, British Commandos," he said.

One of the men responded, "I just received a calling telling me to expect a visitor from a British unit; from your accent you are definitely him. Dan Smith, U.S. Special Forces, Team Leader. I understand you and a team are a short distance from here. What's your story?"

"Probably the same as yours. We were track a group of enemy fighters we believe were firing on the Kandahar base. We trailed them to this mountain where they are holed up in a cave about a third of the way up," Rick answered. "What about you guys, similar story?"

"We were on a routine scouting assignment looking for fighters. We surprised a group about forty-five minutes ago as they crossed ahead on the same trail. We engaged them in a running fire fight, then they took off and ended up here. They climbed the mountain path fairly quickly, so we guessed this might be home to them," said Dan.

Rick asked, "Do you have a game plan yet?"

"Well," said Dan, "We have a CIA guy with us who's reaching out to his command. I get the general feeling from talking to him that they would like to take out this position. The CIA believes this is a major weapons storage place in addition a place for the fighters to hide out."

"That's what our intel people think as well. Where is the guy?"

"He's over there on a sat phone," said Dan pointing toward a large rock formation. "Come on, I will hook you guys up."

Rick followed him over to the general area he was gesturing to. As they approached the operative rang off his call. "Hey," Dan said, "This is Rick Williams, British commandos. He and his team were tracking a group of fighters who scooted up this mountain like the guys we followed did. He thinks this cave may be a weapons storage are. Now he's also struck here wondering what the next move is."

He gave Rick a quizzical look while extending his hand; like doo I somehow know this guy? Probably not. "Jason Cameron, CIA," he said.

Rick grabbed his hand and said, "You remind me of a CIA operative I met several years ago. Different name, so it had to be a different guy."

"I was thinking the same thing, that we crossed paths somewhere in the past; just not sure. Maybe it will come to me later."

Dan jumped into the conversation. "So, what's the plan?" he asked Jason.

"I talked to U.S. intel back at the Kandahar base. They agreed with our thinking that this could be a high value target. However, they would like a more positive confirmation if possible.

"They the Brits are running an op with a team out here, that must be you and your guys Rick. They have a drone they can use to guide us up a path on the right from here. We should be able to get within a couple of hundred yards of the cave. Hopefully we can get a good look see from that vantage point. You guys ready for some mountain climbing?"

They both nodded yes with Rick saying, "Let me contact my team and let them know what's going on. Also, our intel has a drone in the air, they can provide support to scale that hill."

Five minutes later Rick is leading the three of them up the mountain under Kate's guidance. They stop about two hundred feet from the cave entrance; Smith starts surveying with a pair of high-resolution binoculars.

BINGO! What they can see into the cave indicates a large cache of weapons, munitions, generators and so on. And, if they can see a large amount of equipment near the entrance and a short distance into the cave, you can bet there is a lot they can't see deeper into the mountain. Plus, the weaponry is arranged to give the appearance they are ready to battle.

"I'm convinced," said Cameron. "Let's get the hell out of here before we spotted." To Williams he said, "Let them know we are on our way down."

They stared skidding, sliding back down the path when the gunfire breaks out. "Shit," said Dan flies over his head. "We've been spotted. What do you think, should we return fire or not?"

"Let's keep going," replied Williams. "Another two hundred feet or so and we are out of their rifles range. I don't see them lobbing mortar shells at us."

A burst of machine gun tore up a rock formation, kicking up shrapnel. "Keep going by sliding down on your butt if necessary," said Cameron. "We're almost home free."

A roar overhead emanated from below them, going up the mountain, then a loud BOOM! "That's sounded like a bazooka shell exploding," said Smith. "Where in the hell did that come from?"

No answer because nobody new.

"At least it brought silence and stopped the machine gun assault," Williams said. He stood up, no more fire coming down the mountain. "Everyone alright?" he asked.

"My ass and right hip are sore and probably bruised, but I'm alright," answered Smith. A minute or two later Cameron stopped his downward slide and walked up with a bit of a limp. "Alive and healthy," he declared.

They walked back to where the rest of their men where located. Williams looked up and saw a newcomer among his comrades who had joined the Americans. The guy loaded and fired another bazooka round up into the mountains. Another loud BOOM! "If nothing else I drove them back into the cave. Hoped it helped you guys a bit," the new guy said.

"Who are you," asked Williams. "You're not one of my regulars."

"Nope, the man replied. "CIA, the name is Ja.

"Jacobs," Cameron bellowed. "Good timing. I didn't know you were in the neighborhood. What's your story?"

Jacobs answered, "Just out for a stroll with my bazooka when I overheard the radio chatter."

Ahh, that Yank humor Williams said to himself; not sure I'll ever understand it.

"We need to get our collective asses out of here ASAP," Jacobs continued. "As I said, I was monitoring your conversations and decided we needed to finish this mission completely. I talked to command and told them this is the area we had pinpointed for containing one of the largest weapons depots I've seen here. They have two B52," he checked his watch, "which will take off from Bagram in about five minutes. They are going to drop the heavy stuff and try to level that cave. If everyone is ready let's boogie."

Everyone stood up and walked about five hundred feet to relative flat terrain, then started to run. They took shelter among a grove of trees as they hear the B52 streaking above. They watch the rocks begin to blow apart and the smoke and dust as the bombers drop their loads. A quick swing around to the west as they attack from the back of the cave and dropped their load, then they headed back toward the base.

The late afternoon sky was beginning to gray, signaling nightfall was near. Explosions were still coming from the mountain; probably the ammunition inside the cave was being ignited. The men stood and watched as orange flames and dark smoke billowed skyward. Gasoline and who knows what else, has caught fire; it was quite the conflagration. "That place wouldn't be used as a hide out for a while, if ever again," Cameron said. "Let's go home."

Chapter 9

Early the next morning Maya is awakened by a loud pounding on the door to hers and Kate's quarters. "You ladies awake and decent?" a voice called out.

"Rick?" asked Kate.

"Yes," came the reply. "Let me in, I have important news for you ladies."

"If you've come to tell us you love us, we already know that," Kate sassed. "Besides, won't your wife be jealous if you're found in the company of two beautiful women?"

"Shut up doofus; you definitely need a date," said Maya in a hushed tone so Rick wouldn't hear her.

"Rick, what the hell are you doing here so early?" Maya called out.

"As I said, if you're decent let me in and I will tell you."

"Ok, give us a minute and we'll let you in," said Maya.

Rick started pacing a bit outside their door. Women, sometimes it takes them forever to do nothing. Finally, Kate opened the door to let him in.

"What's so important that it couldn't wait for a decent hour? And, what's that smell? Beer and smoke, cigars, I'll bet" she paused to sniff, "and sweat. What a lovely aroma to wake up to."

Before Rick can say anything Maya piped up. "You look like hell. Were you up all night drinking?" She yawned, stretched and grabbed her watch to check the time, 3:15. "What the fuck. It's still night. This better be good."

A bit agitated Rick said, "If all you ladies want to do is bust my balls and aren't interested in my earth-shaking news, then I'll leave you in the dark."

"All right, Maya, let's give him a break and hear him out. It better be good."

Kate stepped back and opened the door wide enough for him to walk in. She looked round outside to make sure no one was watching, then closed the door.

"Oh. It is," said Rick. "You ladies know all about the mission I just came back from, right?"

"Uh-huh," they both replied.

"The group that was to our left at the mountain was a Green Beret team."

Clearly interested now and wide-awake, Maya said, "Go on."

"They had a CIA officer working with them. I just spent the last three hours drinking with him and several of the guys." He stopped and sniffed. "You're right," he acknowledged; "I am a bit gamey. Oh well, rough afternoon. Maybe I'll go shower first."

"You take one step toward that door to leave, I'll tackle you myself," Kate said.

Maya brought her hand to her face. "You're forgiven if you say what I think you're going to say," she said.

"Yes," replied Rick. "The CIA operator's name is Jason Cameron. You were correct Maya. He's running operations between here and the Pakistan border. He operates from both sides of the border."

Maya could feel her pulse start to speed up. She took a deep breath to calm herself before speaking. She started firing questions as fast as any machine gun. "Tell me what happened? Did you introduce yourself? Is it Dirk? Did he recognize you? Did you recognize him? Is he really alive?"

Kate was also sitting upright on her cot; she too was very interested in what Rick had to say.

"Whoa, slow down, slow down, one question at a time. Yes, the Green Beret leader introduced us. When Cameron heard my name, he reacted like he recognized it. He really eyed me, like he was searching his memory trying to piece everything together. We agreed we reminded the other of someone we had met in the past."

"Well, what do you think, could it be him?" Maya anxiously quizzed Rick some more.

"I told him he reminded me of someone I had met in the past, perhaps on a mission. He responded he had a similar thought, that we knew each other from somewhere."

"Did you question him further?" Maya asked.

Remember, it wasn't just Cameron and myself. There was a group of us unwinding from our mission; it wasn't like I could interrogate him or anything like that. And, I probably wouldn't have bombarded with twenty questions any way."

"Tell me more," Maya said. He looked at Kate who nodded in agreement, she was almost as interested as Maya.

"It's possible he's Dirk. His head is shaved clean and he sports a short, reddish beard now. The sharp wit is still intact, and I still don't understand all of it. He also mentioned about working with British troops in the past; maybe that is when we ran into each other."

"I'm convinced," said Kate.

"It could go either way, but, if I had to venture a guess right now, I would believe he and Dirk are one and the same."

Maya listened intently to everything Rick said. The more he talked, the greater the emotions flooded over her. Her eyes reddened, she could feel tears starting to form at the corners, tears of joy and hope. Rick noticed and said, "Before you get too carried away, the only thing I know for sure is Jason Cameron is a CIA operative and is working along the Afghani-Pakistani border. Anything else is purely speculation and conjecture at this point in time."

Kate said, "It's him. We can both tell. We know these things; women's intuition."

Maya, unable to speak right now while trying to hold back the dam, nodded in agreement. Finally, in a hesitating voice she said, "I know it's Dirk, everything in my body says it him. Besides, you said you were convinced."

"It's still not proof positive, just a somewhat half-assed, educated guess. The only way to know for sure is for you, and only you, to talk to him."

"How do I arrange that?" she whispered.

"Come on Maya," Kate said. "We're two cracker jack intelligence analysts. It's what we excel at. We'll figure out something."

"Ladies, I will take my leave and go try to get some shut-eye. Let me know what the next step involving me is when you figure out."

****

Several days go by while Maya worked on her plan. The combat monitoring had slowed, allowing her and Kate to work in a rotational manner rather than in a nonstop, hell kicking fashion.

Maya decided the best course of action would be to arrange a meeting with Cameron; either through an accidental/ambush event or where a friend sets up the encounter. A couple of days ago she ran into Rick and asked if he had seen Cameron since their mission.

"No," he replied, "was I supposed to?"

"Nah, just hoping." Maya then told him of her plan. "What do you think?"

"I guess it's as good as any plan but there is one major problem."

Only one, Maya thinks. "What's missing?" she asked.

"If I'm the friend you have in mind to set up the meeting, just keep in mind I certainly have no advanced knowledge of his schedule, nor do I know anyone who does. Remember, I ran into him the first time quite by accident. You are going to need to find someone to help bridge that knowledge gap."

"Good point, do you know anyone with the CIA?"

"Nope, not really. Those guys just seem to appear when needed and then disappear just as fast."

"See you around, and thanks," said Maya as she began to walk away. As she walked across the compound she had an idea. Why it took so long to think of this she can't fathom.

"Kate," she hollered as she walked into the computer room. Kate bounded over, "What's up," she asked.

"I just talked to Rick about my plan to contact Cameron. She told me I needed to find someone who would have an idea how to find him. As we talked it occurred to me how to arrange a meeting. That Green Beret team leader, Smith, I believe, is here at this base, correct?"

Kate paused a moment then answered, "Yes, I believe that's right; Dan Smith. Why?"

"If I connect with Dan Smith, I can tell him I know Brian Stone, the current team leader of Dirk's old unit. I don't tell him of our conversation, just use his name as an icebreaker. Then I can tell Smith that Rick and I know Cameron and would like to catch up with him over some beers, and would he know how to reach him."

"Kinda iffy, I would call it a long shot at best."

"Better than no shot at all, and, besides I believe it will work," Maya responded.

"Why would you think that?" Kate asked.

"I remembered Dirk told me he always had admired the Green Beret and the time spent with them. In the CIA he worked with their teams whenever possible. I'll bet, if Cameron is Dirk, he would have established relationships with the Green Beret teams over here. Smith, therefore, would likely know how to locate him."

Kate nodded while Maya spoke, then said, "That long explanation actually made sense. I also know these guys become close friends as they have to trust their teammates with their lives." She paused then said, "Alright, let's find Smith."

"Any idea how?" Maya asked.

"Yep."

Kate walked to her desk and shuffled through some papers before finding a phone listing. After a minute of searching she stopped and placed a call. While waiting for an answer on the other end she said, "I met a guy here who works in the IT unit."

"Another Steve?"

Kate smiled, "You never know." She stopped talking as her call is answered. She asked a few questions then started writing down information on some paper. "Okay, got it, uh-huh, yep, thank you sweetie." She handed the paper to Maya.

"Sweetie, huh?"

Kate, a bit flustered said, "Never mind what you think you overheard on the phone. Remember, I said you never know. Just read the damned note."

Maya read the note and looked at Kate. "Where is this," she asked.

"Across the compound. Smith and his team just came back from a quiet reconnaissance trip. You should catch him if you hurry."

"Do we have anything happening right now besides this?"

"I thought this was the real reason why you volunteered to come here."

"Funny girl, haha. In case you've forgotten, I didn't volunteer to come here; we were assigned." She grinned. "Sweetie, huh? We need to talk about that."

"Shut up and move your ass, lady."

Maya stood, walked to the door and left at a brisk pace. "And, good luck," Kate called out.

"Thanks," said Maya as she started toward the far end of the base. Hope this isn't crazy she muttered.

After about an hour Maya returned. "How did it go ask?" asked Kate.

"Great," said Maya. "Smith is doing some reconnaissance work with Cameron tomorrow afternoon. They usually stop for some colds ones when they return to the base. He will discreetly call me after they have been there for a while. I will walk over and into the place. Once he sees me, he will call me over to their table."

"Huh," said Kate. "You know, it's corny enough that it just may work."

"I suppose you have a better plan?"

"Nope," replied Kate.

****

The next afternoon Maya received a call. Dan said they have been at the base for half an hour and would be going for some beers soon. Give us about twenty-five minutes, then come over. When I see you come in, I will stand up at the table and wave you over. After a few minutes I will make an excuse to leave. After that everything is up to you.

Dan ended the call. Maya looked at her watch, twenty-five minutes would be 6:15. I can putz around the office, check out tomorrow's work, then leave at 6:00. That would give me plenty of time to cross the base.

She searched through some paperwork and pick up a letter from the personnel office. She read the letter which was official confirmation that Jason Cameron wasn't employed by the British government. If you still have a need to fill an analyst position please contact them promptly for job candidates.

"Good to know," she said to an empty office.

She briefly pondered what to wear so Smith would recognize her. A silly idea she concluded. No matter what I wear I'm still the only six-foot tall female in the place. She checked her watch; time to leave. Just as she started to reach for the door, Kate opened it and stepped in.

One look at Maya's face, a bit of tension had appeared, told her everything.

"Tonight?" she asked.

Trying to inject a bit of humor Maya nervously responded, "Ohh, what gave me away?"

"How about the apprehension that is showing itself on your face. I know it's difficult but you have to try to relax, otherwise he'll see the look on you face and head for the hills."

Maya forced a smile.

"Better," Kate said, "but try not to force it. Got a game plan?"

Slowly shaking her head, she replied, "Nope, not really. Just going to play it by ear. I really hope I don't chicken out first and never show my face."

She inhales deeply and slowly exhales, trying to calm her nerves. "It's now or never," trying to convince herself not to bail. She checked her watch and announced, "It's showtime."

"Good luck," said Kate and then she gave her a hug. "I love you like you're an older, much older, sister."

That comment caused Maya to smile, a real one this time. She nodded and said "Thanks, I'll try not to hobble," as she went out the door for perhaps the longest walk of her life.

****

As she walked, what seemed like a million thoughts ran through her mind, seemingly all at one time. She stopped briefly and shut her eyes. She was trying to slow down her mind to regain a sense of focus. "Has it really been some twenty years," she thought. "It doesn't seem that long."

Twenty years…..

Even now she still vividly remembers that night on Al-Faw, like it happened last week. Again, she closed her eyes and remembered the night and early morning, actually, when her world came crashing down on her; when her will to live momentarily stopped.

They were to take down an Iranian missile site overlooking the Strait of Hormuz. It was a dangerous raid, as they all were, but the latest satellite photos and the human intelligence from the Iraqi allies indicated the site would be sparsely guarded. The goal was to hit the target hard and fast during the late night-early morning hours, render the site inoperable, destroy any missiles they might find and then make their way back to Basra. Simple and straight forward until it wasn't.

The actual battle was particularly nasty as they encountered much more resistance than expected. They were outmanned and outgunned; still, Winter and another operative managed to slip behind the building and breached the outer wall. Everything was fine until the secondary explosion happened.

There was a loud roar and then a fireball shot high into the early morning sky. Maya immediately had a sickening feel in her stomach. She staggered to her feet, she thinks, throwing caution to the wind; she had to find Dirk. Fortunately, the shooting had ceased shortly after the first explosion, eliminating the concern of being shot as she stood.

As the memories roared back, she unconsciously stopped walking and stood still reliving that night.

She was told she walked away in a stupor; they had no time to search for the bodies, why not? She was quiet the entire way back to Basra; her state of mind was later classified as Post-Traumatic Stress Syndrome.

Some tears started to form at the corners of her eyes. Unconsciously, she had started waking again. She looked ahead and realized she was standing outside the meeting place. She blinked the tears back and dried her eyes the best she could.

Twenty years of searching, wondering and hoping was about to hit her square on the chin. She had to pull herself together. "It had better be him," she said, "otherwise, I'll.. It just better be Dirk."

Hesitating just a bit before reaching for the door, she sighed, took a deep breath and turned the knob.

Chapter 10

She entered the room and allowed a minute for her sight to adjust to the darker surroundings. She quickly looked around the place, and saw no one she recognized. She rescanned the place then noticed a guy as he stood up from a table; from where she stood it appeared to be Smith. She nodded and headed toward him.

As he walked past her, so much for an introduction, he mouthed good luck and headed for the bar. She drew in a deep breath, strode to the table and sat down.

"Excuse me miss," the man said. "I don't think you have the right table." He looked closer at the woman and immediately froze as their gazes locked.

"Perhaps you can help me," Maya said. "I'm looking for an old friend, a man I haven't seen in twenty years." It has to be him!

The man stared, as he searched his memory bank. Softly he asked, "Who are you and who are you looking for?"

Is that crinkling at the corners of his eyes a signal he has recognized me and is waiting for confirmation? She swallowed and answered, "My name is Maya Thernopolis."

She watched as his eyebrows raised in response to her name. "The name of my long-lost friend, the person I'm looking for is," a brief pause as she tried to maintain a strong voice, "Dirk Winter." There, she finally said his name.

The man sports a shocked look on his face, his mouth wide agape as neither speaks. He finally realized he was staring and closed his mouth and settled back into his chair. He shakes his head as he processed everything he just heard.

Maya is determined not to say a word, it's his turn to either confirm what his body behavior has confirmed or attempt to lie his way out of it. She's convinced he won't lie. She flashed her biggest smile. Combined with her flashing green eyes, it was the woman he had fallen in love with all those many years ago.

As the shock wore away, they still stared at each other. He finally drew a lung full of air and let it out. He leaned forward and said, "My God, is it really you Maya, after all these years?"

Still smiling that big smile, she clasped his hands with her and nodded affirmatively. "It's me Dirk," she answered as the tears started to flow slowly down her face. "I'm here and I've finally found you. And, in case you ever doubted, the one true love of my life." She noticed tears had also formed at the corners of his eyes.

Not knowing what exactly to do, he kissed the back of her hands and placed them tenderly on her face. "You've always been my love, always," as he smiled through his own tears. He dabbed at his eyes and said, "I thought I would never see you again. How?"

"I never gave up believing. If anyone could have survived that blast on Al-Faw, it would be you. I just somehow knew."

He nodded slowly. Not sure where to take the conversation, or what to say, he decided to listen and let Maya continue on her roll. She always liked to talk.

"After the inquest into the incident concluded I was reassigned home and shut down with Post Traumatic Stress Disorder. PTSD or not, I never believed the official results. Something was missed somewhere, someone fooled someone. I've spent the past twenty years re-examining the evidence and recounting what happened. The officials were so certain you were dead, yet never did I find any mention of your body being returned to your parents, or that your parents had even been notified of your heroic death.

"I wasn't a hero. I just did my job; what you or any good operative would have done," he sheepishly interjected.

"That was the only conclusion from the inquest report that I fully agreed with. You saved my life and the lives of three other soldiers selflessly. That, my friend, is the definition of a hero."

"The CIA told me you died in the battle. And Rick," he paused, "Williams and everyone in your position, in front of the building, was killed in the battle. Everyone died but me they said. I tried to push the issue for about a year. Eventually I was shut down; told I had no evidence and to mind my own business if I liked my career. So, with nothing to go on, I accepted the order and stopped looking.

"And that British commando from the other day, I thought I recognized him but wasn't completely sure. That was Rick, wasn't it? He must have thought I was crazy; while I thought I was looking at a ghost; hope he'll understand."

Maya nodded in the affirmative. She broke their clasp and placed a finger on his lips, which he kissed.

"I revved up my efforts a few months ago when I met the current team leader of you old Green Beret unit. He told me he and Eddie had the same doubts I harbored. They also received a lot of crap just like I did for not believing, for being inquisitive. This time I didn't stop until I found you."

"Those dirty, lying sons of bitches, why?" he spewed.

"We can cuss them out at another time. Tonight, if you have the time, it's just about us. To hell with them."

****

And they talked and talked, hours and hours. Although they didn't order food, burgers and fries appeared at their table at one point during the evening. A most fitting add-on to their liquid beverages.

It's impossible to cover everything that has happened over a twenty-year period; so, you do your best to hit the highlights. Perhaps the most intriguing fact was that neither of them ever married. Both had attempted romance and love, but the demands of their jobs always interfered. Or, was the real reason they never had permanent relationships was due to the fact they had lost their one true love.

Maya mentioned that she was a single mom, having raised a wonderful son with great support from her parents, sisters, and Rick Williams and his wife. Even though she didn't leave London to go on assignments until he was older, it was still difficult. The best part was the time away rarely lasted longer than a month.

Dirk came close to marriage once but everything ended when he told the woman that his job required assignments around the world; sometimes at a moment's notice. When she asked for an explanation, he told her he couldn't offer one; she would have to trust him that the work was extremely important. The woman finally decided that if he couldn't leave the job that it was either too dangerous or he was engaged in illegal activities. Regardless, he should stop immediately. Dirk didn't accept the ultimatum and left, never to return. Maya definitely understood.

Wow! It had been nearly five hours when they decided they needed to leave. They walked out together and stood outside talking for a while. It was there where Maya had an opportunity to look Dirk over. He looked as fit as ever which was to be expected as he was still a very active operative. His tee shirt showed his powerful chest and the big arms. He showed some age around the eyes, probably sun related she surmised; and since his head was shaved there would be no gray to worry about.

After a few minutes of silence Dirk offered to walk her to her quarters.

"Why Mr. Winter," she teased.

"I promise to be a gentleman," he grinned. It seemed like the old days!

As they reached her place Maya asked, "Would you like to meet again?"

"Absolutely," he answered. I have to go back to Pakistan and check in with the CIA group there. I expect to return in 10 days or so.'

"It's a date," Maya said.

****

"Beautiful, just a beautiful story." Kate said when Maya finished. Kate had showed joy, happiness, all the emotions while she listened completely enraptured. "It's sounds like you just clicked all over again."

"Pretty much. It really was just two friends getting caught up after not seeing each other for a long time. I'm so excited right now I could just float away on a cloud."

"Remember not to push too fast, it been twenty years," Kate reminded her.

"The biggest thing is he's alive. No longer do I have to wonder, holding onto hope that may have been misguided."

"I wonder why the higher ups lied to both of you with the same story, Killed in Action?" said Kate.

"That is a good question, but I not sure if it's one that needs to be answered now.'

"Oh Maya, you not thinking clearly right now. Your emotional high is overriding all rational thoughts," Kate exclaimed. "It's imperative to learn everything you can about the lies; they are the real key to unraveling this twenty-year mystery."

A bit of anger creeping into her voice Maya responded, "What on earth are you talking about me being irrational?"

"Think about," Kate said. "You were both told the same coverup story so it not hard to reason that the CIA and MI6 got together on the same story. And, you and everyone else who tried to look into this incident were shut down. Come on, you know as well as I do that is not a coincidence. This is a well-planned coverup. Why?"

Maya went silent, mulling over what Kate said. Finally, she nodded her head. "You're right," she said. Dirk and I briefly talked about it but not in any great detail. We were just so ecstatic to see each other." She smiled. "If you remember, I told you I needed you to keep me centered through all of this."

"That's what I'm doing; isn't that's what friends are all about?"

"That's for sure," Maya said. I just can't believe I was so stupid, so naive, so …"

"Human?"

"Touche!"

"What now?" Kate wanted to know.

"Not much at this moment. I will think about what you said and then discuss with Dirk the next time we meet. Something did happen during that mission and right now I don't have a clue what it could have been."

"It had to quite serious to keep two people apart by making them believe the other was dead."

"Indeed," said Maya.

Chapter 11

Kate grabbed the mail when it came in and started to sort through it. She stopped when she found an official envelope with the markings for the recipient only. I'm a recipient she surmised; besides, it's probably just personnel records. She opened it and read the contents. Oh shit, she said to herself, Maya isn't going to be happy when she sees this.

At that moment a cheerful Maya, with a spring in her stride, walked into the office. "Looks you're holding an official envelope; anything I need to know?"

"Oh yeah," said Kate. "Remember to keep your cool when you read it."

"I always keep my cool," she responded. She quickly read the missive, then reread it to make sure she had read it right the first. "Mother fucker," she bellowed. She began waving her arms as she walked heavily around the office.

"So much for keeping your cool," Kate said.

"Shut up," Maya snarled. "No way, no how; he's not ready for an assignment to a war zone. No, I won't allow it; he's not ready for Afghanistan."

"You won't allow it; are you the prime minister today or the queen herself?"

Maya looked at Kate who appeared like she's dancing around the office. "What the hell is wrong with you, have you lost all your marbles?"

"Just trying to keep at least two feet away from you at all times."

"What the hell for?" Maya demanded.

"So I can observe you keeping your cool and flailing your arms from a safe distance."

"You read the letter don't you think I have a reason to be upset?"

"Yes and no. Maya, he has completed his Advanced Combat Training; top of his class. He's been a soldier now for eighteen months. What did you expect, a desk job with us?"

"He's still my baby and not ready for this," she railed through clenched teeth.

"He's been in Germany for the last two months on advanced maneuvers," Kate said.

"He's too inexperienced."

"If I remember correctly, you told me you were deployed a few months earlier than he has been, Kate said."

"That was different," Maya fumed

"Really, how?

"I was older, more mature, a college graduate," replied Maya.

"But you both had the same level of training. Look, I get it, he's your only child. But, if command didn't believe he was ready, he wouldn't be enroute."

Maya, steam still coming out of her ears, had clammed up as she continued to stomp around the office.

"You know," said Kate, "this might be partially your own fault."

Maya glared at Kate. "How in the hell did you reach that dumb ass conclusion?"

"He's a sniper, trained by you, the best sniper in the British ranks; perhaps the best anywhere. You encouraged him to be the best and greatly assisted him in that endeavor. He's your son and now he wants to prove himself just like you did twenty some years ago."

Maya had stopped stomping and took a seat at her desk. "You're right," she softly said. "Truth be told, I'm the only one who isn't ready for his assignment. It's tough when your kids grow up and leave the nest."

"I hope to find out someday," Kate responded. "I just hope you're still around to help me through when I become crazed."

Maya smiled. "I wouldn't miss it for anything. Besides, isn't that what friends are for?"

****

While momma bear was busy preparing for the arrival of her cub, Maya now realized her next get together with Dirk would have to change a bit. She was sure he would hear about another soldier with the Thernopolis surname, so she wanted to be the first to inform him.

She then began making mental notes of changes she would have to make to operational protocols. She decided to let Kate have the privilege of monitoring Nick's actions in the field, but she would be right there to monitor her decisions; just in case.

The CIA recently had added their own analyst to the mix in her group. Maya didn't really know him. He might be good, but she knew Kate was excellent. And, it would be easier to step on Kate's toes if she thought it was necessary; she would understand without much disagreement.

While she continued her office procedures realignment exercise, Kate walked into the office. "Hi Kate, have a seat. I have some changes to our work assignments to discuss with you."

Kate said, "I have something important to tell you as well." Seeing the impatient look on Maya's face she said, "By all means, you go first."

"I decided to assign all of the monitoring of Nicky's field missions to you; of course, I will be real close by just in case you need my help."

As she explained the other changes she had in mind to Kate, Kate realized had Maya bothered to stop to think about it, the truth of the manner is that the British commanders wouldn't let her group be involved in Nick's assignments because of the familial ties. Plus..Oh well, time to burst her bubble.

"That's real nice of you," Kate said, but it's not your call."

"What do you mean, I'm the senior in this office."

"I know and your decision is based on you trying to take extra steps to protect your son, Kate said. But had you read the letter more thoroughly, you would have noticed that he is being assigned to Bagram, not here with us. You know, the whole prohibition against close family members serving at the same base."

"Damn, your right, I did forget. I guess I let myself get a little too worked up."

"Just a little?" came Kate's reply.

"Okay, maybe a lot. I just reacted like any soldier responding to the assignment of green recruits to their command."

"Except for the fact that you're the only soldier who is the mother of one of the recruits. Just proof positive why the rule exits."

Maya just sat silently, all of that planning shot to hell.

"My turn," Kate said. "I just got back from a meeting. We have a drone to track on a routine scouting mission. The border has been too quiet the last few days so command thought we should have a look see. The drone arrives in our airspace in about thirty minutes."

"Whose camera is it, ours or the Americans?" Maya asked.

"Since it's strictly a recon flight it will be ours." Kate walked over to the big screen and sat down. Several keystrokes of information resulted in the screen showing the pictures from the drone.

Just then the CIA analyst walked in. "Are you ladies tracking the recon drone?"

"It's live on the big screen as we speak," Kate responded.

"What's the focus?" he asked as he peered down at the screen.

"The flight path is a quick swing around the base and then up to the Pakistani border," Kate said. Command thinks things have been too quiet lately, so they want to get some mechanical eyes on the area."

"Mind if I sit in?" he asked.

"Not at all," Kate replied. "Pull up a chair."

Maya joined them and they tracked the drone for about fifteen minutes with no discernable results noted. The area looked devoid of all activity.

"This doesn't make much sense to me," Maya said. "Less than a week ago we had firefights all over that area. Even after taking out their mountain hideout the fighting continued. Now, nothing. I don't get it."

"Nor do I," said the CIA analyst as he turned to face Maya. "Yet here we are looking at nothing. I agree, it's strange. Maybe it's time to send the drone elsewhere and send out a team."

"Hold on," said Kate pointing at the screen. "There, In the lower left side of the screen, there's a clump of heavy vegetation. See that strange shadow? Now, follow it across to your right."

"I see it," said Maya as she scans the image to the right. "That shadow doesn't connect to the background. It looks like it doesn't belong there."

The CIA analyst concurred. "Can you contact the drone operator?" he asked.

Maya grabbed the phone and called the pilot. "Can you make another pass around to the west and about two hundred feet lower?"

"I should be able to. Find something?" the pilot asked.

"Maybe."

The drone swings around to the west and they watch while the pilot dropped the altitude. "How's that view?" he asked. "I was able to drop it about three hundred fifty feet."

"Beautiful, much clearer," Kate said. She pointed to the same position she saw earlier. "See that vegetation? Well, that shadow is covering what appears to be…" she counts, two machine gun mounted pickup trucks and a mortar. And two feet behind that position the shadows look like a group of fighters."

"I agree," said Maya. To the pilot, "thanks, we confirmed what we were looking at. Thank you."

"Good spotting, and thank you," the pilot replied.

The CIA analyst nodded in concurrence with their conclusions. "Nice work," he said.

Maya; "Can you contact your people running along the border and inform them of our findings. It looks like they will be putting together an operation soon."

Dialing his sat phone he answered, "I'm already on it." Then, rethinking his statement he answered, "What makes you think we have assets out there?"

"Come on," said Kate. "That's our job, we are intelligence analysts too."

The CIA analyst headed out the door as he started to talk in an attempt to ensure privacy. He wasn't sure if the ladies were bluffing him into revealing more information then he should or if they really had inside intel.

Maya smirked as he headed out the door. In her mind he had revealed his hand. As he disappeared around the corner of the building, she said to Kate, "We'll never reveal our source." She smiled. "Bet Dirk will be busy in the next day or two."

Chapter 12

Maya learned after the fact that Nicky didn't have to wait to see action. He had been at the airbase less than twenty-four hours when he was sent out on a patrol. His team met with an enemy force about two miles out. He carefully scrambled himself to an elevated plateau and from there took out the enemy's machine gun nest. Once that was cleared the team was able to overrun the position and captured a small cache of weapons and several Al-Qaeda fighters.

The new hero had little time to catch his breath as he went out with another patrol the following day to set up an ambush. The target this time was a high-ranking Taliban commander. Nick and a spotter were accompanied by two other commandos. A drone helped guide them into position. The spotter found the target and Nick dropped him with a clean shot from over seventeen hundred yards away. The remaining Taliban started firing blindly; they were unable to determine from where the shot originated. In the meantime Nick and his teammates packed their gear then slipped back onto the base.

Maya thought things were going as well as could be expected considering she was operating in a war zone. Her prior military experience meant the action near the base didn't bother her. Maya found out about Nick's missions two or three days after they concluded, thus preventing her from fretting over his mission the entire time he was out.

Kate had overcome her concerns about being in Afghanistan, and although she would never like it, and still blamed Maya for her being there, she was thriving working with the drone pilots. She was building a new skill set by tracking the drone's flights paths on their reconnaissance work. Plus, she had served as the point person on several missions; in fact, she had more assignments in this arena than Maya had. In addition, on a more personal note, much to her surprise she had been able to remain in contact with Steve back in London. Who knew a relationship would develop long distance like that.

Nick was also doing well. Maya had only talked to him twice since his deployment; he was adapting well to the routine and liked being a sniper. Although she never received an update any soon than forty-eight hours after a mission ended, all the reports she read that had been filed by his superiors were all positive. He was on his way to becoming a valued operator.

As for her personal life; Maya had her two more meetings with Dirk. They seemed to fall into a groove, as simpatico as before. They enjoyed just walking and talking, trying to learn more about the other. It seemed very much like they were looking at the other as a new person, even though they had that personal history. They had changed but appeared to have the same feelings for each other.

Heck, the time apart even worked in their favor, at least that's what Maya believed. The absences prevented them from any attempt at overwhelming the other if they were together on a near daily basis. No matter how hard one tried, you can't recoup twenty years in four or five hours every two weeks or so. Besides, they both retained their passion toward their work. The new assignments meant everything was fresh, providing them plenty to talk about when they got together.

Yep, all-in-all things were going smoothly. And then BOOM! All hell broke loose and an event that may turn out to be worse than al-Faw came from nowhere and landed a vicious blow that threatened to destroy everything.

Chapter 13

The calendar was careening toward mid-August. The weather was as stinking hot as ever, maybe even hotter than when then they first arrived. Sometimes you got can lucky and the temperatures will back off a bit from their mid-ninety degrees highs, but not this year. The temps were still soaring, even reaching the high nineties on occasion. The only thing that was predictable about this country, Maya thought, was that nothing was predictable. After five minutes in the office, Maya wished the biggest concern she faced today was the weather.

She threw the envelopes on her desk after reading its contents for the second time. Maya stomped around the office like a crazed woman. It was strange. The whole damn thing was just fucking strange, even bizarre. It made no damn sense.

She had received two envelopes this morning and was in a state of disbelief after reading them. She then re-read the ciphered message again, nothing had changed from the first two times she had read them.

"Kate are you sure this is accurate?" she bellowed.

"This is what the code breaking unit sent to us so it should be legit. Besides, if it's not correct word for word, the contents of the second envelop supports the claim." Before Maya could say anything else, Rick walked in through the office door. He looked at Kate who just nodded.

"I got here as fast as I could," he said. *What the hell is going on?"*

Maya handed Rick the contents of the two messages she had received. He looked at everything, "My God, is that your Nick they're referring to?"

"Has to be, I didn't have any twins!"

"What the fuck; what possible value would he have to the Taliban or Al-Qaeda?" Rick asked.

"Well, Maya does receive after the fact summaries of his missions. On one of them he took out a high-ranking commander on one of his missions," said Kate. "Maybe that's it?"

"Maybe, but how did Al-Qaeda learn his name? That information is classified, so unless they had an inside source, there has to be another explanation. Maya, you've been quiet; what are you thinking?"

Maya has sat down at her desk. "I'm thinking I have to follow the instructions and go get my boy."

"Not by yourself," they both respond.

"I pretty much have to according to the message." She started to drum her fingers on the desk. She typed several keystrokes into the computer, the coordinates from the message and a map popped up. She manipulated the images, then printed out several screen shots. As the printer rattled to life she said, "Don't worry, I not crazy, but I need a plan." She took out her cell phone and punched in a number.

"Who are you calling?" asked Rick.

"The only man, besides you, I would trust with my life and Nicky's.

"Hello, Dirk? Maya. A major emergency has cropped up; can we meet tonight?"

A pause.

"No, I'm not busy right now," she answered.

Another pause.

"Okay, same meeting place in ten minutes." She ended the call.

"Kate you stay here and hold down the fort. If I'm needed, you're free to make up any excuse to cover my absence. Rick, I need you to come with me. Time for you to meet an old friend again and get the trio back together."

Rick believed he understood the message and followed Maya out the door. Kate didn't get Maya's drift, so she stayed in the office. Left alone, she started to pace.

****

Maya and Rick are waiting at a table, maps spread out, when Dirk walked in. The crowd was sparse, there was only three other people on the premises. Perfect, no one to overhear them.

"Sorry about our meeting a few weeks back. I had to adjust to the fact that someone I thought was killed twenty years ago was standing in front of me. It was surreal. Hope you weren't offended," he said while extending his hand.

"Of course not. I had the same thoughts, plus I wasn't even sure if you were the right person, Jason," Rick replied while grasping Dirk's hand.

Dirk chuckled. "Yeah, well there are now two people who know my real name." To Maya, "This must be a real serious problem; you've never called me on the cell before."

"It is," she replied. "And, there are now three people who know you are live."

"Who's the third person?" he asked.

"A real good friend of mine. I will tell you someday when I introduce the two of you."

"Okay, but this circle of trust keeps getting bigger. Just three, right?"

Rick nodded, "That's all."

Not really sure how to proceed, she just went straight ahead. She hands the note to Rick and gives him a moment to read it. As he looks up she says, "That's umm…my son who has been kidnapped. He's stationed at Bagram Airbase,"

"Wow!" said Dirk, "I didn't realize he was that old." He handed the note back to Maya. "Of course, you can count me in. Military huh, sounds like a chip off the old block."

"More than you know."

"Come again," Dirk said.

"You better sit for this, you too Rick."

Puzzled, Dirk sits down first, then Rick. "Rick, you and Megan probably guessed what I'm about to say. If so, you were sweethearts not to broach the subject, thank you."

Maya, still standing, takes a deep breath, rubs her forehead, then said, "Dirk, you're Nicky's father."

Dead silence as Dirk's lower jaw almost dropped to the floor, his mouth agape.

Not knowing what else to say Maya threw her hands in the air and exclaimed, "Surprise!"

Looking around to make sure no one else in the place was paying attention to her, no one was, Maya sat down and squirmed a bit in her chair.

Dirk closed his mouth and swallowed. He switched from a shocked expression on his face to a wide smile. "I kinda thought it was possible especially when you said nothing about his father. What took you so long to work up the courage?"

"Well," Maya began. "I've seen you three times in the last twenty years. I didn't think that you be the first thing to hit you with. I would have gotten there eventually, unfortunately circumstances forced my hand."

"We never married," she continued, "and you were supposedly killed before our relationship reached that level. And, I didn't find out I was pregnant until I returned back to London. Nicky was born seven and a half months later."

Rick said, "The thought entered my mind when you had morning sickness during the inquest; you looked just like my wife. It cinched it for me when Nicky was born."

"Alright, that just increases the importance of this mission in my book," Dirk said. "First, we have a few questions to puzzle through."

"Such as?" Maya inquired.

"One thing that has always bothered me was that raid on al-Faw. What happened, why did everything go to hell in a hand basket?" Dirk asked.

"I stopped thinking about the why after the inquiry was over, to be honest about it. I originally thought we were given bad intel and we dealt with it the best we could. But apparently it has crossed your mind there was an ulterior motive behind it and I can understand why," Rick said.

"While I expressed a moment of being pissed off at both the CIA and MI6 for their joint lies, I never told you the totality of what really happened and my thoughts about the whole situation, Dirk said."

Enraptured, Maya and Rick listened intently to Dirk's recollection of that night twenty years ago.

"Myers and I both survived the two blast. Myers suffered a broken leg and contusions on his right side. He later passed out from the intense pain of the femur bone thrusted through his thigh.

"I was knocked out and suffered a concussion along with several contusions. I was told a Navy Seals unit arrived moments before an Iranian team showed up in response to the explosion. A brief firefight ensued, and they eliminated the enemy combatants. They treated us at the scene and returned to their ship with us. From there we were transported to a Navy hospital ship, then to the Landstuhl Regional Medical Center in Germany. Anything you guys were told to the contrary was a lie."

"We were told about the Navy Seals eliminating an Iranian unit but nothing about survivors; in fact, we were told just the opposite, there were no survivors," Rick said.

"My point here," Dirk said, "is that those missiles never should have exploded based on my detonation. I didn't use enough C4 to have caused that type of a secondary response; regardless of where those missiles were placed inside that building."

"Are you saying there was another denotation that was triggered by another event, such as a remote detonation?" Maya asked.

"Exactly the conclusion I came to as well as the CIA investigators," Dirk said.

"So, it was a trap the entire time; I'll be damned," said Rick. "I wasn't thinking along those lines. Any idea who may have been behind?"

"No," said Dirk. "I couldn't come up at a plausible scenario nor could the CIA. This outcome is what lead to me going off the grid and returning as Jason Cameron. Apparently, the CIA did a good job with their cover story as no one came after me or found out my real name until you did."

"Sorry," said Maya.

"No, don't be sorry; I'm glad you didn't give up, I wish I had your tenacity."

Rick nodded in agreement with that statement while Maya sheepishly smiled.

"I always wondered what happened to you. The official bullshit story that you died, Maya, never washed with me. I even talked to the Navy Seals team that rescued me and Myers. They did manage to recover two bodies buried under the rubble in the front of the missile site. They said both bodies were male. Since they were the first people on the site after everything was over, that told me at least you survived."

A waiter showed and delivered a large pot of coffee that was paid for. He left when he couldn't interest anyone in a late breakfast.

"This is the second time this has happened here without us ordering; someone must like us," Maya exclaimed.

"Probably the bartender thinks you cute," said Rick. Maya responded by flipping Rick the bird as she smiled.

Returning to the storyline Rick asked Dirk, "Does the past somehow tie into today?"

Dirk stirred his coffee and took a sip from the steaming cup. He nodded and answered. "I believe so."

"Who the hell do you think it is?" Maya blurted, then, "Sorry, just a little pissed."

"You have every right to be and so am I," Dirk replied. "I've been thinking about your twenty-year saga as compared to mine. The one thing that really stood out was how Maya Thernopolis continued to be. You have been out in the open all these years with no repercussions.

"Dirk Winter, on the other hand, was removed from all official CIA records; reason, KIA. The CIA didn't want to lose me, nor did they want me exposed to whoever betrayed our team. Therefore, I returned as Jason Cameron; essentially, I've operated undercover all these years.

"Then, you solved the riddle and found me operating in Afghanistan. Several weeks after we meet, our son is deployed to Afghanistan. He completed a couple of assignments, then, wham, is kidnapped."

"I see your point. I've been out in the open all these years and never encountered any problems because of who I am. My only involvement in this matter was when I joined in the assault on al-Faw. If I lived or died it didn't really matter. So, in this case, I'm not relevant." Rick offered.

"Agreed," said Rick and Maya nodded in concurrence.

"To play this out," Rick asked, "who did you and Maya encounter when you guys were operating undercover prior to al-Faw. If my memory is correct, you were in Cyprus?"

"Correct," said Maya. "I initially had the same thoughts, including the Cyprus operation, myself. At our appearance in front of the inquest panel, Sir Hilary himself said all British personnel involved in Cyprus, including those not working with us, were investigated and cleared. The CIA officer in Cairo at that time, Rob Wilson, was also a member of that panel. He didn't disagree or dissent from the findings and conclusions.

"I did some checking on my own about a year after that mess. I developed several theories the panel didn't consider and conducted my own investigation. Regardless of how hard I tried to grasp every little detail I came across, I found nothing to contradict the panel's conclusions. Yet, I always have harbored this nagging doubt in the back of my mind."

"Everyone was silent for a moment before Maya spoke up. "That means I'm the target and they took Nick to get at me. Some type of a revenge thing from our work together?" Maya inquired.

"I believe so, but I also don't believe our kidnappers were unaware that I existed when their mission was planned out" Dirk said. "If so, they probably would have taken a shot at me before now. This should be a big plus for us."

"It now seems that my hunch, my 'women's intuition' was correct," said Maya.

Both men silently agreed; they weren't going to argue something that proved to be right.

Dirk asked Maya, "How did you receive this notification?"

"It was delivered to my office," she answered.

"Do you know who sent it to you?"

"An individual's name, no. But it came from our code breakers."

"Do you trust their work?" Dirk asked.

"This particular group is one of the best I've worked; so yes, I trust them. Why?"

"I'm not casting aspersions, I just making sure you believe them," Dirk responded.

Having been silent for a long time, Rick offered his opinion. "Whoever is behind this wants us to believe that Taliban fighters are responsible for the kidnapping of Nick. Why? Supposedly it's in retaliation for his sniper hit on one of their top field commanders. I don't buy the whole story. I'm not saying that some how the Taliban aren't involved in some form; however, someone else is the true master mind."

"Right," said Maya. "In my book, whoever Dirk and I pissed off twenty years ago found out their trap on al-Faw didn't work as we both survived. So, they've come back to finish the job. And this time they added a handicap to our side."

"Alright," said Dirk. "Let's game this out. Someone, somewhere, unknown to you at this time, received a coded message. It was received elsewhere or received here, again we don't know, and it doesn't really matter." He drummed his fingers on the table. "Regardless of the reason, someone knew to direct this message to Maya at the base."

"An insider?" Maya asked.

"Or someone with access to British communications systems," Dirk answered.

"Highly suspicious," Rick opined. Maya nodded in agreement.

"That's my belief," replied Dirk. "Whoever is doing this is screwing with your mind, playing head games. Think about it this way Maya. You and Rick return to Afghanistan, close to where you first encountered me. Then Nick is assigned to Afghanistan at the same time, and if they could have arranged that, they are indeed very powerful and very connected to the upper levels in the British military. To set your mind at ease, I don't think that is the case. But once the two of you were in this country, they wouldn't have to extract their revenge on sovereign British territory.

"Look, this person(s) knows about our first encounter over here twenty plus years ago and have used that incident to drag you through a rerun of what occurred, a rescue mission of me. They correctly deduced that I was someone you were very close to. And, maybe they even guessed that I am Nick's father. If so, the dagger is further twisted into your heart.

"It's poignant, your demise occurs trying to save your son, in the area where you first meet his dead father. They want to harm you, Maya, break you mentally, then probably kill you. Nick is simply the bait to lure you away from the safety of the base."

Maya is clearly shaken by this story and sat silently at the table. Her thoughts hadn't reached this level of disgust and desperation by some sick bastard holding a twenty-year grudge. Who do I know that is that mentally sick, she wondered?

Rick finished his coffee and said, "From what you're describing, this individual is either MI6 or has a high contact in that agency."

"My thoughts exactly," said Dirk. "They and/or someone they worked with, had the ability to pass on the information that Nick is your son and a soldier. Which is why I was surprised to learn that your identity was never changed. It left you open to this kind of a reprisal."

"I had similar thoughts about an MI6 turncoat, especially in the beginning. I didn't pursue that line of investigation because the MI6 was cleared by the inquiry," said Maya.

"Doesn't mean they got it right," said Dirk. "This person may have had the access to the investigation or knew someone who drove the investigators down the wrong path. It wouldn't be the first time it's happened in our respective agencies."

"Gruesome, sick and disgusting," Rick offered. He paused, then said, "I agree with Dirk's assessment."

Dirk checks his watch and announced, "We've been at this for over an hour. Let's develop a plan. I assume those printouts you bought tell us a bit about where he is located?"

"What have you got in mind?" Maya asked.

"The biggest thing is the element of surprise; whoever is behind this doesn't know I'm alive. They believe Dirk Winter isn't here, that he died on al-Faw, so my alter-ego held. I plan to use this to our advantage. They have planned to deal with you and you alone. Nick's father plans on kicking some ass."

Chapter 14

An hour and a half later, early afternoon, Maya walked into her office. She found the CIA analyst glued to the big screen. He was watching a live transmission of activity at what appeared to be the Pakistani border. She looked surprised that he was viewing that area and wondered if the CIA somehow knew something was going to happen tonight. Turning away from the screen, she looked around and noticed Kate wasn't present.

"I need to leave in an hour to go to Bagram," he said. "Either you or Kate will need to take over. Should be easy the rest of the day, just a simple drone reconnaissance flight that is scheduled for late this afternoon."

"Not a problem," Maya answered; thinking that will make it a lot easier for Kate to be our eyes tonight with no one watching her.

"Speaking of Kate, do you know where she went?"

Spinning around to face Maya, he answered, "Said she was going out for a quick one then back to her quarters."

"Thanks." Hmm interesting, she thinks. Kate's normal routine is to go out for a leisurely lunch then return back here, even if I'm not in the office. Wonder what's bothering her.

"Yeah, no problem," the analyst said. He opened his mouth as if to say something but changed his mind and turned back to watch the computer screen. He wrote some information down on copier paper, then drew what looked like a map. He closed out the images he was watching on his screen, then stood up from the station to leave.

Maya turned her head as he finished the map; she didn't want to be caught in the act of spying on him. By the time he stood up Maya was looking elsewhere.

"See you ladies in a day or two," he said over his shoulder as he walked out the door.

As she watched him leave Maya shrugged her shoulders. I wonder what that was all about, as she scampered to the computer. A couple of keystrokes later and she had accessed the images he was viewing. Her best guess was he was watching the other side of the Pakistani border. She wondered who or what he was searching for in Pakistan?

The CIA analyst had been gone about thirty minutes when Kate wandered in. While not exactly loopy, in Maya's opinion, she believed that Kate had indulged in several cold ones with lunch. Her opinion was confirmed when Kate swayed a bit when she walked across the room.

Maya turned from the computer screen to face Kate. "This is so unlike you to celebrate during lunch," she said. "What's the happy occasion?"

"I'm not happy and I'm not celebrating anything," Kate said.

"I hope you not angry," Maya replied. "You know it not good to drink when you're angry." She was trying to get Kate to open up while not angering her more.

"I'm not angry; at least I don't think I am. I'm not sad, I'm not happy, I don't know what I am.., maybe frustrated."

Keeping her talking, Maya thought. "Okay, what are you frustrated about?"

Kate glared back at her. "Why the hell do you think I wouldn't be frustrated?"

Maya wasn't sure what else to say so she sat silently, allowing Kate to continue.

Kate took a deep breath and let it out slowly. "Did you guys come up with a plan?"

"Yep."

"Care to elaborate?" Kate asked.

"Well, the three of us first tried to understand exactly why what is happening is happening."

"Makes sense, I guess."

Hitting the highlights, Maya continued. "Dirk believes this event is the result of a revenge plot against me based on our working together in the past, our al-Faw mission, to be exact."

"The night when Dirk was supposedly killed," Kate interrupted.

"Right. Anyhow, it's his contention that someone wanted us both dead, but they seemed content they killed Dirk. Something was triggered in this person(s) brain by mine and Nick's assignment here in Afghanistan. They've used Nicky to bait me to leave the base.

"The maps I printed out show Nicky is being held not too far from where Rick and I saved Dirk on a mission that went sideways. Dirk believes the plan is to kill me in the same neighborhood, so to speak."

"God, that's sick. Any idea who?"

"Short list is someone either in MI6 or working with someone who works for the agency. This person accessed military personnel records to link Nicky and me together."

"Boy, if it has to do with al-Faw, that's a real long time to hold a fucking grudge," said Kate. "Okay, that's the reason why, what's the actual plan?"

"I'm going to get my boy."

"By yourself? I thought you knew better than to try such a dangerous mission on your own?" Kate paused for a moment then said, "I'm coming with you."

"I really appreciate your offer, but you read the instructions, it has to be me." Besides, I won't be entirely alone, said Maya.

"Come on, talk."

"Well, for instance, there is a recon CIA drone going up tonight. Dirk has talked to the CIA ground controllers and it just so happens they be flying some recon over where I'm going.

"Dirk will be accompanying me the entire way, about seventy-five yards away on my right flank. And Rick will be ten miles out with a tag team ready to go."

"Then I will follow you in as well, maybe a click behind you guys and ahead of Rick."

So, that's Kate's problem, my best friend thinks she's being ignored. "I expect you to be with me the whole time," Maya said. Your expertise is to be my eyes in the sky, there's no one else I would trust in that position. You will be tracking my movements until I actually enter the facility when I will have to ditch my helmet cam."

Not a bad plan, Kate thinks. Of course, what do I really know about military missions, I'm not a soldier. Maya's right, the best thing for me to do is to watch how it unfolds and provide guidance, at least until they enter the building. "What's your back up plan, you know, just in case everything goes to shit?" she asked.

"Hopefully we will be in a position to fight our way out, even hand-to-hand combat if it becomes necessary. With Rick and a team not too far away, we will have a fair amount of fire power in total." Maya checked her watch and said, "I need to go back to our quarters to prepare myself for tonight." Maya got up from her chair to leave and said to Kate, "I'll be alright, especially with you running things back here."

"Alright, I will stay here and call up the information about tonight drone flight." I'll see you in a bit."

****

Kate sat at the computer but paused before firing up the tracking program. She went mulled over what Maya had told her about the mission. She was aware of Maya's reputation but that was earned in the past, when she was much younger and had honed her body and skills to a razor's edge. She had worked out with Maya and shot targets with her, and she's good, no question. But combat ready is a totally different story. Our joint excursions, over the last few years basically had us being 'cat burglars'. The toughest thing we did was to scale the outside of a building and dodge the occasional security guard; who may or may not have been armed with a handgun. Definitely, there was no one shooting at us.

If Maya had engaged in any "hot action" in recent years, it would have occurred when Kate wasn't providing logistics, like the time in Beirut. Events got screwy over there, but everything happened after the mission was over. And that mission required her to be a sniper positioned several hundred yards away from the close quarter firefighting. Dangerous, yes, but not like this.

If there had been any other similar action, Maya had kept the details to herself. Kate doubted there were others similar to Beirut, she would have thrilled at recounting the details to her.

Kate returned her attention to the computer, pulling up the details for the mission. She carefully looked over the maps; no question the terrain was close to the Pakistani border. She scanned the data for several minutes; memorizing the pertinent details. Definitely doable but also extremely dangerous, with numerous opportunities for the mission to go to hell quickly.

She locked in the drone's flight data, saved it, and logged off. She walked the office to give the room one last look see, making sure one last time everything was good to go. She dimmed the lights and walked out of the office toward their quarters. All systems at her end were ready to go. And, although she didn't like the horrible possibilities that awaited if the plans weren't executed perfectly, she was set. As she walked out the door, she looked to her left and watched the sun start to set. The witching hour was quickly approaching.

****

Maya had been in their room for about an hour when Kate walked in. She was laying on top of her bunk, thinking, going over the plan, preparing herself mentally. She was dressed in dark brown colored fatigues that looked like they would disappear in the dark of night. Kate noticed the military rifle and ammo clips laying on her bunk.

Maya sat up on the bed and swung herself around to face Kate. "Sorry, you came back a bit sooner than I expected," she said as she picked up the gear on Kate's bunk.

After she laid the sniper rifle and clips on her bunk, Maya finished lacing up a pair of combat boots then stood up. She sported an assault rifle, two extra ammo clips and the helmet cam. She looked over at Kate and noticed her fidgeting a bit, with her brow furrowed. The talkative one had gone silent. Guess I'll have to give her a pep talk.

"You okay?" she asked Kate.

Kate nodded she was.

"You're being awfully quiet for you."

"Just thinking," came the reply.

"You know that you play a very important role in the success of this mission?"

"How so?" Kate said quietly.

"I need you here, eyes on the screens, fully alert and watching my butt. A lot of the early success in getting there will be the result of your oversight."

"I can handle that," Kate softly responded.

"Then, why the worried look; do you really wish you were going in with us?"

With a horrified expression, she loudly proclaimed, "Oh hell no. I've seen the plans; the good and the bad. I'm only crazy, not insane." She smiled and said, "Besides, since there's no water for me to dive into or no harbor to mine, I'd only get in the way. I'm just concerned about you; are you ready to handle a situation of this type?"

Maya pondered for a minute before she answered. "I'm definitely mentally prepared. If I lack anything physically, I'm counting on an adrenaline rush to carry me through. Besides I don't really have a choice. You read the note, it demanded I come alone.

"It's like riding a bicycle," she continued, "once you learn these skills you don't forget how to use them." She wasn't sure if she was trying to convince Kate or herself.

"It's not your mind I'm worried about. I know you are a crazed thrill seeker, that why we mesh so well. It's your physical abilities, do you have that razor combat edge anymore?"

"That's part of the reason I still workout and train like I do, to be prepared, just in case. And when shit happened in Beirut, I acquitted myself quite well. So yes, I believe I'm truly ready."

Before Kate can say anything else, there's a soft rap on the door to their quarters, followed by a whispered, "Hey, it's Dirk, you ready Maya?"

"Come on in," Maya whispered back.

Dirk opened the door and entered. He is fully geared, although without his favorite explosive. He was surprised to see two women standing in the middle of the room.

"Close the door," Maya said.

Still feeling wary, Dirk closed the door.

"I was hoping to introduce you guys to each under better circumstances," Maya said. Deep breath then, "Okay, here it goes. Dirk, this is Kate, the third person Rick and I were referring to when we said there are three people who know your real identity. Kate, Dirk."

They each exchanged a "Hey" and a nod as they acknowledged each other.

"Is she okay with this information; she won't talk to the wrong people if questioned, will she?" Dirk asked.

"I don't know what you mean by okay, but we've worked together for the last ten years. I trust her with my life."

"Sorry, nothing personal. It's just that no one outside of our group can know what we are doing. This is a personal battle and strictly off the books. At this time we're not even sure if the British command has figured out that Nick has been taken.

"If none of us make it back alive you've got to swear you know nothing if you're ever questioned." Dirk said.

"Understood," Kate replied. "I've already done that on past excursions."

Dirk raised an eyebrow at that comment; not sure if he was to answer. Puzzled, he said nothing.

"Kate's beyond good, that's why she here," Maya said. She's going to be back here running the visual end of this mission provided by the drone and my helmet cam. She will guide us to the location. Once we are there, I will hide the cam before entering the place. If things work out well, I'll retrieve the cam and she will guide us back out. If things go to hell, she'll at least know where we were when we made our last stand."

"Alright," Dirk said. "Just remember if things go to hell, you know nothing if you are ever questioned. That means you'll have to wipe the computer systems. Are you good with that, destroying evidence, if need be?"

Kate, with a straight face and in an emotionless voice, "Not a problem."

"Good," Dirk replied. He looked at his watch. "Okay Maya, time to go meet with Rick."

Maya picked up her rifle and readied herself to follow Dirk out the door. He looked at her and asked her where her vest was.

"I don't think I will need one. I don't want anyone to suspect I'm contemplating violence."

Dirk grimaced at that statement. "That makes no sense at all," he said. He paused as Maya braced her feet and defiantly folded her arms across her chest.

"Look, at least wear one to humor me; then if you want to dump last minute at the site, so be it." He's hoping once she has it on she will forget all about it.

Rather than starting an argument Maya reached into her footlocker, removed a vest and strapped it on. "Happy?"

"At least you're properly dressed," he retorted while he walked out the door.

Kate gave Maya a hug before she started to follow out the door. "Remember, I plan on seeing you and her grandchildren," she said.

"That's a promise," she said to Kate. "We'll be fine," "See you in a few hours."

They met with Rick and finalized the plan. He's to wait about ten minutes out with his tag team; if events go according to their calculations the three of them will find him and they will leave together. If he's heard nothing after twenty minutes; contact Kate and come to the rescue.

Dirk and Maya load the Jeep Rick secured for them and start the trip.

Chapter 15

About a mile out from the base, Maya activated the helmet cam. "Check, check," she said. "Kate can you see and hear me?"

After a brief moment comes Kate's reply; "I hear you loud and clear; and I have a decent picture."

"What do you know?"

"You're about eight kilometers away from your destination. I see several clusters of vegetation where you can hide your Jeep about four kilometers from the building. The last drone pass showed your guys as the only ones on the road. It looks like clear sailing for now."

"Any pictures of our final destination?"

"Not yet," Kate replied.

"Keep us posted when the images are available of our rendezvous point."

About eight minutes later Dirk pulled off the road and hid the Jeep. Maya called Kate to tell her they had hidden their vehicle and had disembarked.

"Good timing," Kate said. "I just received the photos of the area. The drone pass showed a small compound with three buildings. There is light in one building which is pretty much directly ahead of you on a straight line. The other buildings, both smaller in size, are dark right now. They are located to your right as you approach. One of them is a direct line to the main building while the other is about two hundred feet behind both buildings."

"Roger that," said Maya. "We have started walking toward the site."

After a couple of minutes Kate asked, "Can you see the lights up ahead?"

"They are just starting to come into view," Maya said. "What's does the scenery look like?"

"There is a guard about fifty feet outside the first building patrolling the perimeter. The heat signature the drone picked up shows at least four people inside. One of them is seated."

"Got it," Maya replied. She passed on the message to Dirk.

"The person seated is most likely to be Nick," he said.

"That's pretty much a guarantee," Maya replied.

"I'm moving about seventy-five feet toward the right side of the building. I'm going to watch the guy to see if he's expecting anyone up from the other side. If not, he and I will have a meeting."

Maya has her eye on a small medallion on Dirk's uniform. When he moved his right arm just so, it emitted a faint light. They are about a hundred feet away from the building when they stop in the shadows. They have a perfect visual of the guard who's stopped on the right side of the entrance. Dirk raised his arm so Maya can see the light, he's in place.

Maya said to Kate, "This is the end of our communications for a while."

"I wish you would keep the helmet cam on. I may be able to provide valuable information. It's possible it won't even be noticed."

"I'm going to bet that, based on the intricacies of this setup, the mastermind would immediately spot a helmet cam. Nice thought, though."

"God speed to both of you. Will talk to you guys on the way back home. Over and out."

Maya looked to her right just as Dirk lured the guard into his position by making a noise. He wrapped his powerful arms around the guy's head and neck. Their meeting is over as the once struggling body slumped to the ground, unmoving. He signaled all clear.

Maya removed her helmet cam and vest, then slipped into the building first; ducking behind an object of some type.

Dirk, not happy when he saw her drop the vest, stayed outside in the dark shadows to stand guard and to scope out the surrounding terrain. He needed to determine how much open ground is available to make a fast exit once they grab Maya's; our, son. Through his night vision goggles he doesn't notice anyone in the near vicinity; the enemy appear to be inside.

He briefly looked over the building, searching for the electric source. He entertained a thought of killing the power supply but realized he was the only one wearing night vision goggles. Therefore, plunging the building into darkness wouldn't provide a tactical advantage for Maya.

Off to the right of the building Maya sidled into, he spied another structure, smaller in size than the lighted building. It was right where Kate said it would be located. The area around that building is dark, also with no discernable activity nearby.

He also spied the third structure maybe a hundred seventy-five feet beyond his immediate position; a bit behind the other two as viewed from his vantage point. That building was also dark. He confirmed the compound set up was just as Kate described it; a small compound consisting of three modest sized buildings with the largest structure the place of the action. What's curious to him, the area and the buildings seems empty except for where his son is being held.

If they will need to engage in a firefight, it appears there is plenty of space to maneuver around. He hoped the remaining two buildings could be turned into defensive positions if needed. The only drawback, in his mind, was not knowing what was inside each structure. They must, at a minimum, be some type of storage facilities. Of particular note the immediate ground was unoccupied by vehicles. Therefore, the occupants in the first building must have parked their vehicles behind the building.

CHAPTER 16

Inside and secreted out of sight, Maya sees her son tied to a chair in the middle of the huge open space. The area is bathed in bright, nearly blinding light. She clasped a hand over her mouth to stifle a cry welling up in her throat.

She quietly maneuvered around several containers for a view not directly aligned to the light. She can now see his face as she is in front of him and to his left. Perfect, even if Nicky looked in her general direction, he would be unaware of her presence.

She quickly looked over her end of the building as she tried to determine how much closer she could move forward undetected. She noted several cameras and other transmission equipment clustered off to one side, to the right and behind the chair holding Nick, and directly across from where she is.

Confused by the setup she frowned and wondered what the purpose was behind the equipment; could this be a studio set up? As that thought passed through her mind, she let out an audible gasp she hoped no one heard. Is the Taliban planning a televised beheading of her son? Why? For what purpose? He's just a grunt, a low-level commando of no significant rank. I'm sure he has little, if any, intelligence knowledge and therefore, no value for that purpose.

Just as she began to figure out what's happening, she realized she was fucked. Somehow, she revealed her presence; maybe she didn't stifle her grasp in time. It doesn't matter how, any perception, any semblance of control she thought she had established was now gone. What's next?

A familiar voice, in a heavy British accent, called out form the shadows at the front of the space. "Show yourself, Maya, we know you are here." With that statement her son struggled in his chair, straining to catch a glimpse of his mother, surprised to hear his mother's name. What is she doing here he wondered?

Maya quickly unfastened her ammunition belt, assault rifle and an automatic pistol and dropped them behind her. Slowly and carefully, she extracted herself from the shadows. She stepped out into the light, moving cautiously forward towards her son.

"Now let me see your hands," comes the command. She slowly showed her empty hands.

"Good" says the voice she's still trying to identify. There's now no question this was a planned meeting as they had surmised. Will their reason as why to this specific place in Afghanistan also turn out to be correct?

In a strong steady voice, she called out, "I've shown myself, why don't you do the same." She heard noise, like someone shuffled their feet, then muffled voices that she couldn't understand. Trying to establish a bit of a power situation she called again in a forceful manner as she neared her son, telling him, "Nick, it's MI6 officer Thernopolis, are you alright?"

Nick strained and twisted in his seat, the bindings preventing him from seeing his mother. Not sure why is mother identified herself to his captors with her official rank, he answered, "As you can probably see I'm a bit tied up right now officer Thernopolis; but otherwise I'm okay."

"Come, come Maya, that's very formal tone for a mother talking to her son." She believes she can discern a large figure, still bathed in the bright light. In a taunting tone the man continued, "This is your son, correct?"

No response.

"Of course, he is; after all, how many Thernopolis' are here in Afghanistan in the Queen's service? I only know of two and you are both here with me."

Dirk, who was hovering just outside the door in the shadows on the right, heard the entire proceedings. He checked the entrance, it was clear. Following the same path as Maya, he inched into the room.

Talking into the shadows she spoke in her own defiant manner, "Come on, are you really afraid of a mere woman?" A large man dressed sloppily in military fatigues emerged from the shadows at the front of the room. The bright light directly behind him still hid his identity.

"Maya, I know better than to make mistakes when dealing with you; with the first one being to assume that you are a mere woman. I made that mistake dealing with you once before and it cost me plenty."

Maya had her first clue; this person is someone from her past. And, apparently, they had squared off in some type of a confrontation that she won. If it's really been twenty years or more it's no wonder I am having trouble making the connection. But no, I've heard that voice much more recently, as here in Afghanistan. But who and more importantly, where?

Squinting and turning her head in an attempt to see behind the man speaking to her, Maya identified at least four other figures she believed to be men skulking in the shadows directly behind him. Sarcastically the man continued, "Maya, I know very well you are much more than a frail, helpless, woman. Why, I believe in the day some believed you to be an Amazonian warrior, a very formidable foe, almost mythical as it were."

Several men, including Dirk, had teased about her being like an Amazon. This second clue provided no real help in revealing who he is. Moving very slowly to her left, then stopping Maya replied, "Glad to know you are a fan of mine, but flattery will get you nowhere with me." Still can't identify the voice!

Dirk has found a secured spot from where he can see and hear everything as events unfold. He's mentally trying to device an escape plan from this mess. He calculates his first shot would eliminate the big guy; then if Maya could brush past Nick's chair and knock it over, he could take out a second man before joining her in charging the other two. He sees two problems; are the other men armed, and, how could he signal Maya?

As he approached her son, the captor noticed the quizzical look on his face. The unidentified man continued his soliloquy, "From the look on your son's face he seems to have no knowledge of his mother's past life." He mockingly shook his head, "Tsk, tsk, you have been very remiss in your son's education. Keeping secrets from your family members is never good."

He turned to face Nick, then continued, "Your mother was a tremendous field operative for MI6. She was one of a kind, the only MI6 officer to have been trained in lethal combat skills in addition to learning the traditional espionage tool kit." He paused to let Nick absorb that information. "Actually," he continued, "she was more of a violent killing machine than a spook, at least according to her file."

At that remark Nick restarted his futile effort to escape his bindings. Confusion, along with rage, coursed through his straining body.

"My problem with this is that she worked on a mission with a fuck headed partner some twenty years ago. She stood by and watched as the asshole killed two of my closest business associates. It cost me a small fortune when I lost that arms deal. And, another wad of money was burned when I baited you and your team into that deathtrap on al-Faw; but it was worth it when I knew specifically that moron died there."

Giving her a disgusting, leering smile, he said, "Then, you showed here your still pretty face here, at my British command post, accompanied by an equally lovely blonde pussy. The two of you came here, where I am the chief officer; all without my permission.

"I was okay with that fact, but I monitored your communications because I didn't trust you. And, what a doozy of a discovery you made; you reached into the realm of Hades to resurrect a dead man."

Dirk has figured out the identity of their tormenter. That rotten bastard, I should have killed him in Nicosia when I had the chance. The anger rushed through as he felt his muscles tighten; he was more than ready to spring into action. From the shadows he could kill the British traitor before disclosing his presence. He believed he could kill a second man almost as fast as the traitor hit the floor; then staying low he would move in the chaos from his right. Still, without somehow being able signal Maya before he started. He decided to sit tight. He returned his focus to the scene in front of him.

"So, Maya, you forced me back into seeking revenge, pushing me back into my ugly side. I wondered how to do this, and the answer was so simple; grab your son, lure the two of you here, and trade him for your former lover.

"How, you ask? Simple. To calm your worried mind, you sought out all possible information regarding your son's actions. The contact you established over the secret MI6 communications' network was me. So, as you have hopefully surmised by now, I know all about your rescue plan and I know Winter, who we all believed had been dead all these many years, is indeed alive and is here somewhere waiting in the shadows to be a hero. Speaking of the fuck head, where is he hiding?"

Still with a quizzical look on her face, she continued to wrack her brain to put a name to the face, only to produce a fuzzy memory. God, I must be getting old, she thinks.

A little annoyed with Maya, after all he had produced outstanding clues and hints, he said, "Perhaps this will jog the old brain cells," as he reached behind his back. Gun, Maya thinks, and she instantly ducked.

The man laughed at her silly reflexive action. "Please Maya, I have no intention of shooting you," the man says as he displays a stick of some type. A walking stick thinks Maya. "Johnson? Whit Johnson?" she asked.

He waved his hand in the air like he's ringing a non-existent bell. "Ding, ding, ding. Boy, it sure took you long enough to figure it out; you must be really getting old. I'd always believed you to be the brains of your partnership and Winter the muscle; maybe I had it backwards," he laughed. He leered again, "The gray matter may be atrophying, but at least your body looks fine."

Ignoring that comment and remembering Johnson was cleared in the inquiry, Maya asked, "Why?"

"Why not?" he responded. "Actually, it's always about money, my dear; money makes the world go 'round. Not only was I responsible for coordinating arms sales for our government and its allies, I was also directing a vast number of sales for everyone else in the Middle East, directing others to steal on my behalf; sharing a small amount of the money I was skimming from the legitimate and illegitimate deals.

"And, when Winter killed two of my best partners it put a major crimp in my operations. That, plus the added expense of killing him, or so I believed. Mr. Hero, Mr. Wonderful, had to track that last vehicle, had to watch them pull into the warehouse, at a time, may I remind you, that you had never appeared in the spy nest. Mr. Hero, who saw the four of us argue, just had to insert himself into the situation. Just another stupid Yankee cowboy who probably idolized John Wayne while growing up." Just the thought of it still pissed Johnson off. Which leads us to where we are today.

"When one of my informant's at MI6 told me recently that about a year or so ago you still had the hair-brained idea that Winter was alive, I decided to pay attention. As far-fetched as it seemed, for whatever reason, I guess you never gave up on the idea. Then, you come here, and lo and behold, you somehow find him.

"I needed a new plan to exact, how do they put it? Oh yes, my just desserts. As I stated, to speed up the reunion I found out your son was deployed here and where he was operating. I had him captured after a staged firefight. I sent several signals through your secured system to lure you here. And viola, you both came running.

"So, you see my dear, while fucking you is a thought, I don't want you or your son, I simply want to kill Winter and avenge the death of my former comrades. An eye for an eye, don't you see."

Maya was trying to run scenarios through her mind on how she was going to alert Winter to Johnson's plan. Was he watching from the outside and trying to figure out how the three of them would get out alive? However, if Dirk was in here and saw her take out Johnson, could he somehow save Nick and help her take out the other four; after all, he's armed and a deadly shot. No, no, too iffy. Stall, stall, stall and try to think she tells herself. "So," she said. "Twenty-years, isn't that an awful long time to carry a grudge? You know, in a way, you got what you wanted; you've operated all these years completely under the radar, so, you've won."

"Not really," comes the answer. "Not only did I just lose a lot of money on the deal you two killed, I lost deals and my reputation for several years after that. The Chinese wouldn't talk to me for years after those missiles were destroyed on al-Faw. Word travels fast after events like that and the vultures were quick to pick my bones. But I learned to preserve; until I found out that Winter is still alive.

"Come on, you're just stalling, where the hell is Winter, or do I have to torture your kid to encourage you to cooperate?" With those words a goon walked over to Nick and placed a knife against his throat.

Maya couldn't come up with any brilliant plan. Before she could respond came a voice from behind her. "I'm right here, you old bastard," boomed Winter. Winter had finished scoping the immediate area and concluded any attempt at an escape was too perilous at this moment in time. Winter stepped from the shadows; he was unarmed, having hidden his weapons separately from his current location. He carefully stepped forward, surveyed the situation, then stopped. His perceived advantage at a surprise move had disappeared when a knife was placed against Nick's throat.

"You're just like your fucking dead partners were, no you're worse, because you grabbed a kid to help you with your sick, demented, diseased schemes," Winter said in a strong, authoritative voice. "Let them go and you can have me."

"No, don't, he will only kill you," Maya said.

"I supposedly died once. I just can't let him harm either you or Nick." Winter, with his hands raised, walked toward Johnson at the front of the room. Before he gets within striking distance of Johnson the three other men who were in the shadows rush Winter quickly to try and take control of him. Winter let loose with a solid punch that landed on a jaw but ate two hard fists to the gut in return before he was subdued. Johnson then walked over to Winter and punched him in the face.

"Is that all you've got, you soft pussy? My mother throws a harder right hand," Winter spat. "You've got me, now let them go."

Johnson nodded at his men and one walked over and untied their son. Maya hurried over to Nick and quickly checked him over, he seemed to be in good shape. Surrounded by Johnson's goons, Maya and Nick head toward the front entrance. As they walked by, Johnson grabbed her arm and violently jerked her to him. He kissed her hard on the month. She kept her teeth clenched, basically not moving, desperately fighting the urge to kick his ass and eliminate his dick. Before letting her go he grabbed her ass, squeezed and rubbed it, and then did the thing same to her breasts. He licked his lips in a perverted manner while he rubbed his crotch, then laughed at her. To further show his contempt for her he shoved her away. Caught off guard, Maya stumbled a couple steps then planted her feet in a defiant stance. A short, overweight, smelly goon stepped between them.

"Really? Who are you trying to impress, your lover or your son?" He taunted, "You may have been a good fuck at one time and may still be, but I won't waste my time on you now. Now take your snot-nosed kid and get the fuck out of here before I change my mind. I want to have a little fun with your boyfriend before I kill him," he smirked.

They continued to walk back to the entrance she came in. She stopped before they exited and looked. She watched as Dirk hands were bound with some type of restraints. She will immensely enjoy coming back and killing Johnson and all of his goons. The question is how?

Chapter 17

"Now, with the distractions gone you have my full attention," sputters Johnson at Winter. "My friends here are quite inventive in the art of torture. But first, we will warm up the old-fashioned way." Johnson nodded to his goons and two of them grabbed Winter. He struggled which earned another punch in the face from Johnson. Winter simply smiled and glared at his tormentor.

His hands are bound securely, and the goons hold him in place by the arms. He watched as a rope that is threaded through a pulley about eight feet or so above the ground is brought to where he is held. The end Johnson grabbed is tied to the leather strap around Dirk's wrists and he is hoisted a couple of feet off the ground. Guess the rules of the Geneva convention won't apply here, Winter says to himself as the first fist from one of the goon's slams into his gut and caused him to gasp a bit.

"And now that I have your attention" says Johnson, "a little interrogation. First question, where is your backup right now?"

"There is no backup plan, moron, just me and Maya."

Johnson, having hacked the MI6 communications system knows Winter is telling the truth. Playing coy he says, "That's a very stupid plan, not having a tag team on alert. I guess the two of you are as dumb as everyone said you are."

Winter just smiled. "Lucky for you we freelanced, otherwise an American team would have landed and killed everyone but you by now," he said. "They would have had left the pleasure of killing you to me."

Although the hairs on the back of his neck rose, Johnson ignored this attempt at bravado and moved on. "Next question, are you in charge of tracking my weapons transfers to the Taliban?"

Winter, "It's not me and I don't have any idea who it is."

"Wrong answer." Johnson nodded and the same goon in rapid succession unleashed two more clubbing blows; both are pounded into Winter's torso, causing him to gasp a little deeper for air.

"What base are you working from, American or a multi-country facility?"

"I'm stationed in Afghanistan moron." Another blow to the midsection elicited a cough from Winter. He's a tough son-of-a-bitch; the CIA did a good job with him.

Switching tactics, he decided to add a little verbal abuse and try to enrage Winter. Johnson taunted, "I hope you realize after I have exhausted my time with you, we will track down your bitch of a girlfriend and her son and bring them back here. After we all fuck her, we will slowly kill the three of you so each of you can watch the others die."

At that statement Winter laughed and responded, "You really think these assholes can track them down and bring them back here? Someone as skilled as she is, someone you called a violent killing machine? And, then you're going to fuck her before killing us? Good luck with that half-assed idea."

"What," Johnson replies, "you really believe she that she is god-like, some kind of a Wonder Woman? That was just a character in your stupid American comic books you read as a stupid kid."

"No," says Winter, "But, I'll tell what I do know you dumb ass. Like a fucking idiot, you just decided to screw with a momma bear and her cub. And let me explain this in words even you can understand; you have one fucking angry momma bear on your hands now, shit for brains. And like all mothers protecting their young, she'll fight to the death, your death, to safeguard him."

"Very amusing," Johnson laughed, "we will see. I'm tired of this nonsense." He walks over to a table looking for an item or two to enhance this slow process. He picked up a pair of pliers then walked back to Winter. Just for the hell of it he reached out and spun him, increasing the pressure on his joints. Laughing, he instructed his goons to take off Winter's boots. He looked over his feet and said, "It's looks like you need your toenails cut. Since I have no nail clippers, I guess I'll just have to remove them entirely."

Chapter 18

A soft crackle over his head set then Rick hears Kate's voice. "Rick it's Kate, can you hear me?'

"Loud and clear," he said. "So, tell me what's going on, have you heard from Maya or Dirk?"

"Silencio. They arrived at the compound about thirty minutes ago. I was tracking them the entire way. Once they arrived, I provided an overlay of the buildings from the drone feed. Dirk took out a guard and then Maya took off her helmet cam before entering the building where Nick is being held. Where are you right now?"

"Maybe five klicks from the compound."

"About one click ahead of you, on your right, you'll find a cluster of vegetation. Dirk hid their Jeep in there, then they walked the rest of the way."

Slowing down and carefully watching the scenery on the right, one of Rick's guys in the back hollered out, "Hey boss, over on the right; it's looks like the trees may have been moved to camouflage something."

"That something should be the Jeep we are searching for," Rick said. He pulled off to his right, stopped the Hummer and turned off the engine. He signals to the team to exit the vehicle.

The team searched the perimeter area while he approached the Jeep cautiously. He saw nothing to indicate it had been found by the enemy and booby-trapped. He reached out and touched the hood; it still emitted a small amount of heat. Confident he has found Dirk's Jeep he waited for the guys to report back.

After three minutes the team gathered together. Each guy walked out twenty-five yards and came back. They covered all four directions and found nothing. At this time no one, friend or foe, knows they are here. Time to call Kate.

Kate had barely answered the phone when Rick hit her with a verbal barrage. "We found a Jeep hidden like you said it would be. I checked it over, it wasn't booby trapped and the engine still radiated some heat. My guys surveilled the general area and found no signs of friend or foe. We.."

"Slow down," Kate said. "Let me process what you said and compare what you found to.."

"Hurry up," he interrupted. They've been on site close to forty-five minutes. Our plan was to give that amount of time and then to make our way in. We're ready to move."

"Okay, okay, but a just little bit of patience," a flustered Kate replied.

"I can't have patience; time is of the essence. Every minute we waste is another mark against getting them out alive and home safely."

"Hey, you called me, remember? Don't forget I'm part of this team even if I'm not on site."

Rick could hear the anger in her voice. She's right, her role in the success of this mission is paramount, she's the only one who can see everywhere. "I'm sorry, it's just, I'm worried something as gone wrong."

"So am I. Now, before you go all 'Rambo' on me, listen up. First, the drone conftrmed about five minutes ago that you team is the only traffic on this side of the road.

"The second thing is the last pass of the drone showed several vehicles behind the main building; there could be several hostiles on site.

"Third, it's very likely your plan wasn't properly executed. The last drone feed showed only two figures leaving the main building. Two is not the ideal number for our side. The way they moved would indicate they are hiding as they left.

"Before you go crazy and storm the position, I ask you to wait a little longer."

Rick attempted to cut her off, "But.."

"But nothing. Let's see if we can somewhat lucky and assume the people who left are ours. Either Dirk or Maya would know to search for Maya's helmet cam. Mark time for another five minutes then call me before you do anything. This would allow someone to provide us with real time, on the ground, actionable intelligence. As you know, this option is a thousand times better than flying in blind and creating a bigger mess. Deal?"

"I not sure, what about..

"I said Deal?"

"Deal."

"Good. Look, I know it difficult waiting but when you stop to think it over, you know it's the right course of action," said Kate.

"Keep me posted."

"You're the first call I'll make."

Rick turned to face his team, the look on his face indicates he's clearly unhappy. "What's up," one of them asked.

"The early information is there was a problem with the plan as only two people have left the area. As you know there are three good guys from our side."

"Let's go pick them up," another commando chimed in. "I'm ready, the rest of the guys are ready and so are you. Right?"

"Right, however, there's one problem before we can move to the compound."

"What's that, are we outnumbered? If we are, we beat those kind of odds on a regular basis."

"I didn't ask if we are outnumbered; at this point it doesn't matter. The problem is we have no idea of the identity of the two people who walked out of the building, are they friend or foe."

"Oh shit."

"Exactly, that why, hard as it is, we need to wait a little longer. The belief is if they are friends, they will contact us with real time information."

Chapter 19

After they have exited the building, Maya was steaming, seeing red, spitting fire as she walked the grounds. She started searching the grounds.

Whether it was the degrading fondling she was subjected to or just anger at the entire situation, Nick's pretty sure he's never seen her this mad in his life. "I'm sorry I didn't do more to stop that mom," he said.

She waved him off. "Sorry about what, not getting shot or killed? I like you the way you are. Look, what just occurred in there is an unfortunate part of combat. The crazy bastard who has Dirk, I mean Mr. Winter, was definitely over the top. His actions were an attempt to break me through humiliation and to thoroughly intimidate you.

We were placed in a situation where there was nothing any of us could have done to change the outcome at that moment. We were at a decided disadvantage; which was a calculated mental attack on our psyches."

She walked in a small circle, then squatted down and picked up an object that she placed on head. "Helmet cam with a mic," she explained to a puzzled Nick. "Kate is back at Kandahar tracking us. I had to hide this so if shit happened inside, nothing could be traced to Kate."

Maya flipped the night vision goggles and scanned the ground. Nick, watched then asked, "What are you looking for?"

"I noticed that Dirk had nothing on him when he walked in and gave himself up. Since he had an assault rifle and an automatic pistol when we arrived, that means he left his gear somewhere nearby."

With her back against the building she scanned the area further, noticing something in the grass. "Over there", she whispers, "right in back of you. Grab it and let's go." After Nick retrieved the rifle, they continued to move among the shadows. After they cleared sight of the building, she whispered, "start a slow run."

They quickly jogged away, staying in a semi-crouch. While running she tested the system. "Kate, Kate, can you hear me or see anything? Kate, are you there?"

They stopped running once they were out of sight of the building's lights, about two hundred yards away. A crackle and she heard Kate's voice.

"I can you hear but I have a scrambled picture." She fiddled with the feed; better. "I can see you; you appear to be running."

Breathing a little harder, Maya answered, "Good, you can see us. Yes, we are running."

"So, everything worked out?"

Maya slightly turned her head.

"Wait," said Kate. It looks like you have Nick; where is Dirk? Is he out of the camera's range? You guys are headed home, ready to be picked up, right?" Kate asked.

Maya and Nick came to a clearing and stopped running. "Shit happened Kate. Our assumptions were pretty much spot on. We found out that asshole, Whit Johnson, the guy who we met on our first day at Kandahar, is behind the plot. Long story short I have Nick and they have Dirk and are probably torturing him as we speak."

"Oh shit. What's the game plan now?"

"I don't have one right now," Maya responded. "I'm going back for Dirk and will improvise once I get there. What's the status on Rick, is he enroute with a team?"

"I'm have great news on that front. About ten minutes ago, Rick and his team, five guys total, reached the place where you guys had hidden your Jeep. They are chomping at the bit and ready for some action.

"I convinced him to stay put until he heard from me. I told him the last drone pass showed two people leaving the building; we now know it was you and Nick. I wanted him to wait in hope that you or Dirk would contact me. I want us to formulate a plan before I make contact again."

Maya paused, as she mulled over an idea, nothing is coming quickly. She checked her watch; each minute wasted makes it that much worse for Dirk. Finally, she said, "Tell Rick to give me twenty minutes before coming in."

"Why so long?"

"I'm going back to get Dirk. The plan is to sneak in. I'm armed with an assault rifle. I can release Dirk and then extinguish the lights in rapid fashion. The darkness will be an advantage to me as I will be wearing the night vision goggles.

"Once freed Dirk should be able to roll under a table and I should be able to take them in a fast attack. If Rick arrives too early the captors will hear their vehicles which may cause them to kill Dirk."

Kates hesitated for a moment. She's trying to shoot holes in that plan but has no counter argument. She reluctantly said, "Makes sense, I guess."

"Is the drone still up?"

"The last flyby, roughly ten minutes ago, showed no change in your area or five hundred yards around it."

"I'm leaving the cam on so you can quickly advise me if anything changes on the ground," Maya said.

"I will," Kate responded. "You two stay safe and good luck."

****

"I'm going back for Mr. Winter," Maya said to Nick. That bastard Johnson wants him dead and will kill him for the fun of it. Besides, as you know, no one is left behind."

"I'm going with you Mom; two armed soldiers against five are better odds than one alone."

She shook her head no. "Kate has been in contact with uncle Rick; he's ready with a tag team about four klicks straight ahead. You need to go meet him and bring them in. I just need to get back as fast as possible and execute a plan to stop the torture."

Maya turned around to start back, Nick is matching her stride for stride. She glared and opened her mouth to speak but Nick spoke first. "Mom, I'm trying to piece this whole situation together in my mind. I believe Mr. Winter was a very special person in your life and probably still is. I'll bet the two of you have a very interesting story to tell me."

Maya noticed he's still matching her step for step, so she stopped. She turned to face him and said, "Yes he is, and we'll talk, the three of us, after we are safe. What right now you need to turn around and go back."

"But mom," he protested.

"Soldier forget that I'm your mother. I outrank you on this mission and I have given you a direct order. End of discussion." She reached out her hand. "Give me Dirk's rifle." He handed her the weapon.

"Now, go back four klicks and you will meet uncle Rick. Tell him to wait five minutes and then drive the vehicles in."

"Then what?"

"Hopefully we'll be assembled in the compound when you guys show up, ready to go. If not, he'll know to set a perimeter. You guys will probably need to fight your way in at that point and clean up the mess. Your knowledge of the building's interior will be invaluable to Rick to plan out his entry."

She removed a small sat phone from her pocket and gave it to Nick. With that she left her son who was sputtering and mumbling something unintelligible under his breath. It's just as well, she probably wouldn't want to hear him anyways. Besides, there's no time for an argument right now.

She circled the area, turned around and headed back toward the building. As she started back at a run/jog pace she thought, now what? She admits to herself what she told Kate may be nothing more than a half-assed idea. She was trying to assure her she had everything under control. She realized she will just have to make it up on the fly when she gets there. For Dirk's sake I hope I'm not too late.

Chapter 20

Nick walked back in the direction Maya told him to go. He picked up the pace and started to run. He stopped after a couple of minutes. The run didn't help clear his mind. He walked around a bit, kicking his right foot at the ground, at nothing really. He placed his hands on his head and exhaled deeply. "Screw it," he said to no one. "I'm going after my mother." Order or no order, he convinced himself it was the right thing to do. She can have me court martialed later if she thinks that the right response to being insubordinate,

He hadn't gone more than a hundred yards when he heard a noise coming from his shirt pocket. Puzzled he reached into the pocket and pulled out Dirk's sat phone; he had forgotten his mother had given it to him before she left. Hesitating a bit, he answered, "Hello?"

"Nick? It's uncle Rick. Why do you have Dirk's sat phone? What's going on out there?"

While Nick continued to walk back to the compound, he explained to uncle Rick what had happened.

"Son of a bitch," he exclaimed when Nick finished. Their plan had allowed for the fact that everything could wrong; that's why he was to come in at the end with the tag team.

"Okay, I have a very important message for you to deliver. Go tell you mother I'm ten minutes out, max. Help her stabilize things and save Dirk." said Rick.

Nick smiled from ear to ear. Just to be clear he heard the message he asked, "Is that an order?"

"Get your ass in gear, now," Rick bellowed. "I'll take care of your mother's objections."

Nick picked up the pace to a moderate jog; he didn't want to sprint as he assumed he would be in the middle of some type of combat action when he arrived. He figured his mother had no more than a three-minute head start on him and he would make up the ground fast.

After five or six minutes he sees first the building's lights then Maya maybe a hundred yards ahead. She has slowed her pace to a walk and appeared to be trying to determine her best point of entry. She swept to her right, then is motionless as she catches a glimpse of Winter hanging from the ceiling; he doesn't appear to be moving. I'm too late, is her first thought.

She spins around at the sound of a slight rustle; damn, I told Nick to stay put. Creeping up ever so quietly beside her and before she can say a word he says, "I got uncle Rick's response; he's about eight minutes away. When I told him what happened, he ordered me to come here to help you save Dirk first. If you need to punish me do so after speaking to him."

Lessening her intense glare, Maya says, "You're correct and while it's still dicey, it will be better odds with the two of us against five or six of them."

Nick peered into the room over his mother's shoulder. He sees the same scene that Maya had, an unmoving Dirk hanging by his arms from the ceiling of the building, unmoving. "Is he dead? he asked.

"God, I hope not, I really hope not. I lost him for twenty years, I can't lose him again after just finding him." She wiped away a small tear running down her check. "I'm going in," she whispered.

"Hold on and wait just a minute Mom. Just charging in will accomplish nothing but getting all three of us killed because you know I'm going to follow you in. Now listen, there's a back entrance where the guy you called Johnson was hiding with his men; there are five of them total. I can make out three figures with Mr. Winter, that means the other two are hiding somewhere near the other entrance. I can sneak around there and ambush them. I'll have the element of surprise on my side as I don't believe they thought we would be back so soon, if ever."

Maya nods her head in agreement. "Not bad. Just be careful. One question, did you see any weapons in the back area?"

"A massive number. The entire back area is teeming with weapons. There are so many different types of weapons, light and heavy, that its looks like a military depot."

"Wow, I'm really surprised he lured us to a major warehouse like that. He must be awfully convinced he going to kill us."

"No offense, but if the sides were switched, wouldn't you be convinced you would win any fight?"

She nodded in agreement. "Then we have to change those odds until Uncle Rick and the tag team arrive."

Maya is quiet, she can't think of a plan of entry for herself other than straight ahead. Sensing her hesitancy Nick piped up. "I've got an idea."

He's on a role so listen to him. "Go ahead."

"Are you a good shot?"

"Better than your instructors as I taught most of them," she responded.

"Okay, I will take out the two in back and quickly cross your sight line from back there. You shoot the leather bindings holding up Mr. Winter and then charge in. We figure the rest out once we breech the room. Who knows, maybe Uncle Rick will get here sooner than he thought he would. And mom, if Mr. Winter is anywhere close to being as tough as you are, he's still alive."

Before Maya can object, Nick hightailed to the back of the building. Damn, she's too much like his mother; or for that matter, his father.

****

"Wake him," Johnson commanded, "he needs to enjoy what we are going to do to him as I'm not done yet."

Maya watched as one of the goons throws water in Winter's face and then Johnson slaps him twice across the face. She looks around, waiting for Nick to signal he's in place. She noticed that Winter is barefoot and surmises that one or more of his toenails have been plucked from their nail bed. She shudders, that would be a lot of nasty pain. Stall, Maya says under her breath.

Winter spits, sputters and moans, slowly regaining his senses.

"Ahh, good to see you're still with us. I know the pain of electric shock is unbearable, but you chose not to cooperate; therefore, you suffered." Johnson leaned into Winter's face and whispers to him, producing a pair of pliers.

Looking around to clear his head, he exhaled and said, "you guys ready to quit while you're ahead?"

"Still an asshole, I see, right to the end."

Winter turned himself so he faced the front entrance. Still groggy and trying to focus his vision, he thought he saw movement near the doorway. "Nope, not an asshole, well maybe, who knows." Looking to turn up the heat he added, "But I think I can sense a momma bear nearby."

Maya has seen enough. Dirk is alive and signal or no signal she's going to act. She aimed her weapon at the leather bindings. There's a noise, some kind of commotion in the back room. Johnson and the others turn their attention ever so briefly and she fires. Crack, a clean shot, the bindings are cut, and Winter dropped to the ground, trying to roll away and find cover. In rapid succession Maya lets loose a second shot and drops one of the goons trying to flee toward where Nick is.

Maya left the helmet cam on, aimed at where Dirk was hanging so Kate watched the action live. Nice shot she called out as Maya dropped one of the goons, but no one was there to hear. While she watched, transfixed, she called Rick. "Where are you," she asked.

"I'm at most at least a klick out from the hiding place. The road, what there is of it is in real bad shape, full of big holes and ruts, so we're hardly advancing forward. What's up?"

"Maya is in the building and Nick went in from the back. She left the cam on so I'm watching this action live. Maya found Dirk hanging from the ceiling and not moving. She shot through his bindings which dropped him to the floor and started a gun fight. Continue to drive the vehicles straight in as close as you can and set up a perimeter. No one will hear you as your team will be joining a hot battle."

"Roger that, good to hear everyone is alive and fighting," he replied. To the other guys he said, "The action on site is hot, so I'm driving straight in. I'm not sure if our side is winning or losing so be prepared to immediately engage hostiles once we have stopped."

The second goon returns fire at Maya, as a bullet whistled over her head. She ducked behind several containers, looking for Nick, Dirk and another target.

Johnson, at the first shot, scurried toward a work bench as he swore up a storm. Winter, unable to get to his feet, spins on his ass, hoping to trip Johnson. His effort is a little too late and Johnson jumped over his leg. Johnson reached the bench. grabbed a hunk of pipe and thundered it off the side of Winter's head and right shoulder. It wasn't a direct blow but was solid enough to put him down with a thud. As Winter slumped to the ground he turned and rolled under the bench.

Maya followed the action and lined up a shot at Johnson, but before she squeezed the trigger, Nick is pushed into the room by a goon holding an automatic pistol on him. In broken English he bellowed out, "Hold it."

Johnson looks up, see his side is in control and mockingly calls out, "Come out, come out wherever you are Maya. As you can see, I have complete control of the situation again."

Maya dropped her weapon and stepped into the light. A quick look around shows Johnson is right. It's three against three with his team definitely in control. Winter is just starting to rub his head, no blood; he partially blocked the blow to avoid his head as he turned away. But, what an ache in his shoulder and neck. Nick has a pistol pointed at his head and she just gave up her vantage position.

Without a plan in mind she sat her helmet cam on a nearby crate and started to walk towards the front of the room. She rubbed at her crotch and loosened her belt. She stopped about ten feet away and screamed at Johnson, "You've wanted my pussy, for twenty years, you worthless piece of shit. If you think your man enough come and take it."

"Maya," Kate screamed as she watched, "What the fuck are you doing you dumb shit." To Rick she yelled, "Get your asses moving, Maya is about to put her life on the line."

"We're doing the best we can. We had to back up and circle to the right, but we are back on track and moving."

Chapter 21

As Maya started to walk again, Johnson, with an evil sneer on his face, started slowly, carefully moving towards her, wielding the pipe he used on Winter. They get about five feet apart and Maya unbuttons the top two buttons on her shirt, while pulling it out of her pants, hoping to distract him.

"Looks like we're going to get our wish with your girlfriend," Johnson screamed to Winter. "Watch as I lead the parade."

"Come on you bastard," she hissed. Johnson moved first, wildly swinging the pipe. Maya easily avoided the blow and delivers a quick kick to the back of his thigh. Johnson buckles a bit and Maya moves in, delivering a kick to his ample stomach. She goes low, grabbing the arm holding the pipe. She turns her back into him, striking him in the face with a back elbow; then violently yanks and twists his arm down across her shoulder. Clang, he dropped the pipe!

However, before she can dance away, Johnson delivered a clubbing forearm blow across her upper back and shoulders, sending her stumbling forward toward the floor. As all eyes are on the fight, Nick noticed his captor's grip on him has relaxed some.

Maya, unable to quickly establish her footing, breaks her fall with a rolling somersault. Johnson, showing more quickness than anyone thought possible, pounced on her, unleashing a hand swing towards her face. Maya only partially slips the punch; while not a flush blow to her face it nonetheless puts her on her back. Johnson, in a semi spread leg crouch, towered over Maya. Smiling, he reached down and grabbed her, picking her up by the throat.

Just as he started to lift her up, he abruptly stopped, letting go of her throat and placing his hands over his crotch. Maya dropped back to the floor. She had delivered a hard, nasty kick between his legs; for good effect the combat boots intensified the blow.

She slides away, scrambled to her feet and then delivered a hellacious front thrust kick into the front of his neck, crushing his windpipe. Johnson slumped to the ground, gasping and flailing around as he struggled to breathe. "Wanna fuck me now, you stupid bastard?" she bellowed as he slowly stopped struggling. Turning around she takes one step and then collapsed from exhaustion.

In a state of total disbelief that a mere woman just killed their boss, the goon holding Nick in a loose chokehold tries to step away and aim his gun at Maya. Nick quickly reacted by ramming his head back into his nose, blood trickling down his face. Nick grabbed his gun arm and violently yanked his arm over his shoulder. The weapon clanged on the concrete floor. The goon closest to Dirk turned his attention to watch the new struggle. Not wanting to shoot his partner by mistake he kept his weapon ready but lowered.

Nick reached the gun first and his captor jumped on his back, driving him to the floor. As they struggled over the weapon the gun goes off, and Nick staggered backward, falling to the ground, shortly before the other guy falls. Unsure what happened, Winter screams "No" causing the goon closest to him to spin around at the sound of Winter's voice. Before he can react Winter, who by this time had recovered his boots and removed a knife, rose to his knees and whipped his weapon. It sailed through the air and into the goon's chest, causing him to immediately drop to the floor. Winter slowly got to his feet and limped toward Nick who sat up. "I'm fine," he said. "Go check on my mom; remember she collapsed after the fight."

Winter nodded, put on his boots and turned his attention to Maya who started to pull herself up at the sound of gun fire. Winter takes a couple of steps then sits down, still breathing very heavily. Maya sees this and rises to walk over to Winter with a bit of a limp that she ignored. As she reached him, she noticed he smelled like he had been on fire. "What happened?" she asked.

"I have some injured ribs, maybe broken, from the work-over they gave me; it's killing me to breathe. The burning smell is where they were trying to brand me, for lack of a better description. Guess I was singed a bit. Fortunately, you interfered before they went after my feet." Winter grimaces and grabbed his ribcage.

"You're going to need medical attention, and soon," Maya said.

"Not going to argue with you but I'll be alright for now once I catch my breath. He laced his boots, stood up, grimaced and said, "Come on, we still have work to do."

Chapter 22

As Nick started to make his way over to his mom and Dirk, they hear the rumble of vehicles and see lights coming from the road in the back of the building.

"Sounds like this battle isn't finished yet," Nick said. "This could be unwelcomed company coming soon to pick up their weapons stashed all over this place. And we still don't have backup. At a minimum we need to pull back to the other building and try to establish a defensive perimeter until help arrives."

Smart kid, Winters thinks as he pulled on his boots; someone trained him well. He stands with Maya's assistance. Together and leaning on each other for support, they started laboring toward the front of the building where they entered.

Nick watched as they stumbled together, not making much progress. They stopped to retrieve a rifle and ammo clip for each of them, then proceeded forward. They take a few more steps and stop again, this time next to Maya's helmet cam. She put it on, adjusted the gear and started walking again.

The cam crackles, then, "Maya, Maya, is that you?" Kate asked.

"Yep," she answered.

"I didn't see everything, but it looked like you wiped out somebody, was it Johnson, is he dead? I assume everyone is alright. Why is the picture bouncing?"

"That was Johnson I fought; he won't be terrorizing anyone anymore. If you mean did we all survive, then that is true; however Dirk and I suffered injuries. As for the camera bouncing it's probably because I injured my leg and as a result I limp when I walk."

"Has Rick arrived yet?"

"Not yet," Maya said as she and Dirk stopped to rest. "He told me earlier they were having trouble negotiating the road, more accurately, the lack of an actual road. We expect him and the team soon."

"I'll try to reach him and find out if they are moving or stalled out. Gotta go, keep me in the loop." She signed off.

Maya returned her attention to the task at hand. She's clearly struggling with Dirk; at this rate they'll never leave the building. Nick finally said to his mother, "I can get Mr. Winter back to the other building, are you good to go on your own?" She nodded yes and yielded her position. They pulled Winter to his feet and Nick got under his shoulder to help him walk while Maya gathered up the rifles and ammunition clips.

She started walking by herself, actually limping is a more apt description. She moved gingerly, definitely favoring her right leg, the one she kicked Johnson with. She hurt like hell but gritted her teeth and sucked it up. She was moving much faster alone.

As they reached the front door, they heard a couple of vehicles stop and the engines shut off. Speaking in clipped English a voice calls out, "Johnson! Johnson? Are you here?" After a brief period of silence, they heard, "The weapons are here so Johnson can't be far off; we'll wait."

Dirk said, "They'll soon find the bodies we left behind. I doubt I will make it to the front building in time. There is a smaller shed directly to our left. I will go there, enter from the front and clear the place if needed. You two circle behind the building and enter from there." He grabbed a rifle and ammo clip, took a deep breath, winced and bolted toward the closest structure.

He ignored the pain as the they scrambled for the other building, then Nick and Maya left him to prepare to go in from the back. An adrenaline rush allowed him to walk a bit better as he reached the shed. He pushed through with his assault rifle raised. He looked over the area and determined the place was emptied. Finally, something went our way. He went to the back where he found a stuck window. He spied a pinched bar, banged on the frame and got the window to rise. He stepped to the side and helped Maya through the window and sat down beside her on some crates, the adrenaline high had run out. He sat and watched as Nick followed closely behind his mother.

After a respite Dirk stood and ambled to the window. He looked out and studied the sky. "It looks like there should be enough darkness to provide cover until Rick brings in the tag team. Who's got my sat phone?"

"I had it, but it was smashed during the melee in the other building," Nick said.

Dirk frowned at that piece of news. "We need to fortify our position the best we can," he said. They began the process of secreting themselves in, moving empty crates that were probably used to haul weapons to the site.

They had just finished moving several pieces of wooden pallets against the door, leaving two windows unblocked, when Winter sees a dozen or so men come streaming out of the first building. They spread out; several men went behind the building to search for clues to find who killed the men inside while the others looked immediately ahead. The shed is soon spotted, and several men sprinted towards it.

"Time to make some noise and keep those bastards out of here. We don't need to, and most likely can't survive a long firefight. We just need to buy enough time for backup to arrive," Dirk commanded.

"Kate, Kate, can you hear me?" No response. "Damn, won't you know, she can call me but I can't call her. I was hoping to get a message out to let her know we will soon be trading gunfire," said Maya.

With Nick at his own window and Dirk and Maya across the room, they opened fire on the enemy, cutting down the first wave of men running towards them. The firing attracted the attention of the other men who came running toward the front of the building. They knelt down, returned fire and then scrambled for cover.

Inside the shed they ducked behind their cover and waited out the return barrage. Maya had the only pair of night vision goggles. When the shooting ceased, she cautiously rose to scan the grounds. She spotted movement to their left and began firing, as Dirk and Nick followed. Once again, they ducked to avoid the return fire.

"Shit, Dirk said. "What is happening is exactly what I didn't want to happen, even if right now we are eliminating them and taking no casualties in return. We are running low on ammo so we can't trade exchanges with them for too much longer. Damn, where is Rick?"

A crackle sounded in her head piece and a familiar voice rang out; "Maya, can you hear me?"

"Kate, finally, I tried calling you but got no response. In case you can't see us, we are holed up in a shed type building on the compound facing an unknown number of enemy fighters. We have begun exchanging fire."

A brief pause followed by; "I can see everything in front of you. The last time you stood up I saw at least ten men immediately to your left. It looks like you have killed four of their fighters so far. Don't worry, there are plenty more in reserve."

"Gee, thanks," Maya replied. How about something to cheer me up?"

The guys are silent as they listened to half of a conversation. The worried expressions on Maya's face doesn't paint a happy picture.

"Sorry friend, I'm afraid the bad outweighs the good. The drone has circled your position for the last fifteen minutes. There are more fighters coming your way. It seems that Johnson had arranged for a major weapons exchange with the surrounding enemy."

"What's the good news?" Maya halted at the sound of vehicles approaching from behind them. "Shit, we have fighters entering from a rear position."

"Hold on," said Kate. "That's the good news. The noise from in back of your position will be Rick and the tag team about to enter the fracas." Before Maya can respond the shooting starts again.

A nasty firefight is underway as Rick pulled in with his Hummer and Dirk's Jeep. They piled out of the vehicles, staying close to the trucks for protection as they see to divide the Taliban's attention and take away some of the firepower that was concentrated on the shed. Their night vision goggles provided Rick and his team with an advantage and they started to score kill shots. They absorbed a return volley, then returned the favor, then silence.

Rick spotted a window at the back of the shed. "Give me some cover guys; I'm going into that building over there to see if that's where the gang is holed up."

His men let loose with a hail of fire as Rick crouched low and headed straight to the shed. For some unknown reason there was no return fire.

As the shooting stopped Nick looked around at their position. Although the last volley did major damage to the door it still existed. His mom and Mr. Winter seem well secured and are talking in low tones. He checked the back of the shed. It's solid so the bullets haven't hit back there and caused damage.

He maneuvered his way toward the back window to do a little canvassing of his own. As he made his way there, he watched as someone sneaked through the shadows. Not sure if it's friend or foe he raised his rifle. He noted the figure hasn't raised his weapon, so he assumed the guy is a friend. About fifteen feet out he can make out an insignia, recognizing the British markings, then Uncle Rick.

Just as Rick reached the window the shooting started back up. Maya and Dirk ducked at the sound of the renewed fire, staying tight to the floor. They were low on ammo and didn't return fire. Interesting, the fire wasn't directed at them.

The enemy, without the aid of night vision enhancement, appeared to have figured where Rick's tag team was located and was shooting at them. The enemy's volley was short, ending as quickly as it started. It was answered by Rick's men who were much more accurate.

Realizing they weren't taking fire, Nick and Rick stood up at the window again. They both tried to pry it open with no luck. Nick yelled at him to stand back and he broke the glass. He removed the sharp pieces and helped him in.

Rick made his way to where Maya and Winter are barricaded just to the left of where a door was once located. A quick assessment by Rick revealed Maya and Dirk both have injuries but are functional. The shed appeared to be a solid structure. There are multiple objects to hide behind for protection; however, most everything is wood and with the door now pretty much obliterated from the hostile fire, their long-term safety is non-existent.

Time also is starting to turn against them as the dark sky is slowly beginning to fade away. When it's gone so is their advantage of fighting under the cloak of darkness. They need a plan to extricate themselves out of here and fast.

Maya finished with up a call she had fielded from Kate. Kate had reported the battle and its location up the chain of command. She informed command that Jason Cameron, aka Dirk, was running a surveillance op when he found a remote place near the Pakistani border. Sneaking onto the premises with a small party, he had an opportunity to confirm the existence of a major cache of weapons in the back area of a warehouse. The inventory included a plethora of rifles, RPGs, and shoulder launched missiles being stored there.

Before his team could leave, they encountered a group of Taliban fighters who were looking for their resupply. They were able to fight them off before retreating to a nearby outbuilding where they established a defensive perimeter. They are severely outgunned and outmanned.

The report Kate received back detailed that the latest intel had established this compound as a major weapons exchange point that they had walked into the middle of. An unknown arms dealer, who it is believed to be Whit Johnson, had set up a major transaction point where cash was to be swapped for the weapons. The group they are trading shots with now are the first of what is expected to be several more buyers along with their fighters. They are to remain in place and await further intel data.

The gunfire started again, this time it's the British commandos who initiated the action. Dirk and company take shelter and waited a moment for the return fire, which was sparse. Again, no shots are fired at the shed. They hoped the reason for the tepid response is that after the earlier ruckus ended, the commandos had been able to zero in on where the enemy fired from. The assistance of their night vision goggles should have allowed them to site their targets; their response and offensive actions should have been more accurate and deadlier.

When the shooting died down Maya received another contact from Kate, this time with a dire warning.

"I just got a message from base," Kate said. "They have eyes on your position as well as the road behind the building. The drone data showed more unwelcome company is coming your way. There are no nearby troops who can come to your aid.

"Therefore, command has called for an airstrike to totally demolish the compound and all buildings. You have approximately twenty minutes to get your asses out of there before all hell breaks loose.

"Your best bet is to head for a cave roughly two klicks out; you may have seen it on your way in. One there you should be able to ride out the bombings. After the raid is concluded an Apache helicopter will come in for the rescue."

Maya relayed the message to the others. "I'll go inform the other men," Rick replied. "We'll leave out the back and meet behind the vehicles. We will leave as a group."

In about three minutes everyone is huddled behind the vehicles. Rick told the group about the latest intel and how they had to move out now and quickly. "Not only do we have to move fast but we will also be on foot," he said. "If the Taliban hear us start the vehicles, the concern is they will attack en masse. Since they have us outnumbered, I'd rather sneak out as stealthily as possible."

To Maya and Dirk, he asked, "Can you both walk?"

"We'll suck it up and do the best we can," Dirk said.

"Good, let's get out of here."

Rick helped Dirk to his feet and the group prepared to depart. The rest had helped Dirk recover somewhat and he started under his own power. Right now, he was walking and breathing a lot easier.

Nick helped his mother stand. Her face showed she was still in a great deal of pain as she started walking with a still noticeable limp. He would definitely have to keep an eye on her condition.

They started down the road in the general direction of where the cave should be. Three of the commandos were in front, Rick, Nick and the fourth commando guarded the rear, with Maya and Dirk in between.

The sky has brightened quickly as the sun's journey is in a rapid race to shine gloriously. The group travels about five hundred yards when they hear weapons being fired behind them; it sounded like the shed was assaulted. Two- or three-minutes pass and the firing started up again; now the shots are being directed at them. Maya turned to look back, they were being followed; their secrecy of movement had been lost.

The helmet cam was activated; soon Kate was talking. It was a good time to stop and rest, Maya thought.

"The news isn't good as more fighters have arrived looking for the weapons. They examined the carnage and set out looking for who's responsible.

"Your immediate problem is that there are five men following you. These fighters set out in your direction for scouting purposes and found you. You second problem is they appear to be on a phone; I'll guess they are reporting that they found you. They could have reinforcements very quickly."

"Thank you, little miss sunshine. Anything positive to report?"

"You know what they say; don't shoot the messenger. To your point, the cave is still about a klick ahead. Your lead guys should be seeing some small rock formations and dirt mounds on your left. If you can't continue to the cave, then you need to take cover and be ready to fight it out. The war planes should be there in five minutes. If you are stuck behind the rock formations hopefully you be able to survive the bombing run. The pilots have been informed of the situation on the ground and to not fire on the front group."

Maya relayed the message and they turned left. The shots kicked up debris as they dove for limited cover behind mounds of dirt and rocks. There is a brief pause, which allowed them to catch their breath. The decision is made to continue trying to push ahead; this time Dirk is in the lead as he recognizes the territory.

Another volley is let loose at them from behind a cluster of trees about four hundred yards away. Then a thump, a whistle and a loud explosion about seventy-five feet to their right. Shit, that what the delay was for, to engage a mortar unit.

Dirk held up his hand and shouted so everyone could hear him. "Enough. We are still three hundred or more yards away from that rock formation. They are obviously moving faster than we are, plus they have a mortar setup. We each have weapons. I'd rather fight it out and die here, taking as many of them as possible, than try to run, fighting back at half strength and still dying." A grim assessment!

Before anyone responded, Kate, still watching and listening to them, shouted, "Duck, now." Maya relayed the message and they all dropped down. Mere seconds later the Taliban unloaded some more heavy weapons ordinance against them, which pounded their position unmercifully.

A loud noise is heard overhead, foreshadowing an A-10 Warthog is screaming into position. "Here comes the Calvary," Kate announced.

The Taliban stopped firing on them and trained their weapons on the war plane overhead, to no avail. A few seconds later several massive explosions thundered around them, it sounded like a direct hit on the stored weapons. They looked at the sky too see another Warthog streak ahead, then more ground shaking explosions. A few seconds later they hear the same thing, and again a few seconds later; explosion after explosion.

The pilot of the first Warthog saw the buildings had been leveled and are aflame with munitions exploding into the morning sky. He swings back and peppered the fleeing Taliban soldiers as they scattered in different directions. Several were in small pickup trucks, the rest fled on foot. He dropped one more load on the grounds then flew away.

The second Warthog followed and performed the same assault on the fleeing fighters. Seeing no further movement or weapons fire from the ground they returned to their base. A few minutes later a US Army helicopter lands, disembarking four soldiers. They spread out, combing the area and calling out, "Hello, we are American soldiers. Are there any survivors?" No response.

Chapter 23

London
Two months later.

Maya was back home in London recovering from her leg injury suffered in the rescue of Nick. Her fight with Johnson resulted in a tear of her right hamstring muscle which required surgery to repair. The surgery was a day surgery procedure performed in the morning with her being released in the late afternoon. The injury ended up being worse that initially thought due to the additional trauma inflicted from the combat activity engaged in after the injury occurred. The only good thing, Maya thought at the time, at least it wasn't an open surgery operation which would have required a minimum of an overnight stay in the hospital. That would have really driven her crazy.

The rehabilitation required her leg to be braced for just about three weeks, then she walked with the aid of crutches for another four weeks. To describe her as a pain in the ass as a patient was perhaps a mild term. She was used to being in control when it came to training and taking care of her body.

She thought the rehab was too slow; in the beginning due to the swelling she had to endure then, after the swelling subsided, simply because she wanted to go faster then the doctor and physical therapists recommended. Her only gear was high speed; when she tried recklessly on her own to advance the process the swelling returned, and the pain increased.

She finally listened to the experts when Dirk showed up to a session and watched the results of a particularly grueling session on her own. Near the end she collapsed from the pain. He gathered her in his arms and carried her back to the therapy office. The staff called the surgeon who concluded after an examination that she had overexerted the muscle but didn't notice any tearing. She left with a warning from the surgeon to slow down and follow the therapists' instructions; otherwise the next occurrence could result in re-tearing the muscle.

Dirk took her home and gave her a verbal undressing. At the rate she was going the muscle could tear again because she was a stubborn, mule headed, albeit beautiful, jackass who won't listen. With her jutted jaw, her lower lip protruded, and hands on hips In a defiant stance, he expected an argument. She started to speak, then stopped. She sighed and agreed to follow the therapists' instructions to the letter. Maya stayed home, without complaint for seventy-two hours while taking anti-inflammatory medication.

As she promised Nick, the three of them had that conversation where she introduced Dirk to him and told him he was his father. She explained that the story she had told Nick about his father was true to the best of her knowledge. The official story explained to her was that he was killed during the raid on al-Faw; that he died as a war hero, saving her life and the lives of several others, including Uncle Rick. She, however, never believed that story and kept searching until, twenty years later, she found him in Afghanistan about four month ago.

Dirk followed by telling the official story from the CIA regarding the al-Faw events. He was informed he had been knocked out by an explosion, and he and his partner were recused by U.S. Navy Seal Team. He was diagnosed as suffering a concussion along with some contusions. Your mother and the others had been killed during the firefight.

I too had doubts as I had left the team in good shape before sneaking to the back to breach the storage building. All of my questions were shutdown when I inquired into the truth. Fortunately, you mother persevered by tracking my special tactical work.

Nick wasn't really sure what to say. He had his suspicions from his mother's actions after he was first rescued, thus he wasn't totally surprised. Yet, to suddenly learn that his father was alive, after twenty years, was, he, he, just didn't know what to think.

Speaking of Dirk, he was a doll as far as Maya was concerned. Dirk was there when she was wheeled into surgery and, with Nick, the first to see her after she hit the recovery room. Nick was given five days leave to spend time with his mother and father then had to return to his assignment in Afghanistan. Maya would need a lot of help, especially with doctor appointments, physical therapy and so on.

Dirk let Nick do the heavy lifting early on. He made sure Nick understood he wasn't there to disrupt his looking after his mom. Nick appreciated that and decided he would like to get to know his father better. Whatever developed, their relationship was going to be unique.

Dirk spent the first few days convalescing from his own injuries. The doctor told him he really lucked out, he had two fractured ribs and other contusions including three scars from being burned by Johnson's cigar. The ribs fractures were non-displaced, which was good as a displaced fracture could have punctured a lung. He would be good once the healing completed.

When Nick shipped out, Dirk was more than willing to step in as Maya's caregiver. The first night Maya didn't want to be alone, so he agreed to stay and slept in Nick's room. One night turned into two, then three. They both agreed it was fun spending time together; just getting to know each other again. However, on the fourth night, Dirk went back to the base. Maya asked if anything was wrong, he said no; he just didn't want to rush things. She said whenever he got tired of the base, he always had a place to stay.

He returned everyday day to drive Maya to her physical therapy appointments; after a while it became three times each week. As the healing progressed Maya patience began to grow thin. She was still unable to return to work; they had placed her on an indefinite leave of absence, and she was becoming stir crazy. Kate had called nearly every other day from Afghanistan to keep her involved with the action from afar. The new lead analyst was okay to work for but lacked Maya's knowledge. At least he was cute, Kate said; it sounded like she had gushed a bit when making that statement.

Things came to a head after six weeks of physical therapy. Maya had gotten real cranky, bitchy, whatever word you wanted to apply to describe the situation. She would have been climbing the walls if it wasn't for her leg. Actually, if the leg was fine, she would be back at work instead of going to stupid rehab three days each week.

Dirk was doing his best to roll with the punches. It was hard to describe the state of their current relationship. He enjoyed staying with her and spending time together. In many ways it was like twenty years ago and yet it wasn't. The biggest difference was with his age his thinking had changed, more mature and thoughtful. He had different feeling this time for Maya and he wasn't sure how to proceed.

As Maya was nearing the end of the worst of her rehab, and with the leg responding better to the treatment, Dirk felt it was safe for him to leave for a while. He explained to Maya he needed to go back home for a variety of reasons. First; he hadn't seen his parents in over a year, so a visit was overdue. The best part was going to explain to them they had a twenty-year old grandson. Second; he had to spend some time at Langley (CIA headquarters) to discuss a few things. When Maya asked about what, he demurred. Lastly, he just needed to sort through some things by himself, uninterrupted.

Maya wasn't entirely sure how to react. Was she the problem? She realized she had been a major pain in the ass, but that was due to the forced inactivity and the rehab work. Had she subconsciously been pushing Dirk too fast? They seemed to fall in a comfortable friendship rather naturally, but a lot can change after such a long time apart. She finally asked, "Have I done something wrong, are you leaving because of me?"

"I don't know; maybe, kinda, I'm not really sure. I just need time to be alone and think."

What the hell does that mean, I'm not sure, she thought to herself. Softly, almost in a whisper, she said, "Are you coming back?"

"Yes, absolutely. And, don't worry about your appointments. I checked with Rick; between him and his wife they will get you where you will need to go. Plus, I hear Kate will be back here in about ten days."

"So, how long will you be gone?"

"Probably a week to ten days." He smiled, "Don't worry, it will go fast." He leaned in and gave her a kiss, then headed out the door.

Maya hobbled on her crutches over to the doorway where she stood and watched him leave. She had mixed feelings, confused about their relationship, that is if one really exited and wasn't a figment of her imagination. He had better not be running like a coward, she muttered.

****

Ten days had passed with no word from Dirk. Maya watched the calendar initially but grew frustrated, and, decided to focus her energy elsewhere. The day after Dirk left, she was visited by her boss at MI6. The purpose of the meeting was to discuss the take down of the turncoat arms dealer, Whit Johnson. Maya knew there was an active investigation as Rick mentioned he had spoken to the investigators. Her recitation of Johnson's confession to being a rogue officer for at least twenty years closed a major illicit, long time operation but established another embarrassment for MI6. The agency fell victim once again to lax oversight of its field officers. The most surprising fact to Maya was how when she implicated Johnson as potentially involved with the al-Faw debacle, explained how he had the resources and knowledge to mastermind the death trap, her concerns were dismissed out of hand. Who screwed up that portion of the investigation?

Maya's physical therapy had been progressing quite well; she was completely off crutches although she still had a limp that doctors said would eventually go away. One late afternoon after a session, she came home to find the back door to her apartment unlocked. Strange, she thought; she had always locked the door and was positive she had done so this time. Alright, maybe Nick came home to surprise her, but no, he was in Germany. She searched around the kitchen for a weapon, finding none she cautiously tiptoed into the living room. "Hey gorgeous," said the voice from someone stranding in the bedroom doorway.

"Dirk," she said and scurried over to give him a big hug. Then she pushed him in the chest, and in a sterner voice she accusingly asked, "What the hell are you doing here?"

His head cocked to the left with his eyebrows raised he replied, "The last I remember my girlfriend lived here. Did I miss something while I was gone?"

"Well, you tell me. You said you would be gone a week to ten days, and here you returned after two weeks. No communication, phone call, letter or anything, and now you expect me to welcome you back with open arms?"

Dirk was completely confused, but he had learned from a few of his married friends that women could be like that. He looked around and noticed she came in without crutches; progress but still painful, especially if she had just returned from a 'torture' session. Thinking quick, he responded, "Who just hugged who?"

No response.

"I got back as fast as I could; it took longer at Langley then I thought it would. Plus, my parents were off on a trip to Hawaii when I first arrived. Anyway, I tried to call several times. When I came in I found a notice from the phone company on the kitchen table; your service was shut off because the bill wasn't paid while you were in Afghanistan. And you don't have international service on your cell phone."

"I guess I forgot, things have been a bit crazy. Still, two weeks without a word was rough; I didn't know that maybe you decided not to come back, and…" Then it dawned on her, "Wait, did you just call me your girlfriend?"

"Yeah, I did, about five minutes ago."

"Really?"

"I figured before we went too far it would be nice for you to be my girlfriend first. I mean; in Nicosia, we pretended to be married, and it was cool, but, one step at a time."

They took a seat at the kitchen dinette. He went on to explain his trip, how his parents were stunned to learn they had been grandparents for a long time. He also spent time seeing several old friends, and so on. The trip to CIA headquarters was interesting.

The take down of the weapons smuggling operation was another feather in his cap. I reminded them it was another successful joint operation as MI6 and British commandos played a key role. No, he didn't mention that we found each other alive, it wouldn't have benefited him, or her, or anyone to disclose that information.

Also, they were very interested to learn that Whit Johnson was behind perhaps the biggest illegal arms trading ring in the middle east. Rob Wilson had flagged him as possibly being involved with al-Faw, but never found anything concrete on him. He was good, hid his fingerprints for nearly thirty years. You took out a really bad actor.

"I also stopped into the personnel operation before I came back, he said."

Puzzled, she asked, "What would you be going to personnel for?"

"Just wanted to learn about benefits I've earned, Dirk replied. For instance, because of my assignments I can retire after twenty- five years, counting my army time I have twenty-six years."

Maya's eyes widen at that comment. With a little laugh, she said, "Retired? You? Aren't you a trifle young for that?"

"I don't know, but, yeah, been thinking about lately. Not retire, retire, but you know, maybe retire from the CIA and putter around, try something else. You mean you haven't thought about doing something different with your life?"

"Truthfully, yes, twice," said Maya. The first time was right after I found out I was pregnant with Nick. The director told me to think about, don't rush into anything. He said that the service wanted to keep me as an analyst and would accommodate my desires on the job. They made it real easy for me to stay."

"And, the second time?"

"When you were gone. I started to wonder, if it worked between us, what kind of a wife would you want? I'm sure I don't want any more hot action. This last round. with the injury, convinced me of that. I'm also a twenty-five year person, so I could leave, freeze my pension and go try something else."

"Well, great minds think alike. Speaking about retirement, I couldn't imagine you not working, going to tea with the girls, meetings with teachers, and so on," Dirk said.

Maya made a face at that. "Ugh. You're right, I couldn't picture myself doing any of that. The part of meeting teachers isn't going to happen."

With a sly grin, Dirk replied, "You don't think you'll ever need to meet teachers in the future?"

"Trust me on that one. So, what comes next?" she asked.

"I don't know, we play by it ear, I guess. At some point you will have to accompany me to the states to meet the parents."

"And likewise for you; except you won't have to leave the country," Maya said. "Plus, we'll have to tell Nick."

"Yes, that's very important. I'll let you figure that one out," Dirk replied.

"Thanks," she replied. "Hey, come rub my neck, will ya?"

Dirk stood up, walked behind her and began to message her neck.

It felt so good, Maya thought, those strong hands knocking out some of the tension. She let out a low, soft moan. After a few minutes she purred, "That's not my neck."

"You can always call the front desk and complain," Dirk said, then kissed her neck.

"There isn't a front desk with this operation. Besides, didn't we already play out this scenario once before?" she asked as she shifted her body weight.

"Something like that, I believe. How's your leg, is it stronger?" Dirk asked.

Maya stood up, turned to face him, then took him by the hand. "I think so. Why don't we, you know, give it a test run, to find out for sure?"

"There's nothing like finding out first-hand," Dirk said as they walked toward the bedroom.

www.ingramcontent.com/pod-product-compliance
Ingram Content Group UK Ltd.
Pitfield, Milton Keynes, MK11 3LW, UK
UKHW041228200426
11947UKWH00034B/397